Praise for Stacey Swann's

OLYMPUS, TEXAS

"An action-filled, devastating tale of homecoming."
—*Minneapolis Star Tribune*

"Cleverly reimagines the gods as down-home personality types. . . . A unique way to disrupt the conventional family saga."
—*USA Today*

"This debut novel is a great combination of rollicking entertainment and timeless philosophical questions—a big, messy family saga about home and love and how we mere mortals fail each but try, try again."
—Lone Star Literary Life

"A total page-turner. . . . Swann's debut is rich in Texas flavor and full of nods to classical mythology."
—*Kirkus Reviews* (starred review)

"Luminous. . . . This epic makes the most of its vivid Texan setting, becoming as well a love letter to the state's rugged beauty and homegrown familiarity. . . . This teems with skillfully evoked drama and tragedy."
—*Publishers Weekly* (starred review)

Stacey Swann

OLYMPUS, TEXAS

Stacey Swann holds an MFA from Texas State University and was a Stegner Fellow at Stanford University. Her fiction has appeared in *Epoch*, *Memorious*, *Versal*, and other journals, and she is a contributing editor of *American Short Fiction*. She is a native Texan.

staceyswann.com

OLYMPUS, TEXAS

OLYMPUS, TEXAS

Stacey Swann

ANCHOR BOOKS
A Division of Penguin Random House LLC
New York

FIRST ANCHOR BOOKS EDITION, MAY 2022

Copyright © 2021 by Stacey Swann

The Library of Congress has cataloged the Doubleday edition as follows:
Names: Swann, Stacey, author.
Title: Olympus, Texas / Stacey Swann.
Description: First edition. | New York : Doubleday, 2021.
Identifiers: LCCN 2020032600 (print) | LCCN 2020032601 (ebook)
Classification: LCC PS3619.W3566 O49 2021 (print) |
LCC PS3619.W3566 (ebook) | DDC 813/.6—dc23
LC record available at https://lccn.loc.gov/2020032600
LC ebook record available at https://lccn.loc.gov/2020032601

Anchor Books Trade Paperback ISBN: 978-1-9848-9740-4
eBook ISBN: 978-0-385-54522-8

Book design by Anna B. Knighton

anchorbooks.com

Printed in the United States of America
10 9 8 7 6 5 4 3 2 1

FOR MY FAMILY

A PARTIAL BRISCOE FAMILY TREE

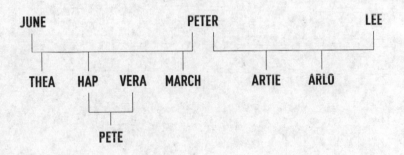

"But then, is everyone not his own god?"

OVID,

The Metamorphoses,

TRANSLATED BY ALLEN MANDELBAUM

FRIDAY

ONE

Drive down in the dark, in the fog—thick white against the headlights and the windshield. The world without form and without shape. Follow the sound of gravel grinding under tires as it slips and shifts. Smooth and quiet means you're headed into the ditch. Cross over metal pipes, the thump-thump-thump of the cattle guard. Downhill, into the bottomland, the gritty crunch now covered by the bawling of frogs and cicadas. Stop the car. Wait. The sun will rise and burn the land into relief.

When morning comes, the view is a tangle of trees and underbrush—bur oak and cedar elm, pecan and supplejack, poison oak and mustang grape vines. Not a hiking forest but scratchy impenetrability, like a ten-acre fence gapped only by this dirt road. Cow pastures lie somewhere near, in this border between oak savannahs and Gulf prairies, but here is just a small clearing with a large white house guarded by a sextet of cottonwoods. Wind lifts the cotton from the trees, and it snows down on the house: two stories with four large columns careening up the front, broken in the middle by a spindle railing and balcony. Windows peep from the gabled roof. Bermuda grass covers the lawn, interrupted by square flowerbeds lined out with railroad ties—the smell of roses and creosote.

The house is bounded by the woods on one side and the Brazos River, slow moving and brown, on the other. The fluff from a cottonwood lands, rides a mud-saturated current, and then gets sucked under. The rise and fall of the water level has left the clay banks patched with only fast-growing weeds. The river—not Mississippi-wide, but too wide to throw a stone across—generates a steady white noise.

And inside the house? Peter and June in their bed, old and brass, columned like their home. The brass rises like prison bars from the head and the foot of the frame. The bed sat forgotten in his parents' barn for decades until Peter found it. He was eleven months into dating June, and he jokingly said to her the bed, with its feeling of enclosure, spoke to him of marriage. He dragged it to his own place, polished and polished until he had a heap of rags stained with the green that had eaten the brass. Knowing he'd never want to undertake that task again, he shellacked the whole damn thing to keep it from tarnishing. It worked for a long time, past the births of all three of their children. But as the years passed, the tarnish crept back, and now it is the tarnish being protected by the coating. June still likes it. Or she likes Peter's frustration whenever he stares at it too long.

June and Peter in a bed too small for him. Stretched out, he must either cram an inch of his head between the bars of the headboard, point his toes through the bars at the foot of the bed, or bend his knees. Peter's a big man, nearly six and a half feet. Wide, too. June has never seen a man so wide and yet not fat. When they were newly married, she straddled him and lay her palm at the edge of one nipple, then her other palm, crossing over and over again. Five hands between, an expanse of a man. Even now that his belly grows soft and extends farther out and down—another two pounds every year—nothing can dwarf that chest.

Or perhaps this should be a study in contrasts, the before and after. Flat stomach to non-flat. His hair, always curly, turned from fat rings of black to ones of gray. The beard fading to white, only black above the lip. Green eyes, sharp and hard as always. Really, he has not changed so much. A partial softening, a partial lightening. June also hasn't changed much, at least if viewed while sleeping. Her blond hair still the same shade at fifty-five as it was at twenty. And when relaxed in sleep, the lines are less visible, no skin sags. Upright and awake, things tighten and crinkle, others droop—thanks to the three children she carried, the years of being outside with toddlers, with cattle, with her own dissatisfaction. But asleep, she is young.

There in bed: a sixty-year-old man and his wife. She's ten inches shorter than him; the bed fits her fine. Her foot rests lightly against his calf. His hand lies close to her hip, sharing heat. Then something in him shifts, the brass feels like a constraint, so he turns over to curl up. This wakes June, and before he can swing his heavy arm over her chest, her hair under the weight of his head, she slips from the bed. Time for coffee.

Downstairs now, the percolator wheezes. She drinks a glass of water, makes toast with butter and dewberry jam. The kitchen, like the rest of their home, is farmhouse meets minimalism with a healthy sprinkle of antiques from both sides of the family. June pours the coffee, walks softly back upstairs, passing Peter, still asleep, and what were once their children's rooms (now a guest bedroom, rarely used, and an office). At the end of the hallway, she opens French doors to the balcony, a big rectangle of white-painted wood enclosed by a low railing of more white-painted wood, shaded by the eave and its extra attic space above.

By the time she's finished her toast, started on the coffee, the front door opens below her. She has more time alone in the winter, but Peter gets up early in the summer, gets up with the sun. He wants his cup of coffee, his large slatted wooden chair, while the air has any chance of being cool. The front porch is identical in size to the balcony above, but it doesn't catch as much of a breeze. He pulls the chair close to the house, far enough that the creeping, slanting light cannot reach him. As he settles in, June waits for his good morning. Instead, Peter's cell phone rings, rattling the glass-topped table it sits upon.

"Hayden. Everything okay?"

Peter's brother. As the crow flies, their neighbor, but because the Brazos lies between them, they may as well be miles away. This suits June fine. She's not uneasy with the cemetery and funeral home that make up Hayden's livelihood. She's just not a fan of the man. In his defense, though, he's not the type to typically call this early.

"He's with you?" Peter says.

June is skilled in making out the missing half of her husband's phone calls, yet she's not sure what to make of this—who the *he* is, why Peter sounds near joyful about it. Or maybe she does suspect but chooses to ignore that whiff of doom now in the air.

"Noon would be great. Can you put him on?"

Shit, June thinks.

"Okay, then. And thanks, Hayden."

She hears Peter set the phone back down on the table, waits for him to speak. His long silence confirms it's news she doesn't want to hear. She holds out her half-full cup, a foot away from her wicker chair and her bare feet, and tips it, watches the coffee spill out and down, slipping straight through a gap in the boards of the balcony's flooring. Though she can't see her husband, she knows his exact location, something confirmed by his swearing as the hot liquid finds its target. Her small acts of violence, a near-weekly occurrence, aren't premeditated. They surprise her even more than they do him.

"I want to point out, before we even begin, that none of this is my fault. I woke up all innocence this morning," Peter says. Their first words are often spoken this way—through her wooden floor, his wooden ceiling.

June snorts, not because she really blames him for the news he's about to share but because she can't ever see him as innocent. Peter is a man who loves with deliberation, but his lust is not so orderly. Their three children make up only half his offspring, and all were born after he married her. Though he has managed to leave those indiscretions behind, they still worm into June's thoughts. Thus the acts of violence.

"March is back?" she says. Their youngest, exiled and silent these past two and a half years.

"He wants to come to lunch today."

"No," she says.

"I already said yes."

"The vet's coming out for the calves. We might not be done by noon, much less leave time to cook."

"I'll pick up barbecue. And it's fine if you're late." He pauses. "If you don't feel like you can reschedule to see your own son."

She wants to tip more coffee, but then she'll have none left to drink. "I haven't forgiven him yet, and I doubt I can pull that off before lunch. And what about Hap?" March's older brother, the one with the most to forgive. Peter, she knows, is well past any hard feelings, if he ever had them. The man had soaked up too much of other people's forgiveness to begrudge it to anyone else. If forgiveness were something to garner and hold on to, Peter sat atop a stockpile.

June has chosen to believe that distance can create safety. March, away from Olympus, was a safe March—safe for Hap, safe for her, safe for March himself. She doesn't like the fact that her carefully built sense of security can evaporate between one sip of coffee and the next.

"You can have lunch without forgiving him. We can't refuse to see him altogether," says Peter.

She sorts through her feelings to find a bit of happiness: a sign she is looking forward to seeing her son. She goes to the balcony railing and scans Hayden's property across the river, wondering if binoculars would let her see March and trigger a more maternal feeling. She's distracted by a peacock—the second-most prevalent animal on their land, after the cattle—stalking across the yard. It comes up close to the porch, its fan folded behind it. She hears her husband suck up a mouthful of coffee, and, mustering experience from years chewing tobacco, he shoots it in a hard stream, hitting the bird in the neck. It doesn't flinch, keeps still, then turns its ass toward her husband and slowly struts farther onto the lawn, spreading out its fan. The sun, not far from the horizon, hits the feathers from behind, muting the colors into a dark lattice of lines and circles, light coming through the cracks to spread another lattice on the lawn. It's too lovely to let her deny her son's request. Still, she lets her silence act as her consent. Silence and a sigh.

TWO

KNOWING HIS UNCLE would take offense at the dogs marking cemetery headstones as their territory, March takes his mastiffs to the field across the street. The dogs wander into the Johnson grass, which, at four feet, just covers their heads and reduces them to moving spots of shaking stems. March watches Hayden pace from the edge of his house's front lawn, across the empty parking lot, to the edge of the funeral home. Halfway back through the unpaved lot, he stops, sliding his cell phone into his shirt pocket. Beyond his uncle, across the river, March can see the small white shape of the house he grew up in.

The dogs return, already panting and staring at March with what, to him, feels like blame. If they could speak, they'd ask to go back to the mountains. Like most non-native Texans, the dogs likely see the heat as a personal affront rather than simply the weather. His uncle appears at his side.

"You're invited to lunch, twelve o'clock." The dogs sniff Hayden's hands, hopeful for another round of petting. Upon being ignored, they drop heavily to the ground, using March's shadow as shade.

"That easy?" March says.

"It was. But I don't think Peter checked with June."

"So you might get a call to uninvite me?"

March is close enough to his uncle to come asking favors, unannounced and early in the morning, but not so close that his prior disappearance affronted the man or requires an apology. Though March hasn't exactly articulated that to himself, it is indeed why he stopped here first rather than at his parents'. Hayden has always preferred March to his older brother, and March isn't too proud to rely on that. The favoritism comes from how much March looks like their father, a slightly reduced copy: an inch or two shorter, features a little sharper, and the same green eyes and dark curly hair. Hap takes after their mother, blond and not as tall, though without her beauty.

"She wouldn't turn you away. If not to see you, then at least to browbeat you." Hayden smiles but March doesn't. "You haven't talked to any of us this whole time?"

March shakes his head. When his affair with his brother's wife came out, he expected Hap's wrath, but he was surprised his entire family seemed to will him away. He, in his typical fashion, hadn't thought that far ahead. In defense, he put a state line between them, so their absence in his life would feel chosen instead of forced. He bought this idea of it having been his choice so fully, he thought he could also choose to come home. It wasn't until he exited I-10 for Olympus this morning, after driving through the night, that he realized he might have made a mistake. He viewed his exile as a prison term served, but he had no proof his family would see it the same way.

"I need another favor. Have anywhere I can store my stuff for now?" March tips his head toward his truck bed, half-full of boxes.

"Plenty of space in the storeroom down the hall from my office. I've got to shower, though. Meeting a family to talk through arrangements at eight. When you're done unloading, come over to the house for breakfast. Grab a nap before lunch if you need it. Stephanie and the kids are spending the summer in Iowa with her mom, per usual, so you'll have plenty of quiet."

Stephanie's absence increases the appeal of Hayden's offer. She considers March a bad influence on his cousins, two boys not yet in junior high, and he can't say she doesn't have good reason. March's affair with his sister-in-law, Vera, was the most recent in a long series of mistakes. Starting a riot on the high school football field that lost the state championship; the Titans had been on the five-yard line, first down, a minute and a half on the clock. The fistfight that led to a fire, destroying the town's one-hundred-year-old domino parlor. His dishonorable discharge from the Army. March doesn't flinch from thinking about his bad behavior because it's like thinking of a separate person. When he becomes truly angry, his body keeps moving while his brain fritzes out, like he's blackout drunk. After a few minutes, he'll be conscious of himself again, now less angry but with no memory of what he's just done. It's hard to own what he can't re-create in his mind. He can't even own his diagnosis: intermittent explosive disorder. Though he believes the people that insist it's true—his entire family—in his heart it all feels like a misunderstanding.

After Hayden heads to his house, March moves his belongings from his truck into the storeroom, getting in and out of the silent funeral home as fast as he can. By the time he lets himself in Hayden's front door, his uncle has showered and is pouring two big bowls of cereal.

"Leave the dogs on the porch?" March does as he is told, but he feels bad shutting the door in their faces. Hayden, in boxer shorts and T-shirt, holding a box of Frosted Flakes, seems suddenly twenty years younger, reminding March that Hayden had his own profligate youth. Probably another reason March is his favorite.

"You think my coming back is a bad idea?" March asks, only now feeling the many things that could go wrong with his return.

"Course not. Facing up to your responsibilities is a good thing." Hayden thuds two bowls and a gallon of milk on the kitchen table and nods for March to sit. "It's hard, I know. Me and Peter weren't that different from you and Hap. Peter seemed like he was born on the straight and narrow—building a business, finding a wife, starting a family. Just like Hap. It took me a while longer to find mine. But I made it in the end, and you will too."

"Wait," March says. "Hap's started a family? Vera's still here?"

Hayden, about to take a bite of cereal, sets the overloaded spoon back down. "They didn't divorce. They have a baby." His uncle watches him for something—jealousy maybe?—but all March feels is shock. "Could be it will make things easier," Hayden says. "Help Hap forgive and forget."

March imagines the next Thanksgiving dinner, Hap and Vera and child across the table from him. It seems the opposite of easier.

AFTER HAYDEN LEAVES FOR WORK, March tries to nap in the recliner in the living room. Leaving aside Hap and his newly expanded family, he still has to contend with his mother, her seething anger now finally presented with its rightful target. That's too much to bear lying down. Besides, every time he opens his eyes, he sees the dogs staring at him from the front window, betrayed and panting.

He rises from the recliner hoping to bolster his spirits as well as the dogs'. They follow him from the porch to his truck and hop and whine around the tailgate, knowing that with the boxes gone, they'll be liberated from the small jump seat where they rode all the way from New Mexico. Even the heat won't bother them when the wind is rushing past. March slides down the thick piece of plywood that was under the boxes, a ramp for the dogs to get their one-hundred-fifty-pound bulks aboard.

He takes the one-lane, barely paved road slowly, enjoying the excited faces of the dogs in his rearview mirror and being surrounded by the land he hasn't seen in so long—big pastures separated by windbreaks of trees, farmers baling hay, the dogs barking first at goats, then at cows. He doesn't pass a single car for ten minutes, until he hits the bigger farm-to-market road which loops him back to the Brazos. The sun is glinting off the water's murky surface like spilled glitter as he crosses the bridge and hits the city limits of the only place that's ever felt like home.

Olympus was settled in the early 1800s, back when Texas was still part of Mexico, but its heyday was over before Houston, its prosperous neighbor to the east, was even founded. First, it was burned to the ground during the Texas Revolution. Forty years later, the rebuilt town was bypassed by the new railroad, which enriched nearby Bullinger instead. Then, it was nearly wiped off the map by the Brazos Flood of 1899. In the hundred-plus years that followed, even being the county seat couldn't prod it into something larger. The town settled at a population of two thousand and stuck there.

In fact, Olympus is so small, March knows if he drives around too long, he'll either run into Hap or into someone who will quickly pass news of his return on to his brother. Even now, Hap's auto body shop is only five blocks east of him. So he turns west and drives the half mile to his father's real estate office—March's workplace, too, in the years just prior to his leaving. What he wants is one more person happy to see him before he must begin facing the unhappy.

As he walks up the three porch steps to the old Victorian and sees *Briscoe Properties* etched on the glass window of the front door, he feels again the knock of nostalgic serenity that the city limits prompted. But the office is locked. He turns back to find his dogs staring at him, their front paws propped on the roof of the cab. He should have left the truck with its dark paint job in the mountains where he bought it, got a lighter one, more heat reflective, for his return. Another thing he should have thought through ahead of time.

Still three hours until lunch, but March tells himself to man up. Best to rip off the Band-Aid. Besides, arriving early isn't the same as arriving unannounced. Another fifteen-minute drive, zipping back to I-10 and then down more one-lane roads that lead to the house he grew up in. Crossing onto their land, he spots some of his mother's cows seeking shade in the middle of the pasture, clustered under a big oak. He rolls down a small hill, past the marshy bottom with its standing water and skin of algae, and then toward the big house, already visible through the trees. To March's great relief, Artie's Jeep is parked in the driveway. Artie and her brother Arlo are Peter's kids but not June's. That his parents favor Hap and their older sister, Thea, over him has never surprised March. But his mother even prefers Artie, the product of his father's early philandering. She's been a frequent visitor to their house for as long as March can remember. While Artie is sure to give him shit for his radio silence, she'll be glad to see him. They've always been friends more than half siblings, and in March's experience friends are more forgiving than blood. Also, March doesn't see his father's vehicle. Artie's presence is a piece of luck that keeps him from a one-on-one with his mother.

He parks a little way from the house, under a tree. Before he can loose the dogs, he hears Artie's loud voice. "March! You asshole. Going to see everyone else before you come to see me." She and his mother appear at the railing of the balcony above. Artie smiles so big he can see it from all these yards away. June does not smile; she crosses her arms. Her distance from him, up on the second story, makes her look small. But she doesn't feel small, not to him. His hand stays on the tailgate, the dogs pacing while they wait to be freed.

"Take those animals to the kitchen," his mother yells. "Don't let them run after the peacocks. They're housebroke?"

"Safer than me," he yells back.

"Not exactly a high standard."

"Some welcome for a son you haven't seen in more than two years." March knows better than to say such a thing. His mother doesn't respond well to chiding in any form, but he can't exactly shout his apology, can he?

She uncrosses her arms, leaning on the railing and lifting up on her toes. To March, she looks like a mountain lion about to pounce. "As if you left town for no reason. As if—" She stops, though, and just turns her back to him. But Artie sweeps her arm toward the house, beckoning him in.

He drops the tailgate, and the dogs thud down and follow him. After climbing the porch steps, he opens the front door and heads through the entryway to the kitchen. March can hear his mother and Artie coming down the stairs. He sits at a barstool at the island, knees jammed underneath the granite. Everything in the room is exactly the same, from the blue glass telephone insulators on the window ledge above the sink to the sugar bowl next to the coffeepot.

Artie, having taken the stairs two at a time, grabs him from behind in a half hug then drops to her knees, scratching each dog's chin. Artie doesn't look the same—her face thinner, smile lines deeper. How can they both be approaching thirty already?

"Two years and not one call." She looks up at him, and Remus licks her unguarded cheek.

March fishes his phone from his pocket. "Had to buy a new one—didn't have anyone's number." He doesn't tell her where his old one wound up: a gas station trashcan on his way out of Texas because he couldn't trust himself not to call.

"Bullshit and excuses." She takes his phone from him, adds herself to his contacts. Then she crouches down next to the dogs again. "Names?" Artie uses a thumb apiece to smooth out the dogs' wrinkled foreheads.

March identifies the fawn one as Romulus and the brindle as Remus.

He's grown so used to the dogs, he's surprised their bulk has made the kitchen crowded. They tower over the kneeling Artie, and she isn't a tiny woman.

His mother enters the kitchen, walks past him without even a look, then rifles through cabinets until she finds a large metal bowl. She fills it with water, and the dogs follow her to the hallway to drink. June moves a pan of biscuits—minus two already—in front of March, brings jam and butter from the fridge, and pours him a cup of coffee. Hostess duties done, she sits on the stool next to him while Artie pulls herself up on the counter, legs dangling.

"You're early," June says, finally looking at him.

"I am."

"And you've been where? Doing what?"

"Working in Ruidoso, New Mexico. Security at a casino." She frowns at him. "It's a nice place. There's a lake, a golf course. Whole resort." She still looks disapproving. "Arlo even played there, last weekend."

"He didn't tell me he saw you," says Artie, joining his mother in her frown.

"He didn't know I was there. I wasn't, actually. Was out of town."

March didn't keep up with the music calendar as no one he wanted to see ever came, just bands like Three Dog Night and Foreigner, Elvis impersonators, and old comedians. He'd gone camping with the dogs near White Sands, and when he'd returned to work, his half brother's name was still on the concert venue's sign from Saturday night.

"You weren't there too?" March asks. Artie manages most of Arlo's tours, the bigger ones, at least. She shakes her head, begins to answer but is cut off by his mother.

"And you've come home," June says. "Why now?"

March would like her to understand what he felt when he saw Arlo's name, part of home there in his place of exile. The force of everyone he hadn't seen in thirty months coming on him all at once. Within days he had quit his job, sublet his condo, and packed up to drive home. His mother's eyes are still narrowed, and he wants to say he had missed her, missed them all. But even that small sentence is too much to articulate.

Artie saves him. "We're glad you're back," she says, stretching her leg to kick his knee.

"And when are you going to talk to your brother?" June says.

"Is that possible?" he says.

"Not possible, but inevitable." His mother is distracted by Remus laying his big head on the counter as he sniffs hard at the biscuits. She pulls one from the pan, breaks it in half, and tosses the pieces in opposite directions. The dogs slide and skitter to the food. "Though if you're as lacking in apologies with him as you are with us, I don't really see the point of your coming back."

He has always felt June's anger like a concrete thing, a hot lead blanket against his skin. Years of exposure had cured his urge to flinch, but now, having had such a long break from her, the urge returns. "I *am* sorry," he says, but it's to his mother's back as she heads to the kitchen window. They all hear the sound of an engine approaching.

A car door slams; a gruff voice yells "Motherfucker." His mother sighs, turning away from the window with her eyes shut. The dogs lift their heads to listen to the sharp rasp of metal scraping metal, then breaking glass, then the hollow thud of something heavy crashing into something heavier. March sprints onto the porch with Artie following close, Rom and Remus tumbling after. June shouts at him to call the dogs off before he has time to fully register what's going on.

"Boys, heel. Now!" The dogs freeze though their hackles are raised. He grabs both by their collars and they consent to be yanked back into the house. March closes the door to block them inside.

Outside, on the lawn, Hap is attacking the side of March's truck with a sledgehammer. March knows he has it coming. Hap didn't force him to leave town, didn't take a shot at him. If there's festering rage, a truck's not a bad thing to take it out on. March even has a moment to reflect that, as Hap is the owner of the town's only body shop, he'll have to pay his brother to repair the damage. But then Hap pauses, looks up at March there on the porch, and puts all his strength into a swing that takes out the entire windshield. March feels violated, then feels himself dropping into that hidden place he won't remember. He tears across the lawn, making straight and fast for Hap, yelling so loud the dogs bark from the kitchen, pawing at the door until it shakes. March, a good half-foot taller than his brother, rams into him while still running.

By the time March is aware of himself again, he's lying on his back, breathing hard, his shoulder hurting. Hap is a foot away, on his hands and knees, his lip bleeding and dirt and grass smeared across the left side of his face. A shaken-looking Artie stands between them with a shovel. Hap scrambles up, but their mother steps in front of him. March focuses on the cloudless sky through the pecan's branches, deep-breathes himself into a calmer state.

"Backstabbing piece of shit," Hap says. "Moral fucking vacuum."

March is trying to craft a reply when he sees his mother's face above him wearing such an expression of expectation that March, to his annoyance, cannot ignore it—so long as it requires only staying quiet.

"One of my guys saw you at Dad's office," Hap says. "You think you can just step back into your life? You think you deserve it?"

March notes with pleasure that their mother is glaring at her favorite. "You came over here looking for trouble?" she says.

"He's owed trouble."

March sits up, steadying himself by sliding his hands into the grass and holding on. Hap tears a sticker burr out of his beard. Behind Hap, there's a middle-aged man standing next to a vintage truck, neither of which he's seen before.

"You think Artie and I are owed trouble?" she says. But then she, too, looks at the stranger by the truck, and her cheeks flush red. "You're early," she tells the man. "Go wait up by the cattle pasture." After taking in the scene in front of him again, the man nods at her and climbs back in his Ford.

Hap avoids his mother's question by hefting the sledgehammer into the cab of his truck. But he goes to Artie and whispers in her ear before telling June, "I'll get back to town." Then he gives March a look that implies he'd rather be hefting the hammer at March. Still, he gets in his wrecker and follows the stranger's truck up the road.

"You can still go back the way you came," his mother says to March. "I can't make you, but I can remind you it's an option." She tips her head up to the sky, rubs her neck, then heads toward the cow pasture on foot.

Artie picks up a jagged piece of headlight and settles on the ground beside March, dropping the glass in his lap. "You may be needing a ride." They both are transfixed by the destruction. March's windshield is a concave and opaque mass of lines with a gaping hole in the center. March understands that his two-year exile wasn't his penance; his penance hasn't even begun.

"Stupid black truck was too hot, anyway," he says, getting a half smile from her.

THE ORIGIN OF MARCH'S RAGES

. . . serving to efface itself, ripe grain
provides the fuel that abets the blaze

❧ OVID ❧

MARCH WAS FOUR. Hap was six.

That day, while at school, Hap had missed his brother. He'd been
excited when, after walking the quarter mile from the cattle guard,
where the bus stopped, his mother met him by swinging open the
screen door and setting an impassive March on the porch. "Go play,"
she commanded before she went back inside.

"What happened?" Hap asked. March shrugged, reached out and
gave their father's chair a shove, then leaned back against the house
with a look he wore more and more often, one not quite angry but not
quite sad. Hap placed his hand on March's head, rubbed once, and
then said, "You're it." He bolted off the porch, calling "*All* the trees
are home base!"

Close to the house, the trees were spread apart, and the brothers were almost equally matched. March was already as tall as his
brother, better at a sprint, while Hap's two additional years gave

him more coordination. But then Hap headed to the cluster of cottonwoods farther from the house. There, March trailed his brother from tree to tree, never able to touch him in the half second Hap traveled between trunks. After five minutes, March moved from calling his brother names—*chicken* and then *coward*—to just grunting as he lunged. But Hap's elbow still ached from March's last tackle, and so he leaped to another giant cottonwood, his hand tracing a full circle around the trunk as he swung around. He stopped when a deep holler of frustration came out of his little brother, too big for his body.

March was standing with his feet apart and his head thrown all the way back, raging at the green leaves forty feet above. He screamed and screamed. Hap would have thought he had been bitten by a red wasp or a snake, but there was no pain or fear in the sound. Just an ocean of anger forced into one flowing tap.

Hap felt a little less scared when he heard the screen door bang. Their mother had come out on the porch. He slowly approached March and touched his shoulder. "I'll be it now," he said. March slammed Hap in the chest with his elbow, still yelling. Hap went to shove his brother back, but he stopped when he met March's eyes.

Hap didn't even see his brother move. He just knew suddenly the ground was under his back, and March was on top of him. It was probably good he didn't know he had decades in front of him in which he would find himself, over and over, in this same position. He would, before long, figure out the best strategies to extricate himself, but this first time, he lay there stunned as his brother choked him. This feeling wasn't like being submerged, when you chose not to breathe to avoid inhaling water. His brother's small hands were so tight around his neck, he had no choice. His ability to breathe was out of his control. Just as he was overwhelmed with panic, their mother was there, grabbing March and pulling him backward. Still March wouldn't let go, and Hap felt his shoulders lift off the ground.

JUNE SAW HER older son's face turning red, saw that he was getting no air. She let go of March, but instead of moving to face him, to reason with or threaten him, to pry his fingers from Hap's throat, she reached around with both hands, clapping them down over March's mouth and nose. She could feel his jaw struggling, unable to open wide enough to bite her, but it was ten long seconds before he let go of Hap and began clawing at June's fingers. She dropped her hands then and picked up his struggling body, still faced away from her. Hap sucked in wheezing lungfuls of air. "I'm okay," he gasped. "Get him away."

She tried to head to the house, but March was flailing so wildly, she nearly fell to her knees. She manhandled him, turning him toward her body, and she pressed him tightly to her, pinning his arms, as if she could squeeze out his anger. Still he struggled, yelling but without any words. She lengthened her strides, thinking that if she could close him in his room by himself, he would calm down.

She hadn't seen him rage like this since he was very young, before he could talk. Even as a three-month-old, there were times he would rock his crib with the violence of his tantrums. At first, June tried what she had always done to quiet Thea and Hap as babies—nursing, changing diapers, picking them up and rocking them—but she soon learned that, with March, she had to wait. Go to him too soon, try to pick him up, and his cries would increase. But wait until the storm lessened, leave him on his own, and he would consent to be comforted eventually.

As she opened the screen door with her foot, March abruptly stopped yelling and she felt him nestle his head into her neck. She came into the house, hoping he had begun to calm, but then she felt his mouth open wide against her skin before he bit down and jerked back. A pain pulled so hard at her neck that, for a moment, she thought she might faint. She stood still, two feet inside the door, and looked at her son, his mouth smeared with blood and his eyes completely empty. Without thought, she heaved him away and didn't even wince as his small back hit the floor and skidded, his cheek banging up against the wall of the hallway. He sat up, and she left him there to run to the bathroom. She could feel blood sliding down the side of her neck, curving to the front, and dripping into her shirt.

After grabbing a washcloth from the edge of the tub, she wet it down as she peered at the wound in the mirror. There was too much blood to tell what her son had done to her. Her neck throbbed, and when she placed the cloth on it, the throbbing turned to a fire. She flinched and said, "Little lunatic." She pulled the cloth away, trying to see the damage before the blood welled up and obscured it again. It didn't look deep, but an exposed circle roughly in the shape of a four-year-old's mouth was clearly visible. "Crazy, evil lunatic," she said.

"Mom?" Hap stood in the bathroom doorway. When she turned and revealed the splatters of blood, he blanched.

"It's okay, baby. I'll be fine."

Hap pointed at the floor. Behind her sat March, his legs stuck straight out in front of him, his fingers tightly clenching the bathmat. His cheek was bright red from where it had hit the wall, his mouth still smeared with blood, and he was shaking with tears but not making a sound. She knew she should pick up her son, but instead she turned and rinsed the cloth, returning it to her neck and taking a deep breath before facing him again. Hap had knelt down next to March, put his hand over his brother's.

March looked at Hap, then her, then turned back to Hap. "We were by the trees. How did we get inside?"

Though June's first instinct was to think her youngest was lying, she knew deep down it was something worse. They took him to the doctor, then a child psychologist in Houston. But being told he had rage issues did little but state the obvious. After a year, Thea announced she was done being understanding and they weren't allowed to punish her and Hap if they fought back with her aluminum softball bat. Peter compromised—no punishment if the injuries didn't warrant a doctor's visit.

Peter's strategy was to tiptoe around his son when needed, while June refused to cater to his moods. She could not so abdicate her parenting philosophy to reward bad behavior. The older March grew, the rarer his tantrums were. But June couldn't credit her son for this, even though she always blamed him for its opposite. His continual refrain of "But I don't *remember* doing it," as if that should let him off the hook, never varied. But it was using that line that saved him from a Bad Conduct Discharge in the Army, and it finally got him a diagnosis of intermittent explosive disorder. Still, it was hard to say if his family saw him as having an affliction rather than being an affliction they sometimes had to bear.

THREE

INSIDE HER JEEP, Artie and March shift hunting gear around until there's space for his dogs. They drive past June as she walks to the cow pasture, but they don't stop.

"That could've gone worse," Artie says. Her hands throb, still feeling the chafe of the shovel's wooden handle and the weight of March as she levered him off Hap. She doesn't mention this, though. She was always reluctant to tell March what he missed when his mind was absent, as if only then would he become culpable.

"I could have knocked you unconscious?" March says. Though she turns to him, March won't meet her eye.

The dogs whimper as they bump over the dirt roads, beaned by fishing poles and soft rifle cases.

"I'm sorry you had to break that up," he says.

"Not the first time, not the last. Refereeing is the price of admission when I visit you Briscoes. Where to, captain?" she asks.

"Unless you want to chauffeur me around indefinitely, better drop us at the car lot. Time for a trade-in."

"Aye, aye."

"You're not managing Arlo's tour?"

"Not since February. His schedule started picking up exactly when I was wanting to slow down. Arlo got himself a new guy, a real professional."

"You don't like him?"

"Nah, I'm grateful for him. Arlo was a little hurt, I think, that I wanted to stop. But this guy has more venue connections, more clout to throw around. So, win-win. But the drummer called me last month to complain that he wasn't as fun to drink with."

"And you?"

"Finally trying my hunting guide idea. Turns out tour managing has given me all the relevant experience—group therapist, logistics expert, provider and organizer of all things equipment related. But now, I get to do it outside, doing what I love, instead of trapped in a van with hungover assholes."

"But your new assholes all have guns."

Artie laughs. She had gotten her first taste of hunting with Peter, him eager to have some kid, any kid, go out with him. Hap and Thea had refused after the first deer-hunting trip, both appalled at the seeming injustice of it. March pretended he had no desire to even try, though everyone knew his parents wouldn't entrust him with a gun. Artie suspected this was why March had chosen the military rather than college after graduation, to show them he could've been trusted all along.

"Some are bowhunters, and some fish, so it's not all guns. But there's not enough of a market here for it to be more than part-time. So I'm still putting my animal husbandry degree to use, helping with the breeding programs at a couple of ranches."

He grins at her. "You mean you're still ruining the bulls' fun with artificial insemination."

"Yep."

Artie takes the back road into town. She's never felt Olympus to be small in a confining way, but she realizes her road choice, avoiding the highway as she prefers to do, will give them a view—across a sorghum field almost ready for harvest—of the back of Hap and Vera's house. Then, once they reach the town proper, take them within a block of Hap's shop.

"What's that smile for?" March says.

"What smile?"

"An unfamiliar, un-Artie smile. Sly, maybe?"

The shop must have reminded her, though her conscious mind hadn't tracked there. "Just a guy," she says. "Ryan. He moved here a couple of months ago, started picking up shifts at Hap's." She likes saying his name aloud, the way it makes her feel like he's there in the car with them, his cedar-smelling aftershave and those strong, quick hands.

"*Just a guy* never made you blush like that." Now it's her avoiding his gaze. "What does Arlo think of him?"

Artie loses her smile. "Arlo's been gone so much they haven't met." She pauses, trying to decide if she wants to hear his answer to her next question. "You might know him, though. Or his family. Ryan Barry, went to school in Bullinger? He was a year ahead of us."

"Not Lavinia Barry's son?"

March's troubled tone confirms Artie's own hazy memory of Lavinia Barry. "He is. I haven't met her yet, though." Years ago, the Barrys had lost their land in Olympus and Mrs. Barry had blamed Peter for it. The kids were young enough that they didn't know the particulars, just that she was bad-mouthing Peter to anyone who would listen. When Artie asked Ryan about it, he shrugged it off and said it was his own father's fault, unpaid property taxes.

"I remember running into her at the post office," March says. "It was just me and Dad. She cussed him out there in the line, kept it up until it was her turn at the counter. Dad just ignored her like she wasn't even there."

"Yeah, but that was years ago. Besides, I'm not even technically a Briscoe." Artie slows as a car passes them on the narrow road, returning their hi sign with a wave.

"She'll still know you're his daughter," March says.

Ryan's theory is that his mother will be more predisposed to like her given her family history, will see her as another of Peter's victims. Walking collateral damage from a man who always thinks he can have anything he wants. That interpretation makes her uncomfortable, though, so she's been in no hurry to test his theory.

"I can't say I remember Ryan. Was he on Bullinger's football team?"

"Yeah."

"Maybe I'll remember him when I meet him."

They crest a small rise, and Artie can't help but look to Hap's house in the distance, sky-blue paint and butter-yellow trim. March finds interest in a cattle-crossing sign out the passenger-side window.

Artie hopes he won't remember Ryan. She hopes Arlo doesn't either. Even setting aside the family history with Lavinia Barry, Ryan's reputation as a womanizer (a reputation not fully deserved, in Artie's opinion) was enough to make Hap concerned, to have him instigate an awkward conversation with her when he learned they were dating. But even if Arlo doesn't know Ryan, he'll still think Artie has turned a fool. It's why she didn't introduce Ryan the last weekend Arlo was in town. She and her brother both have their patterns, although they never discuss them as such. Even the town sees them: Arlo interested in all women, but never a specific woman, and Artie showing no interest in anyone. (She prefers to think she's discreet. It isn't as if she's a virgin, after all.) The gossip would blame their mother, in both cases, her showing them a disastrous definition of love.

Their mother, Lee, had adored Peter and had almost a year with him—a hidden, secret one, but a year nonetheless—before she got pregnant. She loved him so much, she gave him up because his own marriage, own family, started to crumble. His happiness was more important than hers, and her temperament was amenable to martyrdom. Besides, she would have two reminders of him, her twins, *her* family. But what an example to set: a shrine of pictures on her dresser (Polaroids, the cheater's souvenir); the way she preferred the school photos that most showed their resemblance to Peter; the wistful way she responded to March, his father's double. And, if asked, Artie wouldn't argue with the town's opinion. If romantic love contained so much foolishness, waste, and want, why seek it out? It seemed a natural disaster on par with a hurricane—one would deal with it only if evacuation proved impossible. Except. She doesn't feel like she's been visited by disaster. She feels happy.

As they enter Olympus, Artie wants to slow as they pass the narrow road to Hap's shop, peer down to see if Ryan's in one of the open bays, but March has seen enough of his brother today. Three blocks later, they reach the main thoroughfare, with the town's only car lot tucked beside the Dairy Queen.

Neither March nor Artie is a hugger, so she waves as he steps out of the Jeep, waits as he frees his dogs. He reappears at her window, but whatever he is trying to say stays trapped inside his throat.

"It's good you came back," she says.

"You promise?" He takes a step back, whistling at his dogs to follow.

Artie makes a U-turn and heads back out of town. She has a small house on ten acres of land, enough to keep her view free of other houses, other people. The former farmhouse has two bedrooms, one for her and one for Arlo when he needs a place to stay. To have no home at his age, rented or otherwise, should be a bit sad, but his home has always been with her. And he was so often on the road, even before his first radio hit six months ago.

Arlo's pale blue Bronco sits in her driveway. While his car in front of her house isn't a rare occurrence, this morning it's an unexpected one. He texted a few days ago from Flagstaff, starting week five of a six-week tour. She pulls up behind him, uneasy. If Ryan hasn't picked up a shift, he'll be here before lunch. It should be the perfect chance to introduce the pair, but instead, she finds herself pulling out her phone.

"On my way, beautiful," Ryan says by way of hello. "Hap wasn't around and work seemed light. Not worth sticking around for negative confirmation." She hears his tinny radio, Kenny Rogers in a tuna can, through the blown-out speakers, knows he's already driving her way.

"Better rain check." She picks at the leather of the steering wheel.

"How come?"

"Arlo's home, unexpectedly." She pauses, and a lie comes to her. She tells herself it's easier, quicker, of no importance. "I haven't gone in yet, but I figure something's wrong. He may want to talk."

Ryan sighs. "Will the talking take all day? Don't say it'll take all day."

She smiles. "Probably not."

"I'll head over to fish the river, our usual spot. Meet me when you're done? Or bring Arlo with you? We should meet." He pauses. "Shouldn't we meet?"

A twinge in her heart, on his behalf. Ryan manages to exist on the earth and never presume he's automatically entitled to anything—not the last piece of chicken or the control of her remote. Not even that it's only right that his girlfriend would introduce him to her brother.

"I'll invite him." She feels the lie in this too, even though she could make it true.

But he believes her. She can hear it in his voice, the mix of happiness and nerves underneath his "see you soon." A voice so incapable of concealment, it never fails to make her feel safe.

But all she wants to do is conceal. To her brother, her sudden love for Ryan would be like her becoming a Scientologist or joining a polygamist cult. Arlo will see her as a dupe. She and Arlo have always been the clear-eyed ones. Artie can feel his disappointment with her before it even exists.

She drops the phone in her drink holder before getting out of the car, in case Ryan decides to call back, and travels up the flagstones to her front porch and unlocked door. Unsurprisingly, her brother is asleep on the living room couch, and the sun from the wide front windows highlights the dark circles under his eyes. Her brother has always loved early mornings, watching the sun rise, but being a musician means never getting to bed early. Since he also can't bring himself to stay up until dawn, his sleep is a fragmented thing.

Arlo's head is on one armrest, his body angled so that his feet are on the hardwood floor. She's slept in the exact same position before, too lazy to chuck off her muddy boots but too fastidious to put those boots on leather upholstery. The constant touring, with the countless hours driving and the stream of truck stop food, has made his face a little fuller. His left arm is sunburned from being propped by the window while he drove. Despite her unease about Ryan, she's still, always, happy to see her brother. She doesn't even mind the wall of equipment he's moved into her living room—amps and guitars, a big speaker cabinet, even the duffel bags full of extension cords and miscellaneous tools. He's clearly home for a while.

She pulls a Topo Chico from the fridge, admiring the spotless kitchen. Before his nap, Arlo had washed the dirty dishes cluttering half the counter. On the way to the bathroom, she finds another duffel bag. She hefts it into the closet in Arlo's room to get it out of the way, squatting down to move her brother's carefully arranged shoes.

Above her hangs Arlo's brown leather pants, a favorite pair on his tour through Europe. A long black feather runs down the outside seam of each leg, the lines of the barbs and the center quill stitched in sturdy, thick thread. She remembers joking with him the first time he wore them, asking when he was having sequins added. The back half inch of leather is blackened and stretched from getting caught under the heel of his boot. Arlo always wears his pants too long, careless of the extra wear it entails. She puts her finger on the dirty edge, touches New York gutter water, Dublin floor polish. Souvenirs from the surfaces of the world.

She remembers that bar in Cork, the last time she saw him wearing these pants, when she first knew that she no longer wanted to do what she had been doing. The thick wood bar, slightly damp from beer. She pressed her elbows in, lifted up on her toes to catch the bartender's eye. She was crushed and jostled, loud Irish voices bouncing off her ears, shoulders pressed against her spine as people struggled past, moving into the adjoining room with the stage. The heavy Guinness expanded in her stomach, an awful fullness though she hadn't eaten since morning—a pool of mushy Weetabix and a dried-out blood sausage. All she wanted was a Scotch and ginger ale, stiff enough to clean off her tongue but weak enough to settle her stomach.

She looked to the stage—Arlo slicked down with sweat, grinning at the sea of heads. He was at his happiest on tour, but with her there. To him that felt like home. Olympus feels like home to her whether Arlo is there or not, and the weight of that had kept her traveling with him even after she knew she wanted to stop. Almost another year before she finally told him.

Returning to the living room, she sits on the edge of an armchair and watches him sleep. His face wears her own nose, her own lips. Her own curly hair, if he would let it grow out longer than an inch. While Olympus is always home to Artie, it's better when Arlo is there too. That's when she feels one hundred percent herself. It's being with the person who knows you best, in the place that you know best. She can't remember a time when she desired anyone's company above his. And yet, today, her thoughts are already at the river.

She writes GONE FISHING on a Post-it and sticks it to Arlo's shirt.

IT'S HER FAVORITE PART of the Brazos, a quarter mile down from June and Peter's house. She bumps her Jeep onto the grass beside the road, figures Ryan's truck is on the gravel pull-out up ahead, hidden by the swarming mustang grape vines that swallow the trees. She stands on the bank and looks down, the river low enough that a sandbar peeks through. On that island: a spot that is Ryan.

Artie moves down the steep embankment, slapping tree trunks with her palms, a grab-and-release to prevent her progress from turning into a headlong tumble. The harsh buzz of the cicadas blots out any birdsong, almost blots out the sound of the river itself. At the bottom of the embankment, she crosses a few feet of weed-studded mud before the slow flow of the Brazos begins. She takes off her backpack with her fishing pole strapped to its side, stuffs her shoes in, takes off her jeans to keep them dry and stuffs those in as well. The river is too sluggish today to draw an audience of canoers or kayakers, and there are no houses nearby (making the place a favorite of Ryan's for skinny-dipping). She wades out. The mud pleasantly sucks at her bare feet, and the current, though not swift, is enough to make her pay attention as she walks, keeping a straight line to her destination. Artie reaches the island without the water rising above mid-thigh.

Ryan has his back to her, earbuds in as he fishes for gaspergou. She drops her backpack and leaves her jeans inside it as she roots around for the bag of Funyuns and a Dr Pepper. She stands behind him, leaning forward enough to drop the chips into his lap. The fishing pole doesn't even twitch. He just looks up at her with an almost-pained smile and blinks. And blinks a little more.

She might have been able to fight off her attraction, to focus on Ryan's unsuitability (her own family situation made her pay zero heed to gossip, but it was an actual fact that Ryan had never had a relationship that exceeded five months), if not for this trait. He was a man long accustomed—due to his taste in friends, to the nature of the women he had previously been drawn to—to expect kindness only attached to ulterior motives. Add to that a mother who saw the world as always tilted against them, ready to chip away at any happiness they'd managed to get for themselves. A couple of days after they first met, Hap told her Ryan was out sick with a fever, and she showed up on his doorstep with soup and Tylenol. When she offered to take his temperature, he made her leave because he couldn't stop the tears from leaking out. In the coming weeks, she discovered it wasn't the fever. Every unasked-for kindness, every proof that she took pleasure simply in his pleasure, made his eyes turn red, made him abruptly leave the room. It was the tears that had felled her, though it is the trait Ryan most wishes he could shuck. And she understands that, too. Hard to get through life when a bag of Funyuns slays you.

By then, Artie understood the ways Ryan's life had shaped him. Kindness slew him because his mother had raised him insisting life held no kindness. And his recklessness, even the womanizing, was born from a person who had been taught the world was hard and dangerous no matter how much you tried for safety. So why be careful with yourself or with others? He told Artie she had changed him, though. He loved her so much that to not be careful, with her and with himself, was suddenly inconceivable to him. Maybe his mother was wrong. Maybe sometimes things could work out better than you ever imagined.

She sits down next to him, her thigh resting on top of his leg, and hands over the Dr Pepper. Then she puts her head on his shoulder, removes his earbuds for him.

"Arlo wasn't up for coming?" he says. He plants his fishing rod in the sand and opens the chips.

"Already asleep. Didn't want to wake him."

As Ryan nods, his chin brushes her forehead. "Maybe tonight?"

"Maybe," she says.

He nods again and holds a Funyun in front of her mouth. She eats it out of politeness, can't admit even to herself she likes them.

Artie knew of Ryan before she laid eyes on him. Her mother, Lee, had remarked on seeing a new man in town, quite handsome. And June had mentioned Hap hiring Lavinia Barry's son and her worry over it. But Artie hadn't connected the two and neither mention stuck. Later that month, she had been about twenty miles outside of Olympus, rabbit hunting on land that belonged to someone else, but a someone who didn't use it and didn't care who did. She sat underneath a pecan tree, eating lunch, when she heard a crackling deeper in the woods. She was reaching toward her rifle when she saw jeans and a bright T-shirt, tan skin and blond hair, instead of something with fur or feathers. They smiled at each other, and Artie didn't so much recognize her attraction to this man as recognize that she felt like a solid that had suddenly become liquid.

Artie and Ryan hadn't dated. They had gone fishing. They had hunted squirrel and feral hogs. Prior to him, if Artie wasn't working as a guide, she preferred to hunt and fish alone. Being with other people made her aware of herself rather than letting her sink into nature, sink out of herself. And Arlo got more irritable in nature, so she rarely coaxed him into it.

But Ryan was different. She could still sink out of herself, but with company. That was echoed in how she felt when he touched her. It was as if all of her receded except for the span of skin that connected them—she was both not there and completely there, her entire self compressed into a handprint on the small of her back, the shape of his lips on the side of her neck. Now that she had felt this way, it would be a hardship to return to a life without it. To not be as she was at this moment, by the river, with the warmth of his hand on her thigh. That, and the sharp bite of fake onion and salt on her tongue. She drank from his soda. Then she stood up, put on her jeans, and baited her rod while she told Ryan the story of her morning, her feat of strength with March and Hap. She told him she knew March could be more than his history, and she kept to herself her hopes that the same held true for him and for her.

FOUR

WHEN THIS MAN, the one June is now walking toward, drove up in time to see the last of Hap and March's fight, she could guess who he was. Joe, their usual vet, had told her he was sending someone else, a fill-in while Joe recovered from a busted hip (compliments of an ornery donkey). She's embarrassed a stranger has seen such an airing of her family's dirty laundry, and now it's like she must spend hours with someone who knows she's shoved a pair of worn underwear in her pocket. At least the cows will be there to keep her company.

While Peter never had much use for the cattle on their land, their profit margin being so much slimmer than buildings and acreage, June loved them. Loved their massive bulk combined with such peacefulness, how they seemed like contentment personified yet tested every fence for a weakness, ready at any moment to be slow-motion escape artists. And so curious—any new thing, from hat to hummingbird—getting their full attention. She liked hanging out with them. Liked assuring them happy lives as long as those lives lasted. They were here, her responsibility, before Thea was born, and they were still here, years after March had left home. Until recently, June castrated the calves herself. Peter helped, and, when they were big enough, the kids too. She always wielded the tools, though, as everyone else was too squeamish. Now that she has transformed the herd of fifty or so into organic and grass-fed, she makes enough supplying farm-to-table restaurants in Houston to rationalize the expense of professional help. And today, this must be the help: a slim man, wearing jeans and work boots, her age or a bit younger. He moves from leaning against his old F-1 to hopping up into the bed of his truck, his head disappearing from view as he leans over to sort through equipment.

"I'd planned to have the calves culled into a separate pen before you arrived. You're a whole hour early." She peers into the bed, seeing him kneeling as he sorts through a mess of medical implements.

He answers, his back to her: "Sorry about that. I was supposed to check out a horse with a mystery bite—there's been some rabid skunks in the area—but they canceled when they realized the horse was biting itself. So I came on over."

June lays her forearms on the edge of the truck bed and leans forward to get a better view.

"I'm sorry, too, for intruding earlier," he says. "If you want to reschedule, it's no problem."

"Nothing needs my time right now besides these calves." Though he has offered only politeness, June feels at such a disadvantage, she lobs a judgment. "Tidy ship," she says.

The man is leaning forward, head still down, when he locates his Newberry knife—a tool topped with a wide metal U, plus a blade— and stands up, victorious. June gets a better look at his face, which is so damn pleased, she almost finds herself smiling. He has lost most of his hair, cropping the rest close but leaving his beard big and bushy. He grins at her and then drops the castrating tool on his foot.

"Son of a bitch!"

"Language," she chides.

"Sorry." He plops down beside her elbow. "But it's your fault for startling me."

"I've been standing here for ages."

"But I hadn't gotten a look at you, not up close."

June holds his eye. "This isn't a bar. No compliments before introductions."

He spins his legs around, away from her, and slides off the truck, his hand outstretched. "Cole Doherty," he says. "And Joe tells me you are June, seller of beef, in need of fewer testicles."

June laughs. "That sounds more truthful than the plain truth."

"Pardon?"

"You saw my sons." She adds, "Also what I might have said earlier in my marriage." Cole's cheeks color, and June realizes that she has said more than she would have to Joe. To anyone, really. She's not a sharer of details, a maker of confidences. Something in his manner cuts through her embarrassment, makes her feel seen in a good way rather than a bad one. Was it simply his unexpected compliment? Could she be that thirsty for praise? "Enough chatting. We have calves to emasculate."

Cole leans over the side of the truck, grabbing a bucket and the rest of the supplies. She walks to the fence to give herself a moment. Cole walks up beside her, standing close and watching the cattle. Her moment of unease slides away into comfortable silence. She turns to him, sees he has put on a straw fedora, and laughs.

Cole keeps watching the livestock. "I know, I know. Vets shouldn't wear fedoras. Even vets in the 1940s didn't wear fedoras. But I'm from Vermont, and it's too hot down here for my knit caps. I can't buy a cowboy hat. That's like buying a beret in France."

"Go without?"

"Not an option for a bald man that works outdoors."

June is charmed despite herself. Her house is generally devoid of self-deprecation. "Baseball cap?" she offers. "They have those in Vermont."

"I hate baseball."

"I don't think the two have to be related."

"That's how much I hate baseball."

"At least it's straw and not felt. That would be ridiculous." June represses the urge to pluck the hat from his head and place it on her own.

"Are we done assessing my fashion sense? Perhaps we could move on to a subject I have more competence in."

With the help of Cole and some extra feed to distract the mothers, they get the fifteen bull calves into a smaller pen. June picks the first one, and without waiting for the vet, she leans over him, grasping his front leg and back flank, pressing into his side with her knee. The calf barely struggles as he falls to the ground with a thump. She softly praises the animal as she pins him.

"Clearly, there is plenty of competence to go around," says Cole as he sets down a bucket of water. He settles in at the back end of the calf. "Want to tell me about the testosterone this morning? This boy can hear a tale of stupid male exuberance that will now, sadly, never be his." He scratches the calf's side before turning to his scrotum.

Surprising herself, June does want to tell him. "That was the first time Hap—he's the one with the wrecker—has seen March in more than two years. Since he caught March sleeping with his wife. I hadn't talked to March since, either." She expects him to stop in shock, but Cole keeps his attention on the calf.

He says, "How do you feel about him being back?"

"As Hap's mother, I feel like I should still be angry with him. I *am* still angry with him. But as March's mother, I feel guilty for wanting March to basically disappear."

"That seems a natural reaction."

"Yeah, a good mother would want to protect her injured son, even if she has to hurt herself by sending the other son away. But what if sending him away is for me too, so I don't have to deal with my unmotherly thoughts toward my own son? That's less natural."

As Cole makes his incision, the calf lets out an aggrieved bellow. Cole pulls the aptly named emasculator from the disinfecting bucket and drops the Newberry knife in. He works quickly, positioning the tool's jaws to crush the testicular cord, while June rubs the calf's neck, thinking that it felt good to say how she felt aloud to someone besides Peter. Her husband would have waved her concerns away, told her that he knows she loves both their sons.

Once he's done and applying iodine to the incision, Cole says, "Our reactions to most things are muddier than we admit. Yours don't have to be all good or all evil. They just are what they are. Sounds like March did a horrible thing to his brother. That's on him, not you."

The tightness that has been winding up in her chest since the phone call this morning pauses for a moment, like a line gone slack. They let the first calf up and move on to the next.

"What's Hap short for?" Cole asks.

June hadn't thought about the story in years. The family had watched *Snow White and the Seven Dwarfs*. Thea was seven, Hap five, March three. The boys had loved it, but Thea had complained that the dwarf names were "boring." Dopey was dopey, Sleepy was sleepy. She had said it would be funnier if they had opposite names. "Like if we called Pete *Happy*." June explains this to Cole.

"He's named after my husband, Peter, but the nickname stuck."

"So Hap was always sad?"

"Not sad, just more sensitive. Even as a kid, he felt things more deeply than his siblings. That trait doesn't marry well with light-heartedness."

They continue on, cutting testicle cords and pausing in between to make conversation. They have only done seven of the calves when the wind picks up. The blanketing calm of the puffy gray clouds and the relative silence have vanished.

"Fixing to storm," she says. "Not even waiting for the afternoon." June lets the animal up, watching him skitter off to the fence, seeking his mother.

Cole says, "You can smell it coming in."

The sky has added black to the gray, and the wind runs and turns, pushing the treetops at the edge of the pasture into circles. Leaves snap from their stems and ride the wind. A patch of thick cloud suddenly lightens, too dense to show the lightning bolt hidden behind it. After a long pause, the thunder trails after.

"Finish up tomorrow morning, same time?" he asks. "I'm afraid my afternoon is booked."

"Tomorrow's fine." She helps him clean his equipment and return it to the truck, and from beneath the mess, he finds a tarp.

"Don't tell me you drove down from Vermont this disorganized."

"This is only five days of disorder." He unfurls the tarp with a snap, and she helps him secure it. "I can clean it up by tomorrow if it bothers you."

"I don't mean to judge. I just have a thing about clutter."

"How so?"

June opens her mouth to explain, but the thunder rumbles over her. "Fix you an early lunch and tell you about it?" She hadn't even realized she was going to ask. If she had thought about it, she would have stopped herself. But Peter will be less likely to complain about March's absence, about her not calling him to relay the morning's events, with company there.

And so, after he drives her to the house, she pulls out the leftovers from last night's dinner, microwaves the mashed potatoes to accompany the cold fried chicken, makes salad, and tells him about her father's small grocery store and gas station, five miles to the north of Olympus. How her father overbought when things were discounted, the crowded store spilling into their house next door, making it a warehouse. Even her bedroom was crammed with canned vegetables and bolts of fabric. The stacks leaned and teetered precariously, her father never good with spatial reasoning or stacking skills.

Cole takes his chicken leg with him as he peers into the adjoining rooms. He sits again. "You have embraced the minimal, looks like."

"I am partial to open floors and half-empty shelves." Outside, the thunder has finally been joined by the promised rain, and instead of raising her voice, June leans closer to Cole to be heard over the drumming.

"So, just the two boys?" Cole says.

"And a girl, my oldest. Thea. She lives in Chicago with her husband, two girls of her own. She's a prosecutor."

"That's far away for enjoying grandkids."

June nods her head but doesn't add that the distance was a deliberate choice by Thea. And after the mess of the morning, the mess of March and Vera's affair, how can she even blame her? Though this is disingenuous thinking, as the distance was always more about separating herself from her parents than from her siblings.

They have cleared away the dishes and are working on a lonely piece of pecan pie, two forks in one pie pan, when Peter swings open the front door. June has the urge to drop her fork but rejects it.

Peter's eyebrows go up, both surprise and an implied question. He's dripping wet and holding plastic sacks filled with Styrofoam containers.

"Raining so hard, I didn't hear you drive up," June says.

"I'm guessing the antique out there is yours," he says to Cole. Peter's boots squeak on the tile as he joins them at the island, setting down the barbecue. He shakes Cole's hand, transferring some of the wet. "But where's March? And I thought I was bringing lunch." He eyes the dirty plates.

"March won't be coming at noon. Don't give me that look, I'll explain in a minute. And we can save the barbecue for dinner." June goes into the bathroom to get a towel for her soggy husband.

When she returns, Cole is telling an extended story of the donkey mishap that led to Joe's injury. Peter is laughing his realtor laugh, the one with no humor in it. She swipes at his hair and then leaves the towel on his head as she rounds up the last of the leftovers.

"How do you know Joe?" Peter asks.

"Went to vet school with him at A&M. Been friends ever since."

"Surprised your own practice can spare you."

"It's been slow. Folks in my area are starting to own more bulldogs than bulls, and there's plenty of small-animal vets. I think Joe is hoping to lure me down here, wow me with the splendors of Olympus." He looks at June as he says this, and she blushes. She brings her blush to Peter, along with his food. He puts his arm around her waist in lieu of thanks.

"A small plate, no pie, and no March," Peter says. "You didn't uninvite him, did you?"

"He showed up early, followed not long after by your other son, in case you've forgotten about him."

"I have not," he says, as he turns to his lunch and digs in. They listen to the rain against the metal roof, the pause in conversation extending more than a beat too long.

FIVE

THOUGH MARCH LACKS the money to buy a vehicle, he walks onto the car lot unworried. His father carries a lot of clout in Olympus simply by owning more of it than most, and beyond that—because of reasons March has never bothered to learn—the owner feels so indebted to Peter any Briscoe can get a car off the lot when they need one. Which, of course, isn't often, Olympus being the type of place where you drive a car until the engine explodes in such a way that fixing it defies financial logic. March can see the top of a man's head, cowboy-hatted, coming toward him. As the man rounds a row of Suburbans, he stops short at the sight of March and his dogs.

Lionel, the owner and sole salesman, looks disconcerted to see him. It's not just that a Briscoe means a loss instead of a profit. Lionel is friends with Hap, gets a good deal on bodywork, and, like everyone else in town, knows why March had to leave. This is the part of Olympus March didn't miss—the way people's definition of you gets glued in tight, unchangeable no matter what you do. Not that March has ever done much to loosen his.

"Lionel," says March, nodding. He touches each dog lightly on the middle of their spines. They lay down on the paved lot.

Lionel motions toward the brim of his hat in greeting, allows a smile, and relaxes into his suit jacket. He sweats in the midmorning heat. "Been a long time. Your old truck finally give up the ghost?"

"Traded it in out west. Needed four-wheel drive for the snow. I was hoping you could set me up with new transportation."

"Don't know what we'd have that'd suit you," Lionel deadpans as he surveys the rows of shiny vehicles.

"Even for a trade-in? I've got a F-150 out at my parents' place, less than two years old. It's got . . . cosmetic issues, but the engine's fine. Get it towed to Hap's and he'll fix it up good as new, free of charge."

"Will he?" Lionel says, clearly skeptical.

"For you he would. But not for me, which is why I'm here."

Lionel nods. "I think I can help you out. Guess you need big, to carry the dogs?" The two men crisscross the lot until March settles on a white Silverado.

"Do me a favor?" March asks. "Wait until this evening to pick up my old one. I'll need to swing back by this afternoon to get my stuff out of it." The men shake hands. Though Lionel looks pained, he gives up the keys and tells March to drop by soon to deal with the paperwork and exchange titles.

Without the ramp, March has to lift the dogs' back ends up to the truck. They aren't too heavy for him, despite their bulk, but he knows the dogs think it undignified. They avoid making eye contact with him in protest, and now March's T-shirt is covered in dog hair.

After leaving the dealership, he drives past the town square and its brick courthouse with arched windows—at three stories, the tallest building in town, not counting grain silos. He passes empty storefronts as well as inhabited ones in the same ratio, if not the same configuration, as when he left. Off the town square, there's the nicer houses of Olympus, including his father's office, and then the big municipal park, a square the length and width of three normal blocks. The park brings up Vera, suddenly and vividly, and the memory of the last time he was with her. Of the dozen women he's slept with since leaving Olympus, attractive women, none could stand next to Vera and still be seen. Her beauty has the violent ability to blot everything else out—every low-cut shirt, every pair of eyes, every thought of loyalty or love. Though, to be honest, he never loved Vera. He loved looking at her, which felt like being shot in the heart with a barbed piece of iron, but in a good way. And he loved spending time with someone who liked him as much for his bad traits as for his good ones, who didn't keep hoping he'd become someone else, someone a little bit better.

But he never expected her to still be in Olympus. He isn't worried about himself; he hadn't pursued her the first time, just given in to being pursued. If she's stayed and started a family, she's clearly made her choice. But not knowing how she managed to broker a peace with Hap, he doesn't know how much his return will upset things. He needs to talk to her. And he needs her advice on the best way to start smoothing things out with his brother.

March heads to Hap's shop, but stops the truck a block away. He consciously tries not to skulk as he approaches. Once he verifies Hap is indeed there, with his welding mask on and spraying sparks, March turns and walks back. Even if his brother plans on going home for lunch, there is still enough time to see Vera.

His motives are pure. A conversation needs to happen, and it needs to happen without Hap there. And without anyone knowing about it. Vera and Hap's place doesn't have close neighbors. He can come in the back way, along the edge of the now-tall sorghum field, as he has done many times. Once he's parked behind the house, his truck will be hidden from sight. He tells himself if no one finds out, there will be no harm in it. For a moment, he marvels at how easy infidelity must be in cities, where you can come upon a hundred people and know none of them.

He drives past the edge of Olympus, and after checking his rearview to confirm an empty road behind him, he eases into a flat field. After a few minutes with only a minimal amount of crop damage, he hits the twin rows of linden trees that lead up to Vera's back porch. Hap's back porch. He reasons that his tire tracks will be washed away by the coming thunderstorm. The air hasn't turned yet, there's no smell of rain, but off to the west lies a pile of grayness, headed this way.

He gets out of the truck, lets the dogs free. They immediately go to marking territory before settling into the shade of the lindens. March turns at the sound of the back door opening, and there stands Vera, wearing only a robe. She sees him but doesn't step onto the porch. No smile, no wave, but putting off warmth like an iron. Arlo had once explained to March that Vera's appeal lay in her symmetry. The wide blue eye, the blond arching eyebrow, the sharp high cheekbone, each with their exact corollary, exactly placed. Why it is powerful is beyond March, but he has always felt its power. Vera's hair is wet, parted down the center and hanging in long blond curls that almost reach her waist.

March finds his voice but stays still under the tree. "I've come home. I was surprised to hear you were still here, still with Hap." He hadn't realized how tired he was—the drive from New Mexico, the twenty-four hours he's gone without sleep, seeing his family this morning—until Vera zapped the tired away.

"That development surprised me too."

"Can we talk?"

She cocks her head at him, silent. Finally, she shrugs, disappearing back inside the house. He jogs across the yard and up the steps to follow her into the kitchen. It feels as if he has never left town, like he has spent the past two years walking behind her, waiting for her to turn around. He ignores Hap's handiwork scattered around the room—the metal kitchen table, the hand-tiled mosaics between the countertops and cabinets. His story to himself as the pursued is shown for what it is, an oversimplification if not a total lie. Magnetism requires two opposing poles. Vera opens the fridge in the corner and leans down, putting the fridge door between them and obstructing his view.

"Guess you thought I might come back sooner," he says. "I know it's been a long time."

"Has it?" March can hear her moving bottles around, an irritable clinking. "I never thought you'd have the sense to leave in the first place, so why bother trying to guess when you might return."

"You think I shouldn't have come back?"

She stands up and looks at him, finally meeting his eye. "Why are you asking my opinion?"

"Hayden told me y'all had a baby. I'm glad you were able to mend things. I don't want to add stress."

She turns back to the fridge, pulls out a pitcher of iced tea, and sets it on the counter. Vera doesn't look like a woman who has been mended. March sees something fragile in the least fragile woman he's ever known. He's horrified to find this encourages his worst impulses, rather than bringing him guilt. So horrified, he immediately convinces himself he's misreading her. She's fine. Surely, she and Hap are fine. Here she is, after all, in the house she shares with his brother.

"If you're asking if I think you should leave town for the health of my marriage, I'm telling you not to worry," she says. "If you're asking if you should leave for your own health, that's a different matter."

March remembers the expression on Hap's face as he stowed away the sledgehammer. "You really think Hap would hurt me?" He tells her what happened that morning. "But still," he says, "it's Hap we're talking about. He always forgives, eventually. Isn't you being here proof of that?"

"Not your physical health, dummy. During the fight this morning, did you black out?"

"I don't want to have that conversation again," he says. His affair with Vera wasn't full of conversations, but the ones they did have were often about his family, Vera of the opinion they both would feel better with more distance from it, including distance from each other. But he never agreed with her about his family. His leaving wasn't about making himself feel better. Leaving town was the easy thing, in one way, avoiding his own fallout, avoiding seeing the pain he inflicted on his brother. But he also didn't deserve to stay, and it seemed like everyone would get better faster without him there.

"All I needed to know was that I'm not hurting your marriage by being back," March says. "I'll head out—" Vera cuts off his farewell with a raised hand. He hears a child's voice, a soft call for his mother, like a question. Vera rounds the corner into the hallway, and March, though he knows little about children, knows that was not the call of an infant. He approaches the photos tacked to the refrigerator with

magnets. There are baby photos but also one that looks very recent—
Vera holding an almost-toddler, dark curling hair and his mother's
lips.

She re-enters the kitchen alone, stands next to him and touches
the photo with her finger. "I thought you were leaving," she whispers.
"That's Pete."

"He's older than I thought. Not a baby," March whispers back.

"Nope. Born just about nine months after you left. Takes after you,
doesn't he? Although, he also could be taking after his grandfather.
Hap is convinced he's the father. He says the baby has his ears, which
is true, but they're June's ears, too. Convenient, sleeping with brothers. Or inconvenient, depending on which side you take." Vera is still
looking at the photo, a small smile almost breaking through.

"But who do you think the father is?" March has such a need to sit
down, he pulls himself up on the nearby kitchen counter. The cold tea
pitcher sloshes against his back as it's pushed to the wall.

"I don't care to." She turns to him, stern again. "If he grows up
impetuous and irritable, then he can be taking after me as well as you.
And if he turns out nice, then it could be all the time spent with Hap.
Covered on all bases."

"I'm going to go," he says, but he stays put. The room feels off-
balance even sitting down.

She pats his knee, almost kindly. "If you're taking to good intentions, that's a sure disappointment. People should stay in character,
should be the person I assume they are." Now she frowns, as if she
has tasted something bitter. Outside, the clouds have rolled in and
the room is getting darker. Vera goes over to the window above the
kitchen sink and opens it, inhaling. The room is soaked in the smell
of coming rain.

She faces him, leaning back against the sink. Then she pulls the
robe's tie at her waist, freeing the bow. It exposes a two-inch line of
flesh from her cleavage to the top of her panties. March grips the edge
of the counter and lets out a shaky breath. The fact of the boy in the
back room, of what his paternity would mean, is so big his brain can't
even see it all at once.

"My marriage isn't going to make it. Funnily, I figured that out just this week. Then here you are, like a sign I am finally seeing clearly."

"I want to stay in Olympus, Vera."

"Then stay." Vera walks toward him, the robe slipping farther and farther the closer she gets, finally dropping at her feet. She leans into his knees until they slide outward and her torso is held between them. "I won't say a word."

Outside, lightning flashes. March counts in his head—one, two, three. Vera leans forward, her breasts almost, but not quite, touching his chest—four, five, six. His hands are on her hips.

"Where are your good intentions now?" she asks.

"I can't keep them around you."

"You can't keep them around anyone." She stands on her tiptoes, pressing herself into his chest, her blue eyes now all he can see in front of him—seven, eight, nine. March feels the cabinets behind his back rattle from the thunder that finally comes. He wishes she would smile, swears there is something hopeless under her emotionless expression. But even that can't distract him as he slides from the counter, circles his arm around her waist, and lifts her up to kiss her.

THE ORIGIN OF MARCH'S EXILE

. . . he began, with subtle care, to fashion slender
chains of bronze—so thin, the net and snare they
formed could not be seen

ᴪ OVID ᴪ

DECEMBER, two and a half years past. March walked along the edge of Olympus Municipal Park. The sun had gone down an hour before, the shrunken December day sputtering out not long after five o'clock. The park took up a large block and massive oaks ran like a fence along its edges, sheathed in white lights like thousands of glowing barnacles affixed to their branches.

The Christmas Fantasy of Lights parade was set to begin in an hour, and families clustered along the road. Unlike summertime parades, there were few lawn chairs. Mothers shoved mittens on their children and poured hot chocolate. Thanks to a strong cold front, the temperature was near freezing and the children hoped for snow, but it never snowed in Olympus.

March found his family. Hap leaned against an oak, talking to their parents. Vera was next to him, listening to Artie. Vera's blond hair glowed in the light of the tiny white bulbs that wrapped the trees.

As March approached, he focused on Hap to avoid staring at Vera. The guilt that had been growing in him since their affair began made everything, aside from Vera herself, feel ugly. Even Hap, with his crooked nose and receding chin, the extra thirty pounds around his waist, stuck fast since he was a teenager. But if his brother's exterior seemed ugly, his own interior was surely closer to hideous. Hap loved him. Hap would never betray him in the way that March had.

This thing between him and Vera, whatever it was, had begun less than a month before, on Thanksgiving. Thea and her family were down for the first time in two years, putting either an extra edge or an extra joy to the festivities, depending on who you asked. His father hadn't bought enough peanut oil to fry the turkey, and March volunteered to drive to the Houston suburbs to find an open grocery store to fetch more. He came upon Vera, tucked between his truck and Hap's wrecker. She wiped her face when she saw him, was already walking away without a word. To ask what was wrong would feel like prying, but he needed to offer her something. So he asked if she wanted to escape the other Briscoes for a bit.

March was used to being no one's favorite in his family. But slowly, after years of knowing her, March realized he was Vera's favorite. She didn't prefer him to Hap, of course—any idiot could see how much she loved Hap—but it was clear that out of the rest of his family, March was the only one she sought out to talk to.

They headed east, Vera silent all the way to the store and March afraid to ask what was wrong. She drifted behind him in the grocery store, too, until he found the oil and turned so quickly he ran into her. She grabbed onto the fabric of his button-down to keep from falling, and without thinking, March put his arms around her to steady her. He tried to step away, having never gotten more than a stiff-armed hug from her before, but she held on to his shirt, pulling him back to her, then reaching up, pulling his head down to hers.

The kiss didn't last long. Vera broke away from him and, by the time he had paid and found her outside the store, she acted as if nothing had happened. Neither spoke of it on the drive back. March hoped if he didn't bring it up, he could more easily forget it. And if he blotted it from his mind, it wouldn't happen again. When she showed up at his house the next day, he told himself that same thing again. He kept thinking it would end soon, and he kept telling himself that Hap would never know because Vera wouldn't want him to know; Vera could always control a situation.

But it was getting harder, each time, to face his brother and pretend everything was normal, pretend Vera was nothing to him but an in-law. As he approached the group, it was his mother who spoke first.

"Didn't expect you to bother with the parade."

"I love Christmas," he said. "What says Christmas more than tractors covered in blinking lights?"

"Santa and a snowman driving four-wheelers?" said Vera. She smiled in the direction of March without meeting his eye.

"Want to see my sculpture in the shop's display?" Hap asked him. March agreed, unsure if he was glad or nervous when Hap took his wife's hand, bringing her along.

The interior of the park was filled with Christmas scenes sponsored by local businesses—plastic reindeer between six-foot-tall candy canes, a nativity with real sheep, "We Three Kings" blaring through speakers. Vera was on the other side of Hap, and without her to focus on, March felt dizzy from the noise and the color. But then he saw what Hap had made. His brother had welded and shaped thin sheets of aluminum into a life-sized angel. Hap knelt on the ground and flipped on two small spotlights. The wings of the sculpture caught the light and somehow amplified it. For a moment, March felt almost religious.

"My metal doppelgänger," said Vera. "All the beauty with none of the internal flaws, being that she's hollow." Vera knocked on the sculpture, looking up at its face.

Hap was saying something to Vera, but March was too distracted to hear it. It was like Vera's cheekbones and nose had been dipped in hot metal. He wondered if the feeling he had labeled as religious was just him being sexually attracted to an inanimate object. He was about to tell his brother how much he liked it when Vera turned to him and started talking about the difficulty of the process. Even with all that was going on, March could see how proud Vera was of Hap's talent. He had the flicker of a feeling that he was just a prop in a scene from their marriage—like a wooden cut-out donkey in the manger. But then with Vera so close, the self-awareness faded away. All he could think of was how much more beautiful living skin was than any work of art.

BUT HERE WAS WHAT HAP SAW: his wife looking at his brother in a way she hadn't looked at him in weeks. He knew he had done something on Thanksgiving, had somehow hurt her, even though Vera kept denying anything was wrong. She carried with her an anger laced with embarrassment that only disappeared around March. Hap's stomach ached, like a spoon was scraping against its lining. He leaned down to flip the second set of lights on. From this new angle, he could see Vera's index finger hooked onto a belt loop on March's jeans. Touching his brother without touching him. As if she owned both brothers, was entitled to them all—their dignity, their histories, their affection for each other now just hers. It lit an anger in him unlike anything he had felt before. He wasn't sure why he needed visual confirmation of what he was so sure of. Maybe because it was still inconceivable to his heart, if not his brain, that Vera could be sleeping with his brother. That his brother could sleep with his wife.

"See that gingerbread house?" he asked, standing up. March and Vera turned toward it—walls made of timber painted cookie-brown, thick ripples of ivory caulk icing lined with ropes of red licorice so meticulously connected, you'd swear it was a twenty-foot-long strand. A window box covered with mosaics of gumballs and enormous multicolored lollipops growing from it. "The guy who built it has been working day and night. He even set up a cot to nap inside. Nuts, right?" Actually, Hap didn't think it nuts at all. Whether a metal sculpture or a gingerbread house the size of a storage shed, it was all art. A person's vision of something beautiful, even if not everyone agreed it was beautiful, made concrete. Real. Maybe Hap thought something as ugly as his wife's betrayal couldn't be confirmed in such an optimistic place, and the house would clear away whatever jealous nonsense was plaguing him. Or maybe he knew it was only such a place that could, finally, show him the truth.

Hap excused himself to check on his shop's parade float, and he left them standing at the angel. When he returned to his family after ten minutes, March and Vera weren't there. On autopilot, he suggested they move to the other side of the park for a better view of the parade. He stopped them at the angel, received more compliments from his family, and then he pointed out the gingerbread house and its intricate details.

"What's that noise?" asked Artie. The house sounded as if someone was snapping off pieces of the roof to eat.

Hap couldn't feel his legs as he walked over and opened the house's door.

Later, when he and Vera were thrown back together, he had wanted to unsee the image, to paint over it, make it blurry, at least. But it was always there, so clear, so easy to pull to mind: his wife's hair spilling over the edge of the cot, her head lifted to meet his brother's mouth, her arms locked around his back. If only he had possessed the sense to look away, as his parents and Artie did. But he just stood there and watched, felt the bulk of his heart collapse in on itself.

SIX

THOUGH THE CLOUDS are getting thicker, the light dimmer, Artie isn't thinking about the weather. She's thinking *catfish*. She had written "gone fishing" on Arlo's note, and so she needs to return with a fish. She casts again, hears Ryan start his truck from the road above. He had kissed her goodbye five minutes ago, smart enough to avoid the coming rain, smart enough to not insist she should too.

But a rumble of thunder proves Ryan right. The wind gusts harder. As she decides to pack it in, something hits. The line spins out as the fish, landed on the hook, sinks down to the bottom of the river. She begins reeling, and the rain moves from threatening to pouring in seconds. She gets the flathead catfish in quickly, but her hair is plastered to her face, the rain working through her shirt to her skin. She holds the fish to the ground with one hand while she pulls an ice pick from her backpack. She slides the pick into the back of the fish's head, angling until it hits the brain. The flathead, not quite a yard long, stops thrashing.

Artie packs her stuff up, not bothering to remove her pants as she wades back across and not bothering to hurry. Wet is wet. She climbs up the bank, now using the slender trunks to pull herself up instead of to slow her descent. Fifteen pounds of catfish slap against the length of her thigh.

Four feet from the top of the riverbank, she loses a shoe to the grasping mud. She teeters on one leg for a second, but the motion of reaching down to retrieve the shoe throws her balance. She slides, and as she pitches sideways, she traps the catfish between her leg and the land. The splayed pectoral fin cuts into her skin, and she curses, scrambling up and wrenching the fish from her. Now she is muddy as well as wet, and the fin's venom makes the wound throb. She looks down to see a small patch of blood already staining the denim.

By the time she gets back to her Jeep, every inch of her drips, every item that can retain water does. She throws the fish to the lined floorboard of the passenger seat and rests her head on the steering wheel. She forces herself to smile, hoping it will break her mood. When that fails, she consoles herself with the knowledge that, surely, she has used up all her bad luck for the day.

She inches home, the hard rain cutting visibility, but by the time she arrives, the rain has stopped and blue peeks out in tiny patches between banks of clouds. When she comes in the front door, she sees a sight so familiar, her bad mood ebbs away: Arlo in the kitchen frying up bacon and eggs.

"Breakfast time?" she asks.

He turns, his face caught mid-yawn, and sees her dripping and dirty. He laughs. "I come home to see you, and you run out to fish in the rain?"

"I saw you earlier, but you were too asleep to notice. I brought us a second course." She holds out the beast.

"You couldn't have chopped its head off down at the bank? Like eating a dinosaur."

"The weather wasn't cooperating. Besides, easier at the cleaning station." She comes into the kitchen, lifting the catfish's belly until it's horizontal, aiming its open mouth at Arlo's cheek.

"Good thing your station includes a sink." He leans away from her. "I'm not eating that unless you bathe it before you gut it."

"Yes, Princess," she says and curtsies.

Arlo holds out his hand for the fish. "I'll put it outside. You shower and change."

Artie hands it over, but instead of leaving, she undoes her jeans and pulls them to her knees. She grabs the fish back from her brother and slides its belly along her puffed-up wound, sighing.

"Jesus," says Arlo.

"It totally works," she says, pulling her jeans back up. "Healing properties in the slime." As she heads to the bathroom, she calls out, "Plug in the Fry Daddy." Five minutes later, she's back in shorts—still damp but no longer muddy, a bandage on the fin injury.

Arlo's single generous serving of bacon and eggs is split in half on two green plates at her small kitchen table. Arlo sits in front of one, drinking coffee. Artie sits in front of the other, picking up the waiting beer.

"Cheers," she says, clinking the edge of his mug. "I toast to the return of the prodigal son." She enjoys his confused look as she snaps a piece of bacon in half.

"No," he says. "March is back and the motherfucker hasn't called me?"

"And he's already gotten his first meeting with June and Hap out of the way. Ugly, but he's still set on staying."

"He's gonna be in Olympus and not see Vera? Or see Vera and everything will be fine? Impossible."

Artie shrugs. "June was worried, but I could tell she assumes he's back permanently."

"Ah. You mean she was pissed." Arlo smiles.

Artie whaps Arlo's hand with the back of her fork. "June loves her kids. She even loves us."

Folding the white of the egg back on itself, Arlo wipes up the remains of the yolk with it. "She loves you, I'll give you that. But not me. And I'm not sold on her loving March, either, at least not when he's at his worst. God bless him, but he can be a lunatic."

"Not nice," Artie says, but it makes her look sadly at her hands, red and chafed from the shovel's wooden handle.

"March is who he is. I don't see a way this can end well." Arlo slips the fork into his mouth, not talking again until he has chewed and swallowed. "So let's enjoy him while he's here. We can all go to My Place tonight."

Artie eats her piece of bacon before she answers. "I have plans tonight." But she knows she could fold Ryan in, that he wants to be folded. Maybe March could be a buffer? Between Arlo and Ryan. Between her and Arlo.

"That's a cagey answer," Arlo says. "What's up? You got a new guy on lease?"

Artie prepares herself to explain a little of what must eventually be told in full, that she wants Ryan to be permanent. And she prepares herself for Arlo's response, that she's picked unwisely even for a rental, much less for a purchase.

"That reminds me," Arlo continues. "Carl says hello. Says he'd love to see you soon." Carl, Arlo's sometime bass player and her sometime lover, handsome enough to be high maintenance, but sweet too. Arlo grins at her, but then his good humor fades. "Aren't you curious why I'm here and not in Los Angeles?"

"I assumed you just dropped in to irritate me."

"Your replacement flaked. We went to bed in Flagstaff with a manager, and we woke up to an empty bed and a vague note of apology. We did that gig on our own, then when I called to confirm the rest of the dates, I learned we had no more dates booked."

"Shit. What do you think happened?"

"No idea. He was never very chatty. Spent most of his time sleeping on the backseat of my Bronco, refused to even ride with the other guys in the van. We were just glad he didn't disappear with our cash box or the equipment. But that brings me to the favor I need to ask."

Artie has a sinking feeling in her stomach. "Arlo," she says, already shaking her head.

"Hear me out. I'm just asking for the summer. I'll have you back before deer season starts, maybe sooner if we can hire someone else who meets minimum standards. You know how important L.A. is— I can't show up to these bigger venues with no manager. I can't even re-book them this late without some professional sweet-talking to call in favors." He taps his fork against her plate. "You're a known quantity to them. They like you."

He has dropped her in a box, and she has no idea how to get out of it. If she tells him the truth—that besides not wanting to return to life on the road, she also doesn't want to be separated from Ryan— he'll be even more inclined to resent her new relationship.

"Please?" Arlo asks. "I'll owe you."

"I'll think about it," she says. She's sure their new relationship can survive the absence, but still, she has no desire to go. She needs to talk to Ryan. To save herself from saying anything else, she lets slip something that she previously had no intention of sharing with her brother. "You and March might want to head over to Terpsi's instead of My Place, sans me."

Terpsichore's—called The Sickery by most, though half are ironic and half, the churchgoers of the stricter sort, are serious—is the closest thing that Olympus has to a strip club. The place avoided being badgered out of business because of its adherence to pasties. The owner even banned the dancers from wearing thongs. Enough left to the imagination to be almost quaint, vintage instead of pornographic.

"God, I haven't been inside in years. What could entice us there?"

"Who's the one person that would?"

Arlo's face goes slack and he puts down his mug.

Artie says, "Laurel started there two weeks ago." What is she thinking, bringing up the one girl who never could stand her brother, the one girl who had cracked him open? She tells herself he was eighteen then, but it's not as if, other than Laurel, he was a reckless eighteen. He's always been Arlo. Always in control of himself. Except when it came to Laurel.

"But why?"

"Her single-minded abhorrence of you aside, it's not like she's a shy girl. I heard she wants to get her MBA. Times are tough and tuition is high. You know it can be the best paying job in this town."

Arlo fidgets with his fork, rattling it against the plate. She has never minded seeing this open wound on her brother's otherwise impervious heart. It makes him more human, less cruel when it came to being a heartbreaker, in her eyes if not in those of the women whose hearts he breaks. But it bothers her that she has taken advantage of his weakness just to avoid responding to a not-unreasonable request. Since Laurel won't be pleased to see him, she's dealt an unkindness to them both. She tells herself that March will keep him in check. In check, and also there until closing time.

"All right. You're free for the evening," he says. He doesn't even look excited about the prospect of seeing Laurel, just keyed up. He takes their empty plates to the sink. "Get on with the decapitation and scaling. We need a second course."

Artie grabs her boning knife from a drawer and slips out the back door to her outdoor sink and table. In minutes, the fish is ready to be fried, the defilleted carcass in a bucket in the sink. She walks with the pail toward a clutch of trees and heaves it out, food for an animal once it gets dark, food for the ants until then.

The back door swings open, and Arlo leans out as he holds on to the doorframe. "Hurry it up. The grease is popping and I'm ready to fry." He snaps his fingers at her, grinning, and then pulls himself back inside. Arlo has never been much for hunting, not because of a love of animals but because of an indifference to them. But he will happily eat whatever she kills. Will that be true when it's her and Ryan out hunting, both of them bringing dinner home? The three of them at her small table? She wants to believe it's true, but she worries it will take them a long time to get there.

SEVEN

MARCH AND VERA have retreated to opposite sides of the living room couch. Over the baby monitor, the boy fusses and falls silent. The rain, which had been falling so hard it sounded like an attack on the metal roof, lessens to a benign drumming.

"I should go," says March. He stands, tugging up his jeans that were bagged at his ankles, his boots still on. He pulls his T-shirt on over his head.

"You shouldn't have come in the first place." She offers him a crooked almost-smile.

"You're right about that," he says, getting the first glimmers of what is going to turn into a much larger regret, a much bigger uncertainty about his future in Olympus. For once, he's eager to not be in the same room as Vera. He starts toward the back door.

"Wait," she says. "I can't let you leave this miserable." March looks over his shoulder at her. "Sit," she says, pointing to the wingback chair beside him, and he does. She retrieves her robe from the kitchen and returns to the couch. "Pete isn't yours. He was conceived a couple of weeks after you left."

"Jesus, Vera," he says. "That was a fucked-up lie to tell me."

"I know. But *you* know my anger leaks out. Me and you, we're not that different."

His high ground thus taken, March sits quietly, enjoying the relief he feels. If only all of today's complications could vanish that easily. "Why did you stay with Hap?"

"I left. But I came back after the holidays. Snared by my own curiosity. All those years of watching him be the peacemaker. Ready to give up what he wanted if it interfered with someone else's desires. Defining himself through what he gave other people, especially his family. And then he turns around and humiliates us in public, even inflicts our mess on Artie and your parents by making them witness it? It was something I might have thought up myself. Made me wonder if he could change, if, finally, he might not need to constantly deny himself to feel comfortable in the world."

Vera was always tight-lipped about her motives, and often about her own opinions. But March had long ago grasped this fact of his brother's marriage: Hap's kindness and his empathy were seen as something darker by his wife, something less than healthy.

Vera tucks her legs underneath her and smooths down her robe. "He gave me enough hope to have a few conversations with him, and one of those led to me getting pregnant. But, of course, he didn't really change in the end. Same old selfless Hap."

"You still could have divorced him."

"I was excited about the baby but not about being a single mother. I saw that up close with my mom."

"Then you can't really be planning to leave *now,* either." If he states it as a fact, maybe he can make it so. Then maybe he can also shake off the knowledge that, just like two years ago, he's become a prop to help Vera get herself out the door.

"Can't I?" Vera says. "It's impossible I've changed my mind again?"

"So you and me, it was just a way to hurt Hap? For being the same man that you married?"

He sees some of her anger there again, but she pushes it down and her face reverts to sadness. "I don't have any desire to explain it to you, even if you could understand," she says. "But it wasn't spite, just my own weakness. And in my defense, we both had to be weak for it to happen. Both then and just now." She shuts her eyes, as if she's tired of looking at him. March feels no better knowing she regretted their affair as much as he had.

His whole life, everyone has always expected him to do things he shouldn't. It's what he expects of himself. Being blamed for things he didn't remember doing felt so unfair, his actual choices began to skew more in the wrong direction, too. It made the world feel less arbitrary and him more in control.

He gets up from the chair and crosses the room to her. Her eyes are still shut, and he bypasses her lips for her forehead. Then he makes himself step back. "You should shower."

She snorts and opens her eyes. "You think I've forgotten the things I need to do?" She stretches her leg back out, runs her toe up and down his thigh. "Get out of my house."

The dogs have moved up on the porch, not so much to avoid the storm as to avoid the growing tide of mud. They follow March into the yard and consent to be manhandled into the truck bed, snapping at the rain and shaking their coats free of drops only to be covered again. March drives west to the truck stop outside Bullinger, where he takes his own advice and showers, leaving the dogs in the truck, under an awning. He buys a pack of cleaning rags, wiping down Rom and Remus as the rain fades away and the sun returns.

He needs to pick up his stuff from his truck. He needs to ask his father if there's an open rental he could move into. He hasn't eaten anything since his mother's biscuits this morning, and he wants to rifle through her refrigerator and eat leftovers on her front porch, maybe invite himself to dinner. But he wants to do all these things with a clean conscience, an entirely new desire for him. Not wanting to be seen as good by others, which is an old feeling, but wanting to see himself that way. Instead, he's been back home half a day and, rather than beginning to make amends, he's made a bad situation into a god-awful one.

The idea of having to leave Olympus again, so soon, makes his brain recoil from the option. It's not difficult to convince himself he deserves a fresh start to his fresh start, and he knows who might help him with that. He drives back to town.

PETER HAD BEEN GRIEVED to not see March at lunch, a disappointment only partially obscured by June's odd friendliness toward the vet. Now back at work, staring at March's old desk, he feels in full his son's long absence.

Peter's own father had been a farmer. He taught Peter that a true vocation was working land, not selling land. His father also taught him, by example, that working the land was no kind of life, meant yoking contentment to things as unreliable as weather, insects, and blight. Peter's childhood years had coincided with the worst drought in Texas history, and even when the rain returned, prosperity didn't, not for them. Despite generations of successful farmers behind him, Peter had no qualms selling the farm when his father died. Hayden had learned the same lessons as Peter and easily agreed. (Though, ironically, Hayden did return to planting things in the ground, having found an angle far more profitable than living crops.) Yet Peter, unlike Hayden, can't take pride in work so removed from actual sweat. He rigs his day to include sweat—refuses to hire anyone for repairs to the dozen or so rentals he owns, for pre-sale improvements to the houses he sells, despite having the income to easily hire them. Currently, one house needs new baseboards, another a gate replaced. Once March shared that work with him, and they would fit it easily into the morning hours. Without March, the work lasts all day. If March returns to his job, Peter won't have to grapple with the question of whether he's aging out of the honorable part of his livelihood.

Peter has grabbed his tools and is heading out of the office to fix a leaky toilet at one of his rentals—unwise to leave *that* repair until Monday—when he sees his son coming up the sidewalk. He opens the door for March, greeting him with outstretched arms. "Stranger! You were supposed to be at lunch, not breakfast."

"I know," says March. "An excuse of a son."

Peter hugs him tightly, a longer one than he would typically allow himself. He even starts talking without letting go, the words spoken next to his son's ear. "June told me about Hap dropping by. Sorry that didn't go better." He steps back. "Come in, sit down. Tell me all about where you've been."

His son looks back at two enormous dogs panting in the bed of a truck. "Mind if the dogs come, too?"

Inside, March tells his tale. His son tends to the factual, the terse, but Peter sees the subtext, sees how much March missed them. Peter scratches Rom's chest, studying his son, and thinks perhaps the boy has changed. At least a bit.

March says, trying to keep his voice offhand, "I wondered whether any of your rental properties were open. I've got money saved, so—"

"Two, in fact, including your old house. And like before, don't need your money. Wouldn't mind if you came back to work, though. Too much for just me, but I never got around to replacing you."

March smiles, like a middle schooler receiving a compliment, and it breaks off an edge of Peter's heart. March approaches him, holding out his hand, and they shake.

"Want to grab some food?" March says. "Then I need to clear out my truck before Lionel collects it as a trade-in. Might be easier with Mom if you came, too."

"We wrested another vehicle from Lionel? Excellent." He claps March on the shoulder. "Why don't we raid the giant bag of barbecue back at the house? It was meant to be your lunch, after all."

"You sure Mom will let me back in the house?"

"Of course. I even think we can convince her to let you spend the night. She wouldn't want you sleeping on the floor of an empty rental." Peter has no confidence in the truth of any of those statements, knows too well how long his wife's grudges can run, but there's no harm in optimism.

THE ORIGIN OF ROM AND REM

For all things change, but no thing dies.

⚔ OVID ⚔

After skipping town, March first loitered a couple of months in Roswell, New Mexico, with an ex-girlfriend he'd served with in the Army. A six-foot-tall former medic and now nurse practitioner, she had too much sense to keep him around long-term. Kicked loose, he went due west out US 70 toward Ruidoso. After weeks of flat brown expanses, March marveled at the increasingly mountainous land. The nearer to Ruidoso he got, the more he saw pine trees. Snow on mountaintops. Ruidoso was beautiful in a totally different way than Olympus. It gave him the feeling he could begin again, that there was life away from his family, away from that small section of Texas he knew best.

He took a room at a house with three guys who worked at the Inn of the Mountain Gods Resort—a bartender, a waiter, a blackjack dealer. They, along with his Army background, helped him land a job in security. It paid poorly but gave his life structure, which he knew he needed, and personal interaction, which he had not realized he needed. All his life, he had so many family members he couldn't shake them off for more than two days running. He hadn't known what it felt like to be really alone, and he didn't like it. So the casino and resort, filled with both employees and a steady stream of visitors—a portion of them at least moderately attractive, moderately young women—helped him forget he was lonely. On the whole, and for the first time in his life, he kept his nose clean. No heavy drinking, no fighting, no getting angry. He had to have an attachment to the world to feel angry, and this new world, while bearable, held no real attachment for him.

Eventually, he saved up enough money to rent his own place—a rundown condo on the edge of town. The only downside of moving out of a house filled with men who never cleaned was his attachment to the waiter's dog—an English mastiff. The dog, and the waiter, had come from Iowa. March so often offered to dog-sit for him, the waiter worried both March and his dog would evaporate from the town. And so when the man's cousin, the sire's owner, mentioned a new litter was ready to be sold, he and March drove all the way to Iowa to get one.

March settled in on the floor of the breeder's kitchen strewn with used and unused pee pads, taking one puppy after another into his lap. In the end, he bought two. It was momentous, being entirely responsible for another creature's food, water, and shelter. He felt ready for that, but not with being another creature's sole emotional support. He would do his best, but they would always have each other if he failed.

They sped out of Rome, Iowa, two big balls of fur sprawled on March's lap. He hadn't thought about the irony of acquiring brothers until they were well out of town. He embraced it and named them Romulus and Remus. They proved to be a pain in the ass and made sure he'd get no security deposit back, with the baseboards chewed and the carpet stripped into bald patches. But they made him look forward to coming home, made the shitty condo actually seem like one.

He knew he was in trouble when he started telling the dogs about

Arlo and Artie. Before long, the dogs also had heard about his mother and his father, even Hap and Thea. But not about Vera. He found himself too embarrassed to confess his betrayal to these drooling and growing masses that would have loved him even if they understood his moral limitations.

EIGHT

HAP COMES HOME to a quiet house. He finds Vera in their bedroom, reading one of Pete's pigeon books aloud, both of them sprawled on the bed. She hasn't noticed their son has drifted to sleep, his pinky lodged firmly in his mouth.

"Hey," Hap says.

"Hey." She smiles, but it doesn't reach her eyes. That in and of itself isn't a sign of anything; Hap knows her smiles for him haven't had much warmth in months, even if he isn't sure why.

"You're dressed up," he says. She's wearing a blue sundress, earrings, heels.

"Could we go out for dinner? Don't feel much like cooking."

Hap doesn't feel much like going back into the world, but Vera gets what she asks for. He nods and, because Pete is asleep, sits gently on the edge of the bed, smoothing the duvet. "March is back," he says. He doesn't want the news to feel like a test. Vera just nods.

"I heard. Ran into Hayden at the post office."

Hap tells the story of the morning, knowing she'll hear about it eventually and wanting to spin it as a joke she's in on and not an attack on her too. He had accepted her apology before Pete was born. He can't go back on it now. But he's still worried. He'd come home wondering when March and Vera would see each other, that it would have to happen eventually, that it could have already happened.

But, at least, Vera seems to find the tale funny. She sits up and listens, her lips pulled into an amused smirk. They are pretending they can talk about March as if he held no more sway on their marriage, a past life with different people than they are today.

He leaves Vera and Pete and showers, still uneasy. By the time he's done, Pete is awake and Vera is packing up his diaper bag one-handed as she holds him on her hip. He takes the boy from her and kisses his nose. His son, who carries his own heart, not Vera's guarded one. Pete is quick to cry over a dog getting injured or a word spoken to him that is less than kind. Quick to offer up one of his own toys if either parent looks sad. He had hoped their child would show Vera that kindness wasn't always martyrdom. It could be pure instinct, a heart that immediately felt what was in another's, even if he didn't want to feel it. But she chose to see it as a result of Hap's nurturing overpowering Pete's nature, and now it was just another thing to fight over.

Vera stands in front of him with the packed diaper bag and her purse. "Ready," she says.

Hap can't read her. For once, he asks what is on his mind without worrying about how she'll react. "What does it mean to you," he says, "that March is back?"

"You know what happened wasn't about March. It was about us, about me. So it doesn't mean much, other than dealing with more crap from your family. With this whole town watching me." Her lips part to say more, but instead of speaking, she takes a deep breath. She holds it, then says, "The current state of our marriage, it's got nothing to do with your brother. It's about—" She stops abruptly when Pete reaches out for her. Their son has tensed up in Hap's arms just from Vera's bleak tone. She says, "We shouldn't talk about this with Pete in the room. He's picking up so much lately. Let me put him in his playpen, turn on the TV."

Just like his son, Hap is tense too. Though he's the one that started this conversation, he has no desire to listen to Vera turn over and examine every flaw in their relationship. "We'll talk later, I promise. Let's just go get dinner. We'll go to that Italian place in Bullinger, less gawking."

"Okay. Italian it is." Vera knows him well enough to hear the *please* embedded in his tone. "Are you surprised he's back?"

"I always thought he'd come back, maybe not for another year or two, but eventually," Hap says. "After the Army, I'm pretty sure March decided he didn't do well alone. Didn't do well when people expected more from him than he could give. I don't want him back, but this is probably the best place for him. A violent version of the village idiot, one we can all take care of."

He thinks his purposeful meanness might pull a smile from her. But she just says, "That's depressing, if true."

"Or comforting," he says. He swings around to the dresser, Pete laughing at their speed, and opens Vera's jewelry box. "Wear your brooch?" He is so relieved when she nods, when she lets him pin it to her dress.

THE ORIGIN OF HAP AND VERA

. . . when covered, fire acquires still more force

ᕯ OVID ᕯ

HAP FIRST SAW his future wife on the night of his twenty-first
birthday. She bartended at a place near the University of Houston
campus. He already knew her by reputation; she had briefly dated one
of his friends in the art department. Over the next year, she went out
with two more of his friends, the best-looking ones. Hap had generally dated women more attractive than himself. He had a kindness,
an empathy, that contrasted well with his exterior. And his extra
weight, especially at that younger age, just made him seem stronger, more solid. A heel lift for his shoe hid the fact that one leg was
slightly shorter than the other. Still, he never dreamed of asking Vera
out. The girls drawn to his kindness had been kind themselves, and
Vera wasn't kind. Besides, she was easily the most beautiful woman
he had ever seen—in real life or in the paintings he studied to improve
his own.

Most of what he knew about Vera came from listening to her talk to his friends. She served them beer, they sat across from her on bar-stools, trying to get to know her. She chatted because it led to bigger tips, not always easy to come by in a bar full of college students.

So Hap heard the same stories multiple times, sitting next to mul-tiple men. She was from Lubbock but moved to Houston after gradu-ation. Her high school drama teacher, who had spent two years trying to sleep with her, suggested she move to Los Angeles or New York City. But Vera was a pragmatist. She knew her odds were slim. She had no talent for acting. Modeling meant New York, and New York was cold. She had always hated the bitter Panhandle winters. Raised poor by a single mother, she knew the things she wanted, made sure to only want attainable things. Warmer weather, green grass and trees, no snow or freezing winds. She would have preferred Florida, but she could make do with Houston. She just wanted to marry well, have a nice home, raise a family. Two people, her and her mother, had felt like an understaffed team.

At times, when answering a familiar question, she would slip in a lie: claim to be born and raised in Key West, or back from a failed mar-riage in Alaska, or to already have a child. As she said these things, she would look directly at Hap and smile. Those were the only times she did look at him, other than when he ordered and paid. That smile told Hap that the man to his side didn't have a chance.

Those evenings were how Hap knew she was born in November. He was taking a jewelry course that semester and he made her a brooch—a big orange topaz sun burning off winter snow. Tiny shards of mirror melted into silver runoff, revealing iridescent green enamel below. The day of her birthday, he came in by himself, the first cus-tomer of her shift.

"Happy Birthday." He set a small copper box, also his construc-tion, on the bar.

She looked skeptically at the gift, then at him.

"I don't find you attractive," she said. It was the longest she had ever held his eye.

"I guessed as much."

"I don't care how much you paid for whatever is in that box. I still won't go out with you."

"I wasn't asking. And the total cost of materials was less than fifty bucks."

This made her smile. "Even if I did want to, which I definitely don't, I've been dating a lawyer for two months now."

"I know. I've seen him picking you up after your shift."

"So you're giving me this out of the goodness of your heart?"

"You gave me the idea for it. No one else will appreciate it as much." He spun the box on the counter.

Vera stood across the bar from Hap, silent, for a full half minute. Hap didn't break, just pasted on a vague and expectant smile. Finally she caved, curious despite herself. She removed the box's metal top, pushed back the tissue paper, and pulled out the gift.

"My mom inherited a brooch from my grandmother. She never wore it, though," said Vera, "because it was too old-fashioned. Like all brooches." But still, she lifted it carefully from the box, and Hap saw, despite her words, that her hands didn't want to let it go. Her fingers kept it from the stickiness of the bar.

"Orange topaz is my birthstone," she said.

"I know. It's also the stone of friendship."

Vera finally looked up. "And the state stone of Utah, if we're listing off irrelevant facts."

"I can't want to be your friend?"

Vera squinted at him like she couldn't make him out. "You really believe that's what you want?" She tucked the box under the bar and started slicing limes at the far end.

It was in that moment, after Vera had diagnosed him, that Hap realized he was in love. It wasn't a pleasant realization, and he had to marvel at his own capacity to fool himself. He hadn't known before, but now he felt it.

He sat at a distant table, back by a broken arcade game, the rest of the night, only going up to get a drink when the other bartender was free. But he watched her get ready to leave at the end of her shift. Saw her pick up the metal box and again examine the brooch inside before putting it into her purse. She looked at Hap, knowing exactly which table he was at, and he met her gaze. Vera shook her head, but Hap was encouraged to see it looked more like a shake of confusion than dismissal.

Six months later, when she finally consented to go on a date with him, he saw the box again. It sat on a bookshelf in her apartment, positioned like a piece of art. But when she left the room and he opened it, the box was empty. It wasn't until a few weeks later, when he made it into her bedroom, that he saw the brooch on her dresser. That night, in bed, she told him, "When I look at that brooch, I know you see me. Not what I look like. Me."

Hap loved her even more then, for the sadness in that statement. That it would mean so much that he could extract this small detail from her and present it, distilled. This thing anyone could know if they cared to.

HAP'S APPEARANCE didn't bother Vera, even though she had only dated handsome men. She knew, better than anyone, what a disconnect there was between a person's exterior and who they actually were. She saw how men could love her knowing absolutely nothing about her. That she cared about Hap without the bonus of beauty made her think it was all the more meaningful. Made her feel bigger than her own beauty. But having never been in love, not really in love, she was confident she was in no danger of falling in love with him.

Two months into their relationship, she was closing up, counting her till, the doors already locked. Hap had come in thirty minutes earlier to keep her company then drive her home. He was drinking a root beer, a straw poking out of the aluminum can, while she complained about the customer who groped her when she was making a daiquiri. The man, a semi-regular, was already prone to touching her hand too much, too long, when money or drinks were exchanged. He had snuck behind the bar when her back was turned and placed both hands on her hips, sliding them forward into her pockets. She was so startled, she knocked the running blender over. It spewed ice and syrup and rum across the bar and ten feet beyond, splattering the backs of a dozen patrons. Before she could even turn around, the bar-back—six foot four and 350 pounds—had yanked the guy up and laid him out on the bar, in the pile of ice and frozen strawberries, like he was using him as a mop. Then he had shoved the guy off onto the other side. Satisfying, though Vera knew it wasn't for her sake. The bar-back had been pissed because he had to clean up the mess, and Vera was supposed to be thankful he directed his anger at the douchebag instead of the person using the blender. She also got no sympathy from the customers, who were either entertained by the spectacle or trying to wipe themselves free of the sticky shrapnel.

It had made her look forward to Hap's arrival. He'd understand, sympathize with the world trying to take a chunk out of her without asking, without even prior warning. Something Hap would have never done to any woman. And he delivered, listening attentively then telling her, "The world is a hard place for women as beautiful as you."

All her life, people treated her beauty like it was a great gift, one they might envy or covet, depending on their own desires. She would hear women at the bar complaining to other women, the horror of being too old or too plain and too fat or too thin. Didn't they know what a gift it was for a woman to not be seen, to skid below the notice of the world? Those women didn't face a city of men who thought they should have her simply because they wanted her, like her beauty broke the lock of herself, leaving her open to be taken by anyone interested.

No one had ever understood that. Not even her own mother, who, plain and made plainer by a hard life, could only be pleased for her daughter, sure in her belief that Vera's life would be easier, better than her own. But here was this man, this burly and not-so-pretty man, who understood her. Understood her even though the same did not apply to men. The world *was* easier for attractive men, men better looking than Hap.

He said it like it was an undisputed fact then lit up in a smile, as if he understood what he said had changed something in her. She realized she was more than a little bit in love with him. He smiled like he could see that love plainly on her face, and then he leaned over the bar and kissed her.

NINE

ARLO NOSES into a tight parking spot up the block from The Sickery, the only open one he sees thanks to the Friday night crowd. He tries March's new cell number, which Artie gave him, but again it rolls straight to voicemail. He doesn't want to be irritable. He wants to pick up where they left off, to pretend the last two years, where March disappeared and Arlo let him, never happened. But that's hard to do when he's reminded of both March's failings to be a good friend and his own.

Fine. He'll go in by himself. He won't be the only one there alone. The building that holds Terpsi's was built in the 1920s as a state-of-the-art cinema. It had struggled on into Arlo's childhood before a fire in the projection booth destroyed the second story. After staying empty for more than a decade, a rich transplant from Fort Worth with a love of burlesque resurrected it as a cabaret.

Since it's the start of the weekend, the place has a decent crowd—

a small line for the bathroom in the lobby where an old popcorn machine pops. He pushes through the swinging double doors and sits at the end of the bar closest to the stage, ordering his first bourbon of the evening. The dancers are slightly better than he expects, and he doesn't recognize any of them. Perhaps because they are near on a decade younger than him, or perhaps because the talent is commuting in from Houston.

He hasn't seen Laurel in years. She didn't return to Olympus after college, as far as he knows. In his head, she's still the girl he first noticed in high school. If Artie had told him Laurel was performing at a strip club in Houston, he doubted the teenage heart buried deep inside his adult one could have borne what he'd see. But here at Terpsi's, he might even be able to engage with the fantasy being presented. If he drinks enough fast enough. He orders another double, pushing down the thought that he shouldn't be here at all, that March could have talked him out of this if he had just returned his call. That Artie shouldn't have mentioned Laurel in the first place.

When Arlo first spotted Laurel in the school's parking lot, the second day of his senior year, he was sure he'd never seen her before. In truth, he had sat next to her in the stands while watching Artie play softball five years before, stood behind her in line at Dairy Queen a few years before that, but those hadn't registered. Unfortunately for him, he had definitely been registered by Laurel.

How could he know that, two years prior, Laurel had often sat on her cousin's bed, listening to tales of Arlo, the new boyfriend? Then, a few months later, after he had broken up with the cousin, Laurel had spent so many hours consoling and commiserating, building up an arsenal of insight into the immoral nature of Arlo, a boy she had never even spoken to.

And so, when he did try to speak to Laurel, repeatedly, she wouldn't even answer. Her face would harden and she would simply walk away. Arlo became obsessed, lost in the idea of her unobtainability. He feels the cliché, even as he sits here at Terpsi's years later: he's a man who only wants what he can't have. He doesn't enjoy being a spoiled child, or worse, a man with a heart so damaged it schemes against him for its own protection, only feeling safe when alone.

The music changes, violins. Nina Simone's version of "I Put a Spell on You." And there she is, onstage. Laurel. He'd forgotten the way she moved, the small bounce in her step, like a kid. But it's not childish here, in a tight velvet dress that touches the floor, gloves nearly up to the cap sleeves. When she peels off the first glove, he leaves his stool and settles into a theater chair next to the catwalk, a stage extension that curves up the incline and cleaves the seating area into two. He is close enough to see that she doesn't look so much like Laurel as like a woman who bears a resemblance to the girl he knew. The second glove comes off, then she reaches back to unzip the dress, still moving up the catwalk. With the first notes of the sax solo, his memory of her solidifies in this new version, and he is seventeen again.

As she reaches him, she pauses to slip the dress off. Her leg is there—white and freckled and close enough to touch. Arlo has always been a man in charge of himself, but as Laurel begins to spin toward the other side of the catwalk, he finds his body standing up. It's like a magic trick. His boot places itself on the old wooden armrest, creaking as it takes his weight. His other foot has found the stage, but all he is aware of is Laurel's bare skin. She's facing away from him, hasn't even noticed him behind her. His hands reach forward, and only then is he aware of how quiet the audience has gotten. All the chatter alongside the music has stopped. Then a single long boo, joined by another. But even that isn't enough to stop his fingers as all ten of them sink into the softness of her hips. Laurel doesn't freeze; she retracts in on herself, as if she possesses the ability to reduce her own volume. One hand moves up to her stomach, and his other hand curves around the side of her rib cage. He has only been onstage seconds, but Laurel's nearness and the float of the bourbon makes it feel eternal.

A bouncer launches himself up onto the far end of the catwalk. Arlo doesn't see Laurel's elbow as it travels toward his face, only feels it as it slams into his still-smiling mouth. He stumbles backward just as the bouncer arrives, and the tall man catches him while the final notes of the song play.

Laurel turns and her face changes as she recognizes him. The bouncer still has a hold of him, but neither man expects Laurel's kick to Arlo's groin. He steps sideways as he doubles over, all his weight on the foot now half off the stage, and he loses his balance. He grabs the wood at the edge of the catwalk as he falls, catching an exposed nail which slices his palm open. He thuds across two chairs, the wind knocked out of him, while the bouncer hops down from the stage. The man yanks him to his feet, just in time for Arlo to watch Laurel leave the stage with her chin up, a dignified walk in her underwear and pasties while a show assistant picks up the clothes she left behind.

Ten minutes later, after being sequestered alone in the manager's office, Arlo stands on the sidewalk with the bouncer. They had let him wash out the cut on his hand, but a small red circle already grows on the bar towel he used as a bandage.

"With a little prompting, Laurel agreed not to press charges," the bouncer says. "But don't come back for a good long time. The manager says he doesn't want to piss off Peter, but he would appreciate the courtesy of your absence."

Arlo opens his mouth to express some sound of understanding, but nothing comes out. Terpsi's must be one of the rental properties Peter owns. The club's lenience is thanks to a man Arlo has no desire to thank. Humiliation on top of humiliation. He does manage to nod, and he's left alone on the sidewalk.

As Arlo returns to his Bronco, he desperately wishes himself back in his sister's kitchen, watching her rub that ridiculous fish on herself, rewinding this night so he won't have to remember it. He pulls out his phone as he opens the car door and sees he finally has a message from March, too late to be of any use. He slides in, propping his aching hand on the steering wheel, and listens to the message.

March's voice sounds flattened, but Arlo can't be sure if it's March trying to be quiet or if something is wrong. He says, "Sorry I missed your call. Glad you did call." Pause. "At my parents now, but let me know if you want to get together later. Or tomorrow." Pause. "Tomorrow might be better." Arlo can hear Peter talking in the background, June responding. Have they actually forgiven him for fucking their other son's wife? It's impossible for Arlo to comprehend, though he has never been able to understand Peter's or June's choices. "Hope you are out with Artie and Ryan, having too much fun to pick up. Maybe try to be nice to him? He seems important to her."

Arlo clenches the steering wheel, forgetting about his hand, getting nothing but pain and a fistful of towel. The man Artie blew him off for has a name, of course, but why does March, who has only been back in Olympus twelve hours, know it? Why has Artie hid his importance from Arlo, but not from March? Had she sent him here to get him out of the house, like he was an object in her way? No, he tells himself. That's the bourbon talking. That's not Artie.

He starts his car and drives through Olympus, past the courthouse and police station, an eye on his speed limit as he knows he's over the blood alcohol limit. The sun had set about an hour before, and the streets are quiet—people in their homes or inside the restaurants and bars. As he takes the road out of town, to his sister's, he can see the lights of the baseball field a mile off, a late-running Little League game.

His stomach roils, but he blames his lack of dinner. He should stop somewhere. He should eat. He should call March and they should go eat together. He should diffuse whatever is tensing up inside him. But he does none of this. Instead, he cuts off his headlights as he pulls onto Artie's long dirt driveway. Seeing lights on at the house, he leaves his car near the main road, walking up toward the house. There's a late-eighties, piece-of-shit Toyota pickup parked next to Artie's Jeep, and Arlo can see the TV on through the front windows. His sister owns no drapes, no blinds, wants as much of the outside to be seen from the inside as possible. And she has brought the outside in, with fichus and dieffenbachia and pots of fern and African violets, watched over by the vigilant heads of deer and elk and an African antelope.

And two more heads, in profile, on the couch. Then Artie stands up, pulling on a man's arm and waving his car keys at him, wearing an enormous grin. She throws a fake punch, missing by a mile, and opens her mouth in what must be a laugh. Then her face relaxes, and she looks at the man with an expression Arlo has never seen on her before. He knows it well, though, as do most musicians with any talent. Not just attraction but adoration. That thing that separates the love you have for family from that other kind of love. Artie is in love, and she didn't want Arlo to know. That was why she didn't want to help with the tour. Why she had sent him after Laurel.

Never before has it bothered him that his only home is not *his* home. He pays no part of the mortgage or bills, has no say in furniture or arrangement. But his home has always been Artie, and he feels as at ease here as if he had been on the title. He knew without her saying that he would always be welcome. But now, standing outside, looking in, he no longer feels that certainty. He hadn't realized that he relied so much on his sister. She has always been so steady, he never had cause to wonder what it would be like if she was not.

He has behaved horribly this evening, he knows this, but at least his behavior wasn't premeditated. And it wasn't against the person he most wants to keep from harm. He turns back toward his car, already realizing he has nowhere to go.

SATURDAY

ONE

AFTER BREAKFAST with his talkative father and his silent mother, March retrieves his boxes from Hayden's and drives over to his prior home, now his again. It's on the north edge of Olympus, not far from where the houses dry up altogether and are replaced by hayfields. He and the dogs get out of the truck and view the 1920s bungalow. He's lucky to have it—then and now—as most of his father's rentals are '70s and '80s ranch-style houses, carpeted and low-ceilinged and sad. This house has thick wood doorframes, hardwood floors, and enough updating to include central air, which March turns on as soon as they get inside. The dogs cruise through every room, sniffing, before settling on an old blue shag rug in one of the bedrooms, clearly so ugly it was left behind. March says, "Your rug, your room. Have at it."

He leaves them and his boxes and drives to Hap's shop. June had tolerated him last night, but he knows she won't warm to his return until he begins to fix things with his brother. He feels like an idiot jailed for arson, who upon being paroled immediately began to set up a bonfire. Not knowing how serious Vera is about leaving Hap, he needs to lay the groundwork of his apology before Vera drops the match. And he needs to pray she doesn't rat out her accomplice.

Hap's business has five large bays, their doors open to the summer heat, four filled with cars. March parks off to the side, near the sign that reads *Briscoe Auto Body and Repair*. Beneath it hangs one of his brother's metal sculptures, which evokes a car while also looking like a crashing wave. Seven years ago, when the shop was new, Hap also displayed his work here, even occasionally sold pieces. His art drew people to it even if they didn't know why they were drawn. But Hap noticed that it discomfited some of his employees, separated them from him. Now he sells his work online, with a rare show in Houston or Dallas where he can charge what it is worth without the buyer laughing in disbelief, as the citizens of Olympus tend to do. March once asked Hap if he missed having the freedom of living in a city, just working on his art, and Hap said if he did that, he'd miss the greater freedom of making art without relying on it to pay the bills. Plus, he'd have to live in a city. It seemed that Olympus attracted Hap, March, and Artie as much as it repelled Thea and Arlo.

March can see Hap crouched by a dented Mercury sedan at the far end of the bays. He ignores the men who stop their work as he approaches his brother, their welding helmets raised, their hammering ceasing. When he's twenty feet away, Hap stands, probably to see why the noise has stopped. Spotting March, he glowers and calls out, "It sounds like y'all think it's break time, so go ahead and take one." The silence is replaced by the sound of tools being set down, small talk, though March can tell half the men wish they could stay. He wonders if one of them is Ryan, but it seems the wrong question to kick off the conversation.

Hap squats down and goes back to removing the car's taillight. "Your truck's around back. Lionel thinks it's his now, but I'm sure you can get what you need from it. Because if you need something from me, that you're not getting." He doesn't look at March as he speaks. Now that the taillight is free, he's stuck his arm inside to feel the dent in the car's quarter panel. This is how his conversations have always been with his brother. They have to be doing something as they talk, have somewhere to focus their attention to make eye contact unnecessary.

"Can I help you with that?" he says. Hap ignores him. "I'm sorry," he says. Hap continues to give him his profile, and March sees the red bruise on Hap's cheekbone is deepening to purple, proof of yesterday's scuffle. Coming home will mean he has to own the pain he causes others, both the things he remembers and the things he doesn't. "I know what I did two years ago was unforgivable, so I don't expect you to let me off the hook. But could you put up with me staying in town?"

"Will you leave if I say no?"

"I will," March says, though he hasn't thought through that particular scenario and so isn't sure he's telling the truth. After a lifetime of Hap forgiving him, March has gotten too used to it to expect otherwise.

The only sound in the shop comes from the metal creaking as Hap's arm presses against the interior of the car's frame. "You could grab that heat gun and keep it moving over this dent. Watch out for the paint. And that's an answer to your first question. I'm undecided on the second."

March's shoulders relax a little, and he has to stop the edges of his mouth from curling up. He grabs the gun, plugs it in, and starts heating the metal. They work for five minutes in silence, Hap using a long thin tool to press and reshape the dent from the inside.

"I won't lie," he says. "I wish you stayed gone. Especially now with Pete."

March wants to tell his brother he'd like to spend time with his nephew—likes the idea of the three of them together, seeing his brother as a father, something he can't see in himself. "I want to be done breaking things," March says. He sees how much easier life would be if he could.

Hap finishes smoothing out the dent and tells March to shut off the heat gun. Wanting to make his brother feel better, to make his own guilt a little smaller, March quietly adds, "It was never love."

Hap pivots and is suddenly there, inches from March's face. "I've spent my life stuffing down my emotions to make room for yours,

doing what's best for you while no one worried what was best for me."
Hap's voice echoes off the metal, carries out past the open bay doors.
"And what do I get for my trouble? A brother that wrecks my mar-
riage, and not even because he was in love."

"You deserve better than me. I know that." March takes a couple
of steps back. "But I always assumed you and Vera would be divorced
when I came back, her gone from Olympus. Maybe you'd even be
remarried, and it would be easier for you to forgive me because you'd
be happy."

A laugh pops from Hap's mouth, but March sees that it's astonish-
ment and not humor. His brother starts toward him again, and March
lifts his hands like he's surrendering, though the cooling heat gun he
still holds might seem too much like a possible weapon.

"You thought you'd come home and I'd be *grateful* to you?" Hap
wrests the gun from March's hand and March backpedals into the car
behind him.

"When you put it that way . . ." His voice falters. "I always regretted
it. I regret it even more now." Now that he has done it again. Now that
he can see what Hap can't, the bigger damage teed up and waiting
to fly.

"Get out of my shop," Hap says, pointing out the open bay. And
March does, before Hap extends the ban to the whole town.

TWO

In my charitable moods, I think of Peter as having been sober for thirteen years. Just instead of no alcohol, it's no other women."

June and Cole sit on her balcony, the day cloudy enough to forgo shade, drinking iced tea. It's only 11 a.m., but they're both grimy and covered in sweat after hours of working with the calves. June doesn't worry about when Peter will be home. She doesn't worry about what she looks like (a mess) or smells like (cow). She isn't enjoying herself because she's flirting with a near stranger. She's enjoying herself because her lack of attraction is allowing her to speak openly, or so she thinks. She doesn't have a great deal of real friends, the ones you can confide in. The women she knows split between those that pity her, those that judge her, and those that pity and judge her. Besides, after their conversation yesterday, going back to small talk would be like eating fast food when offered a five-course meal.

"I doubt a town this size has a sex addict anonymous group," says Cole.

"True. Anonymous and a town this size are mutually exclusive." Her glass drained, she rattles her ice cubes. "And Peter's problem is not exactly that, anyway."

"Thirteen years and you still use the present tense?"

"Don't they say an alcoholic is always in recovery?"

"True." Cole stretches out in the chair, his legs loose and his arms dangling. "When did it start?"

June has never told this story to someone fresh. If mentioned at all, Peter's adultery is always banged against sideways, the audience, knowing all the details, not needing the direct approach. Normally, the facts of it gall her because of how the events make her look, how egregious they are. But she has no urge to hold the information in. In fact, it feels a little like she's spinning fiction, merely entertaining rather than revealing a wound.

"The first affair was for a couple of months just before we were married."

Cole whistles.

"To make it worse, Peter doesn't count that one since all the sex took place before our wedding." June leans over to the table next to her and grabs the tea pitcher to refill her glass and then Cole's. "I think it should count for the obvious reason. But also because the subsequent child was born after our marriage."

"Shit," Cole says.

"Two months before Thea. His name is Burke. Even if Peter doesn't count it, to me it is the biggest of the hurts." She pauses, surprised to not actually feel the pain in this moment.

"Does it make it hard for you to see Burke?"

"We don't see much of him." Though June remembers almost each time—the baby in the woman's arms, across a bin of watermelons in the produce section; the kindergartener streaking past her car as she waited outside of school; the tall boy with Peter's smile in a graduation cap sitting four rows behind valedictorian Thea. "His mother was married. The husband knew, forgave his wife—he had been overseas in the Army—and Burke was told when he got older. He and Peter talk every once in a while, but Burke's never been interested in really knowing him. He lives in Houston now, has a family." She cannot think of Burke without thinking of Thea, and of when Thea found out about Burke, of the blame that Peter deserved being doled out on June instead. "Joe didn't catch you up on all the local gossip when you arrived? Briscoes usually rate high on the hit list. We're not a rich family, but we're wealthier than most here. And small towns seem to expect an inverse ratio of money to sin."

"Vet gossip is different," Cole says. "He didn't tell me about you because you never did anything stupid to your cattle." He grins at her.

"How about you? What's your proportion of sin?"

"I ruined my first marriage. Also cheating, I'm afraid. The second marriage ruined me; I was the one cheated on. So I learned my lesson by age thirty-five. I've been a happy serial monogamist, minus any wedding vows, ever since."

"Children?"

"A son and a daughter from the first marriage, both live in New York. No grandkids yet, which I am totally fine with."

"I didn't mark you as a man afraid of aging," she says, eyebrows raised.

"Not afraid of being called Gramps." Cole rises from his slouch to take another swallow of tea. "Just screwed up parenting enough to be wary of grandparenting. Do a bad job, and you remind them of your past lack of care. Do a good job, and you remind them of your past lack of care and that you had the capacity to do better."

"I hope you're overthinking that," she says. "Though we see Thea and her girls so rarely, I shouldn't worry."

"Does the town gossip bother her?"

"I'm sure. But it's more that Peter and I bother her. Mostly me, maddeningly. Peter has managed it better simply by bearing her spite with a smile. He dotes on her as much as she'll allow." When Peter thinks of his daughter, he thinks of her intelligence and strong backbone, the family and career she's created. June just conjures a string of their arguments. "That the worst thing you've done, the bad parenting?" she asks.

"That was the worst cumulative. The worst single action, I'd have to think a bit. You?"

Does she want to tell this too? It makes a good story. Does she care so little what he thinks of her? No, she cares. Yet she wants to tell him anyway.

"I was eight months pregnant with Thea, had just found out through town gossip about Peter's affair and Burke's birth. I went home, grabbed Peter's rifle from the gun case, and sat on our porch to wait for him to come home from work." She remembered how holding the gun calmed her down, made things feel simple.

"When he finally arrived, I raised up the gun and aimed it. He put his arms in the air like I was robbing him." In her anger, June had imagined the shotgun pellets tearing into his flesh. And suddenly, she felt such affection for that body. It wasn't that chest's fault its owner had a faulty moral compass, an incomplete will. She thought of the company that body provided. The warmth and the smell and the feeling of home.

"He was far enough away I knew I could shoot and not kill him, the pellets would be too scattered. Maybe put out an eye. I thought I could forgive him, then, because I'd have proved his actions had consequences." Her ripped-up heart and his ripped-up skin.

June falls silent for so long, Cole asks, "What happened?"

"In the end, I couldn't do it." The telling of the story has made it real again, and she can't transform the memory into a tale anymore. She can't tell Cole how Peter walked toward her apologizing, how she stood up and pumped the shotgun as he came closer. She put her finger on the trigger and lined him up in the site. Peter didn't even flinch at the sound, kept coming to her, even though June knew how scared he was. She could see his arms shaking above his head. Every step made it harder to shoot because every step made the shot more lethal. Peter stopped in front of her, and she raised the gun until it was level with his heart. She could imagine pulling the trigger, the deafening noise, the hole she might make in his chest, big enough to see daylight on the other side. She closed her eyes, hoped the potential to do it, the imagining of it, would be enough to satisfy her.

She was only twenty-two to his twenty-seven. She opened her eyes, stared at her husband, waited for him to open his own closed eyes. She knew she wouldn't shoot, couldn't kill him, but she would test him. If

Peter reached out, grabbed the gun, pulled it from her giving hands, she would go inside and pack a bag and leave him for good. But if he stood there, waited for her to put the gun down herself, gave her that much, then she would listen to his reasons. She would try to make the marriage work.

"Please," he said, eyes slowly opening. "I'm so sorry."

She leaned forward, the barrel of the gun coming to rest on her husband's shoulder, the closest she could come to touching him. She started to cry. She pulled her finger off the trigger, laying it flat on the side of the gun. She leaned so hard into him, Peter had to shift one of his feet backward to bear up the weight. Later that night, they would sit on their bed, the brass columns still bright and clear. He would promise it would never happen again, that he hadn't touched another woman since their wedding. A stupid last gasp. That the baby boy would be claimed by the woman's husband and their not-yet-born baby girl would be his only child.

She let herself be convinced. But June was changed, and she could feel it in everything she did—preparing the baby's room, cooking Peter's dinner, making love. We all eventually learn how little we control our own lives, but June resented mightily that it had been Peter who taught her that lesson and not fate or bad luck or some version of a vengeful god. It shouldn't have been the warm body, the comfort she folded herself into at night.

Cole puts his hand on her arm, and she knows she must look upset. He says, "I don't know, June. If you didn't actually shoot anyone, that's a candy-ass worst thing."

"Now that you mention it, other worse things come to mind." She forces a smile.

"We'll save those for our next conversation. I should get back on the road. A herd of goats awaits." He removes his hand, but that place on her forearm still feels warm.

"Lunch first?" she asks. "There's barbecue left." She stands up, her left hand pulling her hair off her neck so the right hand can wipe the sweat away.

"Ah," he says. "I can make time for that."

THREE

WHEN ARLO IS HOME, Artie will get up to watch the sun rise with him, then start her day even though he returns to bed. But this morning she slept past ten, not waking as she normally does from the sound of the back door opening. Now she fidgets in the kitchen between prep work for Arlo's favorite, eggs Benedict. As if fancy eggs could make up for what she plans to tell him about Ryan, about his tour. For the first time, Artie can imagine having a family, imagine babies and the children they would grow into. But her capacity to think of Ryan has blotted out part of her capacity to think of Arlo. Arlo, who she has thought of first for her entire life.

The piece of pecan pie isn't helping her mood. She left it on the kitchen island last night, but here the pie is, still wearing plastic wrap. Usually Arlo devours anything left out before he goes to bed. Perhaps last night saw a miracle, Laurel softening to her brother and taking him home with her? She checks from the living room window—there's his Bronco, parked at an odd angle. Artie begins to mentally compile a list of what might have gone wrong in her sending her brother after Laurel. Checking the back patio, where Arlo would have watched the sun rise, she finds a water glass and a slew of bloodied cotton balls. Her disquiet grows. Picking them up, she's relieved the quantity of blood is small. She lets her guilt take her back to the kitchen, starts poaching eggs.

Just as she's fishing the eggs from the water, she hears Arlo in the bathroom. Minutes later, he emerges and settles at the kitchen table. The uncombed hair is expected. The swollen lip is not. She whistles a single note. "You okay?"

Arlo doesn't answer, but he extends his arms to her in a stretch that displays his palms. There's gauze wrapped around his right hand, splotches of dried blood seeping through. Her own hand launches into sympathetic pain, a heated throbbing in the center of her palm. She can't define her brother's expression, another rare occurrence.

"Elbow to the face. Sliced open hand," says Arlo. "And I got kicked out of The Sickery for being an imbecile. Stellar night." Arlo crosses his arms and leans back in his chair. "Thanks for the recommendation."

It dawns on Artie that the expression on her brother's face is anger, an emotion he hasn't directed at her in years, not even when she told him she wanted to quit touring. After a few days of intermittent lobbying for her to stay, he had accepted that choice.

"I'm sorry," she tells him. "It was a bad idea."

"And your ideas are rarely bad. What prompted this one?" The back of Artie's neck prickles at his tone.

His cell, sitting on the table, rings. Arlo checks the name and picks it up. "Morning, asshole," he says, still with anger in his voice. He listens for a moment then says, "You took your time returning my call, so I was taking my time returning yours."

Artie assumes it must be March because something the caller says finally cuts through Arlo's mood. He smirks and says, "World's luckiest miscreant." Then he tips the phone away from his mouth and looks at her. "You free today?"

Artie nods.

"We'll be there," Arlo says and hangs up.

"We'll be where?"

"March needs help moving his stuff out of storage."

"Peter found a place for him?"

"His old one was open."

"March wasn't with you last night?" Artie had counted on him being there. "What happened with Laurel?"

"An amplified version of what always has happened. She told me to fuck off without even needing to speak to me." His nose wrinkles in pain as he fingers his lip. He gets up to pour himself coffee, and he surveys the prep bowls with egg yolks and butter. "You're making my favorite," he says. The edge in his voice softens a bit.

"I am." She stands next to him, and neither of them speaks as they finish up the preparations, her whisking the yolks as he drops in chunks of butter, falling into the comforting routine of two people who know what comes next.

They sit at the table and eat, Artie putting off the conversation about Ryan and the tour by telling him about her clients and the latest gossip from town. She's sure Arlo will feel better with some food in him. Arlo says little, finishing his breakfast quickly. He sits back, watching her closely, and finally says, "Just tell me. It's exhausting seeing you this nervous."

"I can't come on the tour," she says. She pushes her egg-soaked bread around with her fork.

"You could," he says. "For some reason, you just don't want to. Not even for such a short time."

"You can find someone else," she says. "It doesn't have to be me."

"If they're available on such short notice, and they aren't you, they can't be very good at their job." Arlo takes his plate to the sink, turning his back to her. Then he pulls himself up on the counter, flinching when he puts weight on his injured hand.

Her brother looks smaller, almost fragile, up there. Under his anger is a clear pang of hurt. Arlo rarely complains. Not about their mother, not about Peter, not about her own friendship with June. But she knows she's the one responsible for giving Arlo a center, for making him not feel like an outsider in every part of his life. Even when he performs, he's up on a stage, distant from the crowd. Even with a backing band, he considers himself a solo artist.

"Tell me why you won't go back on tour."

Artie wishes she could say she made that decision months before, that she needs to move on for *her*. But she knows the truth: if not for Ryan, she would help her brother finish this leg of his tour. She wouldn't be happy about it, but she would do it. She has to admit this. She joins him at the counter, leaning next to him. "I've started seeing someone. It still feels new."

"The famous Ryan," Arlo says. Artie doesn't like the sound of Ryan's name in her brother's mouth, and she likes even less the surprise of it being there. Arlo nods, like she's confirmed something. "Come on, Artie. No secrets in Olympus."

"I wasn't keeping him a secret," she says.

"Not telling me about him yesterday? Or, more importantly, on any phone call you and I have had since you met him?"

The truth is she wasn't keeping him a secret, she was only keeping him from Arlo. "I'm sorry," she says. "His name is Ryan Barry. And I really like him, Arlo. I need to see where things are going to go."

"Can't you see where it will go starting in September? If the guy is going to disappear that fast, seems like he isn't worth hanging on to. I wouldn't ask if it wasn't important. You know I wouldn't." It breaks her heart to hear the vulnerability in his voice, breaks her heart even more to find she can ignore it. But Artie sees now that this is no longer about the tour. It's Arlo wanting proof he still outranks Ryan.

"I'm being selfish," she says. "I need you to *let* me be selfish, to stay with Ryan."

"Wait," he says. She sees recognition on his face. "You said Ryan Barry? From Bullinger?"

"Yeah."

"Jesus. That guy's a piece of shit."

"He's not," she says, unable to keep herself from banging the counter with her fist. "You don't know him."

"I know his reputation. And his family's. Trouble follows them everywhere. I've dated a couple of his exes, gun-shy and skittish after getting fucked over by him."

When she sees that condescending look on his face, she can't help herself. "How shy were they twice bitten, then? You're going to judge him for doing things in his past that you're still doing?"

"Maybe I was a dick in high school, but I'm honest now, always, about not looking for anything long-term. Besides, I could give a shit what he does unless he's doing it to you. Tell me you could shrug it off if he disappeared tomorrow, and there's no problem."

"He won't disappear. Just like I won't disappear on him."

"I've gotta shower," Arlo says. "March is waiting." He doesn't even look at her as he leaves the kitchen. At least that's what she tells herself to explain why he doesn't pause when she reaches out, her hand extended to him in apology for a conversation that's gone every shade of wrong. He just slips off the counter and disappears from the room.

THE ORIGIN OF ARTIE'S PROMISE

Yet these were but small griefs.

⋉ OVID ⋊

THE HOUSE ITSELF WAS TAINTED, though Artie and Arlo wouldn't realize that until they were a few years older. When they were small, they didn't know Peter was the real estate agent who had sold their mother the three-bedroom in a new development just outside Olympus. They never knew their living room was the first place Lee and Peter had sex, that their mother's bedroom was where they were conceived. They had actually never seen their father in their home; when they did see him, it was always at his house, always with June and without their mother. But for their mother, that house held the entirety of her relationship with Peter, the beginning and the end. And now it contained what she had been left of him: her twins.

They knew they were loved. They saw it in their mother's actions, and her words, ninety percent of the time. But how to account for that other ten percent? When she didn't even see them. When she locked herself in her room. Forgot about making dinner. Forgot to make them brush their teeth before bed. Sometimes even forgot to put them to bed at all. It mystified Artie.

But by age four, even if Arlo didn't understand the details, he already understood it was weakness. It was the same impulse that made him want to lock himself in his room when their mother locked herself in hers. But he wasn't weak, and so he didn't. He concentrated on making Artie feel better. Pulling peanut butter from the fridge, honey and bread from the pantry. Telling Artie when it was time for bed and putting toothpaste on her toothbrush as well as his own. Arlo's anger at his mother's weakness armored him against the hurt of her neglect. Artie wasn't capable of that anger, so he had to be her armor.

By age nine, Arlo wouldn't even go to Peter's. It wasn't out of loyalty to his mother, though it bothered him she wasn't even allowed out of her car when she dropped them off. He couldn't shake the feeling that the invites came from June, not Peter, like he and Artie were a mess that she kept trying to make Peter clean up. It was hard, too, to suddenly share his sister with three other siblings, a full set of pseudo-parents. Artie enjoyed the visits, so she kept going; he would never begrudge her that. But he didn't, so he wouldn't.

Age eleven. It was one of Lee's bad days. They had become less and less frequent as Arlo and Artie got older. They were lucky to have no memories of their first two years, to have no idea how frequent the bad days could be. But the fact they had not seen their mother like this in so long—even a year is forever if you are eleven—had made it all the more upsetting. Their mother, sobbing in bed, no breakfast, not even acknowledging their questions and offers of food and drink—Artie at the coffee pot, guessing at measurements, Arlo making toast for their mother with three pats of butter and too much jam.

They didn't know what had brought it on, hadn't seen their father the night before at the school's Christmas band concert. They hadn't noticed what had so pleased their mother at the time—Peter quick with the camera, waiting until his three children were all in the same frame to aim and shoot: March, Artie, Arlo; drums, trumpet, guitar.

She had gone to bed happy, but she had woken resentful. She didn't have a picture with Peter and her kids. She never got to watch them together, hear their conversations. Couldn't even spend an hour on their porch as a fellow parent. Still ashamed of her long-ago affair, she couldn't bring herself to ask for more, even if she was also hurt that Peter never asked on her behalf.

And so Artie and Arlo—leaving the watery coffee and overloaded toast on their mother's dresser—went to the porch. Arlo grabbed his guitar on the way out, but Artie shook her head. She knew he would play something sad, and she couldn't stand to hear anything sad.

"We're going hunting," she said. She had brought her rifle out of the gun safe, where her mother always insisted it stay when at home. Arlo hated hunting but followed anyway.

She remembers clutching the cold metal of the rifle. She and Arlo in the woods, convincing him to take the gun, to fire at the targets she had hung on a tree trunk. With the safety still on, he flipped the gun in his hands like one of the drill team's parade rifles. It spun faster and faster as Arlo slapped and twirled. She reached out and stopped it, the force of it an icy bang to her hand. She tried to pull the gun away, but he yanked it back.

"So now we don't just have to take care of ourselves, we have to take care of her too?" Arlo said. He started crying, a rarity at any age but unheard-of since he turned eight. He wasn't hurt as much as embarrassed; he had started to trust their mother to take care of them. He hated feeling like a fool. But Artie didn't understand that; she only saw his pain. She took off her scarf and wrapped the scratchy white wool around his neck, looped it over his head, and tucked the end inside his coat. She pressed her forehead against his, the gun caught between them and pointing out into the woods, its hard wooden stock muffled by thick coats.

And she had promised him. She would always take care of him. She would always put him first, and he would put her first, and their mother didn't have to be their responsibility. They could always count on each other. Nothing could change that.

.   .   .

THEN, AGE NINETEEN. Artie came home for the summer after her freshman year while Arlo stayed in Austin—summer school at UT, plus he was already picking up gigs, coffee shops and the occasional bar (you didn't have to be old enough to drink to be old enough to play). After finally getting away from their hometown, he had no desire to return, but Artie looked forward to time at home. At first, her mother seemed to, as well. But after the loneliness of the whole freshman year—the suddenly empty house and empty dinner table and empty life—Artie's return made Lee despair over what the future held as soon as those summer months were over.

By now, Artie was old enough to know her mother's behavior for what it was—not being lovesick, not feeling blue, but battling depression. For a month, Artie consulted Arlo on the phone daily. He had little sympathy. He said it wasn't their fault she hadn't made her own friends, didn't try to date. It wasn't their job to set those things up for her. But Artie began to panic—their mother was getting worse, would do nothing but sit and stare at the TV or sleep. Soon Lee would need to return to her own classroom of third-graders. What would they do if she lost her job?

Arlo heard his sister's panic. For her, not for their mother, he withdrew from his summer classes and came home. With pressure from Arlo, who could be so much more blunt than Artie, Lee went into outpatient treatment and onto medication. Artie knew she wasn't solid enough to be left alone yet, so she told Arlo she'd commute to the nearby junior college for the fall semester. And Arlo, without even being asked, said he'd do the same. His responsibility to Artie had made him responsible for their mother after all, but he never complained. He just did what they had promised each other.

FOUR

Driving home for lunch, Peter smiles as he remembers March in the kitchen that morning, all of them eating breakfast together. He hadn't thought of himself as particularly unsettled while March was gone, but he's always been a man who can easily convince himself of things whether they're true or not. And now, as there's no denying his relief at his son's return, he mentally notes his good cheer. Better to realize unhappiness after it's already gone. But when he pulls in front of his house, his mood sours at the sight of the vet's truck.

He leaves his vehicle, taking care to close the door quietly though he knows June always hears approaching cars. Unless she's terribly occupied. It hits Peter that the feeling burrowing into his shoulder muscles, making him close his hands into fists, is jealousy. And swiftly, his jealousy changes to anger at June, anger at this new man, that their banter at yesterday's lunch has evoked this in him. Has turned him into an insecure idiot.

When was the last time he felt truly jealous? It must have been thirty years. If a man's wife is constantly tearing about in a jealous rage, he's never in doubt of her feelings. Now on the porch, he hears his wife's laugh. Not the flirtatious laugh he can still sometimes pull from her. This laugh is full and open-throated. He knows this should reassure him, but it doesn't. He enters and finds her and the vet sitting on barstools on opposite sides of the counter. They both turn to him, both still smiling, and Peter's shoulders tighten more, seeing his wife had again eaten without him, again sat down with this man instead.

But he won't show her his jealousy. She would enjoy it too much. She would keep up whatever it is between her and the vet just to nettle him. So he smiles and asks, "Get the calves done? Beautiful morning for it."

"All done," says June. "Here. Take my seat. I'll fix you something."

But Peter doesn't want to sit. He hovers next to the barstool, enjoying the vast height difference this gives him over the vet. He has an excellent view of the man's bald head. He smells livestock, the odor coming off of both this sweaty man and his sweaty wife. This bothers him too, but for no reason he can articulate. So he sits and asks the vet about his plans for the rest of the weekend, not caring about the answers.

As June listens to Cole talk, punctuated by polite questions from her annoyed husband, she reins in her urge to hum. She shuttles things out of the fridge, all while wondering what in the world she's feeling so good about.

June has always been wrong in her assumptions about love—so wrong, in fact, that at this point she should assume the opposite of what she believes and then be right for once in her life. The most ridiculous, looking back, was her assumption that true love bestowed a contentment that blotted out all else. June blamed her assumption on the books she had read from ages ten to sixteen, even though she could blame herself for not noticing what the books showed bore no resemblance to her only firsthand experience of matrimony, her parents. June had figured the problems lay in her parents as human beings and not some defect of love. She hadn't yet learned that since love was the creation of two people, and people were always defective in one way or another, then the love itself was necessarily flawed. She knew that now, definitively.

Another assumption, formed as early as the prior assumption but still standing all these decades later, was that love was a drug. For the first few years of marriage, the simple nearness of her husband, at times just the thought of him, would speed up her heart rate and fill her with a reckless energy. She couldn't sit still, she slept fewer hours. And even after the initial rush had faded, it was prompted again when she suspected him of straying. Unfortunately, that also meant her love and her anger had merged in a way that could no longer be disentangled.

She pops the cold brisket, white fat lining the edges of the slices, into the microwave and heads to the pantry to retrieve the bread. That feeling was proof she still loved Peter. No other man had ever made her feel that way. So, clearly, whatever she is feeling with Cole is something else. Not lust because lust has its own form of agitation. And not recognition of a kindred personality; she's fairly certain she and Cole have little in common, not temperaments or backgrounds or interests. What throws her most is how unlike an accelerated state this feeling is. When standing next to him, leaning against him, even, as they struggled with the calves, she felt calmer than she has ever felt. Right now, she has a wondrous, baseless feeling of well-being. She likes the world more. She likes herself more. She even likes her husband more.

Or perhaps she is just latching on to any distraction, practicing a form of self-medication to weather this feeling of being in a waiting room, or in an audience, before the actors have taken the stage. Only it's a show that could wreck Hap's family, overturn her youngest grandchild's world, force the rest of the family to take sides if March chose not to disappear again. Who wouldn't rather feel that the world is a good place and ignore their worries?

She spoons some barbecue sauce on the bread and then slides the steaming brisket atop it. She sets the sandwich in front of her husband and pulls up a barstool to join them.

THE ORIGIN OF JUNE'S RAGE

I can see—and I approve the better course,
and yet I choose the worse.

⚹ OVID ⚹

IF FORCED TO LABEL the first five years of her marriage, June would call them contented. She loved to see how much Peter loved Thea, but their daughter's birth had been so close to her learning about the existence of Burke. While she loved her daughter more than she had imagined possible, that love contained the shadow of something else. But when she became pregnant with Hap, she had felt somehow repaired. And after he was born, there was something in his little face that made her feel less alone, as if he supplemented that part of her that Peter's affair had lessened. So she was delighted to find herself pregnant the third time, felt her family would be complete at five.

She was four months along, March a small mound on an otherwise flat stomach, when they got a midnight phone call. The repeated rings woke up Thea, who then woke up Hap. June had wanted to listen to Peter's replies, wanted him to answer her repeated question of who was calling, but he leaned forward in bed, the phone to his ear, and turned his back to her. The children called out and so she left the room, sure that someone had died, wondering how bad the news was to come. She bribed Thea into bed with a promise of waffles in the morning, re-tucked Hap while soothing him that everything was fine.

She stepped back into their dark bedroom, saw only the outline of Peter's body, still sitting up in bed. "What happened?" she asked.

"I have to tell you something," he said. The words almost sent her back out of the room. The news was so bad it needed a preface. But June was never, had never been, a coward. "Turn on the lamp, then."

"I'd rather say it in the dark."

And with that, she knew. Of course he hadn't kept his promise. It made her life a lie, the family a lie, the new baby a lie. "Whatever you did, you don't get to admit it in the dark." She slid her hand down the wall until she found the switch and flipped on the overhead light.

PETER HADN'T INTENDED to break his promise to June. He was loyal by nature and assumed he would remain faithful after taking his vows. Even his first affair with Burke's mother hadn't changed his opinion of himself. Lee had started out as just a client, needing a house. But he looked forward to their appointments, even taking her to view houses unlikely to meet her needs simply to see her again. Still, he didn't take it seriously. He understood why he was drawn to her, and that lack of mystery made him feel capable of restraint.

Lee was all softness, the least judgmental woman he had ever met, not just with him but with the world. If he showed her a house that was a wreck inside, the occupants weren't disgusting but "must have been pressed for time that morning." She was warm and affectionate and patient. Asking for nothing, expecting nothing. Their time together, even before they began their affair, was all pleasure and no strife. He couldn't help that he preferred that to the shrieks and energy and demands of a four-year-old, a two-year-old, and a pregnant woman home alone all day with the two of them. Their home, though full of love—for he did truly love his son, his daughter, and most certainly his wife—was not a comfort. It felt, at times, like a thing to be endured, and when we endure things, we start believing that we deserve a reward for that endurance.

The midnight caller had been Lee's mother. The hospital had telephoned her that morning, and she'd driven straight down from Oklahoma. Lee had been voluntarily committed because she feared hurting herself. She had stopped eating, barely even drinking water, after Peter had broken it off two months prior. Peter hadn't known she was pregnant, much less with twins. A fitting end. The ease he had let himself fall into would be transformed into its opposite. More children, more mothers to disappoint.

When his wife demanded he face her in the light, the disgust in her voice made him realize how much he had risked. The whole time he was explaining what had happened, June was shaking—not from tears or grief but from rage. All he wanted to do was get up from the bed, go down to the gun cabinet, grab that old rifle, and bring it back to her. Not just because he deserved it, but also because he could see no other answer. If she didn't hold all the power, how could she forgive him?

"Her mother insists I come to the hospital and convince her to take better care of herself. To tell her that even if I don't want her, I do want her children. She says Lee will take care of herself for me, like a duty, even though she can't do it for herself."

To JUNE, it felt as if her husband was saying to her, *See, that's what real love is. Your love isn't that big, now is it?* She would show him how big her love was. It was so big, when she set fire to it, it would obliterate his life. "Pack a bag. You don't live here anymore. This isn't your house. This isn't your family." She stepped backward and stumbled, and when Peter leaped out of bed to catch her, she spun away hard and rocked into the dresser.

"June, please," he said.

"No more pleases. You get no requests. You get nothing, nothing from me anymore." She rested her palms on the dresser, saw Peter's pocket watch—from his father, his father before him—and desperately wished none of those men had been born. She picked the heavy gold watch up and threw it straight into her husband's face. Later she wondered what would have happened if she had picked up a more substantial object instead. Something that would have drawn blood or knocked him down. It might have pulled a little pity from her, dampened the rage before it grew so large she would never be able to quench it, only contain it. The watch struck his mouth and fell to the floor, shattering. In the next room, Hap called out for her.

June and Peter both looked down at their bare feet, the room still dim enough that they couldn't see the glass beneath them.

"Okay," he said. He leaned over and picked her up, held her in his arms like they were newlyweds crossing a threshold, and she was too stunned to protest. He carried her over to the door, flinching as he opened it, and she knew he had stepped on the glass. All these years, Peter had protected her. He reminded her things didn't have to be perfect to be good and that she didn't have to be perfect either. As he set her down outside the bedroom door, his protection only felt confining. And yet she swayed slightly in the hallway, unsteady without his arms. What he did with Lee stripped her of ever feeling safe with him, yet the experience of her marriage made it impossible to feel safe without him. She heard the door to Hap's room open. She saw Thea already standing in the hallway, a small, dark shape in June's peripheral vision.

She grabbed the doorknob and slammed the door shut in his face, leaving him alone in the bedroom. She walked down the hall, picked up a wary Thea, and took her into Hap's room, shutting the three of them in.

PETER STAYED AWAY for a week, sleeping at his parents' house, bringing Lee home from the hospital, making her promises about everything except returning to her. He watched her, purposefully, haltingly, turn her love for him directly onto the children to come. Meanwhile, June spent that week in a fuming daze. The morning sickness she had left behind weeks ago returned, but she welcomed how the nausea could—occasionally—make her forget herself and only wish for a calm stomach. It took just one evening without Peter there, one morning with no help, no one to hug her goodbye, to talk to, for her to wonder what a future without him would be like. Who would be with her in the delivery room in a few months? Who would fetch the newborn when he woke them up for the fourth time in a single night? Even worse, she couldn't take the ache of waking up alone in their bed, no person breathing next to her, no other body to lean against.

But if she let Peter come back, it would be like saying she saw the pattern of their future and accepted it. As if she didn't deserve better. All week she spun fictional solutions, ones she knew she'd never do but which allowed her to get through the day. She would terminate her pregnancy. Or she would go away and have the baby, give it up for adoption, then steal back in the night and take Thea and Hap from their beds while Peter was sleeping. Take them with her, somewhere far away.

She would deal cards in Reno, she would wait tables in Galway, she would buy land an hour outside of Prague, near the village her grandparents emigrated from, and raise cows. She would be another person, a person who not only didn't love her husband but didn't have a husband to love. She was not even thirty yet. It wasn't too late to craft a whole different life.

On the eighth morning, she came downstairs to find Peter in her kitchen with his suitcase at his feet. They hadn't spoken since he left, though her answering machine was full of rambling apologies and declarations of love and misery. And he looked like a man who would ramble—his normal good humor replaced with a fear so strong it shrank him. She imagined slapping him, having him poof into a cloud of dust.

Her first instinct was to go to him, let him hold her while she cried, and having thus used him, push him back out the door. But she didn't. "Kids are still asleep," she said, grabbing her purse from the counter. "I may come back before dinner." She headed outside to her car, despite not having even brushed her hair yet. Peter trailed after her, only taking her arm after she'd opened the car door.

"We have to talk."

"*You* say. We don't. You can't make me."

"This isn't just about you."

"It's about our children, is it? You're thinking of their best interests? You decided they needed two, no, *three* more siblings? That
they'd be happier with a mother who hated their father?"

"You love me as much as I love you," Peter said. "I could see it in
your face when you walked in the kitchen. It would be different if you
didn't, but you do."

And so, June started to cry. She let her husband hold her. If she
could stop loving him, she could be free. Instead of her holding a gun
on Peter, she held a gun on herself. No matter her choice—marriage or
divorce—there would be a hole in her chest.

"But I can't forgive you," she said.

"I know," he said. "But please. Let me come home?"

FIVE

MARCH ASKED ARLO AND ARTIE to meet him at the storage facility, a place he didn't know existed until his father told him about it at breakfast, a place full of things he thought were gone forever. He's touched his father kept all his stuff, cleaning out his house after he bolted two years ago; March had been sure his mother would've demanded a yard sale. But he's embarrassed too—another mess he left for others to clean up.

The unit isn't climate-controlled, so one chair goes straight in the dumpster, the humidity having given birth to a healthy covering of mold. In New Mexico, he had bought all of his furniture from Walmart, and he'd forgotten how much an object can evoke a whole person. His heavy cherry bed frame reminds him of Vera. He can see her standing, her shirt off, in front of his matching dresser with the wide oval mirror. A burst of self-loathing, remembering yesterday, makes him decide his bedroom won't be in the same room as before.

As if waking to a different ceiling will somehow keep Vera with Hap, will improve his chances of continuing to wake up in Olympus at all.

Arlo's hand, an injury he will not explain, limits him to moving lamps and lightweight boxes, so Artie and March heft the larger pieces into the back of his truck. The next trip, the next layer revealed, makes March feel even stranger. His grandfather's rocking chair that his mother gave him when he came back from the Army. A table held up by copper pipes bent into sharp angles—beautiful but matching nothing in March's home—that Hap had made him while in art school. A dining set he had found with his father at a garage sale while they were shirking work one afternoon.

Once everything is back in his house and wiped and Windexed, Artie and Arlo, both having far superior eyes for aesthetics, arrange things. His old bedroom becomes the dog's room, and they follow March suspiciously as he drags the blue rug to its new location. He is so pleased to be back with the trappings of his old life, he doesn't notice how little Artie and Arlo are speaking to each other. How Artie's straightforward questions are met with curt replies.

By late afternoon everything from pots and pans to dish towels have found their places, and the three of them split a housewarming six-pack on his porch. He tells them stories of the past two years, and they each tell the stories he missed from their lives—Artie's new hunting business, Arlo's recent tours (including stories that make the recently disappeared tour manager into both a fool and a villain). Three times—twice from Artie and once from Arlo—he is warned that a repeat vanishing, without even phone contact, will not be tolerated or forgiven. Though March hates being chastised, these warnings buoy him against the worst-case scenario tickling at the edges of his brain: that this moving day is just playacting, wishful thinking about a life here in Olympus that someone is soon to disabuse him of.

Arlo ignores a friendly question from Artie about his plans for his next album. This time, March registers the frustration on her face, the look of her biting her tongue. She stands, dropping her empty bottle back in its cardboard carrier. "Got prior plans, boys, so I will leave you to your evening," she says.

March is about to ask if her plans include Ryan, and if she wants to invite him over here instead, but Arlo beats him to speaking.

"Ryan, I'm guessing?"

Arlo's tone is sour, but Artie ignores it and says, "Come fishing with me tomorrow morning, Arlo? I've got an early pig hunt, but I'll be done by ten."

"I can think of better things to do," he says.

"Come on. I'll bring the gear. My usual spot."

"Fine." Rather than look at her, Arlo spins his empty beer bottle like a top. Artie attempts a smile at March, waving goodbye to them both before she heads to her car.

They watch her drive away, and March waits for Arlo to explain. Instead, Arlo nods at the drained bottles by their feet. "How should we rectify that?"

"Haven't been to My Place since I got back. Interested?" It's March's favorite bar, not just here in town but anywhere. The place he bought his first underage drink as well as his first legal one.

They decide to walk there, a mile away and off the town square, so they both can drink as much as they want. Neither of them speaks on the walk; they are longtime practitioners of comfortable silences. Theirs has always been a friendship of balance: Arlo may be smarter but March was stronger, Arlo could be meaner but March was more dangerous. All faults on both sides were accepted as perfectly natural. However, after the third time Arlo kicks away the litter in his path—Coke bottle, Lone Star can, another Coke bottle—March has to admit this quiet is not the comfortable kind.

"What's up with you and Artie?" March says.

Arlo gives him a side-eye and asks him a question in return: "What do you know about her and Ryan?"

"Just that she's seeing him."

They continue to walk down the edge of the county road, dipping farther down into the ditch when cars approach. "Apparently, it's so serious that she won't pinch-hit as my tour manager this summer. I asked her this morning."

"That sucks for you, but good for Artie, right?"

"You ever hear anything good about Ryan Barry?"

"Artie's got a good nose for bullshit. She doesn't need us to save her." March thinks for a minute. "Though Dad may need our backup if Ryan's mother gets invited to Thanksgiving."

"What are you talking about?"

"Lavinia Barry hates him. Real estate fallout, I think."

"Great. Quite the choice Artie has made." Arlo kicks another can, sending a shower of beer into the air. "She's just not acting like herself."

March isn't sure Arlo is right, and even if he is, it doesn't mean Ryan isn't a good thing for Artie. He can tell that's something Arlo doesn't want to hear, though.

They reach the bar. It's dark, as always, and still smells of cigarettes from the prior century, as always, and, though March has been gone for nearly two years, he knows the barstools hold the exact same men they did the last time he was there. The fluorescent lights still hang eight feet down from the thirty-foot ceilings, and the cash register from the 1940s still lives behind the bar. Both sets of his grandparents had two-stepped across the thin-planked wood floors. Old men play dominoes at the three tables that front the stage, oblivious to the band's performance.

They have a few drinks, play a few games of pool. People stop by occasionally to welcome March back, or to ask—with poorly hidden skepticism—whether he is back for good. Even more shoot him curious looks. Occasionally women come up to talk to Arlo; his reputation has a way of bringing people to him whereas March's tends to keep them away. None of the conversations last long because the town is too small for random pickups. These women are someone's daughter, someone's cousin, tomorrow might be their checker at the supermarket, their teller at the bank. They move to a table by the back wall, adopt the posture of men who don't want to be bothered.

Several of the women had told Arlo how much they liked his new single. "I guess I'm not listening to the right stations," says March.

"Peaked at number twenty-seven on Billboard's Country chart.

Not earth-shattering, but it's upped my tour dates the past six months. Won't last too much longer, as I've already sunk back out of the top fifty. And if I can't get the tour back on track, I'll miss the last of the momentum."

"What's it take to manage a tour? In case my mother makes my father fire me?"

"A tricky balance of drill sergeant, group therapist, and accountant."

"Might be able to pull off the first one."

"For the sake of our friendship, let's not try."

March clinks his bottle into Arlo's then drinks until it's empty.

Arlo scans the room. "Any chance one of these women is from out of town?"

"Don't look at me. I'm out of the loop." March leaves the booth to get another round. When he returns, a heavyset blond man is standing by their table, talking to Arlo. March recognizes him from the shop, one of Hap's employees. He nods at March, though he puts on a frown to do it, then turns back to Arlo. "Mighty unwise of you to grab Laurel like that," the man says, laughing. "We thought the law would be called for sure." Arlo scowls in response.

"What's this?" March asks. "Does that explain your mysterious bandage?" March is smiling, but Arlo will have none of it. He gets up and pushes past the man, sitting down sulkily at the bar.

As the man leaves without a goodbye, his name finally comes to March. "Nice to see ya, Otis," he calls to the retreating back.

March is headed to the bar to needle Arlo further when Vera comes in through the front door. She's wearing jeans and a white T-shirt, a pair of sneakers, but March can feel every man within thirty feet turn to look at her. She's with a friend, a woman March recognizes as one of Vera's former co-workers. He knows Vera will spot him in another second, so he speeds his pace.

March puts a credit card on the bar by Arlo's empty glass. "Can we settle the tab and get the hell out of here?"

"Man, Vera's already coming this way."

"She's coming and we're leaving. Last thing I need is Hap's employee seeing a story he can retell."

But she's already there, standing in front of March. "Vera," Arlo says pleasantly. He picks up the credit card. "I'll find the bartender," he tells March.

March spots Vera's friend entering the bathroom. He says, as quietly as he can amid all the bar noise, "Hap's not thawing to me yet. I don't want to add another reason for him to chase me back out of town. People are watching."

Vera settles herself clumsily on the barstool next to where he's standing. "Aw, come on. Be of use, March. I can't talk to Kelly about what's really going on with my marriage. But you . . ." She pushes her hair from her face, and March realizes she is very drunk.

"Not your first stop, I'm guessing."

"Kelly makes a mean margarita. Fresh-squeezed lime, no sweet and sour bullshit." She straightens herself, pulls a very serious face. "I'm taking yesterday as a sign. It's time to get moving. Tomorrow I'm telling Hap I'm leaving." She leans in close and whispers, "Don't worry, I will omit the nature of yesterday's sign."

Her assurance brings March a brief surge of relief, but it doesn't last long. "God, not tomorrow. No matter what you say or don't say, Hap's sure to blame me."

"Honey, it's not like you're blameless."

The bar's attention is on them, and March is sure Otis has a good seat for this. Vera feels like a truck that's about to crash into him. Into Hap too.

Vera waves down the bartender, orders tequila on the rocks. "I'm of the opinion that, in this world, collateral damage is unavoidable, no matter what we do. Tough break, Mr. Briscoe." Getting her drink, she raises it at March and takes a sip.

Arlo returns with the credit card and a receipt, but one look at March's expression sends him to wait by the front door. March says, so softly the music nearly drowns out his words, "I want to be on speaking terms with my family again. I want to be able to stay."

Vera squints at him. Her gaze shifts to the pool tables, probably glaring at Otis as he glares at them. "Do you see what you're asking me? To torture myself, to pretend with my husband and string him along, just so you can get what you want, something you haven't done anything to earn?"

For this, March has no answer.

"You want me to do all that, when it's likely no matter how long I wait, you'll be just as fucked."

"I would be grateful if you did" is all he can think to say. "To give me that shot."

"What good is your gratitude to me?" She takes a swallow. "Uh-oh. Kelly is headed over to save me from myself." She looks at March for a long beat, appraising. "Hap thinks you don't have it in you to make a real life away from here. Is that true? You that helpless?"

"I don't know. Maybe," he says, desperate enough to admit the truth he's been skirting, even with himself. He had been so preoccupied with his inability to control himself, he hadn't realized that even when you controlled yourself, you couldn't control other people.

"Kelly," Vera says, with forced brightness. March takes his cue and heads over to Arlo, happy to leave Vera there and start the walk home.

SUNDAY

ONE

HAP'S UP BEFORE HIS WIFE. He hears their son start to fuss, and he eases out of the bed not long after the sun. She had said she was going to Houston to see a movie with a friend, but she brought the smell of a bar into bed with her, liquor and cigarettes. It's not that he cares, it's fine if she wants to have a night out, drink, have fun. But why lie about it?

He carries Pete with him as he makes coffee, then they sit at the kitchen table, his son poking at the corners of his mouth, trying to make a smile. Hap checks his email on his phone and sees he has a text message from the night before, one of his techs, Otis: *fyi March and Vera at My Place*. A few minutes later he had sent another. *March left with Arlo and Vera still here.*

Hap takes a big breath and tells himself that, if he isn't willing to force March to leave Olympus, this is his new normal. He'll lose his mind if he's suspicious of every interaction between his wife and his brother. He has to accept that there will be gossip, and friends who think they're being helpful when they send him status reports on his wife.

Vera comes in the kitchen, yawning and rubbing her forehead, and Hap puts his phone back on the table. She kisses Pete on the cheek and, after a small pause, does the same to Hap. Then she ruffles both of their hair, leaving her hand a beat longer on his head than Hap expects, pressing down so hard he can feel her wedding band's outline. When she steps away, he grabs her hand. The sadness in her expression swallows up all his other emotions. She gently frees her fingers.

"Excuse me while I drink two glasses of water very quickly. I always forget tequila hits me the hardest."

As she fills her glass, Hap says, "Y'all go out after the movie?"

She drinks it down without a pause and doesn't answer until she is refilling. "We wound up skipping the movie. Kelly made us margaritas at her place. She ran out of limes, so we headed to My Place for a bit."

"That all?" If she mentions March on her own, he thinks just maybe it won't sour their whole day.

But she just nods and asks if he still wants to go to church this morning. "If so, I'll need to shower soon." She gets Pete's yogurt from the fridge while Hap picks him up and takes him to his high chair. The boy flails his legs in protest, and, after a couple of attempts, Hap keeps him in his arms instead.

"Otis texted me. He saw you there, talking to March."

"Seriously?" Vera says. She opens the cabinet door too hard, and it bounces back off the other cabinet, closing itself again. "This fucking town."

Pete whimpers and Hap knows tears are not far behind. He tries to pull any anger out of his own voice to keep Pete calm. "You didn't think that was worth telling?"

"A three-minute conversation, mostly March whining about wanting your forgiveness, and me with a monster headache and not wanting to start the day off with this mess? No, I didn't think it was worth telling first thing."

"Better to wait until we were sitting in church?"

"I'm sure it would have come up naturally when three different members of the congregation came up to ask me about it. Perhaps the preacher would have included it in his sermon too." With another tone of voice, Vera might have made him laugh. But his wife sounds two steps from miserable, and Pete begins to wail, and Hap's own misery takes over his mouth.

"How did it feel, y'all seeing each other again? I mean, the first time since . . ." He fades off, unable to finish his own sentence.

"If you have additional questions, take them to your brother." The look on her face is not unkind, though, just exhausted. "No church for me. Pete and I are going to my mother's today. You're not invited." She comes close to them both, wiping Pete's tears and pretending to take a bite from his ear. The boy sniffles and allows a small laugh. Vera says, "I didn't go there planning to see him. Just drop it, please?"

Hap's still at the kitchen table, even after Vera has showered, readied their child, and driven away. He has no stomach for church either.

TWO

PETER AND JUNE go to Sunday services almost every week, have since they were married, and June since she was a child. To run a business in Olympus, at least successfully, means to attend church somewhere. Neither gives much thought to the afterlife but finds the church adds enough to the present: Peter for his love of conversation, June for the community of the women's church group, their work on social causes. Any obligation that wasn't tied to family seemed a respite to her.

Being a small town, it's a small congregation, one that changes little from Sunday to Sunday. They arrive a few minutes before the service is set to begin. Peter nods at Hayden, always in the aisle by the door, whether he is alone, like today, or with his whole family. Then there's Lionel, turning and smiling at him, extending his hand and waiting for a thank-you for March's new truck. Peter continues their trajectory but then spots that damn, now-familiar balding head sitting next to the real vet, Joe, and his wife, Betty. The light from the stained-glass window, tinted blue and purple, hovers over Cole like he's Saint Francis. Peter stops walking up the aisle, can't help it, and his lack of motion draws his wife's attention to that patron saint of animals. Again, that tightness in his shoulders. Peter feels nothing in this moment if not undignified. Is it not enough that the indignities of old age are not that far in his future? Must he be bombarded with the indignities of youth, too?

In his wife's pause, he can feel her thinking. Does she lead them to the open spot behind Cole? It is, he will grant, their usual spot. Or will she lead them close to the front, where they never sit? Peter has no desire to sit behind the man, to monitor if his wife's eyes stray to him. But to move away would mean there was a reason to be jealous. That his wife has something to avoid, and thus something to hide.

Peter hears June take a breath, exhale with purpose. She leads them to sit behind Cole. He wills the group in front of them to keep their eyes forward, but fate again thwarts him. Joe turns to say hello, but Peter cannot keep his eyes off Cole, the way his face lights up when he sees June. In this house of God, Peter feels for the first time the impulse to kill another man—not seriously, not really, but still. Un-fucking-dignified.

THREE

ARTIE PARKS BEHIND Arlo's Bronco on the side of the road and tries to muster a little optimism after a brutal morning hunt. She brings her old .30-30, having heard from June of a rabid skunk tottering around in full daylight not a half mile away. She tucks the soft case's strap over her shoulder then grabs two fishing poles from the back along with a tackle box. Why had she suggested fishing anyway? As if this will make Arlo more amenable. But fishing is what they agreed on, so she must make do.

The feral hog hunt had gone badly. Five tech guys from Houston who claimed hunting experience yet owned no rifles. It should have been an easy gig. She had an arrangement with a farmer who was battling these descendants of domesticated pigs. A menace to farmers and ranchers, the hogs rooted up fields, trampled crops, and left deep holes that tripped livestock. So in the woods adjacent to the farmer's fields, she buried soured corn near one of the pigs' mud wallows. She learned their patterns of movement. She brought the men in early, before the sun was even up, gave them some general advice—the pigs will scatter quick, so shoot fast and shoot often, but don't make bad shots—and settled them into two blinds. Just thirty minutes later, the sounder of hogs arrived. But in their excitement, the men were too loud, spooking the herd before getting off a first shot. As the animals ran, the idiots fired haphazardly, wounding several hogs but dropping none. The pigs might be a blight, but they were also smart, could feel pain as sharply as these men paying her. She'd carry the guilt of her incompetent clients all day as she thought of the animals' wounds, the slow deaths that should have been quick and clean.

Not an auspicious start to the day, and Artie will admit she's a believer in signs. The sun slipping behind a cloud, removing the glare and allowing a perfect shot. Or the wind changing direction, the deer catching her scent and bounding to safety. It's almost enough to have her call Ryan, tell him not to join her and Arlo at the river after all. They had worked it out the night before. His introduction to her brother, a setting that would allow for silence if conversation didn't come easy. Ryan wouldn't arrive for another hour, giving her time to talk to Arlo first and help him see things through her eyes. The conversation would be hard, but they had to move forward.

Laden as she is, she moves slowly down the embankment, through the clusters of hardwood trees, until she reaches the flat sand of the bank. She doesn't see Arlo until she is ten feet from him. The island she and Ryan stood on yesterday has shrunk a few feet in diameter, the water running higher thanks to the rain. Arlo is facing upriver, where the Brazos curves and hides itself behind a bend, his back to her. The wind blows from the east, carrying all the sound away from them. She has to speak up for him to know she's there.

"Hey," she says. "Want to fish from here instead of wading to the island?" She knows he will. She prepares to spend the entirety of Sunday placating, starting now.

"Look at that," Arlo says. He still hasn't turned to her. She follows the line of his finger to a spot almost a hundred yards up.

"Current's strong today," she says. Arlo says nothing, drops his hand. "Hope it isn't that rabid skunk," she adds. At first she thought it was moving, thought she saw splashing, but as she stares harder, it resolves into something small and dark, not moving upstream or down. A pocket of trash caught in the rocks below?

"Does look a bit like a skunk," Arlo says.

Artie smells nothing but the mud of the bank, the humidity in the air. Arlo turns to her, unhappiness on his face, his split lip still puffy and painful-looking. He sees her gun.

"Bet you can't hit it," he says.

With the wind, she barely makes out the words, the emotion behind them inaccessible. She thinks, Just shoot it. Shoot it, and collect the prize she already has in mind—a promise he'll be civil to Ryan when he arrives. She reaches over and unzips the soft case slung over her shoulder, pulls the rifle out with one hand, flicks it from half-cocked to cocked, all in under three seconds. She puts the rifle to her shoulder, pulls the lever forward and back to load the first cartridge, her finger already on the trigger as Arlo lifts his hand. His mouth is open, but no sound comes out. Even if it had, it's too late. She is already lining the object up in her scopeless sight; she is already squeezing the trigger; she has already taken the shot.

She lowers the gun. Arlo's mouth is still open, his eyes so wide he looks like a cartoon version of himself. "What?" she asks, immediately shaky, setting the stock of the rifle on the ground.

"When have you ever shot without knowing what you're shooting at?" His voice is sharp, accusatory.

"No, but—"

"Why did you shoot?" Arlo's voice cracks, full of a panic she's never heard in him before.

Artie looks up river, sees the spot getting a little bigger. Now just a half football field away. Not a skunk. Then it's pulled under, nothing visible anymore, and she feels relief. She doesn't want to know what she has hit. But then Arlo is pulling off his boots, is wading into the river. She's about to warn him that he's headed for a drop-off, that the ground will suddenly disappear, but then he vanishes underwater too. His head pops back out, him spluttering and struggling. The current pushes him toward the bank until he finds footing again.

"Be careful," she yells as she sets down her gun and pulls at her own boots.

Arlo sees her and hollers "Stay put" so firmly she freezes, balanced on one leg. Whatever she has hit bobs up to the surface, still twenty yards away, but she can't wrap her mind around what it could be. There's nothing in the river that long and pale, not even masses of trash. And then she realizes—sitting fast and hard on her ass—she has hit a person.

There's an arm, tan and bare. The water pulls the body back down, the limb disappearing to a wrist, then just fingers. Her body knows who it is before her mind, the pressure of those fingertips on her thighs, on her back, on her cheek. Strong enough to blot out of the sound of the river, the sight of everything. A ragged "no" comes from her throat. Arlo throws himself with a giant splash toward Ryan's body—her mind now understands it's Ryan's body—and he wraps his own arms around that torso that she knows so well. Arlo struggles to the bank, but the dead weight and the rushing water are too much. Both men fall back under and are pushed farther downstream. Arlo comes up with a gasp, his face fixed in concentration, and finally he makes it halfway out of the water, tightening his grip on Ryan as he drags him up on the bank.

They are just two feet in front of her, and Artie rises to her knees as Arlo tips forward, Ryan's body taking him down with him. Arlo rolls away, leaving Ryan lying on his stomach. Her boyfriend's head is turned away from her, and he is so, so still, even as the water flows over his calves and feet. Then Arlo turns Ryan over and pulls him farther up the bank, away from the waterline. He puts his hand to Ryan's chest, leaning down close for a second. Then Arlo scrambles up and back, stopping next to her. Now Artie sees Ryan's face. She is frozen, still on her knees. She has shot enough things to know what is dying and what is already dead.

ARLO IS AWARE of the weight of his wet clothes, aware of the wind, the mud on Ryan's chest and face, how Artie vibrates so slightly it's only visible in her fingertips, aware of forty other things that matter not in the slightest. His brain has shut down his ability to process anything that isn't sensory, but he knows he needs to be thinking. There are things that must be done. Ryan is dead. He didn't mean for it to happen, but it's still his fault. He cannot fix it, but there is damage that needs to be controlled.

It's Artie that gets him moving. She tilts sidewise, still on her knees, and Arlo leans down and loops his arms around her, lifting her up. She stays on her feet, but she looks at him without seeing, a vacancy that scares the shit out of him. He walks her a few yards farther downstream, soaking her clothes with the river water still dripping off him and steadying her as she lists. He sits her down on a massive fallen tree limb and makes sure her back is to Ryan's body. Her view is of an empty river, a brown swath surrounded by green. He is helping, he tells himself. He is taking care of her. He pulls his cell phone from his pocket, but the water has made it useless.

"Artie." He squats down in front of her and takes her chin in his hand, tilting her head so he is what she sees. "Artie." Her eyes focus on him and she jerks her head back, out of his grip.

"Artie. Where's your phone?"

"Doesn't matter," she whispers.

"I need to call the sheriff."

"Dead zone. No reception. Why I like this spot." Her voice cracks on the word "like," and she takes a few strangled breaths, almost hyperventilating. He puts his hands on her shoulders to calm her, but when she speaks again she sounds like she's being choked. "How is it possible? How could you not know it was Ryan in the river?" She leans over and puts her elbows on her knees, sucking in air.

He wants to explain. But if he tells her the truth, that he did know it was Ryan, no one will believe this was an accident. And it *was* an accident. He never would have expected her to shoot, not when she didn't know what she was aiming at. He doesn't want to lay this weight of what he knew on her, but she has asked him a question, and he can't lie to her.

But then he is saved. Because his sister assumes the best of him, even in this worst moment. "How could *I* not know it was him? The chain of things that had to happen. The timing. My stupid impatience." She looks up at him. "It's impossible, what just happened." She doesn't want an answer. She just wants him to agree and turn what they saw, what they did, into a dream.

So he takes her hand. "I know." He gives her a small space of silence, then says, "I'm going to Peter's house to call the sheriff. I want you to not move. I want you to not even turn around." Arlo knows he should bring her with him, should carry her if he has to, but he can't take the chance of leaving her alone with anyone other than himself, not until they have their stories straight. Because he is starting to see he needs Artie to lie.

Her eyes have lost their focus again. "Artie, it's important. You can't touch anything." He's still holding her hand, and he squeezes it. "What are you going to do?" he prompts her.

"I'm not going to move." She is echoing him, still not really there.

"Listen, Artie." He drops her hand and gently shakes her shoulder. "I'm going to tell the sheriff that I shot Ryan. Not you. Me. Can you remember that?"

"Why would you say that? I shot Ryan. It's my fault." Tears spring to her eyes, and she looks at him pleadingly, as if her culpability is a comfort to her.

"No. We're telling the sheriff that I shot him. Let me take the blame."

"But it was an accident."

"Artie, think. If we tell the truth, no one's going to believe it, that you'd shoot impulsively like that. You're too experienced a hunter. It will sound like a lie, that we're covering something up. You know how the town gossips. They'll dig up something, true or untrue, about Ryan, about your relationship, something that would give you a motive. Ryan's family will be the first to do it, too. They'll be screaming for you to be locked up."

"But if I had a motive, people will say you did too. That you killed him for me." Her voice breaks again as she stands up, shaking her head at him.

"No, you wouldn't be that careless with a gun, that impulsive. But I might. They'll believe I could be that dumb, that I could be goaded into taking a shot at something without even knowing what it was. If we tell the truth, there's only two things people will think of you: either you're way too careless, too dangerous to be a hunting guide, and your career is gone, or because you're a hunting guide, this couldn't be an accident. Beyond that, it'll change how every person in town treats you. This is your home. I'm always on the road, and I don't care how the people here treat me. Ryan's family can come after me. I'm the one that dared you to shoot. If there's something I can do to keep your life intact, you have to let me do it."

He can tell what she's thinking from the changes in her face, the fresh batch of tears at the ridiculous idea that her life could ever be intact again. But she slumps in acquiescence. It's not the logic that convinced her, he knows. It's that he's begging, and she can't bear to say no. He's sure if they tell the truth, the whole truth, they could both go to jail. But if he was the one with the rifle, then at least it would only be him in jail. And if they pull it off, there's a chance he won't even be charged.

He sits down on the log and tugs at her hand until she sits again too. "We tell the truth, just with this one change. It *was* an accident. But now it's *me* who took the unsafe shot."

Artie looks up at the sky, like the answer will be there. The post oaks from the embankment rustle above them as the wind picks up. "There's no road straight from here to Peter's, so it will be faster if you walk," Artie says. "I'll wait here. I won't move." Her voice is tiny, but in it he can hear resignation. Arlo needs more, needs their agreement to lift just a little of the guilt that is flattening him. He doesn't move—hoping she will look at him or squeeze his hand. Instead, Artie puts her head in her hands and cries.

FOUR

June's new serenity can withstand much. She's amazed at what it can block out. She's set aside, at least for this morning, her worries over March, over Hap. And she tolerates her husband when he stays in the kitchen to help with lunch, even though she doesn't need the help. She even looks forward to Peter's weekly review of the sermon, his jokes about how it would or wouldn't apply to various members of the congregation, as they eat fried catfish and salad, peaches from the stunted trees behind the house.

But instead Peter is quiet, watchful. Normally such watchfulness would irk her, but today it's as if a thick concrete wall stands between her mood and her husband's. His mood thwaps against it, splattering small piles of peevishness back at his own feet. June remains clean. She doesn't feel obliged to formulate questions to pull him from his silence. He stands next to her at the counter as she lifts the fish from the Fry Daddy and jabs at the jar of tartar sauce with a spoon, scraping the bottom edges hard. "This is kaput."

"On the grocery list. It's your turn to go." They move to the dining room, carrying full plates and glasses of tea.

June hums.

"What's that song?"

"What? What song?" she says.

Peter plunks his glass down too hard on the table, sloshing tea. June sets down her own plate and glass, goes to fetch a dish towel. She wipes the spill and gets no thanks for it.

June returns the towel to the kitchen. She doesn't hum aloud, but her hips sway to the melody in her head as she comes back to her husband.

They hear a rifle shot from down the river. They're so common, neither remarks on it as June sits down to eat. She's particularly hungry.

FIVE

ARLO ARRIVES on Peter's front porch, gasping from his run. Only the speed of his legs and the burning of his muscles have kept him from full panic after he left Artie. Rather than ringing the doorbell and waiting, he launches himself through the front door and finds Peter and June in the kitchen washing dishes.

"Can you call the sheriff?" Being in this room, in this house he hasn't seen since he was a kid, turns his demand into a request, a question instead of an imperative.

"What happened?" Peter asks. "Are you hurt?" He takes a half step to Arlo, and only then does Arlo think about his appearance—covered in mud, still wet, blood smeared on his hands and shirt.

Arlo has the answer, rehearsed on his way there. "Ryan is dead, down on the riverbank. Call the sheriff. I've got to get back."

"What?" June's voice slams into him. "What happened? Where's Artie?"

"She's with him."

"Jesus, Arlo. What have you done?" she says.

It's the question that has dogged him since Artie took the shot. June takes Peter's hand. He's never seen them hold hands.

"You shouldn't have left her with the body," June says. "You shouldn't have left her alone."

Arlo's eyes burn, a feeling so unfamiliar it takes him a moment to understand he's about to cry. He holds out a shaky hand to June. She takes it, drops Peter's, tells her husband to make the call. Then she jogs them back outside, pulling Arlo down the porch steps behind her. They startle a peacock bedded down in the corner of the lawn as they pass, and Arlo stumbles at the bird's screech. The tidy grass of the lawn gives way to taller grass and weeds, then after a few more minutes to the line of sycamores and cypresses. Without a word from him, June knows exactly when to stop and push them through the vines and the bluestem, about a quarter of a mile down from the house. Everyone knows this is Artie's spot.

By now, Arlo is crying in earnest. He's not sure if it's the warmth of June's hand, the safety he feels in her taking charge, or that he has to again face what he's done to Artie. They both look down from the rise of the riverbank on two prone figures by the water's edge—Ryan, facing the sky, and Artie, her body folded over her knees, the top of her head touching the top of Ryan's. She is shaking with sobs, but the sound coming out of her throat doesn't sound human. It sounds like an animal distress call, something his sister would use to lure in coyotes.

June drops Arlo's hand, skids down the bank, leaving him behind. He is grateful to be still, to only have to watch. June kneels by Artie and uselessly checks Ryan for a pulse. Then she reaches over and gently pulls Artie into a sitting position. Arlo sinks down on the upper bank and hears the rustle of Peter coming through the shrubs. The sheriff will be here before too long.

Arlo tries to hold the story in his head. They had no idea Ryan was there, swimming. Arlo shot because his sister teased him he couldn't hit that thing in the river if he tried. He'll look like an idiot, and while he doesn't care what the town thinks, that idiocy will become a part of his history that will follow him everywhere, even in his career. But he can't care about that. He can only think of what's best for Artie.

Peter squats next to him. "They're on their way." He puts his hand on Arlo's forearm and squeezes, but it nettles rather than gives comfort. They watch June and Artie, Artie sitting up and curled into June's side, both facing away from the body. Peter clears his throat. "Let's go down."

Peter is halfway to them before Arlo can make himself stand and begin the descent. Neither June nor Artie acknowledges them, and Peter covers his mouth and walks the few steps to the river. Arlo goes to Artie's side. So much mud coats Ryan from the struggle to get him to shore, he seems almost fully clothed. Arlo's stomach spasms as he spots the entrance wound on the top of Ryan's head, and he sinks to the ground. He hopes Artie will let herself sink against him. Her natural instinct under natural circumstances. But he is still waiting, untouched, when he hears the ambulance arrive.

ONCE THE EMTS have confirmed Ryan is dead, once they've retreated to their vehicle and the deputies move everyone away from the body, Sheriff Muñoz—a woman Arlo has never seen before but who is apparently known to June and Peter—prompts Arlo to start from the beginning. Arlo hopes he hasn't shown his surprise—that she is a stranger to him, that she appears more competent than he expects of a small-town sheriff, that she is a she.

"We met here to fish," Arlo says, looking at Artie and expecting her to nod in confirmation. Instead, Artie keeps her eyes on the deputies milling around Ryan. "And I had pointed out this spot in the water, something dark. We couldn't tell what it was. Artie mentioned that there was a rabid skunk sighting, and I was thinking the animal could have fallen in the river. I told Artie maybe we should shoot it, and Artie said *What do you mean, we*. She said that there was no way I could hit that from here." Again, Arlo turns to Artie, this time not so much for confirmation as to make sure she's not reacting to his lies, making it clear he's spinning a story she hasn't heard before. But Artie is still occupied by the activity around Ryan. "She had her back to me, and she didn't even notice that I was aiming. She didn't turn around until I took the shot."

"Why did you have your rifle with you? If you were fishing?" the sheriff says.

"I don't own any guns. It was Artie's."

Muñoz looks skeptical for a fraction of a second before the expression drains away to leave her face neutral. He wishes he was dealing with the prior sheriff, the one that served with Peter on the Methodist Men's Committee, the one whose daughter graduated with Hap, the one who, the town sometimes grumbled, never seemed eager to pursue anything that could be put to bed instead.

She asks Artie, "Why was your brother holding your gun?"

Artie shakes her head, and anxiety explodes inside Arlo's stomach. But instead of contradicting him, she says, "You never shoot at something if you don't know exactly what it is." Her voice is full of blame, but only Arlo knows it's blame she's directing at herself.

The sheriff nods. "But why did Arlo have the gun in the first place?"

Artie looks at him, and he can see her trying to do what he has asked. But she is too shell-shocked to do it easily. She says to him, "Why *did* you have it?"

"I just picked it up. It was there by me, with our pile of stuff." He says to Muñoz, "We hadn't decided yet where to fish from. We had just arrived."

Muñoz asks Artie, "You knew Ryan might be here? Was he supposed to meet you here, too?"

Artie pulls herself up from leaning on June. She takes a deep breath and runs her hand through her hair, scattering dust from the river mud dried on her hands. "Ryan was supposed to meet us, but not for another hour."

"Why do you think he would come early, without telling you?" Muñoz turns from them to look up and then down the river. "And go swimming while he waited?"

"He loves to swim," Artie says quietly. "He was probably killing time." She shudders, though Arlo can't tell if it is from the word choice or something else she's conjured in her head.

"But he hadn't brought swim trunks?"

"When the current is this strong," Artie says, "it can take shorts right off you. We always swam without clothes when we were here. No houses within view."

But Muñoz circles back again. "Why come early? Without a call or text?"

"He knew I was nervous about introducing him to Arlo. Maybe he thought he could help me by getting the introduction out of the way sooner, so I didn't have to worry over it." Artie's voice cracks.

"Why were you nervous about introducing your boyfriend to your brother?"

Artie looks at Arlo rather than the sheriff when she answers. "I wanted them to like each other." He sees his sister struggle. She wants to explain more, and Arlo knows they are details the sheriff would consider important—Artie not wanting to return to the tour, Arlo's opinion of Ryan. But she doesn't say any of it. She just looks fearful, staring at him. It makes them both look guilty.

"And neither of you saw his clothes lying there?" The sheriff points to a small, dark pile at the base of a tree, down where they took the shot. Arlo had forgotten about the clothing—sneakers, jeans, a T-shirt.

It's Arlo's face Muñoz is watching as she says this, but Artie's reaction immediately draws all their attention. "How did we not see them?" she cries, loud enough for the deputies to look over. She throws out her arms toward the clothes and sags forward, causing Muñoz and June to both steady her, the sheriff leaving her hand on her back. "If I had seen them there, I would have known Ryan was here. None of this would have happened."

Muñoz turns to Arlo.

"I didn't notice them either." He sounds almost as gutted as Artie, but it's because he has never seen his sister this devastated. She leans over, her hands on her knees, and begins dry heaving. Arlo reaches out for her, his arm around her shoulder, but she stiffens and pulls away. June quietly asks the sheriff if they can all go back up to the house.

They sit on the porch, he and Artie and June, while Muñoz follows Peter into the house, offering to help him carry water for them all. Given how long it takes, Arlo assumes Muñoz is using this time to question Peter alone, too. Arlo isn't altogether surprised his plan seems to be working. They do live in a county with many more accidental shootings than actual murders. Yet Arlo feels nothing but doom. He cannot really grasp a man is dead, and what that entails. Any time his brain leans in that direction, it replays, in slow motion, Artie taking the shot. Replicates that feeling in his bowels when he realized what he had set in motion.

When Peter and the sheriff finally come back, and both he and Artie have at least taken a few sips of water, Muñoz sends June and Artie over to the EMTs, now parked in the driveway, to check Artie for signs of shock.

After they've left the porch, Muñoz tells Arlo, "If you had been planning to leave, tour dates and such, you should cancel them."

Arlo nods his head. "Wouldn't think of leaving. Not with Artie like . . ." He points at his sister's retreating back, but he finds he can't keep his arm up, as if his shame had actual weight to it.

"I'm driving over to the Barrys' place now," she says. "Mr. Briscoe has informed me of the history between the two families. So if they come to you, I expect you to do your best to defuse things. Your father seems to think Lavinia Barry will insist on charges being pressed, but I'll tell her what I am telling you, that we don't have enough information to decide on that yet."

Peter looks away from him, embarrassed. He says, "I should have smoothed things over with her years ago. But you aren't me, so she might understand it was an accident." Peter rests his hand on Arlo's shoulder, and it feels burdensome. He can blame Peter, at least partially, if things do blow up with the Barrys. But he knows if he were the son of another man, Muñoz might not be so accommodating, might feel compelled to take him down to the station for more questioning. Maybe even charge him with something right away. And even a scene with Lavinia Barry sounds almost welcome, a thing he can weather in Artie's stead to shuck off at least a little of his shame.

The sheriff eases away, and he and his father are left in the warm dusk. The sun is setting, but everything feels overly vivid, almost lurid, as if Arlo is looking at it with a superhuman pair of eyes. He wishes for darkness, so he can't see Artie at the end of the driveway, huddled on the back of the ambulance with a blood pressure cuff around her arm. Wishes her truth, that neither of them knew what she was aiming at, could be his truth too. And he can't forget the lesson he and Artie both learned from their mother: those absent can feel more present, do more damage, than any warm body in the room.

SIX

THE EMTS HAVE RELEASED ARTIE. Ryan's body has been put on a stretcher, slowly and carefully brought up the embankment, and put into the ambulance. The sheriff and deputies have gone. In the kitchen, Arlo settles himself on one of the two barstools and props up his head with his hands. Artie reaches out to the other barstool and drags it toward her and away from her brother. Peter sees the gesture but can't decipher it. He has heard their story, too, the explanation, but he can't decipher that either. Arlo wanting to take a shot at anything, much less something unidentified?

June, standing next to Artie, with her arm around the pale and shivering girl, gives Peter a look. He isn't doing what he should be doing. So Peter fetches a quilt from the linen closet and wraps it around Artie. He gets bourbon from the pantry. He pours a shot into a glass for Artie, but she shakes her head. He walks around the island, and slides the glass in front of Arlo while placing a hand on his back.

It isn't a comfortable gesture, but it mirrors what a father might do, given the circumstances. Or what he thought a father might do given slightly lesser circumstances—a wife leaving, a job lost. There has always been a part of Peter's heart that wants to belong to Arlo, wants at least the semi-closeness he has with Artie. As a boy and now as a man, Arlo never meets Peter's eye, his gaze only given in passing, as if his father isn't worth a full examination. Even now, Arlo doesn't look at him, but he takes the glass, holding it but not drinking.

June says, softly, "Do you want to lie down?" Artie shakes her head. "Do you want us to call your mom?" Peter can't remember the last time June has referred to Lee, even this obliquely. And when Artie nods her head, he realizes he can't remember the last time Artie has spoken of her either. He feels something in his chest, something buried ten levels deep, crack a little for Lee, so absent from their lives when he knows her life is full of them, even if they aren't present. June nods at him. Peter tips his head toward the front door. He wants to spare Artie from another retelling, but he feels like being out of June's earshot requires approval. He hasn't talked to Lee in more than a decade, a feat for a town this small. June nods again.

Peter goes outside, unhooking his cell phone from his belt. The sky has lost all trace of the sunset, and Peter walks out into the blackness to where his voice won't carry back. Lee's number isn't in his contacts, but he finds his fingers still know the landline.

She answers on the first ring.

"Peter?" Her voice is pitched high with confusion. He thanks Caller ID for not forcing him to speak first, knowing he would have lapsed straight back into their lines from decades ago. "It's me," he would say. "I'm glad," she would reply.

He says, "Something bad has happened to the twins. Ryan's dead. Arlo shot him. By accident." He hasn't called them the twins since they were children. The phrase brings up an image of the first time he had seen them, lying together in the crib, their heads turned toward each other in sleep. He squeezes his eyes shut.

"Oh, God," she says. She repeats it again, and Peter lets them sit in silence. Then Lee asks, "Artie was there when it happened?"

"Yes. Artie wanted us to call you. I mean, June asked if she wanted us to, and she said yes." No matter what Peter says, it feels like a slap in someone's face. That he knows Lee will take a slap without complaining doesn't make him feel any better. He tries again. "She should be with you. Why don't you come get her?"

Lee doesn't answer. Peter can hear her breathing. Finally, she says, "Arlo's there but she wants to come home with me?" Vertigo knocks at him. Even their mother cannot conceive of a scenario where Artie wouldn't be leaning on her brother.

"Yeah," he says, crouching down so that he can lay his free hand on the gravel of the road, steadying himself.

"I'll be there as soon as I can." She pauses. "Goodbye, Peter." She waits for him to say goodbye before she hangs up, though he is slow to answer. Instead of returning to the house, he lets himself sink down to sit, to rest a minute.

ARLO FINISHES HIS BOURBON, gets up and brings his glass to the bottle to pour himself another. He surprises June by pouring her a glass, too. He keeps staring at Artie, his mouth barely open, as if he might speak. Artie is bent toward the counter, her hair hiding her face.

Artie startles, and June wonders if she's replaying the shot in her head. June can pull it up, too, the sound of the shot she ignored, digging into her lunch while Artie's life blew apart less than five minutes away.

Arlo reaches out to grab Artie's hand, but she draws back, stands up. "I'm going to lie down on the couch." She walks unsteadily into the living room and out of sight.

June takes a sip of the bourbon, worried about whatever already seems wedged between the twins. Arlo's expression reminds her of a young Hap, her son's face every time March lost his head and attacked him. The look of a boy whose sibling had transformed into someone he didn't know. That the world couldn't be counted on for even such a basic consistency as that.

Arlo's hand is braced against the counter in front of her. June covers it with her own hand. It's still there when Peter comes back.

"Lee will be here soon."

June gently pulls Arlo toward Artie's abandoned stool. "Sit," she says, and he does. She tells Peter, "Artie's in the living room. I'm going to check on her."

Artie lies on her stomach on the couch, her head turned toward its leather back. June covers her with an afghan and sits down next to the couch, close enough to run her fingers through the girl's hair. She's reminded of how she used to lie on their old orange couch when she was pregnant with March, that week after she kicked Peter out. When this woman in front of her was a fist of flesh inside her mother, nestled up against the flesh of her brother. She keeps stroking her hair while Artie begins to cry.

She stays there even when she hears Lee's knock on the door. June doesn't need to see how this woman will greet her husband. When she hears Lee's footsteps enter the living room, she finally rises and lets the mother take over. She forces a smile and a nod as she walks past Lee, reminding herself they are both trying to do their best.

In the kitchen, Arlo and Peter sit side by side in exactly the same way: boot heels hooked over the metal rung of the barstools, knees tilted out so far June bets they might even be touching each other. She walks around the island to pick up her drink and finishes it off, grateful for the punch of bourbon in her throat that reminds her she is still firmly upright.

Lee and Artie come in, Lee's arm around the girl's waist to keep her steady. Arlo pivots on his stool to face them. Lee says, with almost an apology in her voice, "She's going to stay with me."

At that, Peter turns on his stool too. Separated from them by that island, June sees the family the four of them could have been. Lee speaks again but doesn't seem to like what she is saying: "Artie says you can stay at her place for now."

"Artie?" Arlo says. June can feel the need woven into how he speaks her name, but Artie just heads for the door, walks through it, like no one has said a thing.

MONDAY

ONE

AN ILL THING should befall June for sleeping ten hours straight and waking up without a trace of tired. At a loss for what else to do, June had herded them all to bed before 9 p.m., but sleep hadn't come for her or for Peter until he had the idea to dig out her old sleeping pills, past their expiration but clearly still effective. Peter stirs beside her, and she slips out of bed before he can roll over. But with her feet on the floor, her stomach and chest knot up—a tangle of worries with so many threads she cannot even begin to tease them apart.

Downstairs, she finds Arlo and a full pot of coffee. He has located the components, gotten the pot to brew, but he fell asleep before pouring any, again on the barstool, this time with his head turned to the side, resting on his arms. He had argued to be driven to his car the night before, but June said they'd all had too many drinks to drive and guided him to the guest bedroom.

June studies him in a way she's never been able to while he's awake. He's handsome, but he has more of his mother in him than Peter, her wide-set eyes in a thin face, her lips, which always looked deep pink. June owns both of Arlo's albums, but she only listens to them in her car and has slipped them into CD cases of artists that she knows no one else in her family would ever open—Mozart's Requiem and Joan Baez. She thinks, a bit guiltily, of how she buried his CD cases into the trash, coffee grounds over the handsome face.

The light on the coffee pot turns off, which means Arlo has been asleep in that uncomfortable position for two hours. She pours two cups and brings them to the space in front of him. She tentatively puts her hand on his shoulder and shakes a little. Arlo groans and pulls his arms out from under his head, hiding his face behind his hands. "What time is it?"

"Near eight. You wait to sleep until you got out of bed?" She sits down, wishing she had thought to take one of the expired sleeping pills to him. Had it been one of her children, even March, she would have thought of it. And she wouldn't have been shocked to find March involved in someone's death, either. Yet over all those years, all those fights, and he's never even put someone in the hospital. Instead, it's Arlo with that cross to bear.

"You know you can stay here? As long as you want?" she says.

Arlo looks at her a long while, appraising. "I didn't. I appreciate it even if I won't accept the offer." He lifts his cup and takes a swallow. "Not that you haven't been great. Him too. Just, it's kinda fraught and I'm not up for fraught. I'll stay with March."

"Peter called him last night. He'll be over soon. But do you want to risk getting tangled in March's mess? His life is pretty fraught, too."

"It's the best thing. You know he's a good friend, right? Even him disappearing on us was just him trying to spare me and Artie some imagined burden." He swallows again, draining half the cup.

June feels an unexpected maternal warmth for Arlo rise from her breastbone, that feeling she wishes she could produce on command for March but really only is sparked by Hap. And Artie.

"He may be a good friend, but he hasn't been a good brother. He has left a river of damage in his wake."

Arlo looks quickly away, thinking of his own damage, June guesses. Arlo and Artie have a closeness that March and Hap aren't lucky enough to share. She can't imagine Artie, even in her grief, being unwilling to think of Arlo, how he must be feeling knowing he has killed someone. But then she remembers Artie's coldness to Arlo last night. Something feels off about their story. If there's something lurking just under the surface, June wants it dug up. There's no way to fix what she doesn't know. "If there's more to what happened yesterday," she says, "you should tell us now. Let us help."

Though he sits perfectly still, June feels a flash of heat from Arlo like an oven being opened and closed.

"More than me being the reason Ryan is dead? That isn't enough?" He hops off the barstool and turns his back to her while he rinses his coffee cup. Overhead, they hear Peter's footsteps across the bedroom, loud in the strained silence of the kitchen.

Arlo's facing her again. "I need some air, a walk. If I run into March and don't make it back, thank Peter for his help yesterday. And thank you, too." She's surprised at the sudden shift, his anger mellowed to a sincere warmth. But he's out of the hallway and off the porch before Peter gets to the kitchen.

"Guess expiration dates are approximate. I had the sleep of the well and truly just."

"An unnatural state for you. No wonder a pill that powerful is a controlled substance." She smiles to soften the jab and pours him a cup of coffee. "Should still be hot. At least warm."

Peter sees the light out on the pot. "You been awake that long?"

"Arlo." She hands him the cup. When he pulls her into a hug, she realizes it had been at least three years since she handed him his coffee, wasn't already settled on the balcony when he came down. It only took a death outside their door to shake up their routine.

"Where's he at?"

She pulls back. "Went for a walk. I think he hopes to run into March rather than have to talk more with us this morning. He says he'll stay with him for now."

"He didn't want to stay at Artie's? Even while she's at—" He doesn't finish, and June feels her irritability rise.

"At Lee's. You can say her name. She was standing in my kitchen last night."

But Peter doesn't take the bait, which makes June feel small and ignites her irritability into something bigger. "Artie's going to forgive him. I'm sure she will."

"I would think so, too, if things happened like they said. But she wouldn't look at him last night, wouldn't let herself be comforted by him."

"I'm sure she just needs a little more time."

"You may be their father, but I know Artie better than you do."

Peter raises his voice. "What, you think Arlo is some sort of murderer? That he shot Ryan deliberately?"

"I didn't say that." June goes to the screen door, making sure Arlo is out of earshot. She shuts the door. "I just think there's more to it than we know."

"Maybe it's none of our business, then."

"That would be the easiest thing to believe, so I guess that's what you'll stick to. Just like you think March can move home and nothing bad will come of that."

He fires back: "And you think nothing good can come of it." Peter's cell rings and he gives her a satisfied look, as if he's now had the final word. He pulls his phone from his belt.

"Thea," he says with surprise.

June can hear her daughter's voice, muffled like she's talking from upstairs rather than another state. "No, we were just talking about calling you. But I'm glad Artie already did it."

June shakes her head over the easiness of Peter's lie, always knowing what to say to placate their daughter. And Thea's anger is no surprise. To her way of thinking, information is power. She doesn't take kindly to it being withheld, even by just twelve hours.

"No, we'll come get you. When's your flight?"

Another absent child arriving in Olympus, another chance for her to fail to find joy in it.

"Okay, we'll be there by seven. Love you, honey."

June makes out her daughter's reply, a "love you too." She isn't sure when she last told Thea she loved her. Probably because she worries, if she says it, Thea will confirm June's worst fears and not respond.

Peter is smiling, and June just manages to keep her opinion of his unseemly good mood to herself. "We'll pick her up and then take her over to Lee's," he says.

June wants to see her daughter, has only seen her once in the past year and then just for a weekend. But when the visits are that short, it's so much easier to dote on her grandchildren rather than attempt a better connection with the daughter who keeps shoving her away. Every time, she regrets her distance, and yet now that she has another chance to see Thea, she resists it.

"You should go without me," she says. "It will be awkward if I'm there too, at Lee's house." A weak excuse. Once Lee came into their kitchen last night, she was back in their lives. All her old resentments and territorial claims are too petty for anyone, even herself, to pay attention to. The truth is that Thea's coming feels too much like March's return, prickly and uncomfortable but with Peter turning a blind eye to it. Leaving her to attend to the complications. "Trust me, it's better this way. I'll see Thea tomorrow, her and Artie." She's already won her point, but she can't help getting in one more shot. "Besides, she called you about her flight, not me."

Peter takes his coffee out to the porch.

THE ORIGIN OF THEA'S ANGER

. . . it's he who teaches me what my response must be
(it's right to learn from one's own enemy)

✠ OVID ✠

Thea and a friend, one August afternoon before their senior year, swam in the river then spread their towels on the lawn to watch the peacocks. Hap and March played basketball in the driveway. That spring, March had shot up half a foot and gained twenty pounds. He looked like Hap's fourteen while Hap looked like March's twelve. They began to argue, as they often did, Thea bracing herself to intercede. She preferred to hang out with her friends at their houses. Living in Olympus felt, to her, like living on a stage. Why would she want to bring anyone behind the curtain, too?

"Weird," her friend said.

"What?"

"March looks just like him."

Thea shook her head. "Looks like who?"

"Imagine we're in Economics. Who's there, in the next row?"

Thea stiffened, seeing it clearly and horrified she never noticed before. It was the profile of her classmate Burke, one she now could see was also a mirror of her father, just with white-blond hair and blue eyes. "Fuck."

"I know! Y'all must have some way-back ancestor. Everyone in Olympus is related if you go back far enough."

"Yeah," Thea said. But both girls knew the real reason.

Living on the stage of a small town had one bonus for Thea. She never had to explain her ties to Artie and Arlo. It was like town lore, something pre-baked into everyone's consciousness. But what if the town knew even *more* than she did? Thea thought of her mother, the way sometimes she looked at her father as if he had poisoned the land they lived on.

Her friend left, and Thea went up to her bedroom and changed, moving from dazed to stewing. She knew people saw her as Thea— honor roll student, volleyball player, 2A state champion in Lincoln-Douglas debate. But she was also the daughter of a philanderer, with two, now three it seemed, extra siblings as proof. She knew the ways these things didn't define her, but the town only saw the ways that they did.

Artie and Arlo had been in her life since she could remember, and for years, she accepted the labels half sister and half brother without question. After all, she had friends with half siblings, stepsiblings. It wasn't until she was eight that she realized those friends also had a stepparent. She asked her father and, despite her age, he told her the truth. He said if she was old enough to ask, she was old enough to know. He called in her mother, and they sat together in the living room and told the story. By then, Artie was already like a little sister to her, and so it would have felt like a betrayal to be angry at her father that Artie and Arlo existed. But why hadn't they told her about Burke? Was it simply because she hadn't asked? Was her father just too weak to face the truth unless someone demanded it of him?

But her mother? She could have, should have, told her about Burke. Thea could understand her father's weakness more than what she saw as her mother's pride. That afternoon, after her friend left, Thea searched the house until she found June on her balcony, drinking a Diet Coke and reading a novel.

"Burke is my brother," she said. It was so clear to her, she couldn't even phrase it as a question.

Her mother shushed her and put her book down, but Thea saw her hand tremble as she did it. "Sit down and lower your voice. Your brothers are still out in the yard."

"You don't think they should know, either? You think it's just fine I've spent years walking past my brother in school hallways, having no idea?" She was angry at being lied to—even if only a lie of omission—but deeper than that, she was mortified she'd once had a crush on Burke. Her smiles as she passed him in the hallway, the flutter in her stomach for those months, now shameful things she had to carry with her. She needed to make her mother carry some of that shame, too.

"If your father wanted you to know, he would have told you."

"*You* could have told me." Her mother should have expected the possibility of her crush, a town so small girls cycled their interest through every attractive option. What Thea found most maddening was her mother's refusal to look her in the eye. Thea whispered, "Burke and I have been dating." Her mother flinched but didn't speak. "We've slept together."

Her blow landed. Her mother's face crumpled as she dropped her soda can. It rolled to the edge of the balcony, the liquid glubbing out and splattering the porch below. Thea stood to leave, but her mother stood, too. She finally looked her in the eye. "But Burke knows. He wouldn't."

"Burke knows, but you don't bother to tell me?" Thea seethed. "Jesus, Mom. We never dated. It's still disgusting." And Burke must have thought her disgusting too, attracted to her own blood.

Her mother sagged in relief. It pissed Thea off even more. "How do you know Burke knows?" Thea asked.

"His mother told him."

"How long ago?" Thea searched back into her mind, trying to think if there had ever been a shift in the way Burke treated her. But she could come up with nothing. A quiet boy, good at football but not smart enough for honors. They hadn't been in the same classes in elementary school, and she could only think of two or three classes they had shared in high school.

"I don't know exactly. Third grade, maybe fourth."

He'd known for years. It infuriated her that someone knew more than her about something so big, something that concerned her. "I hate you." This wasn't the first time she had said that phrase to her mother, but the other fights had been over things her mother wouldn't let her do, freedoms denied, rather than things her mother had done. Still, Thea was stunned when June grabbed her arm tight.

"How is this my fault?" Her mother's voice sharpened with anger, the voice she used with Peter and March, not Thea.

Thea pulled her arm free and retreated to the edge of the balcony. "He cheated on you and you stayed with him. And this, hiding this, is your lie too. Your lie to your family." Thea needed her mother to acknowledge that she wasn't the victim here, that she herself was culpable. Thea had not yet messed up in a way that required her to forgive herself, and so she had little patience with the failings of others. "You, more than anyone, should understand how much it hurts to be lied to."

She waited for some rebuttal from her mother, but she got none. June just met her eye, standing tall. That kind of pride, Thea decided, was a form of weakness too.

Thea fled from the balcony. In her room, she soothed herself by adding even more colleges to her application list and taking off the few that were closer to home. There were too many other places in the world she'd rather be.

PETER HAD NO IDEA what was happening up on his second floor. He had been in the living room, watching the Rangers game. It wasn't until the game was over that he went upstairs. The door to Thea's room was shut, loud music leaking through the cracks. Down at the far end of the hallway the door to his and June's bedroom was also shut. Peter felt foreboding, but he shook it off. He had been faithful since Lee. For once, he could enter that bedroom knowing whatever was wrong was not his fault.

He swung the door open, but there was no June on the bed. There was no June in the bathroom. He called her name.

"Go away."

He found her on the other side of the bed sitting cross-legged on the floor, her eyes closed, her head tipped back and resting on the windowsill.

"*Go* away," she repeated.

But Peter had the righteousness of the innocent. He sat down next to her.

"If you don't want me to slap your face, you will listen to me and go away."

"But I haven't done anything."

June snorted.

"I haven't done anything in years. That better?" When he saw that June was about to cry, he wondered if there was false gossip going around. "Whatever you heard isn't true."

"It isn't?"

"Can't be."

"So Thea telling me that she hates me, that can't be true?"

"She's a teenager. She doesn't mean it."

"And her telling me she knows Burke is her half brother. Also not true?"

Peter wasn't prepared, though he should have planned for this eventuality. But he hadn't, hoping that his daughter, like most people, wouldn't see what she didn't want to see.

There would be times during the next few years when he wondered if things might have gone differently had he simply obeyed his wife—stayed silent and gone away. He knew June's relationship with Thea was already rocky, that the fault could be traced back to him and the things he had done to June that made her harder, less forgiving. But it was out of his mouth before he even thought about it: "Did she say she blamed me?"

It's much easier to break a thing that has already been broken once. Mending rarely makes it stronger. Peter and June's marriage had already been broken twice. And now, broken again by this long-delayed ricochet. Peter, never one to actively fix what could be avoided, began again to see if there might be warmth for him away from home.

TWO

IT'S NOT YET 8 a.m., but Sheriff Muñoz sits on the couch next to Artie, her hands clasped and her elbows on her knees, looking as if she's perpetually on the verge of standing up again. Muñoz had sent Lee out of the room, saying it was best if she and Artie talked one-on-one, and Artie waits to hear the bad news coming. "You and your family made the hardest part of my job even harder last night," the sheriff says.

The Barrys. Artie is ashamed she hadn't thought of them once since she'd gotten up this morning after a few hours of partial sleep. Instead, she'd been caught in a loop, her brain unable to move past the riverbank. The feel of the trigger giving way under her finger, the sound of splashing as Arlo struggled to get Ryan to the shore. But Ryan's parents had a night as horrible as her own. "Oh, no," Artie says. "You assumed they knew about me and Ryan."

"You said you'd been dating for months, so it was an obvious assumption. My misunderstanding made me present the news badly. It's my job to do that well. Or as well as possible." She angles herself farther toward Artie, as if she's appraising whether Artie understands the seriousness of it all.

"I'm so sorry." Artie is already playing out how awful the conversation must have been. Ryan's mother not just dealing with the shock of hearing of her son's death, but feeling blocked out of Ryan's recent life.

"You also failed to mention Ryan was working for Hap Briscoe. Mrs. Barry assumed that was where you had met her son, but I couldn't shed any light on that." Muñoz looks at Artie hard. "Lavinia Barry expects to know exactly what happened and why."

She nods at the sheriff. "Could I go with you to see her, to explain more? Does she think it was on purpose somehow? That we had a fight?"

"Her seeing you now might make things worse." The sheriff sighs. "And make you feel worse. Which I'm thinking you really aren't up for yet."

If Arlo were here too, sitting beside her, he'd probably push back, point out that the sheriff has no idea what Artie is or isn't up for. For a moment, she wishes he was there, but surely he would make things worse, just like he had made everything worse since yesterday. Since he came back from his tour, really.

The sheriff continues, "And no, Mrs. Barry doesn't think it was malicious. She assumes recklessness caused it. But she's already saying she's sure Arlo will face no punishment and the Briscoes will go blindly on with their lives, not even noticing they've taken everything from her. I assured her the investigation would be thorough and we do understand what she lost."

Sheriff Muñoz begins again to work through the events of the prior day with her. Her sternness is replaced with a new kindness, but Artie knows she's mentally comparing today's story to yesterday's—making sure they align, but not so closely they sound rehearsed. She is listening for holes, testing for weak spots. And, likely, with her encouraging smiles, her thoughtful squeeze of Artie's knee or hand, giving the witness a chance to mention anything she might have failed to mention the day before, in front of Arlo.

And even though Artie sees the motives, it's an appealing thought. Talking to this middle-aged woman in her immaculate uniform, with her hair pulled back into a gray-threaded bun, her sidearm holster pressed against one of her mother's turquoise throw pillows, makes Artie feel less alone. She, too, is a woman in a man's world. Here is another woman as comfortable as she is with guns, as skilled at putting up with the unease of men who find you not quite acceptable, even as they smile and thank you. It would feel so liberating to simply tell the truth. To be able to say, not just to Muñoz but to everyone, that her brother's thoughtless remark had made her, *her,* kill the man she loved. Now she sees that Arlo's lie has fixed nothing. It feels so small to be concerned about her career, what the town thinks of her, compared to the loss of Ryan. She can't even bring herself to care about possible jail time. She just wants the truth to remove the feeling of that trigger on the underside of her finger.

But Arlo has trapped her. The truth is now more dangerous as well as harder to believe. She can hear Arlo's arguments in her head. That telling the truth won't set her free from anything, won't change her despair or Lavinia Barry's. But it fuels her resentment that Arlo can tell himself he's taking care of her when it's his lack of care that has brought them here.

But there are still some comforts in the conversation. Artie tells Muñoz about Ryan—how they met, what she loved about him, the reasons they had kept their relationship from his family. She has her wits about her enough to mention the issues between her and Arlo— Arlo's skepticism of Ryan's reputation, his request to have her return to managing his tour—and to show them for what they are: minor quarrels and not motives for murder. It's a gift, getting to let her growing anger at Arlo seep out around the edges of her story. She feels like Sheriff Muñoz leaves, finally, satisfied that Artie is telling the truth. She has done the job Arlo wanted her to do. And now she can sit here alone with her anger. Anger at Arlo for daring her to shoot, for making things so rocky between them that she *would* shoot.

The night before, sleep hadn't come for Artie. Even after she closed her eyes to conjure up Ryan lying next to her on his stomach, as he always did, with his sleeping face turned to her, as it always was. But then she found one thing that did feel a comfort: the anger thrumming in her chest, layered below the grief. She had slipped out of bed last night and called Thea. The closest thing she has to another sibling, but also the person most likely to help her feed her anger, nurse it into something even bigger.

THE SECOND TIME the doorbell rings, hours later, Lee is wrist deep in bread dough, making yeast rolls. Artie's fault, as they are a favorite of hers, and she has already refused eggs and bacon, refused toast, refused even coffee. Artie has no appetite for company either, but she lifts herself off the couch, dropping the pillow she had been clutching, her sweaty palms leaving patches in the faux-silk.

She swings the front door open and finds Hap.

"Hey," she says, not able to keep the surprise from her voice. She can't remember him ever being in her mother's house before.

"I'm so sorry," he says, pulling her into a hug. Into her ear, he says, "He was such a sweet guy. Picked up each new thing at work quick as anyone I've seen. And I know how much he cared about you. You made him beam."

She could've called Hap a revisionist; when he first found out his new employee and Artie were dating, he tried to warn her away. He, too, knew all about Ryan's former exploits. But Artie is simply touched, grateful her half brother knows the best way to console her, grateful she feels sure he is telling the truth. Hap has always been cordial, but they've never been that close, and she can feel his surprise when she tightens her grip, latching herself to him.

When she lets go, there's deep concern on his face. "You okay?" he says.

"Let's go to the backyard." She tries to compose her face, keep herself free of tears, walking too fast for him to do anything but follow.

On the back patio, they survey the masses of zinnias and marigolds in silence. Her mother has stuffed the backyard beds with so many clashing colors, it makes Artie anxious. She shuts her eyes, leans back in her chair as Hap cracks open the Coke her mother forced on him as they passed the kitchen.

"It was a stupid question," says Hap. "Of course you're not okay. Is there anything I can do?"

"Just you coming helps," she says. "No one else knew him. I brought him here once, to meet Mom, but it was a quick visit. June and Peter never met him, or Arlo."

Hap sets the Coke can down on the concrete. "Not Arlo? But then how could he have . . ."

Artie's brain fills in the gap: how could Arlo have killed him, shot him, made him disappear. "It would help if you told me how you heard, what you heard." She wants to know what pipes her tragedy is flowing through, the way the news is dripping out over the town. The details the sheriff will inevitably hear.

"I don't see how that will make you feel . . ." Hap doesn't finish.

"I need to know," she says.

"I heard from one of my guys, in the shop this morning. He said there had been a hunting accident and that Ryan was dead." He stops, and the next sentence comes out much more softly. "Shot by Arlo."

She can feel Hap staring at her even though her eyes are still shut. He asks, "Is that what happened?"

"He's dead." It's the first time she's said that sentence, and she hopes to never say it again. "Accidentally shot." She hears the back door of the house next door open and close. The flick of a metal Zippo, the plastic crinkle of a soft pack of cigarettes.

"Can I be honest?" Hap asks. This makes her open her eyes, but Hap is staring at his hands, using his thumb to stroke an old scar that runs down the length of his index finger. She reaches over to him, lays her palm on top of his hand, and cocks her head toward the fence. They watch the exhaled smoke float above the tall slats of wood. It's a welcome break, as Artie's in no hurry to hear his honesty. They both wait, silent minutes, until the neighbor's back door opens and closes again.

"Go ahead," says Artie.

"It doesn't sit right," says Hap. "The sheriff said you were just downriver from Dad's. You and Arlo and Ryan, together."

"The sheriff's already interviewed you?"

Hap nods. "She showed up at the shop. She was still talking to the other men when I left."

A busy morning for the sheriff. "Yeah, we were at the river."

Hap rubs his face hard, like he's trying to erase some thought that's gotten under his skin. "But you don't hunt there. I know you fish there, but you don't hunt. And Arlo never goes hunting, anyway, with you or without."

Her desire to come clean, to tell the truth, won't leave her. But it's too big a burden to shift onto Hap. "We were fishing, but I had my gun with me. Someone had seen a rabid skunk around there." She pauses. "Hap. I appreciate you coming, it's a comfort. But you don't need to worry about these details. You have enough to deal with."

"No offense, but my problems look peachy compared to what's happened to you."

"How are things with Vera?" Artie says. When Hap shakes his head, she adds, "I could use the distraction."

Hap relents. "Vera took Pete, and they spent last night at her mother's."

"That doesn't mean anything. Hasn't she done that plenty of times?"

"Not once in the two years March was gone. And I know she saw March the other night at My Place."

"That doesn't mean—"

"Let's drop it. I know you're glad March is back in town, I know you want him here."

To repay his earlier kindness, she changes the subject. "If you still want to help me, get me out of this house for a while. Between the gingham and the marigolds, I'm suffocating."

They drive out to Hayden's cemetery, a place they frequented in high school, knowing Hayden would never call the cops on them. The universal lure of headstones for teenagers, to feel more alive by sitting among the dead with beer or cheap wine or weed. It's Artie's idea— too morbid, given the circumstances, for Hap to suggest it.

They walk up a long row, heading for the enormous live oak at the far end, out where the headstones ease into smooth pasture, another twenty acres waiting for all those future dead Olympians, to be buried by Hayden and whoever follows after him. Burying her mother, Peter and June, even her and Hap, likely. Burying people not yet born.

Hap asks the obvious: "Will Ryan be buried here?"

"Hayden called me this morning to donate his services—the funeral and internment—and he said he'd approach Ryan's parents about it." She had handed the phone off to her mother, his unexpected help prompting even more tears. "But I can't see them accepting help from a Briscoe. On behalf of a half Briscoe. Besides, I'd think they'd want him nearer to them. Ryan told me once that he wanted to be cremated and scattered in the Brazos, but I don't know if he ever said that to his mother."

Artie knows Hayden's offer would have made Ryan tear up, just as she did, and also to protest, not wanting to be a bother. Instead of the feeling of the trigger on her finger again, her mind gives her Ryan's face, every tiny detail down to his left eyebrow, a pinch higher than the right, the chicken pox scar on the bridge of his nose. The image brings a different kind of pain than the rifle's trigger, deeper but less violent.

She trails her hand over the headstones as they walk, letting the granite and marble slap against her fingers. "Of course, the irony of actually *dying* in the Brazos might have changed his mind on his final resting place." She sees Hap flinch on her behalf. "Sorry," she says. "But gallows humor has to be appropriate in a cemetery." A light-headedness hits her, the lack of food perhaps, and she thinks of fainting with a bit of longing. No dreams when you're unconscious.

Hap takes her arm and links it with his, drawing her away from the headstones.

They settle under the shade of the tree, Artie lying down to stop her feeling of floating and Hap leaning back against the trunk. She tries to ground herself by defusing Hap's worry.

"There's no way Vera left because she wants to be with March. And I'm sure March didn't come back because he wants to be with Vera."

Hap only grunts. Being caught up in Arlo's lie has made her impatient with concealment. Surely talking about these things is the best way to repair them. She says, "What if Vera leaving is a good thing? What if you shouldn't have taken her back in the first place?"

"First March, now you," Hap says flatly. "Her leaving means me not having my son full-time. And if I hadn't taken her back, he'd never have been born. That's your wish for me?"

"You know that's not what I mean," she says.

"Clearly, I don't know what you mean."

She tries a different tack. "Did you ever know why Vera did it? Why March?"

"She said she needed me to end it because she couldn't leave on her own and picking him seemed the best way to ensure that." Hap says it quietly, and Artie can tell it's something he's never told anyone before.

"I don't understand what you could have done to her, that she loved you too much to leave but couldn't bear to stay."

"She loves me but she stopped liking me," he says. "Some of us are built to forgive, and I see that as a good thing. Vera sees it differently."

Artie knows she's not too different from Hap. Their love of home, their desire to keep the peace, to make people happy if they can. Before yesterday, she would have said she was built to forgive, too, but maybe that rifle shot reconfigured something in her heart. Perhaps she'll turn out to be more like grudge-nursing Lavinia Barry in the end.

Artie looks down at her watch. Thea will be here soon.

THREE

AFTER HE DROPS Artie back off at Lee's, Hap returns home. It's the first time he's gone twenty-four hours without his son, and seeing Vera's car still absent from their driveway is another slice from his heart. Inside, at the kitchen table, he finds no note. But he also finds no empty spaces in the dressers or closets, no missing diapers or toys. He calls her cell, listens to her short, clipped message: *Vera's phone. Do your worst.*

In the past, it had pleased Hap to leave sappy messages after her directive, liking that his worst could only be excessive sentimentality. Vera always expected bad news; it was a trait they shared, the pessimism of people who have had their full share. Your mother's lost her job, your father's child support payment is late, your crazy brother has knocked out the principal's son, your mother is not speaking to your father yet again. Pessimism wasn't a negative trait for them. It was a way to consistently feel happier, each mediocre event a triumph over potential calamity.

He hangs up without leaving a message. He doesn't want to go back to work in case Vera and Pete come home, but he needs an activity he can to do with his hands, a project with tangible results to make the wait bearable. At a loss, he decides to clean the bathroom. Vera hates cleaning it, so it's always the dirtiest place in the house.

He tackles the tub with a sponge and abrasive cleaner, thinking about what he said to Artie. If he's built to forgive, then why hasn't he forgiven March yet? Because Vera didn't see that trait as a good thing? His blessed martyrdom, she called it. The thing that had almost driven her away.

He turns on the shower to rinse the tub, watching the grit flow down to the drain. He's back in the thought spiral that consumed him for Vera's entire pregnancy, until the small but concrete weight of his son pushed his thoughts away as less important, less real, than the tiny body and the fact that his wife was still there. Before, it was why March, why sleep with the one person who'd hurt him most? Now, he's obsessing over why Vera is unhappy again. What has made sleeping in the same bed as him unbearable?

Hap moves to scrubbing the toilet, and he notices a wiggle from loose bolts. He goes to find a wrench, switching his thoughts to his brother, an easier book to read than his wife. March had said he wanted to be done breaking things, and yet he had no apologies for Hap that first morning. Even after they fought, March was silent and seething as Hap packed up to go. It was only the next day that the apology actually came. What had made March finally repent?

Hap squats down to tighten the bolts, but then lays the wrench down and goes to the bathroom window. He looks into their backyard, through the field that leads to the country road behind them. The field he, two years ago, realized March had been driving through to hide his visits to Vera. Sure enough, he sees bent and broken stalks of sorghum. His brother has already come to see Vera. And no matter the reason why, *something* must have happened. Something that made March want to apologize.

Hap picks up the wrench. His new anger is righteous and hot and deeply satisfying. Passivity and forgiveness have gotten him nowhere. Not because they aren't good, but because his wife doesn't deserve them. March doesn't deserve them. He stands up and brings the wrench down hard on the ceramic of the pedestal sink, a chunk of it skittering across the floor. He raises his arm and sinks the wrench deep into the drywall next to the bathroom mirror. He is tempted to pull it out, sink it somewhere else, but instead he walks to the back-yard. Leaning against one of their linden trees, he pulls out his cell phone and redials Vera's number. He leaves a message. He does his worst.

THE ORIGIN OF VERA'S BROKEN HEART

I thought my courage was conspicuous,
but all my fame was for mere loveliness.

≯ OVID ≮

WHEN VERA MARRIED HAP and moved to Olympus, she was sure she'd found a man who knew her, the part of her beneath the beauty, and loved her for it. She hadn't yet realized that she didn't know all of Hap.

It started with small irritations. Hap accepting dinner invitations from his parents when they'd both rather stay home. Him picking up slack for one of his workers rather than firing him. At first she chided herself for being annoyed with her husband's innate goodness, but eventually she decided his kindness wasn't generosity. It was self-serving. He was the perfect son. The magnanimous boss. The patient husband with the irritable wife. To feel good, he needed to be better than the rest of them. It likely started with his mother—June modeling martyrdom in her marriage to Peter. Add to that a lifetime of praise, every time he made his parents' life easier to balance out the son who made everyone's life harder.

Vera had too much experience in being a prop, chased by men who needed a high value item on their arm, in their bed, to function in the world. Hap hadn't needed her beauty to validate him, and he was such a wonderful change, it took her a long time to see she was just a prop of a different sort—a hard, often-selfish woman that he could martyr himself against again and again by always being kinder. Always superior to her.

She was disappointed, but she told herself she was adjusting to the same reality all couples do, once the shine is off, once you really see another person. And wasn't she lucky, after all—her own baggage playing so well off her husband's, so that what might be a negative became the thing that greased the wheels of their day-to-day life?

But then she figured out something else.

It was Thanksgiving. Vera stood in front of June's kitchen windows, peeling sweet potatoes, big orange strips piling up in the sink. Behind her, Hap and his mother were chopping vegetables on the kitchen island. Vera watched the Briscoes on the lawn—March and his uncle, Hayden, making wild grabs for the multiple Frisbees being tossed by Hayden's boys and Thea's girls. Thea and Artie and Hayden's wife in a bunch, laughing together as March fell to the ground leaping after a purposefully wayward throw.

"Perhaps March should take a break," June said, appearing beside Vera. "We don't want him getting mad and adding child abuse to his list of sins." Vera was used to these types of comments about March, but, even after several years, Vera had never seen the rage from March that was family lore. She, too, felt the tyranny of low expectations from both her husband and her mother-in-law. She'd had such high hopes when she joined this big family after her lonely childhood. Then she saw how the Briscoes brought out the worst in each other.

A few minutes later, March came in the kitchen with Thea's youngest. She was riding on his back, and the top of her head just grazed the top of the doorframe. The girl was laughing as she rubbed her scalp and slid to the ground, clearly unhurt. But Hap said to March, "No one's going to make a better dad than you." March hadn't realized his niece had bumped her head, and Vera could see the pleased surprise on March's face for a half second. Then Vera noticed the smirk on

June's face, the half-cocked smile on Hap's. Their meanness cut at even Vera's well-armored heart.

March registered the sarcasm, too. "Fuck you, Hap." Then he remembered the young ears in the kitchen, flushed red, and hurried back outside. June scooped the girl up and asked if she wanted to help feed the peacocks, leaving Hap and Vera in the kitchen alone.

"You were being sarcastic," Vera said.

Hap looked at her curiously. "Well, yeah." Vera felt a wave of panic she couldn't immediately diagnose.

"I thought you were never sarcastic. I'm sarcastic, I know. But I thought you were sarcasm-free."

"I certainly wouldn't call it a large part of my personality." He kissed her forehead and moved on to chopping garlic.

Vera scanned through her memories of Hap for similarly off-kilter remarks: the time he had told her she had excellent taste after she bought that bulky Edwardian armoire; the Christmas he told Thea her gift of a sweater showed how well she knew him; when he had finally fired a useless employee, telling him that the shop would miss him. Each time said with utter seriousness, and each time followed by that half-cocked smile. A smile she saw now was a shit-eating grin. It made her feel dumb, those comments she had completely misread, the jokes gone over her head. But her panic came from a different memory. "The world is a hard place for women as beautiful as you," he had said. How she had misread that grin.

She slipped from the kitchen and out the front door to hide herself between the family's cars, unable to reconcile her new knowledge. Vera understood she had negative traits—a temper, a desire to get her own way, a need to control—but those things came from a lifetime of people assuming she was a willing vehicle for their desires. Apparently Hap thought she was that way out of the womb, an easy life and still such a bitch. Not a person who had suffered and sought his kindness. She had loved him for his soft edges, and those edges had turned out to be hard. She wasn't sure she could love a man who was no different from the others after all. That was what she was thinking when March rounded his truck with keys in hand. Though he was wary of her tears, he still asked if she wanted to go to the store with him. She was grateful to be given exactly what she needed: a little time to process what she now knew. But trailing behind March in the grocery store aisle, she saw the best gift Hap had given her—the fact that, since they first got together, she never felt completely alone—had disappeared. Returning to the isolation she'd known her whole life was like hearing a cage door slam shut behind her. She had to do something to bust her way out. That's why she had walked up to March and kissed him. And the next day, it was why she had gone to his house to see him.

She knew it wasn't fair to Hap. She was the one that had misinterpreted him. But she was stuck—she didn't love Hap enough to accept how he saw her, how firmly he was ruled by superiority and judgment, but she still loved him too much to leave him. In sleeping with March, she'd force him to leave her. And perhaps she could help Hap too. He would finally see his urge to forgo his own desires in service to another was unsustainable, no way to live. He would be free of the burden of a selfish wife. He could be good, or he could be bad, all on his own.

FOUR

Thea's waiting at the curb when Peter swings into Arrivals at the airport. He gets out and hefts her suitcase into the truck bed, gives his daughter a hug that lifts her off her feet. With her dark hair and green eyes, she is always pegged as his daughter and March's sister, even though she looks very different than she did at sixteen. Big curly hair straightened and precisely parted. Round cheeks now prominent cheekbones. Her perpetual lack of sleep has left dark circles under her eyes. She's so much like her mother, so prone to bulldogging every problem, to take any wrong personally. It makes her an excellent prosecutor. But how will that translate to this new situation they are in?

When they get in the cab, he turns the air up higher. "Sorry you had to wait in the heat." She has on jeans, and a blazer over a T-shirt, as if she even expects the weather to follow her lead.

"Wasn't long," she says. "You look good."

"Better than a body has a right to?" he says. Thea hates country music, so he likes to drop the lyrics on her when appropriate, or slightly appropriate.

She pulls her phone from her purse and scrolls through her email. "I called Artie when I landed. She asked if I'd stay with her at her place while I was here. I think Lee's house is getting a little claustrophobic for her."

"How'd she sound?"

"Like she had taken a Valium. But when I talked to Lee, she said Artie refused to take anything. Wasn't drinking, either."

"That's good, right?"

"Or she's too upset to do anything to feel better, even briefly." Thea moves the air conditioning back to low, the cab of the truck suddenly quiet. She shakes her head. "How could Arlo do such an idiotic thing? None of it makes any sense."

Back on Telephone Road, the rush hour traffic lingers. "Accidents often don't make sense, though," Peter says. "People are always using the phrase 'senseless accidents.'"

Thea plows on like she hasn't heard him. "You know Artie was worried that Arlo wouldn't like Ryan? She hadn't even mentioned him to Arlo, even though they'd been dating for months."

"So?" says Peter, more irritably than he should.

Thea is quiet. Then she says, "I'm just trying to wrap my head around it all, Dad. No need to be a dick."

"Sorry," he says. "We're all just upset."

"Where's Mom?"

"At home. She'll go see you and Artie tomorrow."

Thea snorts. "Even the woman's driveway is too much Lee for her?"

"I'll come in with you. I want to see how Artie is doing."

Thea snorts again. "I don't think your wife would approve."

"Could you stop that?" Peter says, surprised at the thin layer of anger underneath his words.

Thea runs her fingers through her hair. "Sorry." She squeezes his hand on the console beside her. "I hate coming home because it always turns me back into a petulant teenager."

"You really hate coming home?" Peter asks. She doesn't answer. Not even a snort.

. . .

LEE OPENS THE DOOR for them as they walk up the sidewalk. Thirty years of keeping his eyes from her means that now, with this new permission granted, he can't stop staring. She had often seemed the opposite of June—dark eyes, auburn hair, all curves in addition to her softer personality. Now, even though her curves have expanded, her hair streaked with gray, he still reacts to her like it's decades ago, like he's been wandering around with jumper cables on and someone has just now turned the ignition. He guesses that kind of chemistry never goes away. This gets filed as the first piece of information he will keep to himself when he updates June later tonight. He doubts it will be the last. Lee touches his shoulder as he and Thea cross the threshold.

Thea gives Lee a stiff hug and steps back. Peter, feeling like he and Lee are on display in front of their daughter, just offers her a curt nod. But he holds Lee's gaze a beat too long. "Where's Artie?" he asks.

"In her bedroom," Lee replies. Peter finds he can still read Lee's expressions. Under her politeness, she's not happy to see Thea.

"I'll just say hello before I head home," Peter says. As he and Thea pass through the living room, Peter is amazed by his recognition of nearly every vase, every painting on the wall. So little has changed since he was last there. It looks like Lee has just replaced things with near-identical things when they wore out.

The door to Artie's room is shut, so Thea knocks, calling out, "I'm here!" The door flies inward and Artie hugs her.

"You're here," she echoes. Then she gives Peter a hug too. "Thanks for bringing her over." Peter hears a dismissal in Artie's thanks and feels both relief and a touch of annoyance to be leaving so soon.

Artie is already back at the bed, stuffing a few things into a bag that's more the size of a large purse. It must be Lee's because it's ging-ham with rickrack stitched along the bottom. Peter wishes all the myriad details he remembers about Lee wouldn't float up so easily despite being submerged so long.

"Give us a sec?" Thea says, moving to shut the door behind her.

"But don't go yet," says Artie. "The sheriff had some news."

Peter walks slowly back to the kitchen but stops midway through the living room, watching Lee's back as she stands in front of the stove, stirring something in a large pot. He makes himself move forward, thinking it will be even stranger if Thea finds him loitering and staring in the living room. Lee has to hear him coming, he's cleared his throat a time or two, but she doesn't move. She sniffs, and he knows she's crying. He leans forward so he can pat her on the back without coming any closer. "Making dinner for the girls?" he asks. She simply nods without turning around.

"It's just . . . ," Lee starts. She stops, tries again. "I never wanted Artie to feel this, this kind of loss." He leaves his hand on her back, can feel the warmth of her through the linen of her dress. "She really loved him." When he hears Artie's door open again, he takes a further step back, his hand falling away. Thea and Artie come into the kitchen, Thea raising her eyebrows at him.

"Okay, so I'm meeting Uncle Hayden and the Barrys tomorrow morning to plan Ryan's funeral," Artie begins. Her voice sounds so exhausted, Peter wonders how she is still upright. "And I need to know what I'm walking into. The sheriff said your history with Mrs. Barry is actually still a pretty big deal to her. What *exactly* did you do?"

Before now, what Peter did to Lavinia hadn't caused him much regret. It was just business. He regretted the scenes she made, but there was nothing he could do about that. But he doesn't relish the idea of explaining his long-ago actions to Artie. "It was two separate things. The first was back in the late eighties. Lavinia's father, Andrew Mann, was the biggest property owner in Olympus. But he got upside down after the oil bust. Bad investments. He had to sell off his properties, and I wound up with a lot of them."

"That doesn't sound that unusual," Artie says, confused.

"Well, he had to sell them for a lot less than they were worth, and I got a bank loan to purchase them when he had been denied one to keep them. Lavinia felt like my success, my whole career, was built off her father's bad luck. He died of a heart attack pretty soon after that. The family was left in debt, and Lavinia was newly married to a guy that didn't bring much money into the equation. She went from rich to struggling in a matter of months. Her mother too."

"And the second thing?"

Peter sighs, less eager to tell this one. "The Barrys used to live here in Olympus, twenty acres just outside town. I heard a Houston paper company was looking for land to build a box factory—somewhere with close access to I-10 but outside the city. Around that time, I also heard the Barrys had been falsely claiming an ag exemption on their property taxes. Even though they hadn't owned cattle in years. I might have passed that rumor on to the county tax assessor-collector."

"Jesus, Dad," Thea says. "You snitched them out so they'd have to sell to you?"

Peter bristles. "You think it's fine for people to cheat on their taxes, now? I'm astonished a prosecutor is so flexible about the law. Lavinia got wind of what I had done, and she wouldn't sell me the land. She sold it to someone else for less than I offered, out of pure spite. She got just enough to cover what they owed, and the family moved to Bullinger. Turns out, Lavinia had no idea they weren't paying the taxes. It was her husband. Still, I was the one she blamed for the loss of her homestead."

"She had one life and then, suddenly, you boxed her into a totally different one," Artie says, incredulous. "And Arlo and I did that same thing to her. She was a mother with a son. And now she's a mother who's had her son taken from her." She is shaking her head, keeps shaking it even after she has finished.

"It was an accident. And you lost Ryan too," Peter says. He wants Artie to feel as blameless as she is in his eyes. Because he knows it's not her fault. Just like the exact dimensions of Lavinia's diminished life are not all due to a few choices he once made. The world doesn't work that way. Things aren't that simple. "I think June should meet you at Hayden's tomorrow. She and Lavinia went to high school together. I don't think she blames June like she blames me, and you need someone there to help, in case Lavinia tries to take things out on you. It's strange she even accepted Hayden's help."

He avoids looking at Lee. He doesn't want to know if he's hurt her with the implication that she can't protect her own daughter. But she can't, not the way June can. "With June and Thea with you, it might show we're taking responsibility for things." He can't help adding, "Even though it was just an accident."

"Just because something is an accident," Artie says, "that doesn't mean it doesn't matter. If you hadn't turned them in for the taxes, Ryan's whole life would have been different too. I'm not saying he'd be alive. That's on me. But still." Peter can see her spinning out different lives for Ryan in her head, all better than the one he got. And he's made her feel complicit in it, too.

"Ryan's death is not on you," Thea says firmly. "It's on Arlo."

"It was an accident," Lee says, so loudly that they all jump. She's glaring at Thea. "Arlo didn't mean to hurt anyone." She takes Artie's hand. "Of course it matters. Of course it changes things. But this is your brother. You love him. Have you talked to him today?"

Artie shakes her head. "I just need some time without him."

Peter forces himself to chime in. "I know it's hard to think about it now, but Arlo is suffering too. He took another man's life. Accident or no, none of us can understand how hard that will be to live with." Artie's face goes even paler, but all he can do is slog on until he's done. "He'll need your help with that. And counseling—"

"Counseling," Artie repeats, cutting him off. "Stop," she says. "Stop talking about Arlo. I don't need either of you telling me how he feels. You think you know him better than me? Either of you?"

Artie leaves the kitchen, then returns with her bag over her shoulder, car keys in her hand. Thea follows her outside. Peter is left alone with Lee, who fails to keep the tears back this time. He puts his hand on her back, no patting this time, and sees her readying words of comfort for him despite her own pain. Which is what he wants, he knows, even though he shouldn't.

FIVE

JUNE SITS ON THE BALCONY, ostensibly waiting for the sunset. She has a beer she's not drinking and options she's not taking. She can't imagine sitting alone all evening, thinking of Thea and Artie, Peter and Lee. How she should have gone to the airport to see her daughter. How Artie must be suffering. She wishes she had company, someone who already understood what was going on. Which leaves her sons, who would bring their own problems into the mix, the ones she's been avoiding thinking of. She goes ahead and drinks the beer.

And then there's Cole. The thought of explaining things to him feels like a relief instead of a burden, but she's not comfortable inviting him to her home. Not just because she has no idea when Peter will return. She imagines dropping in on him, but she can't get past the image of them in Joe's living room with the audience of Joe and Betty, perplexed at her arrival. Even meeting him at a restaurant is problematic. People coming up to extend sympathies, dig for details, gossip later about her choice of dining companion. She resigns herself to a miserable evening alone. Decides misery at least deserves oatmeal cookies.

She has the ingredients combined, the oven preheated, and is about to dig her hands into the dough and extract enough to roll into a ball when her cell phone rings. She pulls it from her purse and sees an unfamiliar number, unfamiliar area code. She'd given Cole her number when he had to leave early, in case he needed to change the plan for the next day, but hadn't thought to take his. She smiles at the phone, cannot help herself.

"Hello?"

"Are you busy? I don't want to interrupt."

She likes that he doesn't bother to clarify who's calling, that the knowledge is assumed. "All alone. And glad for an interruption." She can hear the low mechanical buzz of cicadas starting and stopping behind him. "Where are you?"

"I was driving back from a house visit and pulled over a few miles upstream from you. Pretty." He pauses, "I heard about Artie and Arlo. Are you okay? Are they okay?" The order pleases her.

"No one is in jail, so that's good. And no one I love is dead, which is harsh, I know, but true. I'm worried about Artie, though."

"She's at home?"

"Staying with her mother. Thea's flown in, and Peter's gone to pick her up and take her to Lee's." She tries to say it free of rancor or distrust.

"That's good. And tough." His silence is filled by the cicadas.

"You okay? You don't sound yourself."

She hears the rumble of him exhaling hard onto the phone. "Went out to see a horse, but it died while I was there. Distemper. Then the wife brought me coffee and told me all about the shooting with too much excitement and not enough sympathy. I feel like shit, and I'm not completely sure why. The one thing that seemed like it might make me feel better was calling you."

She holds the phone more tightly. "It doesn't sound like I'm helping."

"You are. I'm glad you're okay enough to answer your phone, to humor me by asking what's wrong with my pathetic self."

"You have a sweet tooth?"

He laughs. "Is that essential to being pathetic?"

"Unrelated question."

"I've been known to eat my share of sugar."

She speaks without thinking. "Where are you? Specifically." He tells her. "Stay there." She hangs up then pulls plastic wrap from the drawer to cover the bowl of dough. She grabs her purse, two spoons, and the bowl and heads to her car. She moves fast to outpace the voice in her head telling her that if she's not comfortable seeing Cole in her own home or out in the world, she shouldn't be comfortable seeing him alone, outdoors, either. On the drive, she turns up the radio and does not allow herself to think about a single thing except her anticipation in seeing this man, this stranger, really. This person who seems to always make her feel better.

The sun is setting, and June uses the last of the light to spot Cole's truck, pulled off a rarely used road that dead-ends near the Brazos. She's glad the darkness will soon cover their cars. She didn't want to have to ask Cole to park more discreetly, not because he might get the wrong idea—she feels he understands her too well for that—but because of the furtiveness it would imply. She turns out her headlights, leaves her purse in the passenger seat—after lifting the two spoons from it—and grabs the bowl. She can see Cole's silhouette, him sitting on his tailgate, facing the river.

She hands him the bowl before pulling herself up beside him.

"What's this?"

"A surprise, I guess." She pulls back the cling wrap to expose half the bowl. Then she hands him a spoon. He carefully dips it in and pulls out a generous sampling. June watches his face as he sniffs then takes the whole spoonful into his mouth.

While still chewing, he says, "I haven't had raw cookie dough in twenty years, since my kids were small."

"Sad life," she says, putting her own spoon in, eating a smaller bite.

"My doctor tells me to watch my cholesterol."

"It's oatmeal. Lowers cholesterol."

Cole fills up the spoon again. "You'd make a crap doctor."

They sit in the quiet and chew. But it isn't really quiet, just a sound-scape so familiar to her it might as well be silence. Frogs all around, the burble of the river, those long scratching sounds of the cicadas and the crickets. And spoons scraping against the metal of the bowl.

"One more bite and then I'll stop."

"Have as much as you want." June battles his spoon to take his bite.

"I've already had the equivalent of a dozen cookies, I bet."

"Who can say? It's dark."

More chewing.

Cole drops the spoon with a moan. "Critical mass. I forgot how the raw flour and egg settles in the gut." He hops up from the tailgate. "I've got to lie down."

He disappears from her line of sight, his body now prone and cov-ered by grass. "Better make sure there are no ant beds," she calls out.

"Bites would distract me from my pain," he says.

"Have you ever had a fire ant bite?"

"How bad could it be? It's an ant bite."

"Let's say the word 'fire' is an understatement, but it does linger like a burn."

His head pops back up. She laughs. "Look around. If there are no mounds nearby, you're fairly safe." This is not what she wanted to say. She wanted to summon him back to the tailgate, offer her lap as a pillow.

After some looking and moving of grass, Cole seems satisfied enough to lie back down. "Tell me something to distract me from my discomfort."

"Like what?"

"What you're worried about. The doctor is in. Go ahead. Unload."

"Artie's heartbroken. Arlo's a mess. I haven't even talked to Hap, so I don't know how things are with him and Vera. I can only think of what new problems March may have caused. I can't even appreciate that he may actually be helping the twins." Shining the light on her worries also exposes the ones she can't say—what the sheriff might find if she digs deep enough, how something seems damaged between Artie and Arlo. "And now Thea is home. I'll see, in her every word to me, how much I disappoint her. All that I can control is whether I take it with a smile or if I turn the disappointment back on her."

June pulls her legs up on the tailgate and sits cross-legged. "I know the choice should be an easy one. Somebody's son was killed, not far from my door, and that should make me put aside my hurt feelings and gush love upon all my children. Isn't that what unconditional love does?"

Cole's voice floats up from the grass. "You're asking the wrong person. I don't believe unconditional love is a human emotion."

"Really?" June tends to believe this too, but she's never said it out loud.

"Strongest drive in any mammal, and I limit it to mammals just because they're my area of specialized knowledge, is to avoid pain. It takes a lot to overcome that. But people, and animals, they do it all the time. They put themselves in mortal danger to save their children. But emotional pain is different. If your love is getting pushed back at you, that unconditional river of it, you can avoid the pain so easily by draining out the water."

His metaphor makes her emotions painfully easy to judge. The Brazos-sized river for Hap, the smaller stream for Thea. And March: a dry riverbed that occasionally rises to a shallow crawl. A love that would not cover the tops of her feet. Her throat gets tight. "I'm a horrible human being," she says, intending it to feel so at odds with her opinion of herself that her throat will loosen and she'll be able to breathe again. Instead, it comes out broken, sounding bereft.

Cole is there, so fast she feels spun around. He pulls himself back up on the tailgate next to her. "I wasn't talking about you," he says. "And you're looking at it the wrong way. Even if it's true for you, which I'm not saying it is, it means you're a normal human being. It *makes* you human, not inhuman."

"How's your stomach?" she asks.

"Full as a tick, but it was worth it. As soon as I stop feeling sick, I'm going for a second dozen."

June stays quiet.

"Stop being so hard on yourself. You're overthinking things," Cole tells her.

"Overthinking is what I do."

"When's the last time you did something without thinking?"

"When I came here to see you."

"Oh," he says. She can feel his pleasure in it, just in the one syllable.

"Wait, no. When I answered your question now. I said that without thinking, too. Very out of character. Maybe that's why I like being around you so much. I'm tired of my own company. I'm ready to be someone else." She looks off, up the river, not brave enough to see Cole's reaction.

"I bet June would be about to head home. What would this other person do?"

"Oh, you will get me into trouble," she whispers.

"What?" Cole says. "I could only make out 'trouble.'"

She turns to him and shakes her head. "I don't know what she would do, because if I think about it, I'll realize I can't do it."

"Then we're stuck," he says. "I can't counsel you to act without thinking. It's rarely worked out well for me in my own life."

"You think about it long before you called me today?"

"Thought about it every hour since I last saw you."

A statement that should be as dangerous as a rattlesnake. But it makes June feel safer than she has, perhaps, ever felt. "Before you heard about Artie?"

"A convenient excuse. I took it as a sign. But I have no expectations."

"So you were fated to call, but you have no expectations it will amount to anything?"

"A hole in my logic, I agree," he says. He pulls his own legs up to also sit cross-legged, their knees so close June can almost, but not quite, feel his.

"I don't believe in fate," June says. "Except maybe that character is fate."

"I hate to say it, but if character was fate, we wouldn't be sitting here together. In the dark. With cookie dough."

"I'd have sensibly eaten two cookies, put the rest away. I'd take all my worry over the kids and squeeze it into anger at Peter. That he always has an easier time with Thea. That we're back to being tangled up with Lee. Peter would get home, and despite my best intentions, we'd get into a fight. I'd never hear what happened, or how he felt about it, because he'd withhold anything iffy out of fear and anything good out of spite."

"That sounds bad."

"It does."

"Then act out of character," he says. And so, without a thought, she leans toward him and places her hand against his cheek. She rests her forehead on his forehead and her hand on his thigh. She feels him inhale, but elsewise he doesn't move. It makes her think—don't think, don't think, she tells herself—of how he must be with the cows and horses he tends to, what keeps him safe. He emanates a stillness that removes any feeling of threat. The calm should still her heart, send her back home. She can't help it, even after she's thought about it. She kisses him.

SIX

MARCH SPENT THE ENTIRE DAY waiting for Arlo to talk about the shooting but getting only silence. Silent at March's house, silent when they retrieved Arlo's Bronco from the river, silent on the front porch while they finished the beer in the fridge. When March returns from the liquor store with whiskey and more beer, Arlo is still on the porch, but Hap is there too, his wrecker pulled up on the lawn like he might need a quick exit. March reluctantly gets out of his truck with the bags.

"Join us," Hap calls to him. "I was telling Arlo about my visit with Artie this morning. And also how I'm trying on a new worldview, one that believes forgiveness is overrated. A lot going on today. In fact, a lot going on since you rolled back into town."

Hap's somehow broken the impassiveness Arlo has clung to all day. His face is now caught between grief and anger. Arlo and Hap have never been close, but March isn't used to Hap winding people up. A bad sign. March reaches inside the plastic bag and twists a beer can free. He comes up on the porch and hands it to Arlo, guiding him by the shoulder away from Hap and into the porch swing. Arlo drinks half the beer in one go, then leans to the side so he can see past March. "Have a beer, Hap. Self-medicate with the rest of us."

"I think there's been enough drinking for the day," Hap says. He picks up the unattended bags and takes them into the house.

"What's going on?" March asks.

"Your brother has decided he and Artie are long-suffering heroes while you and I are definitely villains. You already fuck shit up again with Vera?"

March shrugs, then sighs, then nods. Vera must have decided her silence was too much to ask for. Arlo says, "Shit, I guess we *are* the villains."

"If something starts up," March says, "I need you to step in. If I can't . . . you know."

"I know," Arlo says. "Go in low, knock you off balance. Sit on you until you calm the fuck down. I remember the drill."

March heads for the kitchen, telling himself that he can still fix things. He can still convince his brother he's changed. Hap has put away the beer, is wadding up the plastic bags and stuffing them into one another. March's instincts tell him to back out of the room, leave this house, and return to New Mexico. As if his dogs can read his mind, they wander into the kitchen from their bedroom, ready to go with him. Rom approaches Hap to sniff him, still yawning from his nap. Then March sees the dog stiffen, his hackles raising. March isn't the only one with instinct.

"Jerky!" March calls out, as jovial as he can muster. He pulls a sleeve of dog jerky from his pantry—lonely on the shelf with two cans of ranch-style beans and a bag of Fritos. He starts to wave two strips at the dogs, but they're already all over him, lunging and wagging their tails. "Outside," he says, and the dogs rush to the front door. It would be so easy to get in the truck. But there's only easiness in the first step. Each one after gets harder and harder, like a rubber band stretched too far. Rom and Remus push open the screen door and March throws one piece of jerky to the left side of the yard, one to the right, and the dogs jump from the porch in opposite directions.

"Keep 'em out here for me?" March says to Arlo.

"Do my best, but I'm not touching them if they get pissed."

The dogs lie down in the front yard, snuffling for any last bits. March goes back inside, shutting the screen and the door firmly behind him.

He finds Hap sitting up on the kitchen counter, swinging his feet. His work boots hit the cabinets beneath him. Whoomp. Whoomp. March stands in the doorway and waits for things to begin.

"Protecting me from your dogs? You're the one that needs protecting." Whoomp.

"You could have a gun. Maybe I was trying to keep them safe."

"So you've done something worth being shot over." Hap's tone is cold and packed with jagged peaks, a mountain range of disgust. "It would have been better," says Hap, "if I had married a woman that gave a shit about me. I shouldn't blame you for that, but I can blame you for making me see it. Even if it took you a second round to beat it into my thick skull."

All those things March had been hopeful for—working again with his father, returning to his friendship with Arlo and Artie, winning over Hap and his mother, feeling like himself, like he had a life again— are snuffed out.

"What have I ever done to you to make you wreck my life like this?" Hap says. "I know you don't think you're trying to save me from myself. You've never helped a person in your life without being asked first, and usually not even then." Hap bangs his boots against the cabinets again. Whoomp.

"I was honest when I came to the shop. I do want to be done breaking things. I do want to stay away from Vera."

"Since your promise, but not before it."

March nods. If his brother had phrased it as a question, not a statement, he's not sure how he might have answered. But the nod was apparently all Hap was waiting for. He jumps from the counter, knocks into March's midsection, leading with his shoulder, like a football player running into a blocking dummy. March crashes back-ward, falling through the doorway and into the hall, skidding until he hits the edge of a rug. As if in slow motion, he sees his brother's boot headed toward his side. He wonders if he'll black out before the kick. He doesn't, and the pain makes him roll to his other side with a grunt. He hears the door open and slam shut and Arlo's running footsteps and his dogs barking from the porch.

Hap steps over March and drops down, rolling him onto his back. He presses his knee into March's chest, and March can feel Hap's weight transferring to the boot that now rests tightly against his balls. He goes to curl up, but Hap flattens him back out with a punch to the side of his head. He feels Hap's wedding band slice his scalp, hot blood slipping into his hair.

He is so amazed to still be thinking clearly, still firmly in his head and body, he makes no move to shift his brother off of him. He tilts his head back, trying to stretch out the pain that throbs from his groin, and sees Arlo's face. He thinks he hears Arlo yell, "What should I do?" but he can't be sure because Hap punches him again, this time in the eye.

He groans, then looks up at his brother. "Hey," he says. "I'm still here." His relief is great even though his brother still looks more than ready to murder him. Hap smacks him, though the smack is open-handed.

"It's not like you're cured," Hap says. "You just feel too guilty to go into a rage." He roughly pushes himself up and off his brother.

March rolls to his hands and knees, dizzy and sick but still pleased. "Yeah, but it's progress." He can see Arlo's feet in front of him, but he waves him away. He leans his forehead against the floor, catching his breath.

"No fucking progress," Hap calls from the kitchen. March sits up on his knees, watching as Hap walks back past to the porch, carrying the dog jerky and the bottle of whiskey.

"I'm getting the six-pack before we go out there," Arlo says. "In case your brother absconds with the whiskey. Or won't share."

March and Arlo find Hap on the steps to the porch, sitting by the dogs and the empty sleeve of jerky. March eases the dogs out of the

way and sits down next to him. Arlo hands him a beer before returning to the porch swing. March presses the cold can to his face instead
of opening it.

Hap says, "You don't remember that time you stole my X-Men
comics? I think you were eleven."

"Not really."

"I remember, because when I hit you with Thea's bat and you just
calmly gave them back to me, I had this hope you were growing out
of whatever made you such a lunatic. It was a short-lived hope. You
will always hurt the people you're near, March. Always. Leaving is the
only good thing you've done in your life. You need to do it again."

March opens the beer, his relief gone.

They can hear a vehicle coming, fast on the quiet street. March recognizes Vera's car at the same moment Hap does, and he knows from
the way Hap stiffens, the anger that had been released from beating
him up flows right back in. Hap is finally fighting back, but March's
money is, unfortunately, still on Vera. She breaks hard, gravel from
the driveway flying, and blocks March's truck in by parking sideways
behind it. March retreats to the porch, next to Arlo, as she hurtles
toward them.

"Ringside seats," Arlo says with a little too much pleasure. March
shakes his head at him.

"What is this?" Vera yells, close to tears. She's waving her cell
phone in the air, then she throws it at Hap. It hits him and drops
straight to his feet. "You fucking asshole." She leans down and picks
up the phone, and then throws it again, full force, though she is two
feet from Hap. It bounces off, and Remus, intrigued, lifts himself up
and retrieves it, mouthing it on the lawn.

"I'm the asshole?" Hap says, grabbing Vera's arm and pulling her
closer. "Where's Pete?"

"Where do you think?" She jerks her arm back out of his grasp.

"You don't get to be angry," Hap says, "because I finally said something honest to you."

"I can be whatever I want to be. And you don't get to tell me what
honest is. You're a fucking blind man, a fucking simpleton. You're not
the man I thought I married." She is slapping at him now, actually in

tears. Hap pulls back, confused. Poor Hap, March thinks, never with the upper hand. He wants to help, and thinks he should at least get Vera's phone from his dog, but he doesn't want to draw attention to himself.

"You thought you married a man who would always forgive you, no matter what? That's what would make me a simpleton," Hap says.

"You still have no idea?" Then she screams with such frustration March worries one of the distant neighbors will call the police. "You thought because I apologized for what happened two years ago, I was taking all the blame? I *was* sorry, but just sorry I was too weak to leave you that Thanksgiving."

Maybe *he* should call the police. Vera and Hap continuing this conversation seems a terrible idea.

Arlo leans over and whispers, "What did Hap do?" When March shrugs, Arlo looks at him, incredulous. "It can be helpful to know these things. You know, if you're going to go and sleep with your brother's wife."

Vera paces across the lawn, like if she stands too close to Hap she might implode, then she veers off toward Remus. He drops the phone and runs toward March. As she leans down to pick it up, Hap says, "How could you do it again? How could you hurt me like that?" She whips the phone straight back at him, but it misses and hits the siding on the front of the house, the case splitting apart.

"Your beauty won't excuse you this time. Things will actually be hard for you this time," she says, and March realizes she is mimicking Hap, quoting him back to himself. "I won't forgive and try to forget." She twists the words into a simper. Then she is shouting again. "Because *you* are the arbiter of what is right and wrong, Hap Briscoe? Because surely, surely, I have never had to forgive *you* for a single fucking thing."

She looks at March and Arlo for the first time, shaking her head. "I am done with the damaged sons of Peter, the lot of you." She looks back at Hap. "I am done wasting my life on you." She pushes past him to pick up her shattered phone, then leaves without another word.

Hap staggers off to the corner of the lawn and lies down in the grass, face to the sky. March stands, but Arlo puts a hand on his arm.

"I don't think that's a good idea."

"Whatever that was, it wasn't my fault."

"Your brother's marriage isn't a logic problem. You can own all of it," Arlo says, gesturing at his prone brother, "or you can own none of it. But I don't think you get to pick and choose parts."

March wants to think he has evolved in these past few days, but he clearly hasn't evolved enough to follow Arlo's thinking. He eases back in the swing. After a few minutes, Hap picks himself up off the lawn. He gets in his truck and pulls away, not looking at them once, as if the porch is empty of all humanity. Which perhaps, March thinks, it is.

SEVEN

When peter gets home, June is doing dishes. He sees the mixing bowl in her hands as he hugs her from behind. "What'd you make?" he asks.

"Oatmeal cookie dough."

"Are there cookies?"

"No, I ate it raw." She sounds a little distant, a little preoccupied, but he's relieved to find she isn't angry at his lateness. His taking a minute to talk to Lee, after the girls left, had turned into more than an hour.

"All of it?" he joked.

"Stuck the remains in the freezer," she says. He moves away from her, still hungry even though Lee fed him from the stew she'd been making, but June grabs him by his sleeve, wiping her wet hands on his shirt after flicking water in his face.

"Thea staying over there?"

"Artie's place, with her." He looks at the floor. "There are developments." He tells her about Lavinia's anger and the funeral arrangements. He asks her to go to Hayden's with Artie, and she agrees. He doesn't tell her about Lee's tears, about how disorienting it was to stand in her house again, like he was suddenly shot into a parallel existence in which June had not taken him back. How comforting Lee, after the girls had left, made him feel thirty-odd years younger. How he wished he hadn't enjoyed the feeling, yet he had, even while Lee cried against his shoulder. This evening, he has broken his promise to June, one he kept for thirteen years. What would have looked innocent to anyone else would still have been unforgivable for June.

He had cheated on his wife a few times after Lee—nothing serious, one-night stands she never found out about. But when the boys were in high school, she had caught him. He wasn't even sure how, just that she had disappeared and no one had known where she was. Then, one week later, she was back in the house. He found her in the living room, watching an Astros game, with her purse on her lap. Clearly she wasn't staying.

"Don't go yet," he said.

June shook her head, a gesture he couldn't interpret. He reached forward and grabbed the remote, clicking off the game. He thought it might make her turn to him, but she stayed focused on the blank screen.

"Is there anything I can do that will bring you home?"

June pulled something small and blue from her purse and laid it on the couch between them. A passport. They had always talked about getting passports, a vacation to Europe, but hadn't yet done it. Now June had done it without him.

"I can go anywhere I want," she said.

Finally, she looked at him. He saw in her expression that she still loved him. But the love was not as strong as it had been that day with the gun, or the night Lee's mother called. But then, he wondered, did he think that because she looked less hurt? In fact, she didn't look hurt at all. And for the first time, Peter felt real shame for the marriage he had set upon his wife. He knew June never worried about him leaving her, but her fear he would again break her heart must have felt the same. This was the love he gave his wife, a love that made you sick. Yet she had chosen it again and again.

"You can sit," she said, gesturing a foot away from her. So he sat. "I can finally go anywhere I want, and all I feel is tired. I came to see you so I could feel angry again. Anger might give me the energy to find out who I am now, who I can become, after twenty years of being a woman who would stay married to you. All week, I kept asking myself where I wanted to live, what job I might want to get, how I'd spend my days when they were free of you. But so far, all I have is this expedited passport and the desire to go to sleep for years."

Peter reached out for her hand but knew better than to take it. He let his open palm rest on the couch between them. "I can make sure you don't want to use the passport. I can still be the person you deserve."

"You can never have sex with another woman?" And when Peter quickly nodded his head, she shook hers. "No. Not enough. You can never even so much as touch a woman with lust on your mind? I am even banning intent."

"I can."

June's face was so skeptical, it almost convinced him he was lying. But he wasn't. "I can do that. I know I can."

"Then why did you never stop yourself before?"

Peter's cheeks grew red.

"What?" prompted his wife. "You have to say what you can't bring yourself to say. If I'm not convinced, I leave now."

This time Peter did take her hand, and she let him, though it sat limply in his. "This whole week, I've been afraid. Twenty years of marriage and I can finally understand what you've felt. I've been thinking of it too, how I'd spend my days if they didn't have you, and they don't even seem worth living for." He reached out for her other hand, but she pulled both of them to her lap. Peter sat back on the couch and shut his eyes. "You know I've never been willing to lose you."

He felt June shift, her body moving closer to him. "Just once," she said. And Peter opened his eyes to see the blue passport a blur, striking him on the cheek. "Once." She slapped him again. "I so much as see you touch a woman's forearm, and I'm gone. No discussion, no forwarding address, never talk to or see you again. You believe me?"

He raised his head and met her eye. "I do."

With this memory in his mind, Peter tells his wife about what happened at Lee's with many omissions. And all through the telling, he waits for his wife to get testy, to tense up, to push him away. But she stays kind, stays relaxed, pulls him into a hug. "Let's go to sleep," she says. "Worry about tomorrow tomorrow." Her voice, though, isn't exactly right, as if she's reading lines. Still, if she's making an effort to pretend not to be mad, he appreciates that even more than her not being mad in the first place.

And so they get ready for bed, climb under the covers, and though he wants to make love to his wife, he does not want to push his luck, break open her facade to find anger underneath. Or have her think this lust started earlier in the evening, had another source. He puts his arm around her as she kisses his cheek, but he doesn't hold on as she rolls over and away from him.

EIGHT

ARE YOU GOING TO CLEAN yourself up?" Arlo asks. He and March have been on the porch for hours, and even though March has gone inside to go to the bathroom a couple of times, he still has blood crusted under his nose and his hair is a mess. The Ziploc full of ice Arlo made for the lump rising on March's cheekbone melts, unused, on the arm of the swing.

"Come with me," Arlo finally says, finding March too depressing to look at any longer. In the bathroom, they stare at the open medicine cabinet, empty aside from a toothbrush, toothpaste, a hairbrush, and a razor. Arlo closes the plastic lid of the toilet with his foot. "Sit," he says. There's an open box in the corner, and he roots around in it until he finds a washcloth. "Got any rubbing alcohol or peroxide?"

March squats by the box and fishes out a tiny first aid kit. "Maybe in here?" March teeters for a second and has to put a hand to the floor to steady himself. "Yep, time to sit." He settles back on the closed toilet. Arlo wets one end of the cloth, then grabs March's chin. March winces, and winces more when Arlo starts scrubbing at the blood crusted to his temple.

"Sorry," Arlo says. "I never claimed to have a good bedside manner."

March opens his eyes, following Arlo's hand, still clad in a bandage over the palm. "Did you go to the doctor?"

"Nah, did it myself."

"It's seen better days."

Arlo pauses in his scrubbing of March's temple and looks at the graying gauze, now wet from the rag. He peels it off and flexes his hand. The gash has knitted back together, a line of newly formed scab. "Don't need it anymore anyway." Satisfied that he has cleaned the blood off the top half of March's head, he moves on to underneath his nose. "Tilt your chin up."

March leans back until his head rests on the wall behind the tank. "You never told me what happened at Terpsi's."

Arlo explains how he grabbed Laurel from behind, that she countered with what was arguably appropriate force.

March motions to Arlo's hand. "She had a knife? Arguably, indeed."

"I fell and caught a nail."

"Well, that's just embarrassing."

"Shut up," Arlo says, ripping open an alcohol wipe packet that had been nestled inside the first aid kit. He tries to find the cut on March's scalp, underneath the hair. "Does that burn?"

"Yes," March says agreeably.

"Good. Can't see a damn thing in this mess." He tugged at a hunk of March's hair. "Like goddamn fur." He throws the alcohol wipe in the trash by the toilet. "You're as good as you're going to get."

"Time for bed," March says. "Artie put the extra sheets and a blanket in the hall closet, I think. Need anything else?"

Help, Arlo thinks. I need help. I need to tell you things and have you understand them like Artie would. "I think there's one beer left. Split it with me?"

March pauses, clearly expecting a different answer. But he says, "Sure. Dogs could stand to go out one more time. I'll get the beer." Arlo heads to the porch, taking out his phone for the first time that evening. It's near midnight, but Artie always mutes her phone at night. He could text and not wake her. He should text, he knows. It's inexcusable to do what he did and then say nothing to her for the entire next day. He pulls up her name and is about to type something, anything, but then March arrives with a glass half-full of beer and the can with the other half.

March sits down on the wooden porch steps in front of Arlo. He rests against the brick pillar and straightens out his legs.

"I didn't tell the truth," Arlo says.

"About what?"

Arlo knows what he's about to do—voluntarily spread the shit of his life all over March's porch. There'll be no getting free of it. "I didn't shoot Ryan, not technically."

"Someone did, unless you dropped the gun and it went off on its own."

"Artie," Arlo says. "Technically. But I dared her to shoot at something in the river, and the something turned out to be Ryan."

"What?" March says, incredulous. "Y'all lied to the authorities?"

"I took the blame because I really was the one to blame."

"But it was still an accident," March says. "You didn't know what Artie was shooting at."

Arlo hesitates. "Yes and no. I didn't—"

March cuts him off. "Fuck. You knew it was Ryan?" Arlo can see March's horror, how he's about to leap from the steps. For a second, Arlo is back in the rushing brown water, seeing Ryan's face and knowing the damage couldn't be undone. He'd spent yesterday evening, this morning, flailing in the guilt of permanently wrecking lives—Ryan's, Artie's, his own. He can't alienate the one person still putting up with him. Arlo panics and reverses course. "Of course I didn't know! But Artie was already pissed at me that morning. Us not being normal with each other, not for a few days. Not being honest. If I hadn't been stuck in asshole mode, she wouldn't have taken the shot."

"Goddamn it, Arlo. It'd probably be easier for her to forgive you if you actually *had* been the one that took the shot. Instead, you've got her lying to cops, lying to everyone."

"Don't say that," Arlo says, but it comes out so quiet he can barely hear himself.

March rubs the heel of his palm against his eye. "I've had too much to drink. I am too tired and beat up for this conversation. I'm going to sleep."

He stands and whistles to the dogs, all three of them filing inside. March doesn't shut the door, and Arlo can feel the air conditioning leaking through the screen door.

Though Arlo's known most for his love songs, is even viewed as a romantic, his lyrics actually home in on the damage; they detail what he has seen love do to those around him—make you careless of consequences, strangle your life into one half-lived. Love didn't satisfy, didn't provide meaning. His proof for that was both his mother and his sister. His mother's love of Peter had given her just half a life while Artie had always been the most content person he'd ever known, and it was because she held no truck with romantic love. Until now. Her love for Ryan had pulled her away from him, made her lie to him. And now that love has made her turn on him. He hasn't texted her yet because he doesn't want to hear she can't forgive him. What if she never does?

He pulls his phone from out of his pocket and texts Artie.

I'm sorry

He sends it and sits, then types again.

I'm sorry

He finishes his beer, sets his glass beside the rocking chair. He knows he should leave it, but he can't. He sends a third text.

You promised.

TUESDAY

ONE

IT'S MIDMORNING IN THE OFFICE, but Peter can't stop fretting over his exchange with June. Before leaving for work, he went up to the balcony to say goodbye. He couldn't remember the last time he had done that; clearly, June couldn't either, as startled as she was by his appearance. As if he has caught her in the act of something instead of sitting on a chair, her knees pulled to her chest, drinking coffee.

"Didn't hear me coming up?" he asked.

"Guess not," she said, frowning. She put the cup down on the table. "What's wrong?"

"Nothing. Just wanted to say bye."

June stood, but she only took a step or two before stopping. "I'll call you after the meeting with Hayden, let you know how it goes with Lavinia."

Peter nodded. He was about to cross the balcony to kiss her good-bye, but she had already turned away. "Pretty day," she said softly. "So at least there's that."

"Maybe we can go out to dinner tonight?" he said. "Drive into Houston and sit next to disinterested strangers?"

"Okay. But if I need the distraction of making a meal, you can't be disappointed."

"Course not," he said. Then he tried on a grin. "Unless I find that vet hanging around again, as he seems such a fan of your cooking." His evening at Lee's had distracted Peter from his jealousy, but seeing the look on his wife's face made it slide straight back into him.

She's hiding something, he's sure of it. It eats at him even now, here in the office, and he fidgets, spinning from side to side in his squeaky wooden desk chair.

March skulks in the back door, surprising him. He assumed he'd stay home with Arlo. When Peter gets a good look at him, he's even more taken aback. His son's face is bruised and swollen.

"God, what happened to you?" he asks.

March settles himself, somewhat gingerly, in his desk chair. "Do you really want to know?"

"Maybe not. Especially if it was Hap that caused that."

March's silence is its own answer. Peter rolls back in his chair and stands. "Okay." He turns and fusses with the wooden slats of the blinds.

The bell over the front door chimes, and Peter heads to the lobby. Coming through the door is not new business, though. Just a new complication. "Vera, aren't you a nice surprise? What brings you here?"

Peter positions himself in front of the interior doorway to block March from her view. It's all for nothing, though. Vera cants her hip and peers around Peter, looks straight at March as she says, "Hello, Dad." She says "Dad" the way she always has, like it's a pleasant joke no one can take seriously. "I was so sorry to hear about Ryan. I left Artie a message, but I'm guessing she isn't up for visitors yet." She looks back at Peter. "I'm here because I need to list our house for sale and start looking for a new one."

"Today? Seems like it can wait a week or two, with all this going on. Hap didn't even tell me y'all wanted to move."

"I'm in the market. Me. And Pete." She sidles past him to seat herself in front of his desk. Peter lingers, taking in March's alarmed expression and then Vera's back. How he wishes he could just walk out the front door.

"Does Hap know you're here?" March asks her.

"I don't have to ask his permission to move out," she says, now looking into her purse. She pulls out a piece of paper. "I've got a list of my requirements and another list with preferences. I know I can't get everything I want. What are there, less than a dozen houses on the market?" She turns in her chair to face Peter, holding out the list. "I want to look in Bullinger, too, near my mom. Worst-case scenario, we can find a rental for now."

"This is no time for games," Peter says. "I have enough to deal with helping Artie and Arlo."

Vera laughs. "You forget that I know you, Peter. I can't see you doing much for Artie, besides being a bystander, so you might as well perform your actual job for me."

Peter reluctantly crosses to his desk, past Vera's thin hand holding a long white list. He says, "If you really wanted to sell, if you were leaving Hap, you would go to another realtor. There are two over in Bullinger."

"Can't you help clean up a family mess for once? How far and wide do you want me spreading this news?" For all her bluster, Peter can tell Vera's truly upset.

"Does Hap know you're here?" March asks again.

Vera replies to Peter as if he's the one asking. "He will."

With that, Peter understands why March was asking. Real estate help isn't Vera's true aim. She's just expanding her circle of torture, pulling in as many of them as she can. "I'm not your message delivery service," says Peter. "How can you do this to Hap? After all that you've already done? And him still loving you?"

Vera strokes her chin, feigning contemplation. "Likely the same way you could treat June that way, after all you've already done. And her still loving you."

No matter who Peter is arguing with, he seems to never have the upper hand. But Vera isn't done. She says, "You might ask your other son how he could do that to Hap if you're going to ask it of me."

The final shred of Peter's hope for March's return drifts away. He says to Vera, "So Hap has finally tossed you out?"

"You really think your son kicked me out, and I'm here asking you for help? I have left Hap, and that's just the start of my punishment." She slaps her palm onto his desk "For you, dear Peter, I am bestowing the gift of having to get involved."

March jumps in, as if there's anything he can do. "You should leave," March says. "I'm sorry for my part in this. I'm sorry that you think you have to leave Hap, but we can't help you do it. You know that."

Vera twists around in her chair. Her hands grip her purse as if she is strangling it.

"This has nothing to do with you," she says to March. "I did what you asked, I waited to tell Hap I was leaving him, but he still figured out we slept together again. Why are you even here this morning, as if this is a job you will get to keep?" She gets up, smoothing down her skirt, and leans over the desk until she can reach out and poke Peter in the chest. "You'll help me with this or I'll move back to Houston with Pete, make it that much harder for his father to see him. You created Hap, made him wonderful enough to love, then you and June fucked him up, made him awful enough to not deserve it. It's your fault, so now you'll do what I tell you to do." Her voice hovers on the edge of cracking.

"What did Hap even do to you, Vera?" March says. "Why won't you say? What could be worse than what we did to him?"

Vera pivots and strides over to March, grabbing the front of his shirt, bunching it in her fist. But when she speaks, her voice is once again composed. "You wouldn't believe the truth, so I won't waste it on you. You'll just keep believing the lies you tell yourself. That your father loves your mother, and you love Hap, and Arlo loves Artie." She lets go of his shirt. "Piles of bullshit that are now none of my concern."

Vera leaves without another look at Peter. She calls out from the lobby, "Contact me when you get some options put together. I want things to move fast."

Peter and March sit without speaking for over a minute. Then March asks, in a resigned voice that seems to already know the answer, "Want me to head out to that place on Bartlett Road and see if I can get the late rent check?"

"No, son. Go be with Arlo, so he's not alone. Let's get through the funeral, get Arlo and Artie back under the same roof, and then we'll see where things stand." He knows what he is doing, telling his son *once we stop needing you here, we are going to send you away.*

March says, so quietly Peter has to strain to hear it, "Vera leaving isn't about me."

"If they divorce, if Hap only gets partial custody . . . it just seems like it will be bad for everyone if you stay." Not everyone, though. Not March himself. Not Artie or Arlo. But Peter doesn't correct himself.

March rubs his swollen eye. "I'll head out, then. Call me if you need anything?" Peter nods. He has the urge to hug his son, but he worries it will look too much like he expects to not see him again.

After March leaves, Peter thinks about calling Hap. He thinks, too, of calling June. Giving her the further bad news and seeing how things went with Lavinia. But when he picks up the phone, it's Lee he calls. Just a quick conversation, he tells himself, to see if she's okay— home alone while everyone else is at Hayden's. Someone he can comfort instead of someone he will just make more upset. Then he'll move on to the hard stuff.

TWO

JUNE WAITS in the funeral home's family room—all dusty rose and dove gray from the carpet to the tissue boxes. June wonders if this deliberate evocation of parlors and grandmothers helps soothe emotions and speeds planning. Or does it trigger the urge to spend more, a final form of doting? She's so early neither Thea and Artie nor the Barrys have arrived yet. Just her and her regrets on a pink couch.

Technically, she isn't an adulterer. She has only kissed a man who isn't her husband. But for the first time, she understands how you sometimes can't help what you do, no matter how much thought you give it. This has gifted her a small measure of empathy for Peter's mistakes. After thirty-odd years of one unyielding view, such a radical shift in thinking has made her marriage feel like a foreign country.

She hears voices in the hall, then Thea and Hayden come in. She hugs Thea, wishing her daughter would stay in her arms rather than doing her usual squeeze and retreat. Hayden settles in the gray arm-chair, dressed in the type of three-piece suit he favors but that always strikes June as overkill, as does the fact his tie matches the carpet. A small, shallow part of her enjoys the way the vest gaps as he sits. Just a few pounds away from needing a larger size. Thea takes the other end of the couch, leaving a wide gap between her and June—presumably for Artie, though it could be she just wants that distance.

"Artie stopped by the ladies' room," Hayden tells June. "I know we're about to settle into some sad business, but at least we can be happy March is back." He looks at June like he's waiting for her to contradict him.

"I'm not sure Hap is happy," Thea says, letting June keep her own equivocal response to herself. To June, Thea asks, "Or has our Hap already forgiven him?"

June realizes she hasn't spoken to Hap since Friday, not since she lectured him for showing up on her lawn with a sledgehammer. More bad parenting. "I haven't talked to him recently," she admits.

Thea's wearing her look of exasperation that hasn't altered since high school even as the rest of her changed, this grown woman with a bigger life than June had ever thought to hope for. "Ah, but you had plenty of time last night, while you were avoiding Lee."

Her daughter isn't truly invested in this argument, or truly angry. It's just the typical contrariness, the petty carping, that makes up so much of their communication. At the mention of Lee, Hayden begins to studiously scan papers on the clipboard, though June's sure he's taking in every word.

What would her daughter think of her if she knew about Cole? If she could let loose her exasperation on something that big? June's regret over the night before hardens into something like fear. Why is she playing with fire instead of doing her best to help her family? It's madness, letting herself be distracted from what's about to walk in the door—a brokenhearted mother with a massive ax to grind. She won't let herself be distracted any longer. She'll call Cole this afternoon and tell him the same.

The uneasy silence is broken by voices from the hallway. Hayden glides out, then returns with Lavinia Barry and her mother, Mrs. Mann. The women are impeccably put together, black dresses and heels and tasteful jewelry, but their grief pours out at the edges—quaking hands, smudged eyeliner. June imagines Mrs. Mann is a woman who cares about decorum, who kept her funeral best even when she had to sell her other finery. And that she taught her daughter to do the same. June and Thea rise, June saying, "Mrs. Mann, Lavinia, do you know my daughter, Thea?" The women nod at Thea, bypassing the question. Lavinia pauses before she sits on the couch opposite, taking in the empty seat next to June. "Artie's in the bathroom and will be here soon," June says.

"I thought her brother would be here too," Lavinia says. "He's the one who should want to see me, to apologize. I assumed that's what this funeral offer was. Part of a Briscoe apology." She turns to Hayden. "Was I wrong?"

It may have been a bad idea for her and Thea to come, June thinks. Adding more Briscoes to the mix. If Artie was here alone, or just with Lee, perhaps Lavinia wouldn't see her as yet another member of an opposing tribe.

Hayden avoids the question, asking instead if anyone wants coffee or tea. Ryan's grandmother requests tea for her and her daughter, and Hayden slips off again, leaving June to explain their motives.

"Artie wants to help in any way she can. We all do. Whatever you need. She's devastated by what happened."

Lavinia leans over the wooden coffee table and pulls two tissues from the box, handing them to her mother just as a tear leaks from the older woman's eye. "I'd prefer some contrition to another woman's grief. A girl I haven't even met before."

Lavinia's hair is snow white and it, ironically, reminds June of when they were both in high school and Lavinia dyed her brown hair platinum blond. Has Lavinia chosen not to dye it now because it reminds her of being a teenager? Or does it just feel more suited to her personality, a woman robbed of all her possessions, even hair pigment? June has to admit the effect is striking, like a white witch carved from ice. Lavinia had been a girl who laughed often. Those smile lines are still there, even though she wears no smile. It makes her seem all the bleaker, as if someone painted in the wrong expression on a portrait. June has a growing worry that Lavinia is a trap waiting to spring shut when Artie enters the room.

THIS MORNING, Artie had woken up in her walk-in closet with just a crocheted afghan wrapped around her, its waffle print embedded into the side of her face. Hours before, she'd fled her bed—too full of Ryan—and curled up on the hardwood floor. She had been thankful for the closed-in-ness, the lack of windows. And here she is again, in the funeral parlor's small bathroom. Trying to pull herself together enough to face Ryan's family. She wears one of her few dresses, gray knit—hot but short-sleeved, at least. She wants to look presentable for the Barrys, even if they force her right back out of the room.

She hears, faintly, the beep of her phone's low battery signal, and so she searches for it in her purse. She sees a small 3 by the text message icon and, for half a second, her brain tells her they must be from Ryan. Ryan, sitting up in bed in his garage apartment, wondering why she didn't come over the night before. She puts the phone away without even tapping the button to see who they're from.

Minutes later, inside the sitting room, Artie shakes the hands of Ryan's grandmother and his mother. She whispers, "I'm so sorry," which seems a useless statement, inarticulate and lacking, but Lavinia accepts the apology with a nod. The woman waits until Artie has seated herself between June and Thea and says, "I thought your brother would be here too."

That useless phrase tumbles out again: "I'm sorry." Then she adds, "I wasn't sure if you'd want to see him."

Lavinia sets her raised teacup back in its saucer with a clatter. "I would want him to *want* to come."

Of course Ryan's mother wants the person who took her son's life here in this room, some gesture of atonement. And Artie can't explain the truth, that the shooter *is* here in front of her. Artie sees, now that it is impossible, that this meeting could have been a helpful thing for her. To sit in a room and share the grief of other people who also loved Ryan. Instead it's like Arlo dug a wide moat between them and her, interrupting her grief with protective fortifications.

Hayden asks Mrs. Barry where she would like the service—their church in Bullinger or perhaps here at Hayden's funeral home? "We'd like it at the Episcopal church. Here in Olympus," she says pointedly. June gives Thea a concerned glance then composes her face when she realizes Artie is watching her. Lavinia says, almost in response, "It has such a beautiful sanctuary. And this town still feels like my home. It always will, no matter where I had to move to." She pauses, her gaze lingering on June a moment before speaking again to Hayden. "Can you arrange for a choir, Mr. Briscoe? And flowers. We'll need flowers."

Hayden stiffly tells Lavinia it may be hard to get a choir on such short notice, but June, with a frown, counters that Hayden will truly do his best to find one. Then Hayden lays out the further questions for Mrs. Barry. Would they like an open casket or closed? Do they have a burial plot in their own cemetery or would they like a spot here at Hayden's? Or did Ryan want to be cremated? They could bury those cremains, or keep them in an urn, or split the ashes if they wanted to scatter a portion.

Artie tries to speak, but her voice is so quiet no one hears her. She clears her throat and tries again. "Ryan mentioned to me once that he wanted to be cremated and scattered outside." She drops her voice down to a whisper. "Maybe at the river? He liked the Brazos, but we could do the Colorado River instead since it flows through Bullinger?"

The grandmother speaks for the first time, frowning. "I can't remember that we've cremated anyone in the family before. It doesn't seem proper to not have a coffin and a viewing." Her tone sounds conciliatory despite her rejection of Artie's idea.

Mrs. Barry, who had seemed so focused, so self-possessed, looks suddenly at a loss. "Oh," she says. "Afterward. I hadn't even thought about what we'd do afterward."

Artie's hands are balled into fists that she can't relax, even when June tries to lace her fingers into Artie's. Hayden is conveniently engrossed in paperwork. Artie can feel June's irritation beside her. "We could do both," June says. "We can do the preparations for the open casket but still cremate after the service, so his wishes can be carried out. Right, Hayden?" Artie opens her fist to take June's hand and squeezes it.

Instead of agreeing, her uncle says. "We could also cremate, put him in a lovely urn, and have that and a big photo of Ryan up at the front of the church." Belatedly, Artie understands that this has something to do with expense because now Thea is frowning hard at Hayden, too. If Arlo was here, he might tell Hayden he shouldn't have offered the services for free if he was too cheap to spring for the embalming and the coffin. She can even hear Hayden's muttered retort, *waste of a perfectly good coffin*. But now that thoughts of embalming and coffins and Ryan—either headed toward this building or lying somewhere within it—inhabit Artie's head, she has to close her eyes to keep from screaming. And to avoid Mrs. Barry's fractured expression.

But when Lavinia speaks, her voice has authority. She says, "I agree with my mother, we would want an open casket. But if Ryan really preferred cremation, we need to honor those wishes too." Artie opens her eyes to Mrs. Barry evaluating her. She continues, "And your brother will be at the funeral?"

"If you'd like him there," she says. "I'm sure he wants to come." Another lie. She's not sure what Arlo wants. To be there to support her, surely, but not to be put on display.

Mrs. Mann says, "Ryan was never one for dressing up much. Mr. Briscoe, I don't suppose you have extra suits? If they're nice?" She looks at her daughter. "I don't think we'll find anything suitable in town."

Artie quickly says, "I can pick clothes up. I'd like to do that for him."

The women nod at her. Lavinia doesn't look away, though. Finally, she says, "It's my fault Ryan never introduced us. I gave him such a hard time for taking a job from Peter Briscoe's son. I can't blame him for not wanting to tell me he was also dating one of his daughters. My husband likes to say there's no pleasure in a safe life, and we won't be rewarded for one either." She shakes her head. "As if we can tell what will be safe and what won't." Ryan's mother speaks calmly, but Artie can tell there is more than just resignation and grief under her words.

She just can't tell what it is. "I accept that this was an accident. It's important to me that your brother is there. And you."

It crushes her heart, Mrs. Barry trying hard to lighten her burden. Rather than helping, she feels the burden doubled, her loss buried under not just guilt but also shame that she and Arlo have gotten away with something. "But I was so careless," Artie says. "It was my fault." She begins to cry, and she sees the grandmother's face crack, her hand reaching out for Artie even though she's several feet away. Mrs. Barry says, quietly, "Oh, girl, there's not enough care in the world to keep us all safe."

THREE

June's car is in front of Artie's house, and so March sits, stuck inside his truck, watching the lantana in her front yard bend and straighten in the intermittent wind. He should have called, he knows, but he thought only Thea would be there with Artie, not his mother too. Seeing June will only hasten his second exile from Olympus. He's about to text Artie to come outside when Thea emerges from the front door, striding toward him. He rolls down his window, hoping maybe if his mother doesn't see his actual body, she won't be drawn out to talk to him too.

Thea cocks her head, a reluctant half smile on her face and her hands on her hips. "Why are you skulking around out here?"

"It's good to see you, sis," he says.

"You know I hate that word, bro." But her half smile turns into a real one.

"I'm avoiding Mom but I need to talk to Artie."

"You've got a phone."

"I needed to tell her something in person."

"Something about Arlo?"

Has Artie told her who really took the shot at the river? March doesn't think so. Even unflappable Thea would look more agitated if she knew Artie had lied to the police. She just looks sad. "Not Arlo," he says. "It's me. I'm not sure how much longer I'll be in town." Thea's disappointed in him, he can tell. It's a look from her he knows well.

"I wish you hadn't screwed up again so quickly. It'd be better for Artie if you were around for a while."

"I know. I'm sorry."

"It's not me you should apologize to."

"That's why I'm here."

March understands why Thea runs hot and cold with him. She loves him, but it's easier for her to love him from a thousand miles away. He's like an addict who's messed up his recovery too many times. Thea's got no emotional energy left for him.

"I'll get Artie."

"Before you go, got any recent pictures of the girls? I bet they're so tall now."

She nods. "They are. But my phone's inside. I'll text you one later if you don't give me a new reason not to. Be careful with Artie. It was a hard morning."

She leaves him, and March exits his truck to sit on its back bumper. His luck holds, and Artie comes out without his mother in tow. She's in his arms before he can stand up. Why hadn't he come to see her the day before? Inexcusable.

They stay that way a minute before Artie pulls back to stare at his face. "What's wrong with your eye?" She removes his sunglasses, and March tries not to wince as their arm pushes along his cheekbone. "Ouch," she says. She looks suddenly serious. "That wasn't Arlo, was it? Does he look worse than you?"

"No. It's Arlo that patched me up after."

"That leaves Vera or Hap."

"Hap. Things have gotten complicated. I'll probably have to leave town again soon. It'll make things harder for Hap if I stay."

"You can't go," she says, a growing panic in her voice. "I need you to keep an eye on Arlo. I don't have room to worry about him too right now, March. And I don't know when I'll have that room again."

"I know. And I'm sorry. Truly. But isn't it better if you both keep an eye on each other? He's worried Thea's in your ear. He's worried you can't stand to look at him."

"He tell you that?"

"Not exactly, but it's easy to see." He dropped his voice. "I'm worried about that too. He told me what really happened. I know it's gotta be hard for you, not being able to talk about it with anyone. But come over tonight. You can talk about it with him, with me."

"No. I'm not ready to see him yet. But you have to bring him to the funeral tomorrow. It's at the Episcopal church here in town. Two o'clock. Ryan's mom insisted that Arlo be there."

"She doesn't want him strung up?" It's a bad choice of words. It's saying, too, that she'd want Artie strung up.

"No. She just wants to see that he's sorry."

"He is sorry, Artie. You know that, don't you? For everything."

"I'll see you both tomorrow," she says, already moving away from him. She doesn't give him time to put his worry into words. All of them—him and Hap and his mother, Lavinia Barry and their dad, Artie and Arlo—sitting in the same room together. Perhaps there isn't even a way to put that much worry to words.

FOUR

AT HIS SHOP, Hap puts primer on an old convertible, getting ready to paint it candy red, when his father calls his cell phone.

"I don't want to talk about March," Hap says when he answers.

"Maybe you should come over to the office," his father says. "March isn't here."

"I've got work." When Peter doesn't answer, Hap says, "I'll go into my office." His men watch him walk past, all somber as judges. Like they already know his marriage is over.

Once he shuts the door, his father launches in. "Vera was here this morning. She wants me to be the agent that puts your house on the market and finds a new one for her."

"A new house?"

There's a long pause. Then his dad says, "She said she needed a house for her and Pete."

Hap exhales in a rattle.

"I said I wouldn't, of course, but then she threatened to take Pete with her to Houston."

Hap can't feel the phone in his hand anymore. It's like he has evaporated.

"Why don't you come have dinner with June and me tonight? Bring Pete. We haven't spent time with either of you in weeks."

"I don't feel like company."

"You shouldn't be alone."

"I'll be okay," Hap tells him. "I'd rather be alone." But his father won't get off the phone, so Hap lets him keep talking as he leaves the office, gets in his vehicle to drive home. He's been thinking like a fool, ignoring the future.

"I know you've always been more than fair to your brother," his father says. "I know he's used up all his second chances." There's some ambivalence in his dad's voice, but at least he doesn't defend March.

Hap finally interrupts. "It's not just March. Vera's mad at *me,* and I don't even know what I did."

"You didn't do anything, son. This is Vera's doing and your brother's. Your mom might say it's mine too," he says, almost grudgingly. "I welcomed March back into our lives."

"I must have done something," Hap insists. "Vera was so angry with me, and angrier still that I had no idea what had set her off."

"Maybe you just want to think that because it gives you something to fix? Look, it'll be okay if you can't work it out with her. Maybe things shouldn't have to be this hard."

This is not what Hap wants his father to say. He wants him to say that relationships are always hard, but they can still survive. That way he can come home to his son at the end of every day, wake up with him every morning. He thinks of Vera crying on March's lawn, throwing her phone at him. Whatever he has done, his wife is sure they won't survive. "I'll call you later, Dad." He hangs up as he pulls in front of his house. He drove home expecting Vera to be waiting, ready to get the full satisfaction of telling him the awful news to his face, but the driveway is as empty as when he left that morning.

As usual, his wife is two steps ahead of him. His fear that she will take his son from his daily life makes his prior anger—the righteous indignation that allowed him to leave her that voicemail—all but inconsequential. He examines the living room for signs his wife has been there, feels a little calmer that there are none, and then walks to the hallway and looks in their bedroom.

It is an artfully staged scene of a leaving: the closet door slid back to reveal the decimated interior, drawers open to show their swaths of empty space. No empty hangers, so he imagines the pile of her clothes heaped up in the trunk of her car, ready to be pulled out, still with the hangers inside them, and hung up in her mother's guest bedroom.

Her note to him is a Post-it stuck to the bathroom mirror. Vera doesn't waste words. She believes actions speak for themselves, that the world can be tedious, and it doesn't need to be made more tedious by saying aloud what is already known. So Hap's not surprised by the brevity of her note: *You can keep Pete on days you take off work. I'll need 24 hours' notice. Text, don't call.*

Hap pulls it from the mirror and reads it twice more. He checks Pete's room—so much missing Hap can envision not just a full trunk but also a packed backseat.

He knows he doesn't have much time—once Vera gets far enough down this new path, away from him, she won't return. But he doesn't have to figure it out tonight. Tonight he needs to see Pete. He hopes she has enough sympathy for him as a parent to agree to it. He pulls out his phone and texts his wife: *I'd really like to keep Pete tonight.*

He sits in the rocking chair in his son's room—too big for her car, or it would be gone too—with his phone in his lap. Hap knows he's empathetic, usually to a fault. He knows he pays attention. He understands his own motives and knows he loves his wife and wants her to be happy. How can he have no idea what he has done to make her so angry?

Vera doesn't return his text. Hap sits in his son's room for two hours, his work boots flat on the ground, his thigh muscles tensing and untensing as he rocks back and forth. He imagines a life without his son as a constant presence. How had he not understood before that having a child with another person opens you up to a vulnerability that only the ignorant or foolish would enter into? Or those in love, close to the same thing.

FIVE

At a men's store on the west edge of Houston, Artie and Thea have found a suit and shirt, socks and shoes, and are finishing up at the ties—beautiful silk ties in primary colors so deep Artie wishes she could have bought them for Ryan while alive. Only then does Thea press: "When are you going to tell me what's going on with you and Arlo?"

Artie had felt Thea's skepticism about the story of Ryan's death, her worry over Artie's many silences from the past two days. Though Artie had originally called Thea down to Olympus to help sustain her anger, she hadn't yet confessed the truth. It would be like burning a bridge before she's sure she's standing on the right side. Thea will be gone again in a few days. Probably March too. Artie's anger is keeping her moving forward, but does she want to move into a future that is missing not just Ryan, but Arlo too?

Artie runs a finger down a midnight-blue tie with cornflower-blue paisleys. "Are paisleys back in again?"

"They are. And I'm going to get you to talk eventually." Thea leans over and kisses Artie's cheek.

She hopes Lavinia Barry will approve of her choices. She's certain Ryan would have. It's past due for at least one thing to be easy. But when, after she's paid, Artie takes their purchases from the cashier, it stops feeling easy. These clothes won't go in a closet, won't be pulled out for a fancy dinner or an engagement party. Tomorrow, they will be ash.

After all the bags are stored in Artie's backseat, the suit hung neatly from a hook within its plastic wrapping, Artie pulls the keys from her purse and hands them to Thea. "You mind?" she says. She needs a nap. Maybe the recurring nightmares of the river, the feel of the trigger against her finger and the sight of Ryan, lifeless, on the riverbank, won't come during the day.

But five minutes down I-10, Artie's phone rings, and she sees again those three unopened texts as she lifts the phone from her bag. "Hey, Mom," she says. "Thea and I are driving home from Houston. I got the suit for Ryan." Her voice catches on Ryan's name.

"Come by for dinner tonight," Lee says. "I won't keep you long. Besides, I'm sure Thea has work to catch up on and could use some time alone."

Artie hadn't thought about the way this unexpected trip must be wrecking Thea's work schedule. For past visits, it took two weeks of planning to clear her calendar, and even then Thea worked an hour or two a day.

Artie holds the phone away from her mouth. "You need to work tonight?"

She can see Thea eyeing the phone. "If you need to see your mom, I'd get some work done while you're gone."

"Okay," Artie tells her mother. "Let me see how tired I am when we get back. I'll call you in an hour."

"And, sweetie, just so you know, Arlo might be here too. Okay?" She doesn't wait for a reply before saying goodbye and hanging up.

Artie squeezes the phone in frustration. First March, now her mother. She reaches over to the radio, turns up a Motown song, and lets herself think of the beautiful suit behind her, allows herself the indulgence of picturing Ryan, alive and wearing it, her tying the tie for him; in her imagination, she knows how to tie a tie. It's a shame she doesn't believe in ghosts, doesn't even believe in a heaven. Ryan could have picked her to haunt. A friendly haunting, to keep her company.

But, if she's being honest, Ryan would want something more substantial for her. He'd want Arlo to keep her company, even if it was his carelessness and selfishness that started the chain reaction that ended with her pulling that trigger. And so she finally opens her text messages, knowing at least one must be from Arlo.

I'm sorry

I'm sorry

You promised.

What promise? Could he mean the promise they made as *kids*? To always take care of him. That he would take care of her. Was he actually blaming her for shutting him out since the shooting? But the texts were from Monday night, barely twenty-four hours after Ryan died. No, this is something else. She knows the way her brother's mind works, his perfectionism. He can't say he's sorry for things without including why he shouldn't be blamed. I'm sorry I snapped at you, but you knew I was tired. I'm sorry I'm late, but you picked an awfully early time to meet. She knows what Arlo would be upset about. You promised you'd take care of me. I'm sorry I dared you to shoot, that I convinced you to lie, but you chose Ryan over me. She feels something sharp in her lungs, making her unable to draw in a full breath. Something in her body knows what her brain hasn't figured out yet, the link between what he blames her for and a reason for what he's done.

SIX

ARLO WAS LISTENING when his mother called Artie, and he marveled over her ability to trim the corners of the truth. She was attempting to care for her kids in ways Arlo had long assumed her personality wouldn't allow. Perhaps if he and Artie had just caused more trouble growing up—a drug habit, a pregnancy—she might have shaken off her Peter-induced dreaminess and really parented them.

But even with Lee as intermediary, Artie is so late Arlo fears she isn't coming. He calls out to his mother in the kitchen, where she's putting a plate full of dinner in the refrigerator, the one she had been keeping warm for Artie. "Thanks for trying, Mom," he says. She blushes and looks at the tile countertop. He can't remember the last time he thanked her, the last time he called her mom.

"You'll both feel better after you see each other," she says.

Arlo hopes so. He wants to know how to help Artie. He wants to know what happened with the Barrys today at the funeral home, and if Artie's heard anything from the sheriff. And he needs her to see he's not really as petulant as that third text sounded.

But his mother was right in her optimism that Artie would show. Arlo hears her letting herself in the front door.

"I'm so glad you came," their mother says. But Arlo freezes when he sees how Artie is looking at him, the way her hands shrink into fists.

"Come on, Arlo," Artie snaps. She pivots and walks back out the front door. By the time he catches up with her, she's already sitting in her Jeep. "We'll talk out here. Get in." As he does, she turns the key in the ignition and rolls up the windows. But she won't look at him.

"What promise?" she says.

"What?"

"Your text. *You promised.* Were you actually reminding me of my promise from when we were kids? To take care of you, to put you first?"

"I was drunk. I just wanted to apologize."

"You threw out that promise like this is somehow my fault, not yours. You better not be saying I had no business turning down your tour request to stay with Ryan. You better not be saying this is my fault because I fell in love."

"I'm not. I know this is all my fault," he says. He reaches for her hand on the steering wheel, but she raises her elbow to block him.

"You sent the text because you feel guilty, but you also believe I've done something that requires forgiveness too. Now I'm wondering why your guilt is so big you can't handle it alone. You're acting like it really was you who took the shot." In response to his silence, Artie slams the gearshift into reverse, accelerating so hard that Arlo tips forward in his seat. He's pushed back as she brakes, then pulls them onto the road. She stomps on the accelerator. Arlo grabs for his seatbelt.

"Where are we going?" he says, his voice low, to show he knows he has no say in it.

Artie takes the corner so fast that the end of the Jeep fishtails. Arlo sees a young woman and her daughter, dresses made out of the same pink fabric, come out on their front porch, their faces following the car as it flies past. At the junction with the county road, Artie barely looks to the left, barely brakes, as she blows past the stop sign, turning right.

"I don't think you should be driving," he tells her, his fist closing around the grab-handle above the window.

They reach the frontage road, and Artie accelerates again, merging them onto I-10, headed toward Houston. When she closes fast on an old El Camino, she jerks them into the next lane to pass without a glance at the rearview mirror. Arlo finds himself leaning forward, both his hands on the dash, as if he can will the car to slow.

"I can only think of one thing that would make you feel as guilty as you are acting. Somehow you knew it was Ryan in the river. You knew, and you dared me to shoot. Do you think breaking that childhood promise is justification for what you've done? Justification for you being so furious you'd want Ryan dead?"

"No," Arlo says, feeling nothing but panic. "You have to remember my reaction, before you even knew it was Ryan. Did I look like a man who had gotten what he wanted?"

Artie doesn't answer. The speedometer rises to ninety-five, ninety-eight. At least if they crash Arlo won't have to admit he wasn't thinking about her, not when he made that stupid bet. He wasn't thinking at all.

They cross the bridge over the Brazos and she swerves again, flying past the next lane and toward the exit. Now seventy miles per hour. Sixty. They're off the highway. Arlo tries again. "I'm sorry, Artie. Sorrier than I've been for anything in my life. But you have to believe me. I didn't do it on purpose. I didn't intend for you to kill him."

They finally hit zero as she brakes hard at a four-way stop at the intersection. "But you knew it was Ryan, didn't you? You knew." She looks him in the eye.

"I can't believe I did this to you," he whispers. All the answer she needs. Something like a small moan comes out of her, and she turns her face away. She accelerates left, under the highway overpass, then left again. There's nothing out here but billboards and empty fields. And there's nothing Arlo can say.

When Hayden's cemetery comes into view, along with his ranch-style funeral home, Artie eases into his small parking lot, drifting across three spaces before coming to a stop.

"Have all these years onstage amplified your narcissism that much? This isn't about you. Or me. This is about Ryan. Tomorrow, at the funeral, you will sit by me and you will see what you . . . what I . . ." She fumbles to a stop and her pain knifes at his lungs. "I make no promises for what happens between us after."

Arlo nods. Her hand is on the gearshift, and he lays his own palm on top of her knuckles. She doesn't withdraw it.

"And now, you'll get out of this car, you'll grab the suit hanging behind you, and you'll take it inside for Hayden to use tomorrow. I want you to sit with Ryan, keep him company, until the morning. Then you can call March to come get you."

"Okay," he says. "Of course." Because he has not fully parsed these actions, Arlo welcomes the mandatory to-do list. Things she will let him do for her.

She turns away from him, puts the car back into gear with his hand still on hers. "Get out."

And so he does. He gets the suit and another shopping bag and watches her pull from the lot, fast again but no longer reckless. There's a wind coming off the river, and it makes the clear plastic around the suit crinkle and twist, sticking to the sweat on his arm. It's now close on eight, and he doesn't expect to find the front door unlocked, but it is. He wanders into the lobby, a large room with paintings of fields swarmed by bluebonnets and massive brown leather couches beneath. After a few small, empty waiting rooms—notable only for the number of Kleenex boxes in them—he finally finds the office: a large desk with Hayden behind it. Arlo knocks on the open door, and Hayden's mouth opens in surprise. He stands, coming to clasp Arlo on the shoulder while simultaneously relieving him of the suit.

"Arlo," he says, giving the shoulder a squeeze before hanging the suit on a coat rack in the corner. Hayden has always treated Arlo as a nephew, and in return, Arlo has always treated Hayden like an overly familiar stranger in need of better boundaries. But as with his mother earlier in the evening, he finds himself surprisingly grateful for the kindnesses.

"Could I view the body, sit with it awhile? That possible?" He can't meet his uncle's eye, has to stuff his hands in his pockets to keep them from fingering the objects in front of him on the desk—an old metal stapler, a family photo, a small clay screech owl made by a child's hands.

"Sure," Hayden says. "We've finished the embalming. But I recommend a drink first." He gestures to his desk, the uncapped bottle of Crown Royal.

Both men sit, Hayden behind the desk and Arlo in front of it, and Hayden pulls an extra glass from a drawer. He pours for Arlo and adds an extra splash to his existing drink.

"You have any trouble getting the sheriff to release the body?" Arlo asks.

"No. The ME finished his report. The cause of death is clear, so no need for an autopsy, even if there are—" Hayden cuts himself off before he says the word "charges." He tilts his head up to the ceiling. "Artie probably told you, but Mrs. Barry wants you at the funeral."

"Maybe just inviting the perpetrator to the public stoning. From what I hear, she's never been a forgive-and-forget sort of woman."

"True," Hayden says, "But I will remind you that, sadly, this isn't my first funeral for a hunting accident."

Arlo picks up his glass, takes a sip. Thinks about Ryan's body lying somewhere close by and takes a much larger sip.

As he leans forward, Hayden's big forearms take up half the desk's surface. He barely resembles Peter, aside from his size. "I can take you to the body if you feel like that's what you need to do. I can't say I recommend it. We haven't dressed him or applied the makeup yet."

Arlo is astounded by his prior stupidity. Just last Friday, a rough night was getting kicked out of Terpsi's. The worst thing he could imagine was Ryan living in Artie's house. "I appreciate that, but it's what I want."

Hayden shrugs. "People think it gives closure, but what's on the table isn't Ryan. Like chewing on a husk and pretending it's corn."

"Artie asked me to. I don't think closure was what she has in mind."

In the tone of a man who believes himself to carry uncommon knowledge, Hayden says, "Death makes people ask for strange things.

Things that matter a lot less than they think." He takes a drink and looks back at the ceiling. "I can tell anyone who asks that you were here a long time. You staying won't help Ryan."

Arlo shakes his head. "It's kind of you to offer, though. Thank you."

Hayden stares at his glass, as if he's weighing something. "I guess I understand how one action can lead to things you never imagined, how you can always second-guess yourself about different choices you might have made." As if he's decided something, he looks up at Arlo. "I knew Peter was sleeping with your mother, even before she got pregnant. I saw them together once, at his office, and I just knew it was a time bomb waiting to go off. But I never said a word to Peter. Later, when all of us knew about Lee's pregnancy, I almost told Peter maybe he should make a family out of his mistake. What might have changed if I'd just talked more to my brother?"

"Those were Peter's choices to make, not yours," says Arlo.

Hayden shakes his head. "It's not that simple when it comes to family." Arlo thinks of the numberless choices he has made, how Artie's actions might have steered them. And the choices she made, steered by his own. Hayden picks up the bottle, waits until Arlo has set down his glass, and then pours him more.

"Spirits are always good company when hanging out with the dead," he says. "Sorry, mortician humor. Stay as long as you want. I'm headed home, so just drop on by when you're done."

"I might be a while."

"You might," he says. "But I stay up pretty late. If the lights are on, I'm awake." Hayden stands. "I'll walk you to the room."

Arlo picks up his glass and follows Hayden down the dim hallway until they reach a closed door with double signs, both warning of Danger: one, Flammable Liquids, the other, Formaldehyde with a cancer warning.

Hayden leaves him, but Arlo feels paralyzed. Don't think, he tells himself, just do. Don't think, just push open the door. And this is how he finds himself in the embalming room, not remembering pushing the door open, though he can hear it thumping back into place behind him. The look and smell of the room are disorientingly familiar, though they pull up completely different worlds. The lighting is from a dance club in Berlin—rendering everything blue and dark, with startling pops of white, glowing smiles on the packed dance floor. And the smell is pure high school biology. He can almost see the fetal pig on its dissection tray, feel the scalpel in his hand. What must be Ryan is in front of him, and Arlo turns away from the body, desperate to find the light switch. He flips on the unlabeled one, flips off the one marked "UV."

He turns back around to face a metal embalming table. A body with a large white towel draped over his midsection, pale and as unlike the living Ryan as a statue might be. Arlo has never considered what he wanted after he died, but he is a sudden convert to cremation. Seeing Ryan's body without his permission, without Ryan's knowledge, feels like an unforgivable invasion of privacy.

Without thinking, Arlo lifts the glass he's still holding and takes a swallow. He understands his mistake immediately, a wave of nausea pushing him to the sink along the far wall. He doesn't vomit, though, and distracts himself by pouring the whiskey down the drain in a thin stream. He wants to rinse out his mouth, but the look of the clear, empty cylinder of the embalming machine to his left, its coiled tubing, won't let him ingest anything from this room. To his right is a utility cart, cluttered with cosmetics in small plastic baskets along with hairbrushes and hair spray and gel. A box of latex gloves. Ordinary things.

He finds a rolling stool and positions it a few feet away from the body. He sits down and closes his eyes. Now he can smell the strong tang of bleach underneath the formaldehyde, and under that the smell of massage cream. He wants to swivel away from the body, but a silly, superstitious nagging won't let him turn his back on the corpse, as if the reptilian part of his brain expects Ryan to rise up behind him. Artie has found a monkey's paw, and Arlo has turned her into the sort of person who would use it.

He tries to examine her motives more closely: Why, exactly, has Artie placed him here? She wants him to see what he has done, of course, but he can't reconcile the matter before him with the man at the river. They can't be the same atoms. Arlo was the last person to see this man alive, to talk to him. What were Ryan's last words? He can't even remember them.

Both he and Artie have done things the other wouldn't have thought them capable of. Arlo can barely stand up under the weight of what he's done to Artie. And now she needs him to also carry this weight of Ryan, carry it all night and then the next day, carry it into a church and bear it with an audience, too. He doesn't have that strength. Not without her to help him.

SEVEN

A T 10 P.M. MARCH DECIDES it's cooled down enough to walk the dogs. He imagines that after the funeral tomorrow, after Arlo either goes back to Artie's or goes back on the road, his mother will have his father evict him—from this house, from the town. He better soak up Olympus while he can. He heads toward downtown, eventually passing a strip mall that's been there since he was in junior high. It's next to a car wash, and he and the dogs walk along the sidewalk in front of big picture windows—a hair salon, a tanning place. He hears music coming from the end of the building. The video store is now a liquor store, closed. At the very end, in what used to be a laundromat, he finds a new bar. Peering inside, he can see Lionel. The cowboy-hatted car salesman is drinking a glass of wine.

"Can I go in?" he asks the man working the front door. March nods toward his dogs.

"Sorry, man. No animals inside. But there are picnic tables around the corner. A waitress comes around."

March stops in front of the window, sees the name "Nectar + Ambrosia: A Gastropub" etched into the glass. What he sees around back mollifies him a bit, as it's a sure sign all is doomed to failure. There are only two couples, both in their forties. The wives have glasses of wine and no food, while the husbands appear to have brought tall boys of Miller Lite from the gas station down the road. The other picnic tables are empty. He sits at the nearest one, and the dogs snuffle the ground for bits of lost food. The patio is just a section of the parking lot, and there's a faded yellow line below his foot to prove it.

March's phone rings in his pocket. Though it could be trouble, he's grateful someone is calling him. Spending the afternoon and evening alone has given him that untethered feeling of Ruidoso.

"I'm on your front porch," Arlo says. "Where are you?"

"Took the dogs for a walk and wound up at some gastropub. How long has this been here?"

"Uh . . . six months? I played at their opening. They overpaid me by half, which doesn't speak well of the business acumen. Enjoy the sinking ship."

"You forget your key?"

"Nah, just wondered where you were."

Neither of them speaks for a few seconds. Then Arlo says, "I saw Artie."

"How'd it go?"

"Not well."

"You can try again tomorrow at the funeral. I have strict orders to deliver you there." When Arlo doesn't respond, March says, "Come down. Eat something. There's no food in the house."

"Okay, sure."

The waitress arrives, finally. She gives him a quizzical look. "Are you one of Peter Briscoe's sons?"

"I'm March," he says, instead of answering.

"Like a time warp. Mr. Briscoe sold us our house when we moved here fifteen years ago. You're the spitting image."

March isn't pleased with the idea that he looks exactly like his father at age forty-five, but he keeps his mouth shut. "What's on tap?" he asks.

"How is Arlo? And Artie, of course. Horrible what happened."

Score one for town gossip. "What's your name?" he asks. The girl's face closes up, like March is chastising her for some forwardness. He hadn't realized how un-small-towned he had become. She crouches down, talking sweetly to the dogs while they lick her arms and hands. March suspects she must not be a great waitress—beer slops being the only reason the dogs would pay such attention to her skin.

"Could I get two Bud Lights?" He hates Bud Light, but it's a tap standard, and he hopes this speeds the process.

She stands up. "Two? You afraid I'll forget about you out here?"

"Someone's meeting me."

"You should try one of our microbrews," she says.

They can't be any worse than Bud Light. "Sure. Bring me two of your favorite."

She nods. "Be right back."

Arlo arrives, looking like a man set for a morning execution. He sits down across from March. "Parking lot patio? Quaint."

"I ordered a drink, I know not what kind, for you." Arlo raises an eyebrow. "Waitress's choice. You been with Artie this whole time?"

Arlo shakes his head, but the waitress comes back before he can answer and sets the beers on the table. "Hey, Arlo," she says. "I would have brought an amber if I knew this guy was ordering for you." She looks at March as if he had tricked her.

"I'm sure this is fine," March says, picking up his cloudy yellow pint glass. "What is it?"

"Banana Hefeweizen," she says. When March frowns, she says, "It's my favorite."

Arlo picks up his beer. "Trouble you to change this out for that amber, darling? Don't worry about March. He loves fruit." She takes his glass and leaves without giving March another look.

"Fucker," March says, taking a swallow and wincing. "My one hope is that my tongue is so pummeled it gives up and stops registering flavor altogether."

Arlo almost smiles.

"I got you an air mattress today. They're surprisingly comfortable," March says.

"You didn't have to do that."

"Couch ain't comfortable, and I had to go to Walmart anyway. We can put it in the empty bedroom so the dogs won't start sleeping on your legs."

Arlo doesn't respond at first, then says without a pause: "I'm sorry I lied to you about the shooting. I'm sorry if I put you in a bad place with Artie. I'm sorry for being a burden."

All March can do is flush with embarrassment. "Once you start, you can't stop, huh? You already apologized for the lie, and you don't have to apologize for the other two. Artie and I are fine, and I'm lucky to have one family member still willing to put me out."

They are quiet as the waitress returns with the amber.

"It's on the house," she says, letting her hand drop to Arlo's shoulder. "Your brother told me things have been tough."

Arlo shoots him a look, and March shakes his head. After she's gone, Arlo says, "Should've drank the fruit beer."

"Yep," March agrees.

The couples behind them prepare to leave, weaving through the tables, close enough to provoke a low growl from Remus. March begins to apologize, but then he sees the group is looking past him, staring angrily at Arlo. Arlo drops his eyes as they pass.

"Maybe we should both get out of town for a month? Let things blow over," March says.

"Told the sheriff I would stay until all the legal stuff is sorted. And I can't abandon Artie."

March nods. He's relieved at the answer. They'd both leave now with sizable holes in their hearts, too big for the other to fill. "What can I do?" he asks, hoping that, somehow, it is something small enough that he can actually complete it.

"You can accept my apologies," Arlo says, so softly that, at first, March wonders if he's misheard.

"I absolve you," March says, making the sign of the cross in Arlo's direction. But Arlo doesn't smile, and March drops his arm. "I forgive you," he says. "You are forgiven."

Arlo runs his fingernail against the top of the picnic table, cutting a line in the soft wood. Then he scans the area, confirming they are still alone. "Ryan was there when I got to the river. We talked before Artie showed up. I dared her to shoot knowing exactly who she was aiming at. But I didn't think she would. I didn't have time to stop her."

It feels to March like someone has dunked him in an icy lake. "Artie knows?"

"She does now."

March understands now why Arlo needed his forgiveness. Any other may be a long time coming, if it comes at all.

THE ORIGIN OF ARLO'S MISTAKE

. . . but though he is the god of oracles,
he reads the future wrongly

⋇ OVID ⋇

THE RIVER WAS RUNNING FAST, churning with the recent rains
and higher than usual. It was the first time Ryan had done something
that he knew Artie wouldn't like, showing up here early without warning her. But he'd seen how anxious she was, and he hated to think of
her spending even an extra hour that way, not when she didn't have to.
He'd even beaten her there; by the time she arrived, he'd have everything smoothed out.

Though he hadn't been trying to be quiet, he knew Arlo hadn't
heard him as he descended to the bank. Artie's twin was sitting a few
feet from the river's edge, staring at the water. When Ryan said hello,
Arlo jumped. There was so much of Artie in this man's face, it made
him seem familiar to Ryan, as if they were already friends. He waited
for Arlo to stand up so he could introduce himself properly, but he
turned back to the river as if Ryan wasn't even there.

"Artie thought it was time we finally met."

"She didn't mention it to me. 'Finally' seems a strange word, too, considering I didn't even know you existed until a couple of days ago."

Since Arlo wouldn't stand, Ryan squatted down next to him. "Well, now you know." He smiled and held out his hand for Arlo to shake.

Arlo ignored it and abruptly stood, forcing Ryan to follow suit. "To me you're a stranger with a bad reputation, a bad haircut"—he paused here to look him up and down, like he was a bull at auction—"and burn-spotted jeans."

If this man had been anyone else's brother, Ryan would simply have walked away. Artie, though, was worth being insulted over. "Then get to know me. Have an open mind."

"So those stories I've heard aren't true? No trail of broken hearts behind you?"

"My past doesn't have to be my future."

"You want me to believe your intentions are honorable? I'd hate to see my sister gamble her happiness on something so unlikely."

Ryan might not know how to handle kindness, but he knew too well how to handle the posturing of other men. "You're not going to have as much say as you seem to think."

Arlo laughed at him. "Artie's no fool, and only a fool would make a long-term bet on you."

"If you believe that, then why not keep your mouth shut and let her figure it out on her own?"

For a moment, Ryan wondered if Arlo would punch him. Instead, Arlo moved away from him, upstream. Ryan watched a branch float past, the current strong, and it gave him an idea. He was such a good swimmer, Artie joked he was half seal. "Are you fool enough to make a bet with me?" he called out.

"What?"

"I bet you that I can swim one hundred yards upstream." He had made a similar bet with Artie—though that time, he was betting he could beat her there. And he had, her giving up in exhaustion before they were even halfway. He won a home-cooked dinner from her, the first night he ever stayed over.

"I could give a shit how well you do or don't swim," said Arlo, still looking away from him. Then he added, "But you'd have to be stupid to tangle with that current."

"I win, and you back off and go on tour without Artie. When you're proved right, when I leave her for another girl, our whole problem goes away, doesn't it? And you don't have to piss Artie off by trying to run her life." Ryan couldn't conceive of leaving Artie, so the hypothetical was ridiculous to him. She had shown him that fate wasn't just a thing that wrecked plans. It could dispense good as easily as bad. He knew he could fix this. He was a man in love.

BUT WE HEAR what we want to hear. Arlo heard his fears confirmed, and he was made even angrier by the fact that Ryan's assessment was true. He had no choice but to let his sister get hurt.

"Yeah, okay, asshole. And when you lose your stupid bet, you'll encourage Artie to manage the tour. When she gets here, we'll already be fast friends. You'll tell her coming with me is the right thing to do." Arlo was sure Ryan would revert to his old ways, especially without Artie there in front of him. He held out his hand, and Ryan shook it.

"I made the bet because it relies only on me, and I know exactly what I'm capable of. You're the one dealing with unknowns. I'm not gonna lose."

As Ryan began stripping off his clothes, Arlo felt the sting of instruction. Ryan waded into the river. He plunged beneath the surface and was immediately swept twenty yards downstream. Then he found his rhythm. For five seconds, the best he could do was hold steady. But then he began to move forward, every stroke increasing his pace. Arlo watched, his stomach twisting, knowing it wasn't a feat he could have pulled off himself. Soon Ryan was a shrinking blob.

And that was when Arlo did wish Ryan dead. Just for a moment, a fleeting second. Not even long enough to imprint in his memory. The thought, but perhaps not the emotion, was blown away by Artie appearing at his side.

WEDNESDAY

ONE

Artie's mother drives them down a wide street with giant trees and two-story houses. The Episcopal church at the end of the block looks like it belongs in an English village: a large lawn thick with grass, quaint brownstone, a wide red church door, and, all along one side of the sanctuary, bushes heavy with purple blossoms. In front of the building, the street narrows sharply to accommodate two towering oak trees, here long before these roads were paved, long before the town was even settled.

The wide red door is open, but, because they are so early, the inner doors to the sanctuary are still locked. Artie and Thea leave Lee on a bench in the foyer as they go into the main church building and find the narrow wooden door marked WOMEN. Inside it smells of bleach and the green mottled flooring shines. They each enter one of the two metal stalls after tossing their purses on the yellow velvet loveseat crammed by the entrance.

Ever since she dropped Arlo off last night, Artie has been looping around and around the core of anger in her chest. The knot that didn't loosen when Arlo stepped out of the car with Ryan's suit. Confronting Arlo, making him sit with the body, hadn't helped. *He had known. He had known it was Ryan in the river.* But maybe if she tells Thea everything, lays it out for her so they both can pick at the tangles, it will help her breathe.

This is the Thea who let her spend Saturdays in her room when Thea was in high school but Artie was still a kid in junior high. Thea, who was unfailingly fair, who never brought up Lee or what that affair had done to Thea's family. But Thea's unbending sense of right and wrong has also made her a prosecutor. She's a woman who holds her own forgiveness in tight. This is why Artie had called her in the first place. Why is she finding it even harder to tell her, now that she knows the worst?

Thea leaves the stall and washes her hands. Artie doesn't move. If she asks Thea to leave her there, would Thea agree? Artie wouldn't have to see Arlo, wouldn't have to see Ryan in his casket. If she stayed long enough, maybe she'd get locked in the church and could spend the night poking through Sunday School rooms, drawing devil horns on the posters of Jesus and the apostles with a blue crayon. Too bad it isn't a Catholic church. She could sleep in a confessional and wake in the morning to confess her sins.

"Knock knock," Thea says instead of knocking. "All okay?"

"I was thinking we should be Catholic."

Thea laughs. "How come?"

"Going to confession must be therapeutic."

Thea's feet re-enter the stall beside her. The toilet lid closes with a thunk, and Thea sits back down. "Your line's first," she says.

"What?" Artie says.

"Forgive me, Father, for I have sinned."

Artie laughs, but she repeats the words. "Forgive me, Father, for I have sinned."

Thea deepens her voice, and Artie can feel the smile behind the metal wall. Thea was always game for acting but chose the debate team every year over the annual musical. "How long has it been since your last confession?"

"Forever and never," Artie replies. She can hear her own heart beat. All she wants is to tell Thea the truth, either despite or because of the fact that it pushes her further from her brother. Artie says, "I lied."

There's a silence, then Thea says, "How did you lie?" The fun is gone from her voice. "You can tell me. I'm only here for *you*."

Thea will pack up and fly home to her family soon, but Artie will still be here. She can still extricate herself, shut this conversation down. She can even tell herself it is for Thea's sake, to not make an upholder of the law complicit in subverting the law. But then Thea's hand reaches up from underneath the divider between them, waiting for Artie to grasp it.

"That's love," Artie says. "You know I haven't washed my hands yet."

"Yep. And if you love me, you will exit, wash your hands, sit on that scabby-looking loveseat, and tell me what's really going on."

And so she does. She leans against her half sister and tells her the truth. She looks at their hands, clasped in Thea's lap, as she talks. She tells Thea that she was the one who took the shot, not Arlo. And she tells her the most unbearable detail, too: that Arlo knew it was Ryan in the river.

Thea is silent. Eventually, Artie says, "Say something."

"It's not what you want to hear."

"How can you know what I want to hear if I don't know myself?"

Thea squeezes her hand, hard, and Artie can feel her shaking her head. "That's murder. Arlo used you like a weapon."

"He said he didn't mean for me to shoot. The words just flew out of his mouth, and before he could—"

"No, Artie. He said the words. And he was worried enough to lie about it. To ask you to lie. To the sheriff, to all of us. There's no other way to look at it."

"He's not evil," Artie says. As angry and hurt as she is, she can't stand Thea thinking so badly of her brother. Instead of loosening the knot inside her, she feels throttled by it.

"I know he's not evil," Thea says. "People are going to wrong each other. That's what we do. Dad cheats on my mom. Lee sleeps with a married man. Vera and March do the same a generation later. But once someone reveals their true character, then it's *our* responsibility to protect ourselves."

"You're such a lawyer," Artie says quietly.

"Mom was wrong to let Dad get away with everything he did. Hap was wrong to stay with Vera." Thea shifts so she faces Artie on the couch. "Arlo did what he did and, even *if* there was as much bad luck as ill will involved, it would be *wrong* for you to shield him from the fallout, to just accept that he values himself more than you."

"Don't you think people sometimes deserve a second chance?"

"Second chances are just a way to assuage our own guilt: *I gave them every chance, but they fucked up again.* Has Arlo been acting any differently than Dad? Than March? As if each of them gets to exist in his own plane, above the laws the rest of us follow, never suffering any consequences."

"But he's always been there for me," Artie says. "We've always been there for each other." Easy for Thea to say, to judge. With her family waiting at home. Artie has lost Ryan, the person she thought might be her future, and now she is supposed to shake off both her past and the person who has been her constant present? Even though this is why she'd asked Thea to come down, now that the verdict has been handed down, Artie balks. "What if your husband wronged you?" she asks.

"I'd follow my own advice."

"One of your daughters?"

"That's different."

"Why?" She wants to say that's what Arlo is, to her, the one that is different.

"Because I'm their parent. I brought them into the world. It's my job to put them first, always."

"Some people would say that's what you do with all family—spouse or sibling or parent."

"So no matter what, you're duty-bound to forgive?"

A week ago Artie would have said yes. For Arlo, she is duty-bound.

But now all her impulses are tangled together. The only one that feels clear is her strong desire to end this conversation. Artie squeezes her sister's shoulder while she stands, both to show she isn't angry and to steady her shaky balance. "Whatever I decide, I have to get through this funeral first."

Thea stands too. "Whatever you decide, I'll always love you."

"Like you love June?" Artie says. Artie had accepted all those kindnesses from Thea back in junior high, even though being with the Briscoes meant watching Thea and June spar, watching Thea meet June's every attempt at love with a wall of indifference. Thea's face closes for a second, and then she shakes it off. Another person giving Artie allowances, brushing off the truth as simple grief.

She and Thea return to the foyer to rejoin Lee just as Lavinia Barry enters the church. On one side of her stands Ryan's grandmother, leaning on Lavinia's arm, and on the other is her husband, standing close but not touching her. Mr. Barry holds the same shape as Ryan, compact and wiry, and somehow that makes him seem like a much younger man than he really is, even with his hair receding and half gray. Artie introduces Lee to them.

Lavinia looks behind Artie and her frown lines deepen. "And your brother?"

"He'll be here," Artie says, reassuring her. Lavinia feels like a woman full of expectation, though Artie is not sure what she expects. Some closure in finally seeing everyone who had played a role?

"We're going to sit on the left side of the church," Lavinia says. Any warmth Artie had won from Ryan's mother yesterday has cooled. What's just ahead must be occupying her mind. "You all can sit on the right. Up front is fine."

Like there's a bride's side and a groom's, Artie thinks, and she feels sick. But she thanks Mrs. Barry. Would she have liked this woman if they had met over Sunday dinner? For all Lavinia's expectation around Arlo, Artie can tell she is ready to be free of them, already drifting away. Then Lee steps close to Mrs. Barry and blindsides her with a hug. Artie is alarmed by her mother's lack of boundaries until Lavinia finally pulls back; she is gripping Lee's elbow and her upper lip trembles. She can see the echo of Ryan's face in Mrs. Barry—the set of the eyes, the cheekbones—and Artie wonders if that echo of his tenderheartedness is there in her, too. If, perhaps, her life had just taught her how to bury it.

Lee whispers, "We are sorry for your loss," as if it is a secret between the six of them.

Mr. Barry shakes his head. Artie turns to walk inside, but she pauses and lays a hand on the man's shoulder. "I loved your son very much," she tells him. He shifts his body away. She reminds herself that she is a stranger to him. A concept, only, before now. If Arlo died, could she get comfort from a random woman testifying to her love?

Thea tugs open the church door, now unlocked, and a stiff stream of air conditioning hits Artie in the face. She shivers. They walk through the wide double doors revealing an empty church, save for the casket at the front.

Not a large church. Twelve pews on either side. The dark wood of the benches makes the burgundy carpet look shabby and faded. White walls set off the stained-glass windows, four on each side and one in front, a well-fed Jesus smiling behind the altar. Artie doesn't feel comforted by the space. She could see, objectively, the beauty of stained glass, but it made no sense to her—why stuff worshipers in a room full of windows then not let them see out? But churches had always felt foreign to her. Their mother wasn't a believer—a follower of love itself more than a divinity made of love—and Artie's visits to the Briscoes had never happened on Sunday mornings. There was a line that couldn't be crossed, even in Protestant churches: no flaunting of illegitimate children, no bringing in of actual evidence that could thwart your salvation. Like no one ever brought in a six-pack or a prostitute.

As they enter the church, an usher—a boy of twelve, if that—pops up from the back pew and hands them each a funeral program. They are so early, they've even caught the ushers off guard. The picture of Ryan on the program is an old black-and-white high school photo. She's never seen it before, and she wants to laugh at the skinny version of her lover, his nose too big, the spray of acne across both cheeks. Artie wishes she had thought to offer a recent picture herself. Then she remembers she has taken no pictures of Ryan. Neither of them had been the type to keep phones within arm's reach, neither had much use for social media. But now she's going to slowly forget his face; there is no avoiding it. Every time her brain pulls it up, it will get just a little fuzzier, until there's no clarity at all. This thought is so awful, she can't help the whimper that escapes from her throat. Thea puts an arm around her. "Let's sit down," she whispers.

Should she look at the body—get one last view of his face, his hands, his hair? If she picked up his hand, would it be like he was still alive and the whole rest of the world would fall away? She looks at her own hand and wishes it possible while knowing it is not. What is in the coffin is what was with her on the riverbank. It is not who was in bed with her Saturday night. It is not who she loves. She lets Thea and her mother lead her to the front and place her in the first pew, one on either side of her.

After a few minutes of listening to people filter in, the flip of program pages and discreet whispers, Artie texts Arlo: *You need to sit with me up front.* She slips her phone back in her purse as Peter and June materialize at the far end of the pew, by the sanctuary wall. They remind Artie a little of Ryan's parents, standing next to each other but not touching.

Artie thinks again of the coffin. She should go up and see Ryan while there isn't a full audience. Ryan would laugh at her for being squeamish about his corpse. It's just nature, he'd say. Still, the thought of standing over his body wraps her in panic. She had ordered Arlo to do more than that. To sit by the corpse, stripped of its buffering coffin, absent the disguise of a suit and a beautiful blue tie. It did comfort her to know that Ryan wasn't alone last night. Almost as much as it comforted her to think of the pain it must have caused Arlo, forced to see what he had done.

Artie looks to her right, past her mother studiously avoiding Peter's glance. Peter has stopped, not wanting to enter the pew first and to sit next to Lee. June hasn't noticed the delay, her head turned to the back of the church. And there, finally, is Arlo, coming up the center aisle in his most somber suit. She closes her eyes and counts her breaths. She has only reached ten when she feels Thea get up and leave the pew, giving Arlo space to sit. She hears Thea sit down behind them. Artie keeps counting, keeps her eyes closed. At twenty-five, Arlo begins to bounce his leg, making the entire pew vibrate. She puts her hand on his knee and he stops. She wishes that Arlo sitting next to her would bring some comfort, that touching him would finally make him feel closer, some proof that following Thea's advice is not what is best for her. But even with Arlo there, all Artie feels is very alone. She puts her hand back in her lap.

TWO

HAP IS CROSSING the wide green lawn of the church when he spots his son and Vera waiting under a tree. Pete squeals as soon as he catches sight of him, and Vera sets him on the grass at her feet. He streaks toward his father, his face the definition of joy, his little body an ungraceful blur, Hap worrying at every step that Pete will topple over, his enthusiasm spoiled by gravity. The joy is a punch to Hap's stomach, a hook in his heart. He leans forward and picks up Pete and hugs him, all while his brain is caught in a loop of fix it, fix it, fix it. Vera never texted him back yesterday. Hap can't face the thought of all the hours in his future, sitting alone in a silent house, waiting for his messages to be returned.

He carries Pete back over to Vera, still under the tree. She's dressed in the same high-collared, A-line dress she wears to every funeral and heels that make her taller than him. Pete holds out his hands, and

Vera gives him the stuffed donkey she's holding. His son snuggles the stuffed animal against Hap's shoulder and leaves it there, giggling.

"He kept asking for you this morning, so I brought him to see you." She adjusts the shoulders of her black dress, already sticking to her in the heat. "My mom will take him to the park while we're at the funeral. She's waiting over there."

Hap looks to his left, sees his mother-in-law standing by her white sedan, glaring at him.

"Can I pick him up from her after? Keep him overnight?"

"I don't think that's best," Vera says. She doesn't meet his eye, but she's composed. None of the other night's anger or tears.

"Looks like your grief over the death of our marriage is moving fast. You've skipped past bargaining and depression into acceptance," he says.

"Only fair," she says flatly, "considering how long I spent in denial. We can split the stages. I'll leave the bargaining and depression for you."

Hap shifts Pete to his other arm. "How can we know where we stand if I only know your fuckups and not my own." Vera makes a face at his cursing, and Pete cries out as the donkey falls from Hap's shoulder. "Tell me what I did, and we can work on it."

"I take it back. No one gets bargaining," she says. She leans down for the stuffed animal. "Look, I'm not going to insist we sell. It's home for Pete, too, and I don't want to rattle him any more than I can help. But I am going to get a place in Bullinger. I'll need to go back to work, and there are more jobs there. Plus, we'll need my mom's help babysitting during the day."

"But it's a whole other town," Hap objects.

"Don't be a child. It's a fifteen-minute drive. Would you rather it be Houston? Or another part of the state?"

All Hap can think to do is change the subject. "I don't think you being here at the funeral is a good idea." Pete is wriggling, so he sets him back down on the lawn.

"Afraid what I'll do in front of your family?"

"Can you blame me after the scene you made yesterday at my dad's office?" His mouth barrels forward. "And, of course, all those times you slept with March."

"You think you've figured it all out, don't you?" She pauses and glares at him. "You fix the bathroom sink yet?"

Hap nods. "Yesterday. Needed something to fill up my empty evening."

She smiles, one of her icy kind that never signals good. "If you really had it all figured out, you would have pulled that couch into the front yard and burned it instead of tearing up the bathroom."

Now he has another vivid picture he won't be able to stop pulling up every time he sees his brother, every time Hap walks into his own living room. He swallows hard against a sudden nausea.

Vera says, "God, did you have to go so pale? Now I have to feel bad for you again. You always know how to rob me of every pleasure."

Pete, previously babbling, has grown quiet, and Vera leans down to pick him up. "Daddy's tummy hurts," she says, giving him back his toy. He bops her in the head with it.

"Mean mommy," the boy says. Hap almost laughs, despite his pain, until he sees his wife stiffen as if slapped. She takes their son away with her, back to her mother's car.

THREE

ALTHOUGH HE DROVE ARLO to the church, March doesn't follow him up front to sit with Artie and the other Briscoes. He doesn't want to risk stirring up trouble. Instead, he settles on the opposite side of the church behind a tall man, his tall wife, and their small daughters. He assumes the first few pews hold Ryan's family, but he doesn't know them from the front, much less the back. On the right side of the church, he notes the nearly full pew: Arlo, Artie, Lee, then a wide gap and his father and mother at the other end. Thea sits by herself, behind Arlo and Artie, like a chaperone. His mother peeks over her shoulder, but, thankfully, it isn't him she's after. She's looking at a man standing in the back, not even seated in a pew yet. The stranger wears a nice suit, and he lifts his hand to June in greeting. Hap passes the man, not noticing him, and heads up the far aisle to take the seat next to Thea.

A woman barges into March's pew, maneuvering to slide past him and take a seat to his left. It takes March a half second to register the backside ten inches from his face as Vera's. She sits down next to him, setting her purse on the other side of her and crossing her arms. This must be some sort of punishment. Not that Vera's come to the funeral simply to make him uncomfortable. Vera believes in social formalities—never miss a birthday party, never miss a funeral. The small stuff she always had covered. But if Vera had a choice between sitting by herself or sitting next to March, netting the benefit of making him and Hap miserable as well as making his mother angry, she'd go with option number two. Vera's no fool, though. She'd rather have an angry June thirty feet away than a foot in front of her. March turns around to find a new seat, one without the space for Vera to fit next to him.

"You going to spend the whole funeral looking backward?" she asks.

"Is it an option?" He doesn't like how loud his voice sounds in the silent church, but to whisper would entail turning to face her.

"No," she says.

March faces straight ahead. The man in front of him swivels to greet them until March gives him a stony look through his still-swollen eye.

"Your mother have you fired yet?" she says.

"I haven't asked." He's dropped down to a whisper now. "You let Hap know what he did wrong?"

"Nope." She crosses her leg, and the heel of her shoe—thin and black, sharp—brushes against his leg. He recoils and instinctively glances at his family. "Your mother doesn't have X-ray vision," Vera says, finally speaking more quietly.

"I suppose it's too much to ask that you sit elsewhere?"

"Sorry," she says. "I can't leave Hap *and* torture him. But torturing somebody seems to be a requisite for getting through this day."

"Him not knowing why you're leaving, that's torture." There is the faintest shine on her skin, and her lipstick is smudged in one corner, and she is so lovely March cannot believe he ever got to touch her, to be the one that smudged her makeup. They never talked much, and now March is glad they hadn't. Surely he would be in love with her if they had. Her smarts, her humor, and the fact that she's always shown him either lust or bemusement, not disappointment, not hatred. In this moment, though, he doesn't want to feel Vera's heel brushing his leg again, doesn't want to find his brother's wife attractive, still, even as she is tornadoing through their lives. "You love Hap," he whispers.

"Less so, now."

There must be something he can do, can say, to help. If Vera and Hap stay together, he may have to leave town while things settle down, but maybe he wouldn't be exiled forever. He's imagined himself as Arlo's roadie, a life of cheap motels and miles of highway. Even with Arlo there, he knows he will still feel like he did in New Mexico, like he is just floating through his life. But it is the only future that he seems able to imagine, clear enough to him that he is already worrying about logistics. Would Arlo let the dogs come? Perhaps March didn't deserve the dogs, either.

"Why did we do it again?" he whispers.

"I doubt we have the same reasons."

"I hadn't realized yet that I could stop myself."

"You're a bit old to be making that realization," she says. She reaches up and grabs a hair from his head, pulls it out in one swift motion. He knows without looking it will be a gray one. "Ten more years, and you'll match Peter again." She drops the hair on his thigh.

"I don't see what Hap could've done that was so bad."

"I can't tell you," she snaps. "It wouldn't be right."

"You *do* still love him," he says. Vera straightens in her seat, confirming his suspicion. "You have to work it out, then."

"People think love is good in and of itself. Stupid, really. When does it ever work out like that in real life? Maybe I do still love him, but that doesn't mean it isn't a thing to be strangled out of me."

"I can't believe that," he says.

"See. You prove my point. You, a man who has never been in love and has witnessed three decades of your parents' toxic marriage, even you are stupidly in favor of love. What good did love do for your mother? And what good did your mother's love of Peter do for you? She would have been able to love you, I bet, if she had left Peter." No one has ever said it aloud, this thing he has always suspected. That his mother wasn't, isn't, able to love him. He must look upset because Vera says, "Let it go. Live your life like you have no one to satisfy but yourself."

"I've always lived my life like that. This is where it's gotten me."

She shakes her head at him, and then, though he cannot believe it, she smiles and kisses him on the cheek. He is saved from having to respond, though, by an old woman in a bright green jacket and skirt slowly making her way toward the pulpit, aiming for the organ against the far wall. She carries sheet music and an appropriately grim expression. The two young ushers are closing the doors at the back of the church. When the space between the doors dwindles to nothing, the organist launches into "Rock of Ages."

It feels like a certainty that this will be the last time March is in a room with his whole family. All of them—him and Hap and Vera, Artie and Arlo—are caught in one long skid, spinning out on tires with no traction. There's nothing he can do, can say, to help anything.

FOUR

THOUGH ARTIE HAS NEVER BEEN, and is still not, the type of woman to throw herself on a funeral pyre, Ryan's memorial seems a final insult to inflict on the dead. Better to have keening, mourners brought to their knees. She needs some acknowledgment that death is messy for those left behind and weathering the mess isn't a foregone conclusion. Instead, she must abide this minister in immaculate lace-ups, an audience silent while they hear about the glories of heaven—so overdone and utterly enticing that, if true, the entire congregation would stand and pass a pocket knife hand to hand, puncturing their own jugulars and collapsing into the beautiful embrace of God. The minister chastises them on the selfishness, the wrongheadedness, of grief. As if the way her hand aches without Ryan's to hold is a choice she is making. Something she could will away by turning her face to God.

After the minister finishes, Ryan's cousin gives a eulogy. No more talk of God, just stories. Better yet, stories she hasn't heard before, a chance to see Ryan through someone else's eyes. Ryan, halfway to drunk, walking into the Gulf waves of Galveston on prom night; keeping the Bullinger police chief's daughter out all night; swallowing a live scorpion on a dare. The cousin talks of how, to him, Ryan had seemed immortal. Arlo continues to fidget beside her, tapping his foot like he's keeping rhythm to a fast beat. She can feel how much he wants to leave. Can't he acknowledge Ryan's life as worth commemorating? Can't he muster enough care for her to at least act as if he did?

According to the program, they should be moving on to a hymn. Instead, Lavinia stands up. The crowd barely has a chance to indulge its surprise—a communal shifting on the hard pews, a collective inhalation—before she's behind the lectern, already talking into the microphone. And it seems they'll be spared from witnessing a mother's uncontained grief; Lavinia's voice is firm and stronger than Artie has ever heard it. "I wanted to have my son's funeral here in Olympus, my true home. I wanted to say goodbye to Ryan in the same place he was born. And looking out at all your familiar faces, it's like no time has passed at all." Lavinia isn't looking out at *all* the faces. She is staring down one person, Peter. Artie looks across the pew at him. His brow is furrowed, but both he and June appear too astonished to even avert their eyes. Artie understands then that the strength in Lavinia's voice is not from community or comfort but from righteous anger.

"It feels like I could leave here, drive with my husband and mother back to our old homestead, as if it had never been stolen from us. In this daydream, my mother and I inherit my father's properties instead of losing them to a greedy speculator. We never have to pick between paying our health insurance bill or paying the gas bill. I send Ryan to college, maybe even out of state. He works in an office in a skyscraper, downtown Houston or Dallas at his feet." She pauses, and Artie can feel them all envisioning Ryan there. Artie sees him in the suit she bought for him. Lavinia continues, "In that life, there's no chance he'd be dead now, killed by that greedy man's son. I'm not saying it would have been a perfect life, but our problems wouldn't have all come from one man's choices. They would have been because of *my* choices."

Now Lavinia's focus travels down the row, landing on her and Arlo. Arlo's tapping finally stills, and both she and her brother inhale at the same time. She feels his unease, but Artie isn't afraid. She's almost eager for whatever is coming, as if Lavinia is freeing them from the rock they've been hiding under.

"You heard his cousin just now. My son was bold his whole life, but he also seemed charmed. His boldness *never* caused him true harm. Then he took a job with Peter Briscoe's son. Started dating Peter Briscoe's daughter. And now he is gone. I want, just once, here in Olympus, here in front of all of you, for there to be real repercussions for this family's bad actions, ones we *all* acknowledge. My son was swimming. Just swimming. And then a Briscoe chose to fire a gun."

Artie realizes Lavinia's pinning gaze is not on both her and Arlo, but only on him. She wants some of the blame, *she* is the Briscoe that chose to fire a gun. Yet a larger part of her wants this public judgment of her brother, even if everyone in this pew is humiliated along with him. Lavinia levels a steady arm, pointing directly at Arlo. "*You* have inherited your father's heedlessness. His urge to do whatever he wants, whenever he wants. His unwarranted pride and his selfishness. Even now, Peter Briscoe has the gall to think he can sit here with all his family, next to his former mistress, without a stain on him." Lavinia has gathered up all the attention of the congregation and now propels it straight onto her brother. "And you, Arlo, have the gall to act as if this is *not* your fault. You have the gall to sit there like a mourner. I won't allow it. *I am casting you out.*"

The church is still, as soundless as a vacant building. No heads turn to see Arlo's reaction because no one can look away from Lavinia Barry. Her arm shakes as it lowers to her side, then she doubles over onto the lectern. Her mouth is so close to the microphone as she begins to sob, it's like the entire church has become trapped inside her. Lavinia lets go of all the tears she must have been locking down since their meeting when she insisted Arlo must come.

Artie turns to her brother, and he looks shocked but also bristling, sure he has been misused. He leaps up and steps into the aisle, but then he faces Artie again. His hand is outstretched, and he is sure that she will take it, sure she will go with him. He doesn't consider that what she needs in this moment is different than what he needs. She *can't* go. She needs to see Ryan before they close the casket.

Artie looks to the front of the church so Arlo will see, will understand why she has to stay. When she turns back to him, he's already moving away, his gait longer and faster than his normal one, radiating anger even though she can't see his face anymore. And that anger makes him seem to Artie like all the things Lavinia accused him of.

There's so much motion—Arlo down the aisle, Thea sliding back in next to her to replace his empty seat, Mr. Barry half carrying his wife through the side door that leads to the vestry, her sobs still with them until the door settles closed again. The current of stress that ran through the congregation is broken, and the minister returns to the pulpit, ending the service by reading from the Book of Psalms. When he finishes, no pallbearers rise to shoulder the coffin. There will be no procession to the cemetery, just Hayden and his assistant loading the body to take it to the crematorium.

"Ready?" Thea whispers. Behind them is the noise of dozens of bodies taking their leave. Artie can see Thea is relieved she didn't go with Arlo, perhaps even proud of her. And Artie knows it was the right thing to do, but she still finds it hard to look at Thea. And hard to bear up under her mother, too, who is leaning against her, trying to make sense of what just happened.

Artie tells Thea and Lee, "You go on. I want to sit here by myself a little while." They pause, but then they obey. After a few minutes, it's only Artie and the organist left. The woman finishes up "Morning Has Broken." Artie expects her to leave, but the organist begins another song Artie can't place. Then she begins to sing. Not a hymn. A Hank Williams song about a funeral procession, one with dire lyrics disguised by a quick tempo and a cheerful fiddle. But this version is slower, the barest of chords, and the woman's voice is gravelly and only approximately on pitch. *Six more miles and leave my darlin', leave the best friend I ever had.* In one stanza, Artie's anger at Arlo's expectations, that he turned out to be exactly who Thea said he was, becomes no match for her grief over Ryan. Her chest feels empty, yet aching, her heart a phantom limb. The song ends, and though it was perhaps just a minute long, the absence of it is deafening. The organist turns off her instrument, stands, and walks down the aisle. She looks at Artie briefly, giving her not so much a smile as a moment where she doesn't frown.

Artie is at the casket without realizing she walked there, looking down at the waxy simulacrum of the man she bought NyQuil for, cooked with, slept against. She moves to the side of the coffin and sinks down to her knees so all she sees is his hair instead of his face. The hair, always dead, looks the same. She grabs a lock between her fingers and rubs it, the same slick softness as always. She finally feels like Ryan is there, is present. She closes her eyes and says her goodbye. Standing up, she sees his hair is now slightly disheveled. She knows Ryan would like that. She closes the lid.

FIVE

ARLO HAS TO FORCE HIMSELF to not break into a run as he exits the church. What happened with Artie the night before, admitting he'd known it was Ryan in the river and then being with the physical result of what he'd done, laying on a mortuary table, had flayed him. Entering the church was hard enough—seeing Artie and seeing Ryan's parents, seeing the coffin—but being ejected from it was like a flayed man being thrown into a saltwater sea. He can only think of getting to land. He makes it out onto the church lawn, still incensed by Lavinia's stratagem and Artie's abandonment, but he falters in the bright sunshine, feeling alone and unsure where to go. He starts toward March's truck to wait. By the time he makes it to the sidewalk, he realizes someone is following him. Sheriff Muñoz.

"I hadn't realized you were here," Arlo says, stopping.

"I was in the back pew. I like to pay my respects at times like these. You okay? That was brutal in there."

She is good at her job, Arlo thinks. She has the kind of face that you want to talk to, which is not the most common kind of face in law enforcement. It's why he answers honestly. "Not used to carrying this much guilt around with me."

She nods her head, like he's given her the correct answer. "So, I've been interviewing people since Sunday. Nothing turned up on Ryan and Artie—no affairs, no abuse. The relationship looked healthy, and probably too new for the kind of intractable problems that make people think death is the only way out." She puts her regulation cowboy hat, which has been tucked under her arm, back on her head. "And though I can't imagine what Mrs. Barry just did was pleasant for you, I have to say, I'm relieved. She'll feel like she got a little justice, and maybe that will be enough for her when we don't file charges on you."

"There'll be no charges?" Arlo says. He needs her to say it straight, so it feels like a promise.

"No charges," she repeats. "Of course, while what you did isn't criminal, that doesn't mean you didn't make a big mistake. One a lot of people will never get over."

She nods at him as she touches the brim of her hat, then she heads back across the lawn to the church. Arlo no longer wants to sit, waiting for March. He wants as far from this place and its judgments as he can get on foot.

THIRTY MINUTES LATER, his socks sweaty and his heels beginning to blister in his dress shoes, Arlo is staring into the dark windows of the gastropub—the only place with alcohol that's open this early. Halfway into his walk, March had called, but Arlo didn't pick up and March hadn't left a message.

Because it's barely noon, the tables are only a quarter full, the stools at the bar completely empty aside from two old men in short-sleeved Western shirts. George Jones sings from the jukebox, and Arlo sits at the bar, as far from the other men as he can. Still, he is forced to nod an acknowledgment. The men nod back, speak quietly to each other. Surely about Ryan.

Arlo meets his own gaze in the bar's mirrored backsplash. His suspicion that he has made a mistake in coming here is confirmed when he sees Laurel at a table. She's finishing up lunch, laughing with a couple he doesn't recognize. He should leave, but the bartender appears in front of him, so he orders a Scotch on the rocks—for the ice as much as the alcohol.

When it arrives, he gives the bartender a ten and waves away the change. He fidgets with the highball glass before sipping, forcing himself to avoid looking at Laurel in the mirror. He will finish his drink and slip out. As he tips the glass to drain it, the ice collides with his nose. Arlo spins on the stool, wiping Scotch from his face, and finds Laurel standing directly in front of him.

"Leaving already?" she asks, her mouth puckering to the side like she's tasting something awful.

"I didn't think you'd be here," he says. She raises her eyebrows at him. "I mean, I didn't come here looking for you."

"Did I say you had?"

He shakes his head. "I'm going."

"You owe me an apology first." She takes a seat but leaves one stool between them. He spins back around as Laurel notes his empty glass. "Let's step you down a bit." To the bartender, she says, "Two Lone Stars." She doesn't speak again until the bottles are opened and placed in front of them. "I was sorry to hear about the accident. How's Artie?" Laurel isn't looking at him directly; she's talking to his reflection in the mirror. "I saw her with Ryan, God, just last week. In front of Hap's shop. They looked so happy together." Arlo wonders if she is trying to wound him on purpose, but then she adds, "I can't imagine anything worse for y'all. Are *you* okay?"

Though her question is the first kindness Arlo has received today, it makes him feel worse, even more angry at Artie's abandonment, at the unfairness of Lavinia's speech. Arlo shrugs, not trusting himself to answer.

"Did you know Sheriff Muñoz interviewed me?" she says. "The bouncer from Terpsi's too."

Arlo hadn't considered that the sheriff's interviews would dig into his own life as much as Artie's. Attacking a woman onstage then shooting a man two days later. He is the definition of erratic. And would calls to bandmates have led to calls to former bandmates, ex-girlfriends? Though there's nothing *that* dark in his past, he imagines Lavinia Barry taking notes on those calls instead of Muñoz. Heedless. Selfish. He turns to face Laurel, but she doesn't give, her eyes only on the mirror. He swivels back and meets her gaze there.

"What did you tell her?" he asks.

"I told her we knew each other in high school and that you were so drunk on Friday night you forgot yourself. The bouncer assessed you as both calm after the fact and appropriately embarrassed."

"Why would you help me?" he says, quietly enough that the bartender can't hear.

"I might have zero use for you, but even I know you would never hurt Artie on purpose. You may expect to get what you want when you want it, but you aren't a murderer."

Arlo remembers wanting Ryan to stop talking to him there on the riverbank, remembers wanting him anywhere but there in front of him. How much of what has gone wrong in the past week is just about him expecting to get what he wants?

He finds Laurel's face in the mirror again. "I'm sorry. What I did to you."

"Which part? Friday's assault or your high school stalking?"

Arlo looks down at the bar in embarrassment. He wants to push back against the word "stalking," but he stops himself. Laurel feels like a huge part of his past, yet this conversation is the longest they've ever spoken to each other. "It was that bad? All of it, not just Friday."

This gets her to turn, to actually look at him. "Seriously? You've *always* scared the shit out of me." She picks up her beer and drinks, wipes a line of sweat from the bottle with her index finger. "I never found any of your attention flattering. Not even the songs. What does it say about you, to have such an unwilling muse?"

Arlo hadn't named her, but his first album was full of Laurel and his unrequited love. Yet he had never bothered to imagine what she thought of the songs. In high school, he used to rail over the unfairness of her disdain. A punch of shame hits him in the gut. "I'm sorry. I didn't see how much I was taking from you."

She takes a long time reading his face. Then she says, "Funny. That wasn't nearly as satisfying as I thought it would be."

"You don't have to finish your beer with me," Arlo offers. "I can go."

Laurel shakes her head. "I don't have to forgive you to feel sorry for you." She takes another swallow, but when her friends appear on her other side, she stands to greet them. As she walks away without saying goodbye, Arlo marvels at how all that desire he couldn't contain a few days ago has evaporated. He had once thought he deserved her, more than deserved her. But he's beginning to see he may not deserve anyone.

SIX

JUNE HADN'T REALIZED March was at the funeral, but there is his back as he walks away from the church, already shucking off his suit jacket. Did he feel lucky, escaping the Briscoe condemnation from the pulpit in spite of his own heedlessness, his own selfishness? In spite of his own most recent unforgivable act? She had extracted from Peter a blow-by-blow of Vera's performance at his office the prior evening. It was good June hadn't seen March or she would have begun the casting out before Lavinia even got started.

June herself had beelined from the church, not even caring if Peter was behind her. In another mood she might have found humor in the way the rattled citizens of Olympus, here on the church lawn, look everywhere but directly at her. Instead, she just feels dirty. It's like she's been splattered with muck from a puddle hit by a passing car, but in this case, that car was also her husband. Peter comes to stand next to her but says nothing. June doesn't want to leave until they've talked to Artie, made sure they can't help in some way. She also doesn't want to look like she's skulking away with her tail between her legs. The pair of them stand, still being studiously avoided, until Thea and Lee join them. As a group, they watch March reach his truck and drive away.

"I didn't see Arlo in the truck. Did you?" Lee asks Peter, but he doesn't reply. Probably because Vera is striding toward them with an expression of gleeful validation. The town is about to get more spectacle, June fears. She should have skulked away while she had the chance.

Now Cole is also standing by her, on the opposite side from Peter. She doesn't acknowledge him, though she can feel the whisper of his suit jacket against her elbow. He's that close. When she called him yesterday, she told him not to come. That not seeing him anymore meant not seeing him anywhere. Normally when people ignore what she asks, she feels the need to force them to comply. But instead, she only feels grateful he is there. Vera stops in front of them, her look of triumph fading into somberness as she says hello to Thea, who—bless her—gives a single nod in reply. June suppresses an inappropriate impulse to introduce Cole to Vera. To Thea. Even Lee.

"Strange that you're here," Peter says to Cole with a frown, peering around June.

"Strange that you're here, too," June says to Vera.

"I'm here for Artie."

The gall of this woman, as if she can get credit for social politeness after again humiliating Hap. "If you and Artie were ever friends, you're not anymore," June says. "She will choose Hap over you. Especially with your threats to move away with Pete."

Vera raises her voice from calm to angry in a half second. It always catches June off guard, the way her daughter-in-law shifts in and out of moods like they're scarves. June's own moods are typically as intractable as straitjackets. Vera says, "I came because somebody *died,* and that's what you do. You show up for family, even as convoluted as this family is. I'd say more, but Lavinia Barry has already done an admirable job." Vera pauses and gives Lee a gentle smile. "Though I'm sorry other people, like you and Artie, got caught in the cross fire."

Vera turns back to June, the smile falling away. "You're happy to stand here next to Mr. Scarlet Letter, yet you'll still shun your own son, I bet." Somehow, in staying with her husband, June has aligned herself with him against a strange triumvirate of wounded women—Lavinia and Vera and even Lee now on the same team.

"You're just trying to evade blame," June says. "Even now, trying to make Hap think all this is his fault, not yours, not March's."

Vera laughs, her mouth open so wide June can see back to her molars. Then she reaches out and grabs June's hand. Her daughter-in-law's fingers are cool but her grip is strong. "You don't think there's enough blame to go around?" says Vera, squeezing hard. "Some for me, some for Hap, some for his mother—such a role model." June's cheeks redden, the sentence a slap.

In Vera's unyielding grip, June's knuckles shift and bone rubs against bone. Her family is silent, an additional chorus of judgment circled around her. She doesn't want to reckon with how things might have been different if she hadn't stayed with Peter, hadn't shown her children a warped definition of marriage.

Thea, in a tone that implies she can't be bothered with this mess, says, "I'm going inside to find Artie." June hears the clack of Thea's heels on the concrete steps up as she returns to the church. Peter and Lee are both avoiding June's eye. Cole, too, has his eyes cast down. But then she realizes he is staring at her hand, gone white from the force of Vera's grip.

June says, "You're the one who's ripped open Hap's heart by sleeping with his brother again." She struggles to pull her hand away, but Vera keeps ahold of her. Then Cole steps close to them, and he grabs Vera's wrist, tight.

"Let go," he says, his voice calm but firm. "Let go *now*." Vera only laughs. So Cole pulls Vera's fingers back, one by one, until June's hand is free and she feels the relief of blood rushing back to her fingers. Hap has finally appeared, and he stands behind Vera looking flabbergasted. When Cole drops Vera's hand, he gently cups June's. For just a second.

Vera leans forward and says, more defeated than angry, "He had already ripped open mine."

Before she can grab on again, Hap takes her by the shoulders and steers her away, saying, "Let's go." Peter still stands next to Lee. Peter, always just standing there. Doing so damn little. June's hand throbs. The dozen or so people who had been watching Vera's scene turn back to their own groups.

"You okay?" Peter finally asks. She doesn't bother responding. "Uh, Lee and I will go find Artie. I'll tell her you and I are heading home and make sure she doesn't need anything else." He weaves through the dispersing crowd of funeral-goers, Lee following behind. June is left with only Cole by her side.

"I said I couldn't see you anymore," she says quietly.

"I know. I'm afraid that sometimes I don't listen to good advice," he says. "A definite flaw in my character."

She meets his eye and can't stop a small smile coming to her face. "It's okay. I'm glad you're here."

Cole puts his hand on the back of her neck. More dirty laundry for everyone to see. Except for the very strange fact that Cole has made her feel washed clean.

SEVEN

AT FIRST, Hap has to pull at Vera to get her moving away from his mother, but by the time they are halfway across the lawn, Vera is moving so fast he has to lengthen his stride to keep up with her. She heads for her mother's car idling at the curb, and Hap can see Pete in his car seat. There will be no driving them home, no chance to wrest a conversation from her. They have to talk now. Because he could see it so clearly when she was yelling at June: his wife still loves him.

He grabs her hand and stops, leaning back a little to brace himself as she is jerked to a standstill. Before she can tear her hand away and start moving again, he says, "You'll talk to my mother about me breaking your heart, but not to me? If I can try to forgive you, without you even apologizing for sleeping with March again, why can't *you* try too?"

"I don't care anymore what you do. You need to stop caring what I do." She takes her hand back but stays facing him.

"I know you're mad. I know I'm saying the wrong things. But can't we lay it all out? Won't it be better, no matter what happens, for us to understand each other?"

"I *am* sorry," she says, begrudgingly. "I should have been strong enough to just leave you, not to hurt you again." She takes a deep breath. "And I'm sorry I sound angry. I'm angry at myself too. Want your own turn at repenting? I'll listen. Then I need to go home and get Pete fed."

"But a person has to know what he did before he can repent for it," Hap says.

"You're wrong there. We're Methodists. We can repent right before we die, in a wide, well-meant swath, and all will be forgiven."

"Do I have that option?"

"Sure. I'll forgive you right before you die." Vera looks exhausted as she pushes her heavy hair from her forehead, but he knows her so well he can hear her small smile buried behind the line, can feel the part of her that doesn't want to walk away and would rather keep talking to him, even as she sweats through her dress and one of her heels has sunk into the soft lawn. Had he ever thought he could leave her?

"So don't forgive me. But stay."

Her eyes fill and she puts her hand up to hide the tears from him. He's only seen her cry three times in his life, and twice have been this week. "I can't stay," she says.

"Then tell me."

Vera nods and Hap follows her to one of the big trees on the edge of the lawn, away from the path of folks headed to their cars. She leans against it and looks him in the eye. Hap feels suddenly like a man opening the door to a room that could hold anything inside it—a bare closet, a hospital room, the vacuum of space. He wishes he could take her hand again, but he simply waits.

"I'm leaving you because I finally realized you were sarcastic."

"What?" To Hap, it sounds nonsensical, like a punch line without the joke. "I'm barely sarcastic, biannually sarcastic."

"Do you know exactly when I decided I could love you?"

He has always told himself it was the brooch, her realizing he loved her personality as much, or more, than her face. He offers it up but already knows it's not the right answer.

"The brooch made me *like* you, or made me want to like you. It took longer to love you. I loved you that day you came to pick me up, the evening the handsy customer had come behind the bar and I knocked the blender over."

Hap can't recall the night but doesn't want to admit it. "Why then?"

"I decided you were different than any other man I'd dated. You understood my life. You told me the world was a hard place for women as beautiful as me."

Oh, shit, Hap thinks. The line, coming out of his wife's mouth, brings the memory rushing back.

"That Thanksgiving, when I started things with March, I finally realized you get this smile, this distinctive, half-cocked smile, when you're being sarcastic. It took me years to figure that out because, as you say, you are biannually sarcastic. I had always liked that smile, in particular, until I figured out what it meant and felt twice the fool. The moment I fell in love with you, you were being sarcastic. And I didn't even know it."

"But still," Hap says. "That's a small moment compared to the years we've been together. How can that be it?"

"I don't think it's small, but yes, that's not the only reason. You know my life. The high school drama teacher, the two restraining orders, the luck that kept attempted rapes from becoming actual rape. All those things happened, at least partially, because I was beautiful. You think my life has been easy for me because of my face, that the world threw itself, even threw you, at my feet because of it. Which means you think I am a bitch *despite* my treatment by the world and not *because* of that treatment. The person you think you love? That person is not me."

"It is you." He tries to put his palm against her cheek, but she pulls away.

"And who I fell in love with isn't you, either. I can't watch you put everyone's needs above your own and then think that makes you better than all the rest of us. I want a relationship, a real marriage, not to be an object that solidifies your own damn sense of self. I knew I'd have to leave as soon as our son started picking up on your cues, started to see me with your eyes."

Hap flinches at this, remembering all the times that, already, Pete has begun to take his side against Vera. *Mean mommy.*

"And Pete is already modeling you, starting to give up his own desires. Maybe now it's out of kindness, but before long he'll understand how to manipulate people with that. Just like you picked up the skill from June." She stands up straighter, adjusts her purse on her shoulder, and Hap knows she's about to walk away. "I can't respect a man who would fall in love with the spoiled narcissist you envision me to be. And I can't live with my son thinking that of me."

As she leaves him by the tree, Hap tries to process what she's told him. He gathers himself enough to follow her, reaching the car just as she puts her hand to the door.

"I never thought you were spoiled," he says, loud enough for her to pause.

"But you thought I had it easy," she counters. He doesn't answer. It was true. "I had it easy, and yet I was often so mean to you. I had it easy, and yet I have sex with the one person in the world that should be unforgivable even to a forgiving man like you. Then I do it a second time, and you're prepared to forgive me all over again. Because you are beneficent Hap, bestowing your grace upon us." She takes her hand from the car and leans into him to whisper in his ear. Not an act of intimacy but to make her final shot at close range. "Fuck your grace, Hap. It means shit to me." Then she gets in the car, barely getting the door shut before her mother starts driving away.

Hap sees, suddenly and completely, how much his idea of his wife had shaped his idea of himself. He is the unattractive, overweight man who has won the love of a beautiful woman. He is a husband whose kindness allows him to love an unkind wife. He is sympathy and empathy—enough to withstand a partner with none. The world has seen his wife slumming with him while all the while his buried ego has been confident he was slumming with her. When people define themselves in comparison to something else, they become that much more committed to never changing their minds about that something else. At least this is what he tells himself to justify why his empathy never extended to the place it was needed most.

EIGHT

PETER KNOWS BETTER than to hope his family will leave Lavinia's performance contained within the walls of the church. June silently seethes beside him on the ride home, and Thea scowls at him from the backseat when he catches her eye in the rearview mirror. He feels no need to talk about the speech himself. It's not like Lavinia said anything new about him, not like he hadn't been called far worse than a "greedy speculator." Both homes and land carry too much meaning for the people who lived there for *every* transaction to be free of hard feelings. His only true pang comes from Arlo getting extra blame due to his parentage. Without that shared blood, would Lavinia have insisted on Arlo's attendance? Would she have even thought to stave off her own grief by launching an attack? And Lee had to sit there, too, while Lavinia slandered her son. Still, no lasting harm done, Peter tells himself. No one dies of embarrassment.

It would've been hard enough to deal with June, especially after

Vera's ambush, but Artie had sent Thea away with them also. At least Artie hadn't seemed overly shaken. She was a little distant, perhaps, as she explained she and Lee were going to the reception, and she didn't think it would be wise for any Briscoe, even Thea, to attend. She may have been a bit stiff, too, as Thea hugged her goodbye. But she was carrying a heavy load, and those things were to be expected.

June often stews a few hours before starting their arguments, but Thea is unlikely to sit on her displeasure. Sure enough, before they've even made it to the interstate to head home, Thea says, "Hard enough to come back in these circumstances, but I also have to serve as an audience to Lavinia Barry's denunciations from the pulpit and Vera's from the church lawn. Me, along with a slew of Olympians, witnessing the show. A nightmare within a larger nightmare."

Peter waits for June to answer, but his wife stares out the window as if she's heard nothing at all.

"I wish it hadn't happened that way," Peter says. "But I didn't hear either woman calling you out, specifically. Perhaps just count yourself lucky."

"*I've* done nothing to be called out for." She crosses her arms and stares at Peter in the mirror before targeting June. "Who was your savior, Mom? The man that pried Vera off you."

When June still doesn't answer, Peter says, "Our vet got his hip broken by a donkey, and Cole's the fill-in. He helped your mother with the calves last week."

"That doesn't explain why you were so jealous of him."

Peter feels his cheeks flush. "I wasn't jealous. Don't know why you'd think that."

"Doesn't explain why he was at the funeral, either."

Peter had wondered the same thing. Why *had* the man come to the funeral? And why had he joined them on the lawn, like he was family, not just settling into their group but also peeling Vera off June? No one had needed him to do any of those things. Peter could have removed Vera, but he knew June wouldn't want him to. His wife needs protection from no one. Except, perhaps, him. Except, sometimes, herself.

June finally turns from the window, settling her gaze on the road in front of them. "For someone who doesn't want to be an audience, you're trying awfully hard to stir up trouble."

"Whatever," Thea says. But she changes the subject. "At least Artie didn't let Arlo pull her out of the church with him."

Peter had seen Arlo's extended, untaken hand. He thought it was just Artie wanting to stay longer, not some sign of a larger rift, but from Thea's tone, it's clear she took it as meaningful.

"What would you ladies like for dinner?" he asks. "Maybe we should stop by the grocery before we head home."

June says, "Artie needed to stay. I'm sure Arlo understood why."

Thea snorts. "I wouldn't put money on that. And don't you two go pushing Artie to forgive Arlo. Let her make her own decision."

"I doubt we'll have to push," says Peter. "They'll work it out themselves." As he says it, though, he can see Artie in his kitchen Sunday night, pulling her barstool away from her brother.

"Artie may be running short on forgiveness."

"If Artie's given up on forgiveness, I bet she can thank you for that," June says.

"I'm just helping her do what's best for *her*, not what's best for Arlo. And, honestly, do any of us here care more for Arlo's happiness than for Artie's?"

Peter feels the stab of Thea's statement. What she's said is true, but it makes him acknowledge the why—because Artie is kinder to him than Arlo. His preference is rooted in his own selfishness, proof Lavinia wasn't entirely off base in her judgment.

"You're wrong," he says, too loud for the car's interior. "There's no way Artie's happiness isn't tied to Arlo's. And Arlo's tied to hers. They have to patch things up."

Now it's June who's too loud, but her anger is all for Thea. "And who are you to say what we should and shouldn't do? How often do you see Artie, talk to Artie, compared to me? You don't understand the stakes because for you, losing your family would barely register as bad news. You're the one that should keep your mouth shut, not us."

"*My* family is in Chicago," Thea says. "Not here."

"Exactly," June says. "You don't understand us, especially not Artie. And I'm starting to doubt you'll have more empathy for your daughters than you can muster for parents and siblings. Not if they have opinions that differ from yours."

"I think we've had enough talking for now," Peter says. He turns on the radio to temper the silence.

"Drop me off at Artie's," Thea says, her voice stripped of any emotion.

"Honey, no. Have dinner with us," Peter says. "Artie's not even home yet."

"Drop me off."

No one speaks again until Peter's stopped in front of Artie's house. June has shut her eyes, but she asks Thea if she has a key. A small attempt at an apology that their daughter rejects by exiting the vehicle and slamming the car door so hard he and June rock in their seats. Peter decides to take the back roads to their house, as if peaceful views will lead to a peaceful car. June goes back to staring out the window.

Finally, when they are just a half mile from home, his wife speaks. "Do you even care what it felt like, to have to sit there beside you in church? I realize everyone in town already knows each bad thing you've done, but I always thought if they were judging anyone, it was you, not me. Your business decisions, your moral failings. But that was wishful thinking. Sitting there today, I could feel their judgment. That I was complicit. I felt complicit myself. And you don't even seem bothered. You escape even being upset by it, just like you escaped Vera's tirade on the lawn. It all falls in my lap."

"It's done, June. Why worry over it?"

"Because it's not done. Hap's marriage is wrecked, and at least some of that is March's fault. And we have no idea what will happen with Artie and Arlo, how they will weather this." She sighs and covers her eyes with her hand. "I kept thinking one day, if I waited long enough, you'd be more of a help."

The fact that she doesn't say "instead of a hurt" seems a good sign. He reaches out to her, puts his hand on her knee.

"Things are this bad, and you *still* think you can wait it out," she says. "Don't you realize the only reason you get to be so hands-off is because there are other hands still doing their job? What kind of life would we have had if all of us acted like you?"

Likely an easier life, Peter thinks, but he knows to keep his mouth shut.

She says, "The only way I could manage our marriage was to take the same tack, to ride the waves rather than get out of the storm. If I had made you face the consequences of your actions, if I had left you, maybe it would have made you a better man. Your kids would have benefited from that, even if I didn't."

"You sound like Lavinia." He draws his hand back from her knee. "That all in the world would be well if I just got a taste of justice. Like my life hasn't been filled with troubles and repercussions, just like everyone else's. I am who I am, June, and I don't think that's bad." She frowns at him, and her intractability pushes him into anger. "You're too smart to believe people can change. None of us change," he says. He had thought it was a worldview they both subscribed to. Her threat of leaving him had been the gun to his head that enabled him to be faithful, but it wasn't change.

"We do," she said, her voice surprised, as if she is shocked to find she thinks that. "I have."

NINE

Aʀʟᴏ ɪs ʟʏɪɴɢ ᴏɴ ᴀ ʙᴇᴅ in a Houston motel, miserably staring at the ceiling. The air conditioning turned to high but his suit still on. After seeing Laurel, he had retrieved his car from March's, not even checking in with him, and headed east. With the sheriff's assurances that no charges were looming, he could finally get out of Olympus, freedom for at least one night. But on this still-made bed, with his shoes off but his feet throbbing, he isn't feeling free.

Arlo had always assumed he saw the world clearly—understood both his own motives and how his actions impacted others. He had been wrong. Despite Lavinia's words, he knows he isn't like Peter, but being different doesn't necessarily mean being better. He is sure Laurel would agree. And now, Artie too. He can't blame her.

A phone call from March lifts his misery. It's quick, with no time to ask questions, but all that matters is that Artie wants to talk. Arlo can face all his faults, figure himself out, if he has her help. He will do whatever she asks, for as long as it takes, until things between them are right.

He drives straight back to Olympus, to March's house, to March and Artie on the front porch swing. Artie is up and standing by the time he reaches the steps, but her wide stance and crossed arms keep him from climbing up to join her. March also gets to his feet and slips quickly behind her, going into the house without saying hello.

"I talked to the sheriff after the funeral," Arlo begins. "She said charges aren't likely, and she hoped Lavinia's stunt at the funeral might feel like enough payback for the family."

"Stunt," Artie says, her voice impatient. "Is that the term Muñoz used?"

"Her . . . eulogy. I shouldn't have called it a stunt." He had thought starting with the good news would help, but he's already botched things. "I'm so sorry, Artie. I don't even know where to start with my apologies. It's like it's too much to bear, and my brain can't grasp all the weight."

"Too much to bear?" Her voice is calm and flat now, worse than if she'd started yelling at him. "What have you lost, compared to Ryan's mother? What have you had to bear, compared to me? I killed the man I loved. I did that. Then I helped plan his funeral, bought him a suit, and tried to comfort the family I took him from, all the while hiding what I'd done. Lying to people who have every right to the truth of how their son died." She descends the stairs, points her finger at him. "And what have you shouldered? Did you even stay with Ryan at the funeral home? Or did you take one look at the body and bolt?"

She guesses his failings so easily. "I couldn't stand it, not with the weight of you being mad at me, too."

"So that's also on me? Won't you own anything, Arlo? Even your offer to take the blame for the shooting was just a way to avoid telling me the truth. That I took a blind, stupid shot, but that you knew exactly who I was aiming at."

"You can't think it was premeditated," he insists, fear making his voice quaver. "I didn't plan it. I never thought you'd take the shot." And yet, didn't it somehow feel to him like fate? She aimed and fired so quickly. If she'd paused and asked for terms, Arlo would have come clean, told her the spot was Ryan. If she had said anything, one simple word of assent, Arlo would have reached out to place a hand on the rising barrel of her gun. A hundred things had to conspire together to turn her into an unwitting murderer. So many more things to blame than a recklessly spoken sentence. But then why does he feel like he is standing there, lying to her? Some tiny voice, buried deep in him, gives him the answer he doesn't want to hear. He didn't think she would shoot, but that didn't mean that he didn't, just for a half second, *want* her to shoot.

He needs to own this. "I know this is all on me," he says. "I'll spread every bad action, every buried motive, on the table for you. You can help me understand it all."

"How would your understanding help *me*? Even if it allowed me to forgive you, what would that forgiveness get me? You'll say it will make me feel better—and you may even believe that—but the real goal is letting *you* feel better. I don't *want* to forgive you for getting Ryan killed. I don't want to forgive you for boxing me inside a set of lies."

"But we promised each other," he says.

"A promise made by children."

"No. A promise made by you. To me."

She raises her hands in defense, as if he has tried to grab her. "I didn't understand what the promise meant then," she says. "It's not my fault your heart didn't grow enough to understand it even now." She takes a few steps back from him. "You aren't welcome in my house. You aren't welcome in my life." Then she walks past him to her Jeep, as if nothing is wrong, as if she has ended a normal conversation. He drops down on the porch steps, watches her pull out onto the road, and tries to keep the Jeep in sight as long as he can.

The screen door behind him opens and slams shut again. March sits on the step above and hands him a beer. "I know we've been drinking too much, but this is no night to quit. Who knows how much longer I'll get to stay in this house. Or in town. We might as well drink while we can."

"I should be alone," Arlo says, his voice strained in a way that would normally send March off without another word. But it doesn't.

"Maybe she'll change her mind," says March, though with such little conviction Arlo doesn't bother contradicting him. And though he knows he should be grateful for March's support, it feels paltry compared to what he's always gotten from Artie. "Maybe she just needs some space," March says. "Time without Thea in her ear."

"How'd that space solution work for you? Turns out two years wasn't enough—less than a week, and you're back at it with your sister-in-law. If a situation needs space, it's already irretrievably fucked." Arlo puts the unopened beer down on the step. He should go inside, close himself in the guest room. Or go for a drive. Go back to the motel. Anything but continue this conversation. But he's bound up in his insistence that space solves nothing, and he won't prove March right. "She needs your whole family out of her ear. I'd be with her now if it wasn't for all of you."

"If she had no other option, you mean."

He can tell March is sorry as soon as he says it—he won't meet Arlo's eye—but Arlo doesn't want an apology from him. "As if we would have chosen any of you, a walking collection of deadly sins: Peter's lust and June's wrath and Thea's pride and Hap's envy."

"And me?" says March, no longer looking sorry.

"You're the worst of all, the whole collection in one. Your father never slept with his brother's wife, your mother never blacked out from her rage, Hap envies only that Vera briefly picked you, not anything else about who you are." March's face shifts into a deep scowl, and the anger between them is a relief, a vacation from how Arlo felt seconds ago. "Wait, I'm wrong. You're at least missing pride. A man with pride wouldn't have come back, wouldn't be desperate for the love of a woman who'll never give it to him."

"I'm done with Vera."

"I'm not talking about Vera, you dumb fuck."

Though he was angling for this—for March's rage to take over and allow Arlo to punch back with no guilt, safe in the harbor of self-defense—he's still caught off guard by the way March's face turns into a theater mask, all emotion but no consciousness. Then a blur of movement and March's forearm pinning Arlo's neck against the stair railing. The crushing of his larynx is so painful it almost blocks out the realization that he can't inhale.

Arlo tries to push back, to get a grip on March's arm so he can wriggle underneath it, but the noise of the scuffle has brought the dogs outside. Now, besides March's wrathful face, there are two growling heads that sound as if gears are being crushed inside of them. One barks so loudly Arlo can feel his own eardrum, and warm saliva smacks his cheek. He shuts his eyes and waits for contact.

Instead, he hears March's voice, suddenly calmer. "Hey, hey, it's okay," he says. The arm is pulled away from his throat. Arlo thinks March is talking to him, but he opens his eyes to see March holding out his hands to both dogs, trying to soothe them. March lays a hand on each head, stroking them between their ears. "You're a lucky son of a bitch," March says. "I never pop back out that fast."

"You're improving," Arlo says, and though he believes it, it still comes out coated in sarcasm. He tries to swallow but has to cough instead.

"No. I'm no different, no matter how much I want to think otherwise." March moves, sitting down on the lawn next to the dogs with his back to Arlo. "I think you should stay somewhere else for a while." They watch a car drive past the house, flip its headlights against the fading dusk. March pulls the closest dog to him and presses his face into its neck. He hears March inhale the dog's smell, hold it in. Arlo can do nothing but go inside to pack up his things, allowing March privacy with the one comfort he has left.

TEN

IT'S ALMOST DARK when June parks on Joe's lawn. There's no driveway, and everyone else is on the lawn too—Joe's truck, Cole's truck,
and the Buick that belongs to Joe's wife, Betty. June creeps into a
space between the two trucks, an attempt to shield her car from view.
Then she sits, still not sure she can do what she's come here to do. As
the light fades, more details become visible through the kitchen window and she sees Betty's head above the sink. She would have sat for
longer, gathering will, if she hadn't realized Betty was peering back
through the window at her. She has no choice but to get out now.

The door swings open as she reaches it, and Betty smooths down
her hair as if June is an unexpected gentleman caller. She can hear the
sounds of a baseball game in the background.

"June," Betty says. "Got a sick cow? I thought Cole had his cell on
him for emergencies."

"I hadn't thought to call ahead. Sorry for interrupting your eve-

ning. Cole here?" She nods toward the sound of the Astros, the sound
of one of their batters being struck out, before remembering Cole's
hatred of baseball.

"He's staying in our travel trailer. Walk around the side, head for
the flower trellis, and it'll be hidden behind it."

"Thanks," June says. She gives a friendly wave and backs away from
the door, trying to keep her smile relaxed. Nothing to see here, no
woman sneaking out on her husband.

June goes around the side of the house, skirting a flowerbed that
has seen better days, half-wild monkey grass and the dead remains
of some climbing vine. The backyard, though, is a smooth, cropped
bed of Coastal Bermuda, and the edge of the lawn is marked by a tall
lattice covered in vines. The lattice is an entanglement of green with
the pink of morning glories, all the buds rolled up tight, and splashes
of white—newly opened moonflowers that smell like jasmine and
sunscreen. She can make out a light from the trailer, barely filtering
through leaves.

Cole is sitting in a patio chair, eyes shut and oblivious to the swirl
of moths battering around the lighted window above him. Earbuds
snake from either side of his head. His fingers loop around a highball
glass on a tiny metal table next to him. The liquid is the distinctive
urine-yellow of chardonnay, cut with half-melted ice cubes. Cole's
foot is tapping, and every so often he tosses his head.

Though June would like to stay here for an hour, smiling at the sight
of him, she makes herself move. When she reaches him, she crouches
down and puts her hand above his knee. Cole's eyes fly open. She can
tell from his expression that he is well on his way to drunk, if not there
already. She tugs an earbud out. "What are you listening to?"

"Sex Pistols. Clear-my-head music, drives out the thoughts." He
blushes, but he puts his hand over hers, still above his knee. With her
free hand, she lifts the earbud from Cole's lap and puts it in her own
ear. She knows the band name but not the music. She likes how jangly
it is, how it feels so foreign next to the familiar sounds of cicadas, the
familiar feeling of sweat against the collar of her shirt.

There's no second chair, so she sits on the grass in front of him, using his knee for balance, leaving the hand there even after she is settled.

"What are you doing here, June?" He says it with a sort of wonder, as if she has performed a miracle.

She closes her eyes and listens to the music, but after a verse or two, it abruptly stops and leaves her feeling like herself again. She wishes he would have left it on. "I came to see you, of course." She pulls away from him and places her hands on the ground behind her, leaning back.

"Where's Peter?"

"Get me a glass of that wine, and I'll tell you about my evening so far."

"Do Joe and Betty know you're back here?"

"Betty thinks I have a cow emergency."

"She'll figure out pretty quickly that you don't with your car still sitting there."

"I don't care."

"I'll care for you. Betty's a terrible gossip, and I'm afraid today's public stoning might have whetted the town's appetite."

"You want me to leave?"

"Yesterday, you thought it was better that we didn't see each other anymore. I probably shouldn't have gone to the funeral, and you probably shouldn't be here. The last thing I want is to be a source of regret for you."

"Let me worry about that," she says. There's something loose in his gaze, in his motions, that makes June wonder if there's already one empty bottle of wine inside that Airstream. She looks behind him, sees a dirt road that cuts between where they sit and a pasture beyond them. "How about I go back out, drive away, and then swing around and park on the road behind you?"

"There's a barbed wire fence in the way."

"Like I haven't crawled through barbed wire before."

Cole opens his mouth and shuts it again. If she can get one more glass of wine in him, she suspects he will cease trying to protect her from herself.

"I'd appreciate a conversation. I don't want to go back home," she says.

He looks at her a long beat, as if the right answer to her proposition can be seen somewhere in her face, then he says, "Wait here." He picks up his glass and walks up the steps and into the trailer. His path is almost a straight one. She assumes he has gone to get the wine, but a few minutes pass and she still sits alone, her butt starting to feel damp on the grass. She can make out the figure of Cole scuttling back and forth through the screen door. She doesn't feel like waiting.

June opens the door and finds Cole shoving clothes out of a laundry basket into the drawers of a tiny dresser. "They're clean," he says, shutting a drawer as he turns. "Just hadn't stored them." June can see the blue plaid of a pair of boxer shorts caught halfway out of the drawer. He picks up an assortment of dirty dishes and lays them in the sink, the pile growing until it heaps above the edges.

"Stop fussing," she tells him, and she slides into the dining area— a small table and a bench seat on either side.

"I know outside is nicer, but if you want to talk, I don't want our voices to carry." He shuts the door as well as the two open windows above the bed. He turns on the air conditioning, and the hum masks any noise from outside.

"Too hot of a night for Betty and Joe to keep their windows open," she says.

"Still. I told you she's a gossip."

"I've known Betty for twenty years. You don't have to tell me for me to know. I'm telling you I don't care."

Cole doesn't look at her. He peers into his tiny fridge and pulls out a box of white wine. He retrieves another highball glass from above the sink, holds the box above it, and opens the spigot, wine splashing down. "It's fairly bad. I was putting ice in it to cut the cheapness. Want ice for yours?"

"Nah," she says. "I've got no palate, anyway."

He tops off his own and joins her at the table, sliding her glass in front of her.

"How many do I need to have to catch up with you?"

He looks at her steadily. "I don't think I have enough left for that.

Maybe, if I stopped with this glass, which I will not. You're making me nervous." He smiles, though, as if his nervousness is a pleasure to him.

June tells Cole about her argument with Thea after the funeral. "I know I have a million faults, and Thea brings them out in me more than anyone else. But this was too far, even for my own sharp tongue. I did it solely to hurt her. What would Hap think of me, if he knew what I said?"

"Why Hap?"

"He's always been the best version of me, like me on my best day, a best day I might never have made it to. Kind and empathetic, smart. He can translate the mess of his own interior into physical objects people want to look at, even pay money for. My own mess never got translated into anything except bile." June takes a big swallow of the wine, runs her finger over the rim of the glass, squeaking. "But this best version of myself is also married to a cheating spouse. You heard Vera. I warped him."

"That's not your fault. That's just love. That's the story of a million spouses forgiving, certain the betrayal won't happen again."

"But why does the best version of myself get the same shitty problems?"

"Because shitty problems are that common?" Cole takes a drink, forgetting he has refilled his glass. Wine splashes on his face, and he sighs and sets the glass back down.

"You're cute when you're drunk," June says. But the frown stays on her face. "So you're trying to take my blame away from me, too?"

"What else have I taken from you?"

She wants to tell him *peace of mind,* but that isn't true. She feels peaceful here, in this tatty trailer, even when she has no reason to. She tells him, "You've taken my ability to be righteously indignant."

He grins. "What a horrible loss." He picks his glass back up and plinks it against the glass in front of her. "Here's to the glory of righteous indignation."

June sips her wine. Then she gets up and slides into the seat next to him, taking the glass from his hand and replacing it with her own hand. "You've changed me," she says.

She kisses him, and though he doesn't move to embrace her, he squeezes more and more tightly on her hand. Kissing Peter is so familiar to her, it carries no thought anymore, like tucking your hair behind your ear or wiping sweat from your forehead. It might feel good, make you feel better, but you don't experience it the same way. She feels Cole's kisses in a dozen ways at once—the smell, the pressure, the taste.

"Let's go to bed," she says, mouth pressed up against his ear. He tries to pull away from her, but there is nowhere to go on that tiny bench seat.

"Not while I'm drunk and you're so upset."

"I don't feel upset," she says.

"I know you enough to know you're not acting like yourself."

"That's not a bad thing. I'm in need of drastic measures. I refuse to wait this out." She wraps her hand around the back of his neck. "You can tell me to leave all you want, but I will continue to refuse. And you are too drunk to drive. If you go off on foot, I will follow you." She kisses him again then pulls back and waits for him to speak.

"At least go move your car to the road in back. I'll wait for you by the fence."

She weighs his tone. "You think once I get back out into the fresh air, I'll come to my senses. I'll get in my car and go back home."

"I think it's a possibility. I want to give you that option."

She hops up, is out the door and headed to her car before he can say anything else, jogging across the backyard, then slowing to a walk once she reaches the front in case Betty is watching.

She doesn't have a single doubt until she is back in her car. Then looking at the CD player reminds her of Arlo, which reminds her of every other damn person in her family. The legion of them, in here with her.

THURSDAY

ONE

Aᴏᴛᴇʀ ᴊᴜɴᴇ'ꜱ ᴏᴜᴛʙᴜʀꜱᴛ in the car, Peter had given her a wide berth in the house. She scarcely said two words to him all afternoon. To help repair things, he cooked dinner for them both, but when he went to tell her it was ready, she was gone. She had driven away while he was otherwise occupied. Irked, he consumed most of the dinner himself, then stayed up watching TV, or half-watching, until 11 p.m. He didn't want to give June the satisfaction of seeing him waiting up, so he went to bed.

He remembers half an hour of listening for the sound of June's car, being annoyed when the air conditioning kicked on and covered up the outside noises. And now it's 7 a.m., somehow. He often wakes up alone, but not to the blue and white quilt still pulled up on June's side, the pillows plump. There's no smell of coffee. Has June actually been out all night? He grabs his phone from the bedside table and calls her, something he should have done the night before, as soon as he saw her car was gone. There's no answer—just two rings and straight to voicemail. He hangs up.

Downstairs, he tries to shake loose his new fears as he makes coffee, the first time in years it hasn't been made for him. As he waits for it to brew, he calls March. To ask his son to do the undignified things Peter can't bring himself to do. After they talk, the thought of puttering around the house, waiting either for his son to call or for June to wander back home, seems intolerable. He needs to be useful. But more than that, he needs to be around a person who makes him feel better about himself instead of worse. Just for a little while. He tells himself Artie may have spent the night at Lee's, so he'd be checking on her. Seeing if she and Arlo talked after the funeral. Being a more active parent, as June had admonished him to be.

Fifteen minutes later, he stands at Lee's door. He's worried it's too early, that he might even wake her, but Lee answers the door fully dressed. And surprised to see him. She's also—he can tell, even without any practice at reading her expressions for many years—not quite pleased at his arrival. Not quick to invite him in.

"I thought I might check in on Artie. How was the reception?" he says.

"Fine," Lee says. "Lavinia didn't talk to us, but we sat with Mrs. Mann for a while. Artie's not here, though. She's at her house." Peter nods but doesn't say anything. Finally, Lee says, "Want a cup of coffee?" She steps back from the door, and he follows her to the kitchen, where she begins to make a fresh pot.

"I thought you had extra. You don't have to make another."

But she waves him off and tells him she'll join him on the back porch, a trace of aggravation in her voice. Ten minutes later, she arrives with the coffee and sits down next to him. He decides to come clean. "I'm sorry for busting in here. I was at loose ends this morning. June didn't come home last night. She's exasperated with me."

"Oh, Peter," Lee says, and finally she is herself again, looking at him with concern, feeling bad on his behalf. "I'm sorry about that. But maybe you should be out looking for her, not here?"

And he should be. But he feels a desperate need to be around the one thing he's proud of doing well this week. He always assumed Artie had built the wall between his family and Lee—information didn't cross that line, like a separated highway, Artie the concrete barrier down the middle. But *he* was the one that built the wall. There was a better path he could have taken, one that treated Lee like a person rather than a mistake to hide. Being a friend to Lee this week had been its only bright spot, and he had tried to taint even that by showing up this morning just to make himself feel better.

He sighs. "I should be. But I'm pretty sure I know where she is."

"With the man from the funeral?"

"Yes," he says.

"And if she is?"

"What do you mean?"

"Could you forgive *her* for once?"

"Yes. No question," he says. Of course he would. The real issue was whether she would even seek his forgiveness. Whether, this time, she'd just be gone for good.

Lee gives him a weak smile, as if she reads his mind and sympathizes. Then she lights up, a real, genuine smile, but it is focused on something just beyond Peter's shoulder. He turns and sees Arlo sliding open the patio door, yawning but clearly surprised to see his father on Lee's back porch.

"Well," he says. "Since you're already here, stay for breakfast, Peter? I need to talk to you." He pauses, his face tensing up as if he is about to drink something unpleasant. "I may need your help."

TWO

WHEN HIS FATHER CALLS, March lies and says he was already up. He holds the cell away from his mouth as he sucks air into a yawn. He's pleased to have been called on for help, his exile not already in effect. But after he hears what his father wants him to do, his feeling of optimism is undercut by the news his mother slept elsewhere. At this point any thought of his family brings with it the image of a swift knife cutting through a rope. Something heavy, long held in the air, hitting the ground.

"So maybe you could drive past Hap's? Not stop, if you don't want, but see if her car is there."

March can tell how preoccupied his father must be because he doesn't realize March patrolling past his brother's house is a far more dangerous thing than actually stopping.

"And if she's not there, check Artie's?" March asks.

"Oh. She won't be looking for Thea's company, not after yesterday."

His father clears his throat in such a mannered way, March is afraid to hear what he says next. "Maybe you could drive past the vet's place, Joe and Betty's? Just see if her car is there, then call me."

"Why would she be there? She's never been close to Betty."

"No, no. She's struck up a friendship with the guy Joe brought in to help him out. He's the vet that came out last weekend to help her with the calves."

"He's staying with Joe?"

"Yeah."

He doesn't see how his father could even contemplate his mother spending the night there. But there's a detail nagging at March.

"He a short guy, bald?" He can see the man in his suit, leaning against the back wall of the church. His mother's head turning. The same man that witnessed Hap welcoming him home with a sledge-hammer last Friday.

"You saw them together?"

"Just saw him at the funeral."

"Oh, yes. He was quite present at the funeral."

Peter's tone keeps March from asking more. "I'll head out. Report back in within the hour."

"Thanks, son." There is so much gratitude in his father's voice, it hurts March's chest. And that hurt lingers, even as he gets his stuff together, deals with the dogs. What Vera told him at the funeral, what Arlo echoed last night, has sunk in. He has to stop seeking his mother's love and approval, has to accept it will never come. But. What might happen if just this once he has the moral high ground?

IT'S QUIET AT HAP'S HOUSE. March had hoped to see his mother's car, but there's only Hap's vehicle in the driveway. Instead of continuing past, March pulls in behind his brother. He can't bring himself to get out, though, and picks up his cell. If Hap won't pick up the phone, he won't open the door for March either. It will spare March being denied on his front step.

"Why are you calling from my driveway?" Hap says as an answer. March now sees the open curtains, his brother's body blurry behind the glass.

"Have you talked to Mom?"

"Not since yesterday. What's wrong?"

"Another fight with Dad, I think. Can I come in?"

There is silence on the other end. March looks at his phone, sees "call ended" and sighs. But then Hap opens the front door, stands waiting. March hops from his truck and jogs up the lawn. He is happily surprised to follow his brother's receding back into the kitchen.

Hap refills his coffee cup, then sits at the table, scattered with yet another metalworking project—jewelry, it looks like. March sits too, apprehensive, waiting for Hap to insist he stand back up. Instead, Hap says, concerned, "Mom's MIA?"

"Dad said she didn't come home last night. Asked me to look around for her."

"Has he called her?"

"I assumed he had."

"You call her?"

"I didn't try. She's not going to pick up a call from me."

"But you think she would talk to you if you found her?" Hap places his big hands over the scattered pieces of metal wire and gently slides them back so he can lean on the table.

"It's more like recon. Pin down where her car is. Dad seems to think she might be . . . with someone. Maybe that new vet."

"You really think she spent the night at his house? Our *mother*?"

When March woke up this morning, the last thing he thought he'd be doing was sitting at a table with Hap and discussing his mother's sex life. He wants to speed away from the topic as fast as he can. "Who can say? Family members are peeling off at the speed of light, no one talking to anyone." March drops his head in his hands, flattened by the bigness of it all, and afraid to examine the idea that, perhaps, if he had stayed in New Mexico, none of this would have happened. It's silent in the kitchen except for birdsong from outside.

"We're talking," Hap says.

March raises his head, amazed to find Hap is looking at him with something that could be mistaken for affection. "I can hardly believe it."

"Well, Vera's gone and Mom has apparently become some different person from the woman who raised us. I've got to have someone to talk to." Hap drinks from his cup. "I still think you're an asshole. But I'm an asshole too."

"I can't see that being true."

"Maybe it's not best for Vera to be married to me."

"Maybe it's not best for you to be married to Vera."

Hap shakes his head and pulls his phone from his belt. "I'll try calling Mom." March can hear her voicemail pick up from the other side of the table. "Looks like you'll have to do that drive-by." Hap walks him to the door. His lip is slightly curled on one side. The hint of a smile.

"What?" March asks.

"You're easier to stomach when you're swollen and bruised. I'm just saying, if you want to be able to call me, to drop by the shop, it may be necessary for me to punch you in the face once a month."

"I would consider it a fair trade," March says. He has to say more, has to show Hap he isn't making a mistake by forgiving him. "I walk around all the time, now, with the guilt of what I did to you. It's like some new . . . gravity, maybe? I know you think I'm no different, but I kind of am." March shocks himself by giving Hap a hug. Shocks Hap as well, but after a couple of seconds, his brother squeezes him back.

Reaching joe's house twenty minutes later, March slows to a crawl. He doesn't spot his mother's car. He's relieved at first, but he knows his father's fears aren't unfounded. He makes a U-turn and parks on the street.

The front door swings open as he approaches it with Betty grinning at him from inside. He has always liked that smile he gets from older women—appreciation without expectation. "Well, March Briscoe," she says. "It's been years and years. More problems with the cow?"

So June must have stopped by. "Have you seen my mom this morning? She left her cell at home, and my dad's been trying to reach her."

"Haven't seen her since last night when she came to talk to Cole."

Shit. "He go out to check the cow with her?"

"Not sure. He's out back in the old Airstream. Feel free to walk around and ask him."

"Thanks," March says, and he follows the sidewalk to the back of the house, sees the silver of the trailer glinting through the open spaces of a trellis. What's behind the trellis is a surprise, even though he's been preparing himself for the worst. His mother sits on a metal chair, hair pulled into a messy bun, wearing a man's T-shirt and a pair of plaid boxer shorts. She has a chicken in her lap, pinned tight with one hand while the other hand dabs ointment onto a gash on its wing. She hasn't even noticed March, is muttering something half-kind and half-dictatorial to the chicken.

"Mom?"

She looks up, and he expects her to drop the chicken and flee. But she only looks momentarily confused, as if she can't place him. Then, upon putting the name to the face, she smiles. Oh, it breaks his fucking heart right open.

"Hey, March. Want to give me a hand?"

He walks over and kneels in front of her, taking the proffered chicken. The bird swivels its head, getting a better look at him. The hen must find him acceptable because he feels her relax into his hands. "What happened to her?" he says.

"Dog attack. Can't put her back in with the flock until she heals up, or the other coldhearted fowl will beat up on her even worse. She's occupying Cole's chicken condo over there." March sees a dog crate next to the trailer. "Okay," she says, putting the cap back on the ointment. "You can drop her."

March obeys, and the chicken turns her attention to the grass, hunting for bugs. He can feel his mother looking at him, but he's not ready to meet her eye. He wants to tell her what happened last night with Arlo and Artie. That his father is worried about her. That the better future Hap may have just gifted him with—his family returned to him—also feels dependent on her not sitting here, in a stranger's boxer shorts. Instead March stands up from his crouch and says, "Dad wanted me to find you. I haven't called him yet, though."

She nods. "Sorry he roped you into this."

"It was nice to be asked." He's still watching the chicken, and his mother is still watching him. He feels assessed but not, for once, found lacking.

The trailer door opens, and March sees the vet. "This is March, come to find me," June says by way of introduction. Almost brightly. March finally looks at his mother, who is gazing at this stranger with no shirt on, hanging half out of a tiny trailer, and wonders how it is she seems more content than she's ever been.

"Ah. I didn't recognize you without your brother whaling on you." Cole is watching him warily but says, "Do you like pancakes?"

His mother nods in agreement. "Have you eaten? Stay."

"Sure." Once Cole has ducked back inside, he says, "Dad's worried, though. Maybe you could at least text him?"

"I will." She gets up from the chair. "At some point, I will."

To keep her from walking away, March tentatively puts his hand on her arm. "We're coming apart," he says. "Arlo and Artie. Me and Arlo. Hap and Vera." Saying it out loud is bad enough, but it's worse when his mother doesn't disagree. "And now you and Dad, too."

"Me staying with your father isn't what makes us a family," she says, such certainty in her voice. He wants to argue that yes, of course it does. "Staying with your father didn't make me a mother to you. I think it might have kept me from it. My resentment of him always distorting my reactions to you."

March shakes his head. "Everyone was fine before I came back. I fucked things up again."

"Everything wasn't fine. Me being here isn't your fault. Artie not speaking to Arlo isn't your fault. You make amends with your brother, but don't claim all the rest of this." His mother reaches up and pushes his hair off his forehead. It must be decades since she's comforted him that way, but his forehead remembers the feeling of her hand pressed just there. It is only now, when she looks at him without a pinch of judgment, that he realizes every memory of his mother's face he can summon up is freighted with it.

She says, "It will all be okay, one way or the other. Go ahead and text your father that you found me and that I'll be home before lunch. Then help me move some furniture so we can have a proper outdoor breakfast."

THREE

Hᴀᴘ ᴀʀʀɪᴠᴇꜱ at his mother-in-law's house as they are finishing a late lunch. He's nervous, and he assumes it's because this conversation is so important. And also, perhaps, because the jewelry box in his pocket reminds him of proposing to Vera, how he'd been so sure she would say no. The door opening to his mother-in-law's angry face doesn't help, making him feel like a very unwelcome, very unasked-for guest.

Vera's mother used to love Hap, but that was before his Christmas present to Vera of a public shaming, before the woman moved from Lubbock to keep a closer eye on her daughter and new grandson. Nothing that has happened in the past week seems to have surprised her, and she is shaking her head in disapproval even as she's opening the door. Vera joins her, joins in the head shaking. At least Hap can see his son, still in his high chair, smiling at him with real excitement. He bangs the tray in front of him with a spoon, Pete's usual signal that he wants his father to pick him up. Hap waves to the boy, knowing he cannot just walk in.

"Sorry for interrupting lunch. Vera, could I borrow you for five minutes?"

Neither woman says a word. His mother-in-law actually clucks her tongue.

"Five minutes. And I promise I won't show up unannounced again." He doesn't think Vera will agree and that he'll have to make his pitch with an audience, but then Pete calls out for him, sad already that his father hasn't come to pick him up. Hap sees Pete's distress bothers Vera as badly as it bothers him.

"Three minutes," she says and pushes past him. Her mother shuts the door in his face before he even has the time to turn.

The only furniture on the porch is a hanging swing. His wife allows him to sit next to her, and the chains squeak as it shifts with their weight. He leans back and pulls a small jewelry box from his pocket.

"What the hell is wrong with you? We are eons past apology presents," she says, refusing to touch it. "A marriage can't be solved with art, for fuck's sake."

"It's not like the brooch, when I made something for you without even understanding the real reason why." Hap pops open the container, holding it in front of her face. She averts her eyes, still fuming.

"This will not work, Hap."

"Fine. But you're going to have to take a look to prove it to me."

She does, but Hap suspects it's only because she notices his hand shaking, the nerves amplifying as he waits. Inside is an aquamarine pendant, a big stone with its bottom half obscured by a light patina of sand, permanently fused to its polished surface. The faceted top catches the light except where three tendrils of silver emerge, seemingly from the stone itself. Around those spots, the gem is unpolished and raw, as if it has scar tissue. The tendrils wind into each other and form a loop for a chain.

She blinks but she refuses to take it. Hap can't even guess what she's thinking. Then he understands. His nerves are because he actually *doesn't* know this woman. His body is admitting his brain got her all wrong.

She shrugs. "I've seen it. Now I'm going back to lunch."

"I think I've got ninety seconds left," he says. "Tell me what it looks like."

"The sea and the sand. If you tell me you've booked a vacation, I'm going to pummel you on the front lawn in full view of the neighbors. Did you hear a thing I said yesterday?"

Hap keeps the box aloft, still in front of her. "You love Key West. It's this beautiful place. People are drawn to it. They want to possess some small part of it. So people come and cover it with buildings. Tourists flock in, clogging streets, trashing the beaches, vomiting in the bushes. The day-to-day life of the place is worse—harder—because of what its beauty draws."

She leans back, just a little, so her shoulders rest against the swing. "Are you saying our marriage is like you vomiting on me?"

"I have a plan," he says. "I found two apartments for rent in the same complex, right on the water in Key West. One for you and Pete, one for me. I found a shop that was hiring, and my business here can function without me for a while. It should be enough to cover our bills there and keep paying the mortgage here. I propose a six-month adjacent-separation away from all the things that helped make me who I am. Maybe I can change. I'd like to try. For you and for Pete. I'd like to be the man you thought you fell in love with. And if, in a few months, I'm still failing at that, I'll respect your decision."

Vera eyes him. "Is this because you can't stand me and March living in the same town?"

"I know this wasn't about March. I believe that. But if I'm going to have any chance of leaving some of my bad habits behind, I need to be away from my whole family."

"I'm sorry," she says. "I just don't believe you can change that much. That you can model something different for Pete. You can't see even your narcissism. Here you are, showing me all the things you will give up, how you'll uproot your whole life to go to a place *I* want to go."

"I picked Key West as much for myself as I did for you. It's the perfect art scene for me. I'd be miserable in New York, or in L.A. You're always telling me I should try harder on that front, not just hide behind a website. And leaving home will be hard for me, sure, but this isn't about giving up Olympus for you. It's about getting you to give me this chance. I know you're more likely to agree if we go somewhere you already love, somewhere Pete will love, too."

"And what happens when we invest all this money, all this time and effort, and I *still* want a divorce? Better we just cut our losses now."

"You were right when you said my behavior affects Pete. Us divorcing doesn't stop me from being his father. I couldn't forgive myself if I taught him the way to navigate the world was through emotional manipulation. I have a lot of incentive, so much more than just keeping us together. The real question is whether you think I'm worth investing that time in."

"I don't know the answer to that," she says. "I really don't."

"Just think about it."

She shakes her head in exasperation. "Okay, but I'm probably going to tell you no tomorrow."

Hap nods, trying to hide his relief. "Fair enough."

"And just so you know, if we did go, I plan on fattening myself up, chopping off my hair, and wearing ugly caftans. No shaving my legs, no plucking my eyebrows."

"You'll still be better looking than me."

"True," she says. "We aren't changing you that much." She leaves him, and the jewelry box, on the porch, but not before Hap gets a glimpse of a smile Vera thinks she is suppressing.

FOUR

THEA IS WHISPERING, angrily, and Artie's mother is speaking at a normal volume, but also angrily. Artie finds she can't orient herself, can't open her eyes, can't understand a thing, then she remembers Ryan's death, feels herself hit the floor of that reality, and everything else tumbles in. She opens her eyes to find herself in her own bed, in her own home, the other two women looming over her.

"Nothing's wrong with her," Thea hisses. "I convinced her to take an Ambien last night so she could get some real sleep."

"All sorts of convincing you did yesterday," Lee says. She leans down and shakes Artie's shoulder before realizing her daughter is already awake. "Hey, there," she says gently, as if she hadn't just been bickering with Thea. "You need to get dressed. We have an appointment at the Sheriff's Department. I'll be in the kitchen, but don't dawdle."

"I'll come too," says Thea.

"No. You won't." Thea and Lee are locked in a staring contest, and, amazingly, it's Thea who blinks.

"Well. You call me if it turns out I might be useful," she says and stalks from the room.

Lee has never been an authoritarian, and her unexpected spine so stuns Artie, she does as her mother says. Once they're in the car, Artie tries to get Lee to explain what's going on. All she gets is "Best to wait till we get there."

They arrive at the county Sheriff's Department, a squat concrete building a block off the square. Artie follows her mother through the automatic doors, dizzy from the worry or the Ambien or both. A discrepancy in Arlo's story must have turned up, a witness late to come forward. But the sheriff, coming out from her office into the lobby, welcomes Artie with kindness. She says, "Your brother would like to speak to you first. I'll take you back." It seems Arlo has found the only way to make Artie talk to him, by force of the authorities, and Artie begins to seethe.

Arlo and Peter are sitting in what must be the break area—a small white room, painted cinderblock walls, with two round tables and a vending machine. Peter rises and kisses Artie on the forehead, then leaves without saying a word. Arlo looks relaxed, he looks himself for the first time since Sunday, and this makes Artie even angrier. The sheriff shuts the door behind Artie, leaving the two of them alone, but she doesn't move toward the table.

"What's going on?" she says.

"I'm about to sign a statement about what really happened. It says you shot Ryan after I knowingly lied about what you were aiming at. It says I didn't think you'd shoot, but it also says I had to realize there was that possibility. That I acted with reckless indifference and tried to cover it up."

"You're lying," she says, struggling to understand all the consequences of what her brother is proposing. "You and Mom have set this up so I'll have to forgive you because you offered, but that I won't let you go to jail." She feels her fingernails biting into her palms, and she wills herself to unclench her hands, to breathe. "But I *won't* stop you from going to jail, Arlo. It's what you deserve."

"It is what I deserve," he says quietly. "I know it. I've already told the sheriff. There's nothing for you to do or not do. It's over. I have a lawyer, and I'll plead no contest to deadly contact. It means jail time but probably not a lot."

She walks toward the table because she must sit down, feels herself swaying. She drops down too hard and the chair skids back an inch.

"I don't expect you to forgive me," Arlo says. "I know this doesn't erase what I've done. I'm doing this because it's the best thing for you, to be able to tell the truth. And for Lavinia Barry. Maybe she'll get some comfort from a portion of justice since she never expected any justice at all. And I hope serving a sentence will help me handle the guilt I'll feel every day for what I did to Ryan, if not the guilt of what I did to you."

Artie looks up at him. "I'm chargeable too. At the very least for lying to the authorities, lying for you."

"I told the sheriff the truth, Artie. That you let me lie because you were in shock, because you trusted me to do the right thing. And I failed that trust." He pauses, an almost-smile on his face. "I guess I did tell *one* lie, that you told me to come forward or you would tell the truth without me. Muñoz gave me a guarantee: there will be no charges filed against you."

Artie finds herself strangely empty, stripped of the anger that has kept her company since Ryan died. She attempts to channel how Thea would react to this news. Too little, too late. Changes nothing. That she and Arlo will never have the same relationship again. But all Artie feels is numb.

THE NIGHT BEFORE, Arlo had left March's and returned to his motel. He woke up at 3 a.m., uneasy, maybe even afraid. He felt disassociated from himself, as if he had left his identity somewhere else and kept only his body. He focused on the sound of the old coiled mattress creaking as he shifted his weight, the sound of a train whistle on the other side of the interstate. He couldn't shake the feeling that, if he opened his eyes, he'd see Ryan in the corner of the room. Not the shell of him, the man on the mortuary table, but Ryan alive, back in a T-shirt and jeans, sitting against the wall, butt on the worn carpet and forearms resting on top of his knees. Ryan felt more alive in that moment than Arlo did.

But Arlo had blotted that identity out. It was true a hundred unlikely things had to line up for Artie to pull that trigger, but Arlo's had been the only choice with malice at the heart of it, an ugliness not mitigated by its briefness. What he wanted more than anything was to drive to Artie's, to offer hours of apologies, to somehow take it all back. How else to remove this man from the corner of every room he'd ever sleep in?

He turned from his side to his back. He smelled the cheap detergent they used on the sheets. The loud air unit by the window kicked on, making him flinch. And, all at once, he saw it—a way out of this feeling. He sat up in bed, turned the bedside lamp on, embarrassed by his own relief at finding the corner of the room empty. Nothing to do but head over to his mother's and wake her up, enlist her help again.

IN THE WAITING ROOM of the Sheriff's Department, Arlo takes the empty plastic chair between Peter and his mother. Artie is now with Muñoz, giving her statement. The Houston lawyer—the one Peter rounded up for him so quickly—arrives, and Peter and he step outside to confer. After fifteen minutes, the sheriff emerges from her office and waves him in. He joins Artie where she's standing on the other side of the doorway. The sheriff tells them both about the next step—the court hearing on Monday where Arlo will plead guilty. Until then, he is free on bail, an amount small enough that he can, to his relief, cover it himself. Though Arlo knows he can't look to verify it, he swears his sister has moved a little bit closer to him. That they are standing there together instead of separately.

Later that night, Arlo will play at My Place to a full house, as news of his imminent incarceration spreads. He'll be able to keep up his stoicism while he's onstage. It will only slip when the entrance door opens, when he can't help checking to see if Artie's come in.

But Artie is spending the night at home. She gets a text message from her mother and reassures her that she is fine. June has taken

Thea to the airport, and Artie's happy to finally be alone. On TV, a young Val Kilmer hunts a lion; it reminds her of that first day she met Ryan, the rabbit he wound up shooting. She had taken a picture of the tiny trophy with her phone, teasing him about how it was too small to feed more than one person. He responded by telling her all the dinners he cooked were for one, giving her a theatrical sigh and a shy grin. But was it just the animal she caught in the frame? She scrolls through her photos until she finds it. Just his profile, all the focus on the sad, scrawny rabbit. But it's still him, in the second before he turned toward her and implied his availability. She runs the tip of her thumb down his face, grateful for the visceral punch of pain, grateful she will still have this moment to view when the pain is not as strong.

Artie looks out the window to check the size of the moon. She puts on her boots and leaves the house, and her flashlight, behind. She heads toward a line of trees, happy that she can be comforted by the sounds of the frogs, the cicadas, if not happy with the thoughts in her own head. Like the photo, that comfort is something.

FIVE

JUNE FINALLY RETURNS HOME after her impromptu breakfast with Cole and March, but Peter isn't there. She goes upstairs and takes a shower, is pleased to even get her hair dried and be completely dressed before she hears a car driving up. But as she comes downstairs, there's a knock at the door rather than her husband waiting for her. She opens the door to March.

"Two unannounced visits in one morning. You stalking me?"

March doesn't smile, which is what she had, uncharacteristically, wanted to pull from her youngest son. She waves him inside and sits next to him at the kitchen island.

"Dad called. He's down at the sheriff's office. Arlo's giving a statement on what really happened Sunday."

"Peter's not stopping him?"

"Wait," March says, confused. "You know what happened?"

She shakes her head. "No, but it can't be good."

And so March explains it to her, both slightly better and so much worse than her own imagination had conjured. All she can say is, "Oh, Artie. To be the one that fired the gun."

"She's okay, I think. Arlo has been making things worse and worse between them, and now he's making it better. At least Artie won't have to keep up a lie."

"But he'll go to jail."

"He will. But he has a good lawyer. And it's what he needed to do." March stops, running his finger along the edge of the counter. Finally, he says, "Are you going to leave Dad?"

"I think so," she says, without a pause. She is relieved to say aloud what has been rolling through her head all morning.

"For Cole?"

"No, not *for* Cole. Because I like myself better without him."

"You won't be without him. Not unless you leave town. And all of us."

She puts her hand over his. "I wouldn't do that. Your father is still my family, even if we aren't together. More so, probably, because I won't be drowning in my well of anger anymore. My personality will be my own again, not bound up in how I've been wronged."

"Can't you feel that way without leaving him?"

"If I could, wouldn't I have done it already?"

"Maybe you didn't want to before. But now you do." He spins around on the barstool until she can't see his face. "I feel different now. Not the same as even last week."

June understands March's investment in her decision is about more than just her and Peter. She puts her hand on his back. "I believe you. And I'll have plenty of time to verify that, since you'll be sticking around."

Before March can respond, the door opens.

"Hey, we didn't hear you drive up," she says to Peter. "Everything go okay?" Her husband looks shell-shocked, as if he's not quite sure he's come into the right house.

March says, "I filled her in."

Peter nods, runs his hand through his hair, and looks at June so sadly it nearly changes her mind.

March puts his hand on June's shoulder and kisses her on the cheek. To Peter he says, "Where's Arlo now? Did the sheriff let him go home with Lee?"

"I dropped him at your place, his request. That okay?"

March nods. "I'll head over." Her son can't keep the stricken expression from his face, though, as if he's leaving his father to the slaughter.

Before March is out the door, Peter is already moving away from June, up the stairs. Attempting to avoid what he must know is coming. "Gonna change," he says. "Sweated through this shirt standing out in the parking lot with the lawyer and Arlo."

June trails after him, leaning in the doorway while he takes off his short-sleeve button-down and replaces it with another. "The lawyer's optimistic?"

"There will be jail time, so no. But it was like Arlo preferred that. Like he thinks going to prison will make Artie forgive him."

"Maybe it will," she says.

"But prison? He could get hurt. And even once he's out, he'll have a record."

"He's got one of the few professions where jail time can actually help him," June says, "but I take your point. Still, it was his choice to make and it was the right thing to do. It's good you helped him."

Though finished buttoning his shirt, Peter makes no move toward her, stands staring absently at the dresser top.

"Come out on the balcony?" she asks. She waits a beat for the answer, but not getting one, she goes on her own. The Brazos trundles past them, slower today. She walks to the edge and, unexpectedly, spots Hap's truck parked below. She can't see her sons, but she can make out the murmur of their voices below her. She hears Peter step out onto the balcony, shutting the door behind him.

"Hap's here," she says.

Peter comes up next to her. "Arguing?" He peers down through the slats to the porch, but the boys must have moved around the side of the house.

"No, sounded okay."

"Things seem good with you and March. He found you this morning?"

She's not sure what he's expecting. Some innocent explanation? A contrived story that they'll both pretend to believe? She finds she can't tell him the simple truth as she had planned. The truth feels like an act of violence against him, one she's now reluctant to perform.

"I'm sorry I didn't come home last night. You got worry upon worry."

"I can't say I didn't deserve it."

"I didn't do it as a punishment," she says. "I did it to feel better. To figure out an answer to a question that I've avoided for thirty years. One I couldn't avoid any longer."

Peter tenses and she can feel him want to peel away, put off what is coming. She says, "I think I need to move out for a while. See how that feels."

"You're going to move in with the vet?"

"No, but I can't promise I won't be spending time with him."

They can see their sons now, walking down to the edge of the lawn and toward the cottonwood trees. March's dogs trail after them. Their voices grow fainter, and June still can't make out what they are saying.

"You want me to move out?"

"That doesn't seem fair. Maybe I can stay with Artie. Maybe I'll move in with March," she says.

Peter laughs dryly. "You're serious? I was specifically not letting myself say that you're acting crazy, but that statement's crazy."

They both watch as March and Hap turn back to the house, finally seeing them and waving up at their parents. "It could work," she says.

"You stay here. I'll stay with March. It gives me an excuse to see more of Arlo, too, before he starts his sentence."

"I thought you'd be more upset."

Peter says, "I am upset. But it feels more like the other shoe has finally dropped." She turns away from the yard, facing him, sees how much he wants to put his arms around her. He tries a joke, though his face looks miserable. "I can't get mad at this new June. Unfortunately for me, the newness makes her doubly attractive."

"Stop flirting," she tells him. "I'm impenetrable."

"Good to hear. It seems like we're all armed with sharp knives we can barely control."

"Is that any way to talk about your family?"

"Being family just means we don't have the safety of fences between us."

"If you're going to wax philosophical on me, I'm not sure we can even be friends." She looks at him skeptically, her old, unamused expression easily finding its way back to her, but she can't maintain it. She tries a smile but it won't stick either, so she just pats him on the back. "Come on, let's go see the boys." Already she is thinking of tomorrow morning, being up on this balcony with no Peter below her. Free of her anchor, but free of her anger. Finally untethered.

ACKNOWLEDGMENTS

There have been many times over the past two years that this novel's good fortune has left me stunned, sure I was about to wake up from the best dream. The first and wildest of these was Nicole Aragi's belief in this book. A huge and heartfelt thanks to her, Grace Dietshe, and everyone at Aragi, Inc.

My good fortune continued in getting to work with editor extraordinaire Lee Boudreaux, who always understood exactly what I wanted the novel to be and invested *so* much of her time and editorial brilliance to help me make it better than I ever could have on my own. I am so grateful to her, Cara Reilly, Elena Hershey, and everyone at Doubleday. Thank you to Emily Mahon and Ping Zhu for the gorgeous cover.

Thanks to Christie Grimes and Sarah Frisch for always being there to spur me on over the twelve long years of writing the book, and for being the best readers and friends I could ever ask for. To my fantastic writing group for plowing through the first draft and for providing laughter and insight in equal amounts: Angie Beshara, Owen Egerton, John Green-man, Stephanie Noll, Michael Noll, Becka Oliver, and Mike Yang. To Zahie El Kouri, Ammi Keller, and Harriet Clark for keeping me sane and making me smarter. To Stacy Muszynski, Abigail Ulman, Mark Barr, and Ammi Keller for helping me through tricky revisions and being always awesome. To Kristin Lorraine and Laurel Holman for their feedback and for making so many Wednesdays full of so much inspiration. To Kendra Bartsch for decades of belief.

Big thanks to Callie Collins, Jill Meyers, and J. M. Tyree for putting early versions of the opening out into the world. Eternal gratitude to the generosity and early endorsements of Jennifer duBois, Sarah Bird, Owen Egerton, Smith Henderson, and Richard Russo.

Thank you to Stanford University and its Creative Writing Department for the gift of the Wallace Stegner Fellowship and the wonderful classmates who made me a better writer: Molly Antopol, Skip Horack, J. M. Tyree, Abigail Ulman, Sarah Frisch, Jim Gavin, Vanessa Hutchinson, Stephanie Soileau, Justin St. Germain, Rusty Dolleman, Sharon May, Rita Mae Reese, Suzanne Rivecca, and Shimon Tanaka. With gratitude to Stanford's Continuing Education Department, their years of support, and especially to Malena Watrous and Scott Hutchins. In memory of Eavan Boland and John L'Heureux, who gave both the program and all of us in it so much.

Thanks to the MFA program and English Department at Texas State University, especially the early encouragement and continuing friendship of the brilliant Debra Monroe. My gratitude to Blue Mountain Center and the Sewanee Writers' Conference for expanding my community (and to Allen Wier for showing me how to really line edit). To Writers' League of Texas, LLL, and LWA for my Austin community.

Thanks to Laurie Filipelli, Zahie El Kouri, Anne Bingham, Jessica Lamb-Shapiro, Susanne Grabowski, and Marit Weisenberg for the stellar company around tables, small and large, for all those hours of revision. Oh, that we can return to those soon! And to Becka Oliver for having the answer to every question, especially the ones I haven't even thought to ask yet.

And, finally, thanks to my family—Bill and Janet Swann, Lisa Swann and Marc Thiel—for a thousand different kinds of support, large and small, and for helping me believe I could get from there to here.